West Coast Holiday Series

Christmas in Tahoe

New Year's in Napa

Rendezvous in Point Reyes

ELISABETH BARRETT

Christmas in Tahoe

A West Coast Holiday Series Book

ELISABETH BARRETT

ACKNOWLEDGMENTS

Major thanks to all my friends and family who encouraged me to publish this book. Especially Jennifer, who has been with me in all my adventures, including trekking up to Tahoe to do research, and who will forever remain the comma queen. Julie, who patiently answered all my snowboarding questions, and Chris, who was a wealth of information about Tahoe. Tasneem, Suzanne Turner, Lia Riley, and Jennifer Ryan for reading this manuscript, both in whole and in part, and providing invaluable feedback. Jessica Scott, Marina Adair, Sharon Hamilton, Hannah Jayne, Jules Barnard, Shawntelle Madison, Kristin Miller, Megan Frampton, Ruthie Knox, and Jennifer Probst for providing huge amounts of encouragement and support. Nalini Akolekar for being the best agent ever! All of my readers for continuing to take this journey with me. And always, always, always, Jonathan. I love you.

CHAPTER 1

"Mandy, please don't do this to me," Ann Smith muttered to herself as she scanned One World Insurance's well-maintained parking lot for her ride. "Not right before Christmas."

But Mandy Aligheri's little blue Prius was nowhere to be seen. Just the usual panoply of sedans, minivans and SUVs.

And a handsome guy sporting a beard, leaning on a huge truck.

Definitely not her ride.

Her gaze slid over him and toward the entrance to the parking lot. Still no Mandy. It was just like her friend to be late, a pattern since college. They used to joke that if they combined Ann, who was always early, with Mandy, who was always late, they'd make one person who was always right on time.

Oh no. One of her colleagues—a guy named Nick who frequently worked as part of her team—approached, and Ann held her breath. With her monstrous pocketbook and skis on one arm and a giant roller bag on the other, there wasn't a lot of room to maneuver on the path leading up to her office building.

Of course, Nick came right up to her. "You okay?"

"Yes." Short and sweet, the way she always answered.

"Going to Tahoe?"

"Yes."

"Great." Nick sidestepped her and her bags, gave her a nod, and said, "Glad you're getting away for the holiday. Have a great trip, and Merry Christmas."

Releasing her breath, she nodded back. "Thanks. Same to you." Nick disappeared into the building. *And thanks for not dragging me into a ten-minute-long discussion about my personal life.*

Just as she was about to pull her phone out of her voluminous bag to see if she'd missed any messages, Huge Truck Guy peeled himself off his truck and started walking directly towards her.

"You Ann?" he said. Even from twenty feet away his voice carried, a deep masculine rumble.

She nodded stiffly.

"I'm Chase," he said, holding out a hand. "Mandy asked me to come pick you up."

Reluctantly, she shifted her skis to her left side and took his hand. Rough fingers slid over hers and gripped her palm. *Strong. And warm.*

And it wasn't just his fingers that were rough. It was the whole package. Worn jeans, a crewneck sweater, and a pair of scuffed hiking boots complimented his thick, midnight black hair. His beard—somewhere between a five-o'clock shadow and full-on lumberjack—didn't hide his strong jaw and lean cheekbones. His eyes, almost as dark as his hair and filled with intelligence, settled on her.

A crazy pattern of heat played a samba on her skin. When she closed her eyes to get her bearings, kaleidoscope colors flashed behind her lids. Was she having a stroke? The likelihood of that happening given her age, sex, and overall health was less than one percent, as were the odds that she was having a heart attack. A tumor was another possibility, but that was even rarer, clocking in at a probability of zero-point-four-five percent.

Dawning awareness crept over her and, shocked, she blinked once. Then twice. For this was something that couldn't be predicted with any probability whatsoever. Something so creaky and rusted from disuse she barely recognized it for what it was.

Desire.

There was so much she could have said. That she wanted to say, ranging from *where did you come from* to *why you?* But she'd just met the guy and couldn't exactly start spouting off about his sex appeal, so after opening and shutting her mouth a couple of times—not one of her better looks—she settled on something neutral. "Where *is* Mandy? She was supposed to pick me up."

A crease formed between his brows. "She didn't tell you? She told me she called you."

"I was in a half-day meeting," Ann said, frowning as much from the irritation of having Mandy flake out on her again as she was from the effect this big man had on her. "I haven't checked my messages."

"Well, then I guess you'll hear it from me," he said with a shrug. "She can't make it for a day or two. Something's come up at her lab, and since I was in the area, she asked me to take you up instead."

Something was *always* coming up at the lab for Mandy. Trained as a scientist, she now worked as a post-doctoral researcher at one of Stanford's biology laboratories. But a day or two? She wouldn't put it past Mandy to set her up. She'd been trying for ages. Well, more like for a year and a half.

Ann narrowed her eyes at the guy in front of her. Why she wanted him she wasn't exactly sure. Typically, she liked her men with a little more . . . polish. John had been polished. This man just looked rough . . . yes, *rough*. Rough at work. Rough at play.

Rough in bed.

Maybe driving to Lake Tahoe with the mountain man wasn't such a good idea. She was ready to move on—at least, she thought she was. But not with a slab of a man who looked like he owned an axe and knew how to use it.

She must have made some kind of face because Chase just shrugged. "Look, I'm sure she left you a message, so why don't you listen to your voicemail? I'll wait."

Ann pulled her cell phone out of her bag. Sure enough, there was a message. She pressed a few buttons and then put the device to her ear. In a moment, she heard Mandy's cheerful voice squeaking through the line.

Hi, Annie! I am soooo sorry that I can't pick you up today but something's come up. I started this experiment yesterday and the cultures have to incubate for at least forty-eight hours and . . .

Ann zoned out for a moment. She never understood what Mandy was talking about when she spouted biology. Her friend went on for a while about her exciting new experiment and how terribly important it was to the head of her lab to get it done before everyone left for the holiday weekend. When Mandy changed subjects, she switched her brain back on.

I've asked a friend to drive you up. His name's Chase Deckert, and he's letting us use his house, too. I've known him since grad school and he's a really good guy. I normally wouldn't ask this of you, but we've talked about this and you know you need to get away this weekend. Chase'll take care of you until I get there, I promise. I didn't tell him what's going on, but he knows how important you are to me.

Her gaze flicked over to him. He was standing there, arms crossed over his broad chest, watching her with those dark eyes. He still had that little crease between his eyebrows. He still made her hotter than she had any right to be. She turned away.

And Annie, this isn't a set-up. I know you're thinking it, but that's not what happened here. I'll be there as soon as my experiment is over and we'll drink that wine just like I promised, I swear! If you're up for it, we can even try the bar to meet some hot snowboarders. Say hi to Roxy for me, and again, I'm so sorry I can't be there right away, Annie. Stay strong! Love you, babe!

The message ended, so she clicked the phone off and stuffed it back into her bag, Mandy's voice echoing in her ear.

You know you need to get away this weekend.

Yes, she did. She really, really did. Because if she had to spend what would have been her second wedding anniversary alone in her chilly townhouse without John, she knew she'd be tempted to stare at old pictures of him when he was alive and cry all weekend, just like she did last Christmas. But this year was supposed to be different. She was going to start fresh, and Mandy had promised they'd do it together. Now her friend would be holed up in her lab 24/7 until her experiment was over.

This would be the last time she let Mandy take charge.

That little pit in her stomach started to throb. For a while, after John died, it was there all the time. And over the last year, as things had slowly returned to normal—well, except for the fact that the love of her life was dead—it had ebbed. But around this time of year the feeling came back. It probably always would.

Chase cleared his throat. "Look, er, Ann," he said, "No pressure, but we're losing daylight. A storm front's moving in up north. If we want to get there tonight, we have to leave now. You coming or not?"

She'd already cleared her schedule at work for the next couple of days, and if she stayed at home alone . . . well, that wasn't part of the plan. Carefully, Ann weighed her options: flying solo over Christmas or Tahoe with a stranger.

She took a deep breath. "I'm coming."

"Good." Without waiting for her to move, he took her big roller bag, lifted it up, and began carrying it to his truck.

"Wait!" she said, chasing after him. "You don't have to. I've got it."

"Uh-huh," he said, still walking. "Seriously, what do you have in here? Rocks?"

"No, I—"

They were stopped in front of his truck now—a metallic gray Toyota Tacoma with a double cab and a Snugtop covering the truck bed—which didn't exactly scream *Silicon Valley executive*. A loud bark came from the cab and Ann jerked back before she could stop herself.

"Roxy, I presume."

Chase grinned at her. "You got it."

"I'm allergic," she informed him. And she was—horribly, utterly allergic to anything with fur. Just walking by a pet store made her sneeze. But she didn't have any other way to get up to Tahoe, or any practical way to get home with all her gear. A friend had given her a ride to work, and taking the Caltrain back to Mountain View wasn't going to cut it.

Chase didn't speak. He just opened the passenger-side door and rummaged through the glove compartment.

"Here," he said, handing her a box of antihistamine medication. "One of my friends is allergic to Roxy, too. If you still want to join me, you can have some."

"I—" she started, before stopping. She could just ask him to drive her home. Cut her losses before she took the risk of heading up to Tahoe with some guy she didn't know. *No.* She'd promised Mandy. Truth be told, she'd promised herself. She could do this. She needed to do this. She pulled out a blister pack of medicine, pushed the little pink pill through the security foil and swallowed it.

Chase nodded approvingly. "We can stop and get some more at a drugstore. Now let's see about that bag of yours."

He reached down to pick it up, his flesh shifting under his sweater. *Those are his muscles bulging as he lifts your insanely heavy suitcase, Annie.*

Why did she pack half a case of wine again?

Actually, bringing the wine had been Mandy's idea. According to her friend's logic, drinking some of the wine she'd purchased for her wedding—the wine John had handpicked for the occasion that never happened, the wine they'd saved to drink on each one of the numerous Christmas anniversaries they would share together—would give her some measure of peace and help to kick-start the rest of her life. It wasn't possible to forget John, but Ann was ready to emerge from the black hole she'd been living in since his death.

Chase must think her crazy, but Ann didn't care. Instead of trying to explain to him that her bag contained part of her late fiancé's prized wine collection, she merely pursed her lips together, nodded her thanks, and walked around to the front. He did the same and got in, watching as she placed her big bag onto the floor, lifted herself as gracefully into his truck as she could manage, shut the door and fastened her seatbelt.

"Come on, Roxy," Chase said. "Show yourself."

The face of a large black Lab popped between the two front seats. The big animal tilted her head at Ann and regarded her with soulful brown eyes.

"She won't, ah, try to jump into the front, will she?" Ann asked, edging toward the door.

Chase scratched Roxy behind her ears, and the dog closed her eyes and leaned into his hand. "Nah. She likes it back there."

"Okay," she said, one eye still on Roxy. She didn't seem to be going anywhere, so Ann finally slid her gaze away. While Chase got on his seatbelt, she took out a portable GPS device from her big bag. Carefully, she unwound the cord and plugged it into the cigarette lighter.

"What's your address?"

"347 Pinetree, Tahoe City," he answered. "Why?"

She programmed in their destination. "There," she said, placing the device on the dashboard and watching it closely as it calculated the optimal route.

He watched her, his mouth a little open. "What are you doing?" The crease between his brows was back. "Not to be obvious here, but we're going to my house. I'm pretty sure I know the way."

"I like to know where I am and where I'm going at all times," Ann said.

Some folks said it was a disease, her constant need to know in which direction she was facing, but being armed with information meant the probability of her getting lost was lower. She hated getting lost. John had understood.

Try explaining that to the big guy sitting next to you. But it must not have been that big a deal to Chase, because he simply shrugged and turned the key in the ignition. He hadn't even put the truck into gear when a familiar itch tickled the back of her nose.

Then she sneezed. Hard.

"Guess you really are allergic," he said, easing the truck away from the curb. "The medicine should kick in soon."

"All right," she said, fumbling around in her purse for a tissue. She sneezed twice more before Chase stopped the truck and reached across to the glove compartment.

"Here," he said, pulling out a package of travel tissues. Chase was in her space, sucking out all the air in her vicinity.

"Thank you," she said, accepting the package from him as she sneezed again.

She glanced at him just in time to catch his smile bloom. "Mandy was right," he said. "You really *do* need taking care of."

Okay, hot *and* nurturing? Of course he was.

She didn't put too much credence into fate, but maybe meeting this guy was some kind of sign. She hadn't truly been interested in anyone since John died. For the first year, she'd walked around in a haze. And for most of the last year, she'd been so wrapped up in getting her life back, trying to figure out who she was without John, that she'd let her personal life lapse. Now she was coming to the realization that perhaps the reason she hadn't been interested in anyone else was that she just hadn't had the right kind of inspiration.

And despite the fact that he wasn't quite her type, mountain man was definitely inspiring.

She must have been staring at him a bit too long, since he cleared his throat. "Lots of traffic today."

Her cheeks warmed and suddenly the GPS was very interesting. "Yes," she said, fiddling with the monitor.

"Things will be all right until we cross the bridge. The 880 up to Berkeley's always a mess for some reason."

"I don't get up there a lot."

"Work keep you busy?"

She just nodded, her eyes on the GPS. Work did keep her busy, just the way she liked it. Being an actuary was interesting. She was on the life, health, and pension side, and while building statistically-based mortality tables to quantify risks and determine insurance rates might be considered a bit morbid, Ann loved the steady, solid nature of the work, of knowing what was coming down the pipeline months, even years, in advance. Numbers were truth, and work was one of the few things that kept her grounded.

"Ski much?"

"I used to." But not anymore. Not since she'd met John, actually. He wasn't a skier, and they'd found other things to do together. She turned to look out the window.

"Well, the snow's great right now—kind of surprising for this time of year, but I'll take it. Six inches of fresh powder fell over the last couple of days. Just perfect. Some of the back country trails are still pristine, and they'll stay that way with the storm coming in tonight." His voice was quicker now, seemingly excited by the prospect of all that snow. She glanced over to him, but she could only see half his face, not enough to assess whether he was genuinely thrilled or just putting on an act for her.

Ann turned back to the window. She'd checked the weather before they left. There was a seventy-six percent chance of more snow that night, and they really were racing to beat it. Her GPS said they'd be at Chase's house in four hours, fifteen minutes. Mentally, she added in another hour for traffic. It never hurt to be conservative. By her calculations, they'd barely make it.

"Sit back, girl," he said.

"What?" Ann sat up straighter in her seat and glared at him.

"Not you." He jerked his finger at Roxy. "Her." Roxy had her head on the armrest between the seats, that huge tongue lolling out.

"Oh," she said, angling her body toward the window. "You were talking to the dog."

"She's not going to like you if you keep calling her that," Chase said, a hint of humor in his voice. "She's very sensitive."

Just then, something wet and warm coated Ann's ear.

"Ugh, gross!" She grabbed a tissue and wiped at the side of her head.

"Guess she likes you after all," he said with a chuckle.

Ann finished wiping her ear, carefully folded the dirty tissue inside a clean one and placed it on the floor near her foot. "Don't try to tell me that a dog's mouth is cleaner than a human's. That's just an old wives' tale."

"I wasn't going to insult your intelligence," he said, his voice filled with mirth. "And I also won't try to tell you where Roxy's tongue's been."

Nothing seemed to faze this guy, but he sure liked rattling *her* cage. She fished around in her bag for some wet wipes and swabbed her ear afresh.

He laughed a little more at that, so she crossed her arms under her breasts and stared out the window again. They were on the San Mateo Bridge now, driving in the right-hand lane. She looked out at the Bay below, vast and blue, and wondered what in the hell she thought she was doing—

driving to Tahoe in a truck with a dog she was allergic to, and a scruffy stranger with a killer smile and a laugh that slid down to her belly like warm cocoa.

CHAPTER 2

As soon as Chase hit the halfway mark on the bridge, the invisible weight sitting on his chest disappeared. Silicon Valley was in his rearview mirror, and it would be smooth driving from here on out. Technically, Menlo Park was north of what was officially designated as Silicon Valley, but people who lived and worked almost everywhere in the San Francisco Bay Area had the same mentality—the constant drive to produce, succeed, and win, win, win, regardless of cost. And he would know all about that, wouldn't he?

Dwelling on the past always made him feel like crap, so he ran a hand through his hair and tried to focus on the road in front of him.

When he finally got off the bridge, he glanced over at his reluctant passenger again. Ann Smith had her face turned away from him, staring out the window at the Bay, her dark curls guarding her expression from his sight.

A beautiful stranger for Christmas.

Typically, holidays weren't really Chase's thing—more of a reason to get together with family than anything else. When Grandma was alive, she always invited him, his brother Tommy, and their parents to spend Christmas week in Tahoe. This year, without Grandma to hold them together, his parents made plans with friends in Sacramento, and Tommy decided to head to Hawaii, so when Mandy asked him if she and a friend could stay with him over Christmas, Chase agreed. Things got wonky when he'd gotten a call from Mandy saying she couldn't make it up right away and asking him to please pick up her friend Ann.

Actually, he thought Ann would be something like Mandy—gorgeous, brilliant, way too much fun for her own good, and so absent-minded as to be potentially unreliable. But Ann Smith wasn't like Mandy. Not at all.

First off, Ann didn't seem like a whole lot of fun. Before they'd even met, he'd thought that *Ann Smith* was just about the most dull and prim name he'd ever heard. When he saw her carrying a pair of ten-year-old Blizzards, he wasn't that surprised. Granted, they were nice skis—in fact, he knew some pros who used the newer version of the model she had—but she could have bought them used. Maybe she was into skiing for the retro-cool factor. Or, more intriguing—she bought the skis new and they'd just moldered in her place for years. Anyway, that was strike one in the fun department. Next, she was wearing a suit. The only people who wore suits in Silicon Valley were lawyers or bankers, and given that he'd picked her up at an insurance company, she must be a lawyer. Strike two. The jury was still out on *brilliant*, but he could give a big thumbs-down to *unreliable*. She'd made the plan to go up to Tahoe and even though she could have bailed on him, she hadn't. *Not unreliable at all.*

Gorgeous he had a handle on, because regardless of her issues, she was pretty as hell. Her features were delicate—little hands, little nose—set off by a mass of dark hair that was held back in some kind of messy knot. He'd always had a thing for brunettes, especially when coupled with light eyes. Hers were a vibrant blue behind her wire-rimmed glasses. The winter weather—mild in Silicon Valley, but chilly enough—had tinged her cheeks, staining them a rosy pink that matched her lips. No doubt about it. Gorgeous.

Mandy had given him explicit instructions to take care of her, but Dr. Aligheri should have warned him that Ann Smith, who wore her suit like armor, carried her ancient skis like talismans, and tilted her chin in the most challenging manner possible, would do her best to exude an aura of *I don't need taking care of.* Clearly she didn't want him, or anyone else, to help her.

Just then, Ann gave a little sniff and dabbed at her nose with a tissue. Despite all the warning signs, a protective instinct swelled in his chest, knocking him for a loop.

Don't go there, Chase. This is why you live up in Tahoe. No entanglements.

And *definitely* no entanglements with a woman who clearly didn't want any.

As if on cue, Roxy panted right in his ear. He'd gotten the double cab so she could ride with him with space to spare. "My good girl," he said, keeping his eyes on the road while reaching back and rubbing that sweet spot just behind her ear. *My only girl.*

When he'd found Roxy scared and half-starved in the woods behind his cabin, he'd done everything he could to find her owner. But with no tag, no chip, and no black Lab reported missing in the area, it was either put her in a shelter or keep her. Of course he'd kept her, and she'd proven herself. He couldn't have found a more loyal friend and companion.

They were heading north on 880 now. Ann was still staring out the window, at what he wasn't certain. This stretch of road was pretty dull. *If she's going to ignore you, you need to ignore her.*

Crap, this was going to be a long-ass drive, especially since she had been silent for miles. He had way too much time to think. Tomorrow, he'd hit the mountain all day. So he *wouldn't* have time to think.

They passed through Oakland, then Berkeley in silence, and when they got to Richmond, Chase checked on his passenger again . . . only to find her fast asleep. Her head was leaning back on the seat, exposing her long white neck. Her mouth was open, a perfect rose in bloom. The sun hit her face just right, emphasizing her high cheekbones and her long eyelashes. She looked so vulnerable in sleep.

The seat belt seemed to be biting her in the neck, so with one eye still on the road he swept his finger under it so it lay flat. He sighed deeply. It looked like Ann Smith was well and truly his responsibility now.

He'd just turned his gaze back to the road when his phone rang. He picked it up fast, popping it onto Bluetooth.

"Deckert," he answered.

"Hey, Deck!" Mandy's voice came through the speaker. "Did you get Ann?"

"Yeah," he said.

"Hi, Annie!"

Ann didn't answer, and a quick glance over at her confirmed she was still out cold.

"Ann's down for the count," Chase said.

"What did you do to her?" Mandy demanded. "She never takes naps in the middle of the day."

"*I* didn't do anything. It was Roxy."

It took a moment for Mandy to connect the dots. "Oh, no! I totally forgot she's allergic to dander. She took some medicine, didn't she?"

"Yep," he confirmed.

"And that stuff always knocks her out. Any other guy, Deck . . ."

"So you trust me?" he said with a laugh. "I sure don't trust you. Not after the stunt you pulled."

"I'm not sorry," Mandy said, utterly unrepentant.

"You should be," Chase said, discontent rising inside him. Mandy had set up a meeting between him and Phil Markowitz, the larger-than-life founder and CEO of Alliance Biotechnology in South San Francisco, by telling him that Phil just wanted to talk about Chase's previous research. Chase had thought the thrill was long gone between him and science, but when Phil expressed interest in the research, he couldn't resist. That work had been his old life, after all, and somewhere, buried deep, he still had a passion for it.

But the meeting had been a set-up—a not-so-thinly disguised

interview—something Chase had figured out half an hour into their little chat. Talking about his research was fine, but he was *not* interested in joining another company. Not after he'd spent the past three years trying to get away from the specter of his last gig—a start-up that had blown up when his partner, Greg Frobel, sold him out, going behind Chase's back to take his ground-breaking malaria research to a huge biopharmaceutical company.

He hated being played and it burned him even more because Greg was the one who did it. Greg hadn't just been Chase's partner—he'd been his friend and confidant, too. But the grants and the accolades and the press hadn't mattered when Greg double-crossed him.

It's nothing personal, Greg had said. *It's just business.*

But Greg had lied. It was *very* personal, and a lot more than *just business* to Chase.

Losing control over his research had been like losing part of himself. The rage and resentment was overwhelming until he managed to wrestle it into a sort of numbness. There was a reason he'd left Menlo Park for greener pastures, and it was the same reason he didn't want to return. But back to Mandy, who was silently waiting on the line.

"Did you think I wouldn't figure it out?" he said.

"You were *supposed* to figure it out, Deck. You're wasting your time up in Tahoe and you and I both know it."

"I'm not wasting my time," he muttered.

"Oh, no. Tell me you didn't do that thing where you go off on corporate America again."

"I didn't do that thing," he said, even though corporate America and he weren't seeing eye-to-eye right now.

She sighed. "Good. Then you got the job. Because when I talked to Phil, he was seriously impressed with your research. I told him you were the best at—"

"Yeah, I'm sure I got it," Chase said, interrupting her. If he was good enough for MIT, who'd invited him to apply for a post-doctoral fellowship after he and Greg parted ways, he was good enough for Alliance. "But I don't want it."

"Sure you do. When Phil makes you the offer, please take it." He was quiet for just a moment too long. "Deck," Mandy intoned, "do not be an idiot. These kinds of positions don't just come out of nowhere. Alliance Biotechnology is at the cutting edge of malaria research, even more advanced than what you were doing before. Phil is the *man*. You know it. I know it. Everyone knows it. He's been following your career for a while, but he thought you were still in Africa. When I told him you were back in the country, he was very interested. You know you have the chops for this work and you're *perfect* for this position!"

Mandy was right. He would be perfect for the job, an amped-up version of the research he was doing before. Since he'd left, no one—not even the company who bought his research—had been able to develop his work properly. Phil would give Chase the opportunity to pick up where he left off, with a full team at his disposal to focus on the development of still newer malaria combo therapies using alternative artemisinin derivatives.

Chase couldn't deny that on some level it was tempting. Groundbreaking research. Lots of money. Lots of prestige. Not that he cared so much about the latter two things. It was a huge vote of confidence that even though he'd been out of the field for a while, his reputation was still strong enough to warrant a position like this, and returning to the Bay Area biotech arena on his terms would be like publicly giving his old partner the middle finger.

But he knew where he'd be going—right back into the viper's den where greed always won out. And the next time someone took away his research? He'd lose his mind for sure. He couldn't live his life like that anymore. Tahoe, with its laid-back attitude and slower speed was his style now. Not full-throttle, day-and-night Silicon Valley living and all the crap that went along with it.

"What did you tell Phil?" Mandy demanded.

"That I'd think about it," he said, reluctantly. And he would think about it—for the brief amount of time it would take for him to count up all the reasons he shouldn't go back to the Bay Area.

"Don't think too long," she said. "Phil's not noted for his patience."

"I'm well aware of that. But keep in mind that *I don't want the job.*"

"I've heard he's awesome to work for," Mandy said, pretending like she hadn't heard him. "I can hook you up with a friend of mine who's currently working at Alliance. I think you'd get a lot out of talking with him."

Chase just sighed. There was no stopping Mandy when she got on some kind of kick. That was the thing with her—she was usually pretty scatterbrained, but when she set her mind to do something, she went after it with laser-like focus.

"Look, Deck, you've been up in Tahoe for what, a year now?"

"Yeah."

"It's great and I'm sure it's been fun, but don't you think it's time to get back to real life?"

He sighed again. "This *is* my real life, Mandy."

"All I'm saying is that you're one of the most brilliant guys I've ever met, and you once used your immense powers to help save people's lives. Don't throw yourself away on mountain climbing and backcountry exploring and ripping up the slopes when you have all that brainpower at your disposal."

"Snowboarders shred. Skiers rip."

"Whatever," she said. "Just hear me."

"I hear you." he said.

There was silence for a few moments.

"Well, don't be in such a hurry to thank me for handing you this job on a platter," Mandy said.

"Thanks," Chase said, mostly to get Mandy off his back.

"You're welcome," she said, sounding pleased. "But I really should be thanking you for picking up Ann."

Ann. The beauty with the wary gaze. She looked like she needed to get out of the Valley even more than he did.

"When do you think you're going to make it up?" he asked.

"Christmas Eve, maybe Christmas Day at the latest. Please take care of Annie. Seriously, she needs this trip. She's had a rough time of it over the past couple of years. This was going to be our weekend to get her back on track."

"What's her story?" he asked.

"Well, she—" Mandy stopped. "Oh, crap. I need to get back to my cultures."

And without even a *Bye, Deck*, the line went dead.

Typical Mandy.

Guess he'd just have to wait for Ann Smith to wake up to get some answers.

CHAPTER 3

Ann woke up disoriented, stiff, cold, and smelling like dog breath. She opened her eyes. Outside, the skies were dark. Rain drummed a beat on the roof of the truck. She glanced over. Chase was leaning back in his seat, a book in his large hands.

Angle of Repose by Wallace Stegner. *Interesting. Mountain Man was a thoughtful reader.*

Roxy's head rested on the armrest between them. Ann edged away, not wanting to get too close to that tongue.

"Where are we?" Her voice came out thick and cottony. *Curse you, Benadryl.*

Chase glanced up from his book and regarded her with deep brown eyes. She thought she saw his mouth twitch, but she couldn't be sure. "Parking lot."

"Yes, I can see that," she said, flicking off her seatbelt and doing her best to right herself. "But *where?*"

"Auburn."

"Why aren't we in Tahoe?"

"They closed I-80," he said by way of explanation.

"Wait, what?" she said, trying to clear her foggy brain. "They closed a whole interstate? Can they do that?"

"Sure. Happens all the time. Rare this time of year, but it happens."

She rubbed her eyes, trying to make them focus. "Can't we take a different road?"

Chase flipped his book shut and tapped her GPS. "Why don't you have your trusty sidekick tell you what other options we have?"

"Let me guess. There aren't any," she said flatly.

"One way in. One way out."

"So that's it? We're just going to sit here freezing in a parking lot while we wait for the road to open up again?"

His eyebrows furrowed. "You're freezing?"

"Yes." She started to shake. She was always cold when she woke up.

Immediately, he turned on the engine and flicked a few buttons on the dashboard. Heat blasted from the vents. "Better?"

"Yes, thank you," she said, her shivering starting to subside. "Sorry."

"Don't apologize." He gave her a once-over. "So that medicine really knocked you out, huh?"

She nodded, still groggy, but now getting warmer, fast. "Yes. Also, I'm kind of confused as to what's going on here."

Chase sighed. "They close the road, you just stop, wherever you are. I figured it'd be better if we stopped near some civilization rather than just sleep on 80."

"People just stop on the highway?" That did not compute.

He nodded. "Yep. If they close the road during the daytime, it's like a party out there. At night, you just curl up and go to sleep until the cops knock on your window to tell you the road's open again. I've been listening to the weather and monitoring the Caltrans Highway Information Network. The storm's still raging, and they won't be able to clear the road until it's passed. We'll probably be stuck for a while, and Auburn's one of the last towns before the mountains with restaurants, gas, and most importantly, hotels. Oh, and before I forget. Here," he said, pulling a box out from his pocket. "I stopped by a drug store while you were sleeping and picked this up for you."

Antihistamine medication. The non-drowsy kind. "Thank you," she said, fumbling around for her bag. "Let me pay you for this."

She finally got her wallet out, but he waved it away. "On me."

"That's really generous of you."

"Least I can do if you have to suffer the ride up with us."

"I'm not suffering," she murmured. It was the truth. She'd been unconscious for most of the trip so far, and before that she'd gotten to look at him—some of the best eye candy she'd seen in a long time. Except for the whole being knocked out by allergy medicine thing, it hadn't been that bad.

He gave her a wry smile. "Maybe I shouldn't tell you that Roxy licked you a couple of times while I was in the store."

"What?"

"I'm just guessing here. When I came back, your face was a bit wet."

Ugh. That explained the dog breath smell. When she looked over at Roxy, the dog cocked her head and gazed up at her affectionately. She didn't much love the slobber, but having a companion who looked at her like that might be kind of nice. It had been all she could do to take care of herself after John died, let alone take care of another creature, but maybe she could handle it now. Perhaps she'd look into getting one of those hypo-allergenic pets when she got back to Silicon Valley.

Chase scratched Roxy right behind the ears, and the big dog closed her eyes in pleasure. "We're going to be stuck for a while, so I thought we'd get something to eat," he said. "I don't have an umbrella, so you might want your coat. You have one, right?"

She nodded. "It's in my bag."

"I'll get it for you." He reached for the door handle.

"Wait—no. I'll get it." The last thing she wanted was him rifling through her suitcase.

"Your bag's really heavy," he pointed out. "Let me drag it to the edge of the bed and you can open it inside. That way everything will stay dry."

"Okay."

"Wait until you hear me holler, okay?"

She nodded and waited while Chase jumped out of the cab and ran to the back.

"All right, Ann!" he yelled after a few seconds.

As soon as she opened the door she was pelted by chilly raindrops. Maybe she should have just let him get the coat. She ran to the back of the truck, unzipped the suitcase, and pulled out her coat, keeping the wine safely hidden in between her other clothes.

Quickly donning the jacket, she zipped the suitcase back up. A few seconds later, Chase had the doors to the rear bed closed.

"Thank you," she said over the sound of the rain.

"Come on," he said, guiding her to the cab. When he opened the door, Roxy jumped out with a happy bark. "Let's go, girl!"

As they walked briskly to a nearby restaurant, Roxy skipped happy circles around them, droplets of water splashing up from her paws. They were under the overhang fast. From his pocket, Chase pulled out a leash. "Here, girl," he said, hooking it onto her collar. "You can't come inside, but I'll get you some water and a juicy burger."

Roxy barked again, shook herself off, then lay down near the post where Chase had tied her leash.

"I think she actually understands what you're saying," Ann told him.

"We get each other," he said, and held the door to the restaurant open for her.

The door was bedecked in evergreen garlands, and as she walked over the threshold, she stepped on a slick patch of linoleum and her feet skittered. "Whoops!" she cried, just as Chase caught her under the arm, keeping her from falling.

"Close," he said, his hand lingering for a moment longer than was strictly necessary. His strength was palpable, and when he finally removed his hand she could still feel the pressure from his fingers against her skin. She liked the way it felt. "Come on," he said, giving her a half-smile. "Let's get you something to eat."

The place looked to be a burger bar with upscale fast-food. It was pretty crowded—no surprise, given that the parking lot was, too—so they had to wait a few minutes in line to give the girl behind the counter their order. Or rather, Chase's order. She just wanted a coffee, both for the warmth and the caffeine. When she tried to pay for it, he waved her hand away.

"Sure you don't want any food?" he asked, right before he handed the cashier his credit card.

"No. Just the coffee, please."

When they were finally seated at one of the outdoor picnic tables under the overhang, she took a sip of coffee and glanced around. The tables inside were jam-packed with families, kids, bikers and people who looked like ski bums. It was just as crowded outside, and attached to the restaurant was a little market, also full. Christmas lights were strung up on the underside of the overhang and wrapped around the posts. Despite the rain, it was festive.

"What *is* this place?" she wondered.

"Ikeda's. It's pretty famous around these parts. Some folks think it's a tourist trap on account of the hype around the homemade pies, but I've been coming here since this place was a fruit stand."

"So you're from the area?" she asked. The coffee was perking her up.

"Sacramento."

"Ah. But you live in Tahoe now."

"Yep."

He let the silence draw out for a bit.

"So what do you do in Tahoe?" she asked, trying to get him to talk.

"Snowboard."

"Do you teach?"

He blinked and looked at her strangely. "Sometimes. Why would you ask that?"

"It's just that you're very patient, is all."

He didn't speak for a moment.

"Number forty-seven," a voice over the loudspeaker called.

"Food's up," Chase said, looking a little relieved as he unfolded himself from the seat.

He came back in short order with a huge tray of food. He'd ordered a bacon double cheeseburger, a big basket of curly fries, a basket of onion rings, a giant soda, two regular hamburgers, and a large piece of berry pie. Five little paper cups of ketchup lined the tray. He used a plastic knife to cut up one of the hamburgers and put the paper plate on the ground. Roxy started in on it right away, wagging her tail as she ate.

Chase lifted the bacon double cheeseburger. He'd piled it high with lettuce and tomato slices. Then he opened his mouth and took a giant bite, eyes closing in pleasure.

Self-consciously, she took another sip of coffee.

He finished chewing and turned his gaze towards her. "Here," he said, pushing the fries across the table. "Eat something."

She used to share meals with John. Decadent meals like Cowgirl Creamery's Red Hawk cheese sliced onto thick wedges of Acme bread, or olive tapenade and warm, crusty cheese popovers. They'd spend hours at farmers' markets, getting the freshest vegetables for huge salads they topped with oven-roasted chicken. And in their townhouse there was never a shortage of fine Recchiuti chocolates in which to indulge when the mood struck.

Since John's death, all the joy had gone out of eating. Sure, she ate, but just enough to keep up her energy, and this time of year things were even worse. "I'm really not hungry. Truly."

"Uh-huh," he said, his gaze not leaving hers. *Eat*, his eyes were saying.

"Fine," she said, picking up a fry and putting it in her mouth. She chewed and swallowed. Salty. Greasy. Good. "Going to report back to Mandy?"

"Maybe." The corners of his eyes crinkled up. "And speaking of Mandy, why is it that we've never met before?"

Ann shrugged. "Mandy's not noted for her organizational skills. At least outside the lab."

"You have that right," Chase said, taking a drink of his soda. "I got to be decent friends with her in grad school even though I was a few years ahead of her, but only because she showed up to the best parties."

"She did that in college, too. But that's not the Mandy I know."

"How did you two get connected?"

"At Michigan. We were assigned to be roommates our freshman year. She was a brilliant glamour queen from SoCal and I was a geeky country girl from Vermont. We couldn't have been less alike, but somehow it worked."

"Why'd you move out here?"

"A job. And then I stayed." She took another sip of coffee. "It's hard for me to think about going back now, even though my parents want me to."

"Why would you want to go back?" he said.

She just shrugged and ate a French fry to cover her discomfort. The way her parents saw it, coming home would be a good chance for her to start fresh, close to them. They'd begged her to join them for Christmas but she resisted, afraid that on some level it would feel like she was regressing. She loved them dearly, but being fretted and fussed over wasn't what she needed right now.

Chase put his burger down and eyed her. "Country girl, hmm? I'm not really seeing it."

"I don't dress the part anymore."

"But you used to?"

She pushed her glasses up her nose. "Yes."

"I'm envisioning overalls and braids."

"So stereotypical," she said with a little laugh.

He just shrugged. "Sometimes stereotypes are accurate."

"Not in your case. If you went to grad school with Mandy, you must be a scientist too, and I'm not really seeing *that*."

"That's because I'm not a scientist anymore."

"So what do you do now?" she asked. "Aside from sometimes teaching snowboarding?"

"Snowboarding in the winter. Rock climbing in the summer." He picked up his burger, and pointedly watched her. She ate another fry and was rewarded when he nodded. "It's kind of the way of life in Tahoe."

"What prompted the change?"

"Way too much stuff to talk about on an empty stomach," he said, pushing the other burger toward her.

"Oh, I see what you're doing."

"Do you?" His voice was a little huskier now.

She swallowed. "Yes."

He didn't speak again. Just dropped his gaze to the burger in front of her. He was being pretty obvious. *Eat more and I'll tell you what you want to know.* "Fine," she said, flipping open the bun and dumping some ketchup on top of the meat before sinking in her teeth. It was no organic, grass-fed beef burger from Gott's, but the grease and the carbohydrates must have been what she needed, because it tasted pretty good. She took another bite.

"Fast learner," he muttered.

She swallowed. "The change?" she prompted. He stared at the burger again. *Keep going.* "Ugh, you are such a taskmaster," she said, eating some more.

He laughed. "That's what all my students say." She finished chewing, put the burger down, and stared at him. "Fine," he said. "You earned it." He put down his own burger and took a fry. "I've opted out."

"You've what?"

"Opted out. Let me try to explain. You work in Menlo Park?" She nodded. "And you live in . . . "

"Mountain View."

"I used to live in Menlo Park and I worked in Palo Alto. You know what it's like."

She didn't quite know where he was going with this. "I think so. I mean, I guess the cities are similar."

"What I mean is that you go to work in some corporate building in some industrial business park where you wear a suit."

"So? I like to work," she said.

He nodded. "Okay, so you like your job. And on the weekends, you hike in an open space preserve, or go cycling up Arastradero Road with your fancy gear, or meet some friends for coffee at Red Rock?"

He was asking it like a question, so she answered. "Yes. I like hiking and I like coffee." Especially at Red Rock, a downtown Mountain View institution. "I don't cycle though."

"So you do something else."

"Wine," she said. When John was alive, they'd go to wine tastings on the weekend. Napa, Sonoma, Mendocino—he loved it, and she'd loved it too because it made him happy.

"Wine. Pretty typical," he said, nodding. "I did all that stuff, too. The job. The house. The weekend activities. And after a while, I realized it was all a façade."

"How so?"

"It's fake. All of it. There are supposed to be rules. Civilized codes of conduct. But no one follows them. At least in Tahoe I know what I'm getting. If I don't put chains on my tires, I slip out on the road. If I go out of bounds on the slopes without proper precautions, I get killed. The parameters are much clearer."

"Are you talking about the odds of getting hurt?" she asked. Her area of expertise.

"Sort of. Both places will drag you down if you're not careful, but at least in Tahoe what you see is what you get. I had the choice between Silicon Valley and Tahoe, and I took Tahoe."

She sat back. "I'm not sure I understand. Couldn't you have both? Why couldn't you have kept working there and come up here on the weekends or for vacations?"

"I needed to come up here full-time," was all he said. Then he took another bite of his burger. And another.

"That's it?" she asked. "You're just going to leave me hanging?"

He raised an eyebrow. Was this his way of bribing her to eat more? Well, she'd bite—literally. She ate a few more fries and drank some coffee, but he moved on to another topic of conversation and the line about his work was dropped.

After he'd finished his burger and she'd eaten most of hers, he popped open the plastic container with the pie.

"What kind is it?" she couldn't help asking, still a little disappointed she couldn't get him to talk more. Since they'd stopped talking about his work, though, he'd been a lot more relaxed.

The corners of his mouth twitched. "Marionberry. It's a cross between the olallieberry and the Chehalem blackberry. Not too tart. Not too sweet."

He slid the container toward her and handed her a fork. "Go on. Try some."

She speared a forkful, knowing he was watching her closely as she placed it in her mouth. It was amazing—the tanginess mellowing to sweetness across her tongue. She'd tasted this kind of fruit once before, when John had taken her for a picnic up in Mendocino. After hiking around the bluffs in the tiny town, they'd shared some ripe berries and soft, rich cheese while they watched the ocean crash and roll beneath them as the sun sank low in the sky.

It had been a good day.

She blinked, and the Proustian moment was gone. Chase was still watching her eat, waiting for her to say something.

"It's good," was all she could manage with the lump in her throat.

"Glad you like it." He smiled and leaned back in his seat. Lazily, he rubbed Roxy behind the ears. The dog leaned against his knee and closed her eyes.

"You're not going to eat any?"

He shook his head. "Got it for you."

"I—thank you."

He just smiled again.

The pie was so rich and the memories so thick, she wasn't able to eat more than a few bites. After she'd finished eating what she wanted, Chase gave the rest to Roxy who gobbled it up in three seconds flat and smacked her lips.

The sight of Roxy's pink tongue licking up all the dark berry juice made her laugh, really laugh, something she hadn't done in a long while. Strangely, the laughter settled her, took away some of the tension that had dogged her for so long, leaving her lighter. Clearer.

And as she watched the rain come down from under the safety of the overhang with the twinkling holiday lights, sitting there with this man and his dog, she began to think she could get used to this feeling of calm.

After they finished their food, they got back into Chase's truck. Ann was surprised when he started the engine and began to drive.

"I thought you said the road was closed," she said.

"It is."

"So where are we going?"

"I got you a room," he said.

"Just one?" she said before she could help herself.

"If I'd been alone with Roxy, we probably would have stopped in the middle of Route 80 and just gone to sleep," he said, pulling into a hotel parking lot. "Thought you'd be more comfortable sleeping in a bed. I'll stay in the truck with Roxy, and we can start off early in the morning."

"That doesn't seem right," she said, frowning.

He shrugged. "None of these places take dogs." He parked near the entrance and hopped out into the rain. She followed him inside, getting only a little bit wet in the process.

The front desk clerk was a twenty-something guy with shaggy hair, a sleepy smile, and a Santa hat. "Merry Christmas," he said, pulling up the reservation. "Last room, lady. You're lucky. We're typically full up this time of year."

She gave him her credit card. "You don't, ah, take pets, do you?"

"Nope. Why?" The clerk peered at her. "You got a pet?"

"No. No," she said hastily. "Just curious. I'm allergic."

"Oh, yeah. No pets allowed. You shouldn't have any problems."

"Do you have any cots?" she asked.

"Sorry, no," the clerk said, handing her back her credit card along with an electronic keycard. "Just gave my last one away to a family of five."

"Thanks anyway," Chase told him, before turning to Ann. "Come on."

Chase brought her bags in himself, so she wouldn't get wetter, and got her settled in her room. As soon as he was gone, her mind began to whir. He'd been doing all the heavy lifting for her—the driving, the medicine, the food, the hotel room. And now he and Roxy were about to spend the night in a cold truck in the rain. It just didn't seem equitable. Right then and there, she knew she'd be sneaking them in. She had to. It was a matter of principle.

It was definitely not because she wanted another look at his broad chest or his slow, sly smile.

Not at all.

When Chase got back to his truck, he pulled out some blankets from the rear bed and jumped into the cab. After he was mostly dry, he covered Roxy with her dog blanket and leaned his seat way back, his jacket under his head. He'd done this enough times to know exactly which position was the most comfortable, and how to angle his body so his knees didn't hit the steering wheel while he was reclining.

He glanced at the dashboard, where Ann's GPS was still sitting, taunting him, a reminder of the stiff-yet-vulnerable woman who put it there. Surprisingly, Ann had seemed reluctant to have him leave. Was it his imagination, or had she been trying to get him to stay?

The sooner he got ideas like that out of his head, the better. Women like Ann Smith were in the Bay Area for one reason: to get ahead. She wanted the job and the house and the yard and the two perfect kids. Oh, yeah, and the successful corporate guy that went along with all of that other crap.

Sure, her country-girl upbringing had surprised him. And the sad look in her eyes, when she thought no one was watching.

Don't get involved. His mantra. It was better not to think about her at all. He pulled down the GPS and stuffed it and its cord into his glove compartment, then got settled once again.

"Night, girl," he said to Roxy, who gave him a little snuffle. He pulled the blanket up higher and closed his eyes.

And nearly had a heart attack when there was a loud knock on his window. He sat upright in a flash.

"Chase?" a soft voice called. "Chase, are you still awake?" *Ann.*

He rolled down the window and ran a hand through his hair. "I am now." She was standing outside in the dim light, shivering in the pouring rain, one of those plastic hotel ice buckets held over her head like a demented rain hat. "Oh man, Ann, get in the truck."

He unlocked the doors as she ran around the back and climbed in the cab. Water dripped onto the seat and floor.

"Please come inside with me."

He blinked. *Not what he was expecting.* "Roxy," he said, using his head to indicate his companion.

"Bring her. She can't stay out here, either."

"You're allergic," he pointed out, testing her.

"I have medicine, remember?"

"We're fine."

"It's freezing in here. I happen to know the temperature is going down to thirty-five degrees tonight, which technically isn't freezing but is really close, and it would just be cruel for you to stay out here when I have a warm room only a hundred yards away."

"You've thought everything out, haven't you?"

"Please say yes."

"All right." She'd done all the rationalizing for him, anyway.

Relief flashed across her face. "I thought you'd say no. Okay, we have to go around the back way."

He raised his seatback and turned on the engine. "Can't believe you, of all people, are offering to sneak me and my dog into the last hotel room in Auburn," he said. "You're pretty much the last person I'd ever expect to be a rule breaker."

"That's not really fair. You've known me all of," she glanced down at her watch and wiped the rain off it with a damp sleeve, "six hours."

"Oh, I had you pegged from the moment I saw you."

She looked affronted by that. "I can break the rules if the situation warrants it," she said. "And I have never met a man who is so quick to judge a book by its cover. It's right there," she said, pointing to a door with a single bulb hanging from an attached overhang.

He pulled into a nearby parking spot. "I judge everyone by their covers," he said. "It cuts through a lot of crap." Because he'd been burned, and he wasn't going to make that mistake again. "Anyway, you did, too. You assumed I'd say no." Ann had no response to that. "So tell me how you *really* got us in," he prodded.

"It wasn't a big deal. I simply spoke with the front desk clerk."

Chase turned to her and raised an eyebrow. She was staring at the dashboard.

"Where's my GPS?"

"I put it in a safe place. And you're dodging the question."

Her gaze snapped back to him. "I am not. I appealed to his humanity," she said. "It's so cold out here." As if on cue, she shivered.

Chase was silent, watching her watch him.

"He has an English bulldog named Frank Sinatra at home."

Chase just stared at her.

"Okay, fine! I gave him fifty bucks and he promised not to tell his boss. Happy now?"

Now *that* made sense to him. "Money talks."

"I'd like to think it was a combination of money *and* humanity."

He laughed at her naiveté. "Money always wins out."

"What made you so cynical?" she said, pushing back some wet hair. "It doesn't. Not always." She hopped out of the truck and raced toward the overhang, where she waited for him and Roxy to catch up.

Quickly, Chase gathered up the blankets, locked the truck and joined her by the door. "We're going to have to agree to disagree."

"Shh—" she said. She had opened up the back door and was peering inside. She stared for just a moment longer. "I think the coast is clear," she said, motioning for him to come. "Keep quiet. And don't let Roxy make any noise."

She was treating this like a matter of national security, but he wasn't going to complain if it got him and Roxy into a warm building for the night.

"This way," she said, leading him down a corridor. "Wait—" she said, plastering herself against a wall and gesturing for him to do the same. When he merely crossed his arms over his chest and raised an eyebrow, Ann frowned. Roxy was more compliant. She padded around him and simply sat down at Ann's feet. "It's quiet now. Let's go!" She ushered them down the corridor and inside her room fast, then stuck her head back out to look around. Seemingly satisfied, she shut the door, locked it, and leaned back against it. Her cheeks were flushed and one thick, damp curl framed her face. She looked up at him, triumphantly. "I'm pretty sure no one saw us."

Man, she was adorable. This cloak-and-dagger thing had really gotten her riled up. Honestly, he didn't think she had it in her. "Thought you bribed the desk clerk," he said, trying hard not to smile.

She pushed her glasses up her nose. "Yes, well, his manager always stops by around this time and I didn't want to get him—or us—into any trouble. You think she'll stay quiet?" she asked, indicating Roxy. His tired girl had already curled up into a ball in the corner of the room. "She looks like she'll be okay."

"She'll be fine," he said, moving his attention to the king-sized bed taking up most of the space in the room. "I can take the floor, if it'd make you feel more comfortable."

"No. Please. It'll be fine. The bed's large enough to hold both of us. I think." She eyed him up and down. "You're pretty big," she muttered.

He raised an eyebrow. She'd noticed. And now he noticed her face flushing anew. "I've got to get dry." Quickly, she turned away and put the ice bucket down. Then she grabbed something from her suitcase and slipped into the bathroom.

Chase shrugged off his wet coat and hung it up in the closet to dry. She had balls, he had to admit. Sneaking a damp, dander-filled dog into a hotel room so he wouldn't have to sleep outside alone, bribing the clerk—not prim and proper behavior at all. He might have to rethink his opinion of her.

Or . . . not.

She emerged from the bathroom wearing a garment the likes of which he'd never seen. It was like something out of a New England primer . . . a flannel men's sleep shirt with buttons going halfway down the front. It swallowed her body up. It was red.

And it was plaid.

He finally dragged his gaze away from her lumberjack PJs and up to her face. She'd set her jaw as if she were daring him to make a crack. He opened his mouth, then shut it.

Because she had let her hair down, and the whole damp, dark mass of it tumbled over her shoulders, past her breasts, making her look at once ethereal and fragile. Then she turned, and it was like someone had drop-kicked him right in the gut. The long, wavy strands hit mid-back. Did it feel as soft as it looked? He wanted to touch it. Bury himself in it.

Surprised at the heat which had settled between his legs, he went for a laugh. "Wonder what your lawyer friends would say if they knew you were breaking the rules."

She looked back, her lips turned down. "My lawyer friends?"

"Your work colleagues. You're a lawyer, right?"

A confused expression colored her face. "Why would you think that?"

"You were wearing a suit," he pointed out. "And you work at an insurance company."

"No," she said. "I mean yes, I was wearing a suit and I work at an insurance company, but I'm not a lawyer. One World Insurance just has a pretty conservative culture, at least for Silicon Valley."

"Then what do you do?"

"I'm an actuary."

Now that just figured. "You have got to be kidding me." He pulled his sweater over his head and threw it on a nearby chair.

He hadn't meant it as a compliment, but she looked pleased. "So you actually know what an actuary is? Most people don't."

"Probabilities. It all makes sense now," he muttered, kicking off his boots and shoving them under the chair with his foot.

She nodded. "Yes, I calculate the probability of death, illness—worst-case scenarios, in essence—so that my company can issue the proper life insurance policy at the proper rate. There are other actuaries who do the same thing on the property side, but I prefer people. It helps a little, I think," she said, sliding into the bed. "Knowing that bad things happen with the same odds across the board." Most of that horrible gown was hidden now.

"What kind of bad things?" he said, leaving the *happened to you* unsaid.

"Mandy *really* didn't tell you?"

"Nope," Chase said, pulling his long-sleeved T-shirt over his head. "You gonna?" He felt a little guilty that he was pushing her, but truth be told, he was curious. What could have happened to a woman like her?

"I think I should return the favor and not—"

She stopped talking so he turned to see what was going on. She was staring at him—specifically his chest—with an expression akin to awe. Her mouth was parted slightly, and red was creeping onto her cheeks. Her eyes were wide and bright. He knew exactly how to read that look.

How would she feel if he made a move?

Though he wasn't as big a part of the scene as some of his friends, hookups were fairly common in Tahoe. There'd be a road closure, and you'd end up at someone else's house in front of a roaring fire. Or to avoid the avalanche control's inevitable snow dump on the highway you'd stay at a friend's place closer to the mountain . . . and wind up more than friends by morning. It happened all the time, but not with a woman like actuary Ann Smith. A woman who calculated the odds. A woman who was grounded in real life, not flitting from experience to experience like so many people he knew.

Not that there was anything wrong with that.

He just couldn't do it with her.

Quickly, Chase washed up, then slid into the bed. Ann had taken off her glasses and curled up into a little ball. She was as close to the other side as she could manage without falling off. He kept to his side as if there were an invisible line right down the middle, painfully aware of the ache that had taken up residence in his groin. He tried to turn his brain off but it was working overtime now, imagining her in every possible position, but mostly her under him, that hair spread out all around them.

"Chase?"

"Yeah, Ann?"

"Thank you."

"What for?" Shouldn't he be thanking her?

"For . . . for everything. I didn't anticipate things panning out the way they did today, but you've made everything so much better. I'm fed and warm and dry, thanks to you."

He grunted in acknowledgment. The only reason things had worked out tonight was because he had major experience in going with Plan B when things went wrong. At least he'd learned *something* living in Silicon Valley.

"As long as we're doing thanks, let me thank you for the bed," he said.

"Oh," she said. "It wasn't a big deal."

It kind of was, but instead of telling her that, he cleared his throat. "Try to get some rest. We'll get on the road early."

"Okay."

Under the covers, Ann's small body shifted, and shifted again. She was struggling to get comfortable, that was clear. He knew the feeling. His balls felt like they were about to explode and there wasn't a thing he could do about it. Ann flipped onto her back, made a little noise of frustration, and then curled herself up again.

He thought about going over there, wrapping his arms around her and soothing away her anxiety and stress. But he couldn't—he wouldn't—touch her. Not without an explicit invitation.

It took a while, but he finally heard the rhythmic sound of her breathing. In a few more moments, he found himself drifting off to sleep, too.

CHAPTER 4

Ann stifled a yawn and took a bracing sip of coffee, the bumpy ride from the chains on the wheels doing more to wake her up than the caffeine.

It was morning now, the road was cleared, and they were once again en route to Tahoe, climbing up through the mountains. Chase was at the wheel, and Roxy was curled up on the seats in the second row. Now that Ann wasn't sniffling and sneezing around the dog, she was getting used to Roxy.

Not so much Chase.

She hadn't gotten nearly enough sleep, mostly because she kept waking up, hyper-aware of Chase's big, warm body close to hers all night long.

More than once during the night she'd had to stop her own hands from roaming over her body. She'd wanted to—*really* wanted to—but she couldn't find the guts to touch herself while they were lying in the same bed. What if he'd woken up and found her like that, her fingers playing around her most intimate parts while he lay right next to her? Even if he thought she was attractive, he'd probably think that pleasuring herself in a bed with a strange guy was just . . . creepy.

But it had been so long since someone touched her—so long since she'd even touched herself—and that tantalizing glimpse of Chase Deckert's rock-hard chest last night had revved her up like crazy.

Chase had been anxious to get on the road, and that two-minute shower she'd managed to squeeze in hadn't helped a whit with her little—make that big—problem. So now she was stuck with a deep ache, an itch she couldn't scratch—at least not until tonight when she hoped she'd be alone.

Lord, she hoped she'd be alone. Mandy hadn't said anything about Chase's place, but she assumed there'd be at least two bedrooms. She'd heard that places in Tahoe ranged from bare-bones cabins to multi-million-dollar chalets, but based on the state of his truck, Chase didn't seem like the kind of guy to spend a ton of money on a house.

She glanced over at him. Big mistake. He looked even better today than he had yesterday. Like her, he'd taken a quick shower, and his hair was still damp, in thick waves swept back from his face. He hadn't been able to trim his beard, but it really didn't matter. The extra scruffiness suited him. He was still wearing the same sweater and shirt and she knew exactly what was under that shirt—a widely-planed chest with washboard abdominal muscles that rippled when he spoke. Or moved. Or breathed.

She just couldn't stop staring. Like this morning, when she'd gazed with wide-eyed wonder as he dragged out heavy chains to attach to his truck's wheels. Spare and elegant in his movements, especially for such a big man, he looked like he'd done the job a thousand times.

Yes. *Definitely* inspiring.

Just before nine, they pulled off Route 89 and onto a steep, snowy road. Even with the road mostly plowed and the chains on the tires, it was still slow going. Finally, they reached the end of the road where a large wood cabin was situated.

"Rawls," Chase sighed as he stopped the truck, whipped out his cell phone and quickly dialed a number. "You did it again."

After a few seconds, Ann heard a muffled voice at the other end pick up.

Chase jumped in. "Dude, it's nine. I need my driveway cleared, and everyone else on your route does, too. Just throw on some pants and come out here and do it." He hung up the phone.

"Who's Rawls?"

"My neighbor. That's his place there," Chase said, pointing to a cabin through the woods in front of which was parked a big snowplow. "He's in the snow removal business. Except as usual, he overslept and hasn't removed any snow."

"Ah," she said.

A big, blond, sleepy-looking man came out of the cabin. With one hand he rubbed his eyes, and with the other he held up his pants. Ann actually felt a little sorry for him.

"Can't we walk the rest of the way?" she asked, trying to save Rawls the trip.

Chase shook his head. "Nope. Can't leave the truck on the street," he said, backing up to make room for the plow. "It's illegal during the winter. And as for walking, you're not exactly dressed for it."

He might be right. She'd thrown on a pair of jeans and a sweater this morning, anticipating the ability to change before they went to the mountain.

Rawls started the plow, and after a few long moments, drove up. From what she could see of him through the driver's side window, he did not look happy. He made quick work of the snow in Chase's driveway, then drove right back down the street to his own, cut the engine, and stumbled back inside his cabin.

"Idiot," Chase muttered, turning the engine off. "I don't want him losing any more business because he can't get his ass in gear. Well, you can lead a horse to water." He shook his head. "Hang on. I'll be back to get you in a second."

Chase hopped out and quickly dug a path from the freshly-cleared driveway to a door underneath an overhang. He was done without even breaking a sweat. Her mountain man certainly had a lot of stamina. *Just when did you start thinking of him as yours, Annie?*

"Powder's gonna be killer. I can feel it," he said, opening her door and reaching out his hand. "We're going to have fun on the mountain today."

She put her hand in his, and when that little jolt came, she embraced it. "Sure," she said, getting out of the truck.

Surrounded by massive pine trees, the cabin was built of roughly-hewn wood. It blended in with its surroundings beautifully, as if it were an organic outcropping of the landscape. To the left of the structure was a smaller shed, built from the same wood as the main house. Ann looked up. The second story deck soared over the front lawn. "Your place is really beautiful."

"Thanks," Chase said, letting Roxy out. "My grandfather built it." He went to the trunk and opened it. "Wait until you see the view from the deck."

"You can see the lake?" she asked.

"Oh, yeah. Best view in the neighborhood." Chase hauled out her bag. "Let's head up. I'll give you a quick tour, then we can get changed and get onto the mountain."

"Sounds fine."

Ann followed him into the house. The interior of the place was just as lovely as the exterior. In the living room, grommet-studded leather sofas and chairs were accentuated with soft-looking pillows and throws. A huge fireplace took up one side of the room. Another wall held a floor-to-ceiling bookcase filled with tomes and small sculptures. Through a large picture window on the front wall, Ann caught a tantalizing glimpse of Lake Tahoe. And then she saw it in the corner—a six-foot spruce, bare.

Without warning, the sentiment of the season—all the joy, the warmth, and the love she used to have—walloped her senseless. She froze in place.

Chase gestured at the naked tree. "Rawls brought it in a couple of weeks ago. Didn't have time to do anything with it. Come on." She nodded, not trusting her own voice.

Somehow she got her legs to move, and she was able to follow him through the house.

"There's another porch out there, and a hot tub, too," he said, indicating a glass door. "Just be careful going down the steps. It's always slippery in the snow and ice. The tub's always on so the water doesn't freeze, but I keep it covered so the heat doesn't escape. I usually end up in there after I hit the slopes."

They went upstairs next. "Here's your room," he said, opening a door halfway down the top hallway. "There are two twin beds, so Mandy can take the other one when she gets here." *If she gets here.*

"Thanks," Ann said, glad her voice didn't come out all choked up.

He glanced around the room for a minute. "Get changed. We've already missed the best powder, but we can still catch some if we leave soon." And with that, he left the room.

Slowly, she collected herself and went to change.

It was nearly ten-thirty by the time Chase and Ann got to Alpine Meadows. As was typical post-storm, the sun was shining and the hordes were swarming all over the mountain, carving it up. He hoped there was some fresh powder left for him.

"You said you used to ski," he said to Ann as they walked toward the lifts. "How good were you?"

Ann shrugged. "Pretty good."

"Pretty good, huh? Did you ski black diamonds?"

She gave a short nod.

"Good. We could drop in on Alpine Bowl from one of the expert trails. It'd be a nice start to the day."

"Sure."

Without lingering further at base camp, he and Ann took the Alpine Bowl double-chair lift to Ward Peak, Chase more than cognizant of Ann's soft weight pressed up next to him.

She looked different out of her work clothes. When she'd come out of her room, dressed only in a long-sleeved T-shirt and a skin-tight retro-style snow bib, his eyes had nearly bugged out of his head. It wasn't bulky, like other snow gear, and the slim matching jacket she wore on top was just plain sexy. He'd seen a few bibs on the mountain this season, but hadn't paid too much attention until he'd seen her petite form packed into one.

Did she have any idea what that thing did for her ass? She'd taken off her glasses—she must be wearing contact lenses—and her beautiful blue eyes came into full focus. He hadn't realized how long her lashes were.

But her guarded look was back full-force. Maybe she was nervous about the skiing, but it seemed like it was more than that.

As he always did when he got off the lift, Chase took a moment at the mountain's peak, savoring the anticipation of what was about to come. Other people were strapping in and checking their bindings as they got ready for long, deep runs on freshly-dumped powder. Down below, gleaming white slopes were carved out of the dark green tree line, and a few little dots—skiers and snowboarders—weaved and turned in the white. The wind blew across his face, chilling the parts where his beard didn't cover his skin. He breathed in the fresh, clean mountain air. *This* was why he lived in Tahoe—the natural beauty and the freedom he had to do this—take an unspoiled, pre-holiday, mid-week run.

He glanced over at Ann. She had her eyes shut and looked to be breathing deeply. When she finally turned to him, she didn't look as sad as she had before. Satisfied that the mountain was starting to do its work, he clicked his bindings into place.

"You ready?" he said.

She nodded.

"Okay," he said. "I usually like to board out of bounds, but I should be able to catch some fresh powder if I stick close to the sides of the run, especially the day after a storm. You can ski right down the center, and I'll wait for you at the bottom." He peered over the cornice. There was a pretty high lip thanks to the winds last night, and to kick off from here would mean catching some serious air. "You sure you can ski this?"

"I'm sure," she said, pulling her goggles down to cover her eyes. "See you at the bottom." Without waiting for him to answer, she kicked off and went over the edge.

And Chase's mouth dropped open.

Because Ann Smith could *ski*. As in technically perfect and wickedly fast, just like a pro.

It took a moment for Chase to register what was happening before he got his act in gear. He tipped over the lip and started down the mountain. Forcing himself to focus on the course in front of him instead of on Ann's ass, he sought untouched powder. It took a couple hundred yards to find it, off to the left of the run, right at the tree line. It was amazing, and just for the moment he forgot about Ann as he reveled in the twists and turns, carving his own path through the freshly-fallen snow.

The storm's bounty was his for the taking. If he'd been able to get up sooner it would have been even better, but now that he knew Ann was an expert skier, he might be able to let her do her own thing while he headed into back country for some off-piste action. Or maybe he could convince her to join him. With her skill level, sinking into the fresh stuff would be less of a problem for her.

Chase lifted his head from his own run for a moment, following Ann's form down the hill. Perfect, tight turns, even on those old clunkers of hers. He wondered how fast she'd be if she got some new skis. Then the front edge of his board dipped just a hair, and it took all his strength and skill not to let the edge go under the snowline—a sure-fire way to end up in a face-first slide down the mountain. He shifted his weight more firmly to his back foot, and curled up the toes on his front foot. Crisis averted.

Alpine Bowl was pure pleasure. He took a few long, easy turns for several hundred yards, enjoying the spray of powder as it flew up and around him, then gunned it to the intermediate slopes that would take him the rest of the way down the mountain.

Sooner than he wished, he was at the end of the run. Ann was waiting for him at the base. As he approached, she raised her goggles. He could see the brightness in her eyes, the flush of her cheeks. She looked exhilarated and completely blissed-out. Without warning, heat hit him deep and low.

"You're good," he said, trying to focus on something other than her inherent sexiness. "Really good."

"Thanks," she said, smiling up at him. "I skied in the Junior Olympics, but decided to go to school full-time and keep the skiing as an extracurricular, just for me."

"Less pressure."

"I still pushed myself, but yes, a lot less pressure. And just look at me. I'm really out of shape now." She laughed and rubbed her legs. "My thighs are killing me."

He grinned. "Let's see if we can turn them into jelly. Come out of bounds with me."

"Oh, I can't ski off course," she demurred.

"Why not?" he challenged. "You're good enough."

She shook her head. "No. If you don't mind, I think I just need to ease my way back onto the slopes. Why don't you do your thing and I'll meet you back at mid-mountain for lunch? You have my cell phone number, so just text or call when you're done."

Ann wanted to be alone. He got that. "Catch you back at the grill for lunch," he told her. She smiled and headed toward the lift.

When she was gone, he texted his friend Kyle, another instructor at Alpine he sometimes boarded with on their off days. Kyle texted back a minute later, offering to meet up with him. Lucky break. Some out-of-bounds skiing would surely do the trick to get him back on track. He only wished he could be more enthusiastic.

Throw your heart into it, Deck. One celibate night with a woman you hardly know shouldn't change your outlook on things.

But strangely enough, it had.

CHAPTER 5

Snow arced into the air as Ann came to a stop at the base of the mountain. Her heart was pounding and she was breathing hard. Her legs were jelly again after that steep, wide-open, powder-filled run through Bernie's Bowl back to the lodge, but boy, it felt good. She'd forgotten how amazing the thrill of a long, sweeping run could be. With every run she took, the tension and sadness inside her dissipated more.

Which was good, because after she'd seen that undecorated Christmas tree at Chase's place she'd almost lost it. Thanks to last-minute wedding preparations, she and John hadn't had time to decorate their tree either, and after he died it faded to a sickly yellow in their townhouse—a fire hazard she didn't have the will to throw away for months. But the sense of freedom she had while skiing and the simple beauty of the mountain were slowly helping her regain her sense of balance. That, and Chase himself, who was doing his best to make her feel comfortable.

This was exactly what she hoped would happen this weekend—that she would face the past, but be able to move forward.

Ann took a deep breath, pushed her goggles up high on her head and watched a few snowboarders carve up the powder more than competently. Boarding looked to be pretty challenging. Maybe she'd try it one of these days. Maybe Chase could teach her.

She found herself wondering how Chase boarded. In the one run they'd done together Ann had been out ahead of him, and he'd been close enough behind that she hadn't been able to see his style. Did he take the mountain slowly and deliberately? Or fast and hard? Was his boarding technical or sloppy?

This morning's ride up the lift with Chase was . . . challenging. She'd wanted to lean over and kiss him so badly. What was it about that man that made her so bold? She'd really snuck him and his dog into a hotel room last night, hadn't she?

And when was the last time she'd done something because it *felt* right? She'd worked hard to get back on track with her regular life, but she hadn't given herself the opportunity to live. Just locked herself up in her routine, going through the motions.

Until she met Chase.

John was a good man but, like her, he lived by rules. He was a lawyer, after all, with as many legal codes to memorize and employ as she had actuarial rules to use. They'd made a good team, and with their organized life the possibility of something negative happening seemed almost infinitesimal.

Until his death, when she'd been forced to confront the idea that the odds could sometimes *not* go in your favor. That the small chance something bad could happen actually *did* happen every day. To regular people going about their regular lives. To John.

It had taken her a long time to realize that even though it was her job to calculate probabilities, she shouldn't be making decisions or living her life based on chance. Of course, realizing something and acting on it were two completely different things.

Whatever had helped her turn the corner, she was grateful. She'd started to act, and now that she'd tasted what living could feel like she was going to grab on with both hands and not let go. She was going to race down that mountain at warp speed and forget about the naked Christmas tree. She was going to smile and laugh. And if Chase asked her to go out-of-bounds skiing with him again she would accept, the probability of death or dismemberment be damned.

Speaking of the man . . .

Chase walked up to her, looking confident and strong with his big board in his arms. "Hi, glad you got my text. Want some help?" he asked, indicating her skis.

"Yes, please."

With a sharp press of his booted foot on each of her bindings, she was free.

"Have a good morning?" he asked.

She nodded. "Yes." She stepped out of her skis and picked them up. "Did you?"

"Yeah." There was fire in his eyes. From the boarding or from her, she wasn't certain. "Hungry?" She nodded again. "Then let's go," he said, a hand on her back guiding the way to the café at the lodge. She tried not to read too much into it.

Grateful to give her body a rest, she sat down at a table while Chase bought her a wrap sandwich and a coffee with his employee discount. As soon as he brought the food to her, she attacked it.

"Mountain gives you a big appetite, doesn't it?" he said. She caught his smile behind his beard.

"Yes. Don't tease."

"I'm just stating a fact. You push your body hard, you need calories." He took a bite of his own wrap. Within three minutes she'd finished her own. "Want another?" he asked.

She waited a second, gauging her body's hunger level. "Yes," she admitted. "But if I eat another whole one, I'll probably be sick."

"Hmm. Got room for this?" Chase pulled a giant chocolate chip cookie out of his pocket and held it up in front of her.

The man was tempting her. Wooing her with food. And they both knew it. Gently, she took the cookie from him. "I have room for half." With the cookie still in its plastic wrapper, she broke it down the middle and then opened the packaging, taking a piece. He was watching her, so she took a big bite and made a huge deal out of chewing it.

On the mountain, every sense seemed to be heightened, including taste. This cookie was ambrosial, but she barely had the strength to finish eating. She'd pushed herself so hard—harder than she had in a long while—and it seemed her body had finally caught up with her brain. But she didn't want to be the one to beg off.

Chase must have noticed her slowing down because he searched her face for a long minute. Then he stretched his arms over his head. "You look as beat as I feel. Let's finish up lunch and get you home."

CHAPTER 6

Chase never imagined Ann had it in her to ski like that. She'd looked over the edge of the cornice, laughed, and launched herself right off that lip, catching some serious air before landing gracefully back on her skis and carving up the mountainside like nobody's business.

He was lounging on the sofa in front of a fire he'd built with his bare hands—none of that gas-lit crap—with an ice-cold beer in his hand. Ann was sitting on the floor nearby, her knees folded up to her chest as she stared into the fire, Roxy by her side. She looked less tired now, and definitely more relaxed. The firelight danced off her hair, creating licks of red and gold on the chestnut strands. It played all over her expressive face, and cast shadows in the hollow of her cheek. He loved that sound—silence, except for the crackling of the wood as it snapped and popped in the fire. And he liked having her here. Strangely enough, she fit.

Ann cleared her throat. "How long have you been in Tahoe?" she asked, still watching the flames.

"About a year," Chase said.

Ann glanced around. "Seems like you've been here a lot longer than that."

He knew what she was taking note of—the well-worn furniture, the family history in photographs on the mantle, and the artwork on the walls. "I grew up here," he said. Even when he'd had his place in Menlo Park, *this* had been his home—the place he always came back to. The place that always reminded him who he really was. "Like I told you before, my grandfather built this house. He and my grandma lived here until she died a little over a year ago. She left it to me in her will. I think it was her way of dragging my sorry ass back up North."

"But Silicon Valley is in Northern California."

"Grandma considered anything south of Sacramento to be Southern California. Sounds silly, really, but she told me on more than one occasion that living in Silicon Valley was going to rot my soul."

"Harsh," Ann said.

Chase shrugged and took a swig of beer. "She was a pretty blunt lady. But look at me now. I'm back where I belong."

"Why'd you really leave?" Ann asked.

"You want the truth?"

She nodded. "Always."

"My partner sold me out for a couple million bucks and some stock options."

"What?!" she said, turning, a look of shock on her face. "You need to give me more details than that!"

"All right," he said. It wasn't something he really wanted to talk about, but he was willing to tell Ann. She'd been hurt, too. He could see it in her eyes. And somehow he knew she would listen without judging him. "I'd always been interested in the prevention and treatment of malaria. I even did my dissertation on it. It's not a disease many Americans have ever experienced, but for people in many parts of the world it can be a matter of life or death. Preventing the disease from reaching your village or getting quick, effective treatment if you do happen to catch it can mean the difference between being able to plant your crops or dying of starvation. Between being able to tend your fields or animals or letting your village go to ruin. And the prohibitive cost is still a huge problem."

He took a deep breath, getting ready for the tough stuff.

"In my research, I stumbled upon a real game-changer. A new artemisinin derivative that could be used in an Artemisinin Combination Therapy, or ACT. The new derivative really looked promising, so we founded a company, ACT Corporation. Not very original, I know, but at least everyone knew what we were working on. I was jazzed about the research," he said, remembering those times when he couldn't wait to get to work every day, and the vivid dreams he'd have about the research at night. "I let Greg handle all the business stuff. Big mistake. He gave himself controlling ownership in the company we founded, patented the research himself, and then negotiated a deal behind my back to sell the work to a huge biopharm company."

"Didn't you have rights?"

"Sure I did. I could have fought and dredged up my lab notebooks and emails and notes and argued in court for years, but that's not what my work was about. That's not what *science* is about. I went into the field to help people. To save lives. Not to sell off my research to the highest bidder so a big company could make a bigger profit. That medicine needs to get to those who need it most, and now it won't. Not unless some humanitarian organization shells out hundreds of millions of dollars so the people who really need it can have it at an affordable price." He took a deep breath, tamping down the anger.

"That doesn't sound fair."

He shrugged. "What's fair?"

"It just doesn't sound *legal.*"

"Oh, it was legal all right, but the whole thing stank. I realized too late that Greg was never in it for the science—all he cared about was the money. I knew if I stayed in Silicon Valley I'd lose myself. Besides, I had nothing left. No job. No research. Oh, and no girlfriend. Believe it or not, she left me for Greg." He shook his head, remembering the feelings of anger and impotence that had swept through him when right after Greg dropped the bomb that ACT Corp was over, Heather announced she was ditching him for a new prize. "After that, I kind of soured on the Valley. I could've gone to Globalize, the company that bought the research, just like Greg did—they wanted me, bad—but I was so furious at being screwed over that I told them all to piss off and I went to Africa."

"Why?"

"I guess my thought process was that if Silicon Valley couldn't play nice, I'd go somewhere else. I spent a year in Zambia as a Johns Hopkins fellow. The research was fine, but nothing like I'd been doing with ACT. Honestly, I'd rather be in the lab than in the field. Just as the fellowship was up, my grandma died and left this place to me. I didn't like the thought of going back to Menlo Park and getting a job at another biotech company, so I came up here."

She turned back to the fire and was quiet for a while, as if absorbing what he'd said. Finally, she turned back to him. "Do you miss it?"

He took a drink and pondered the question. "Yeah, I miss it. Parts of it, anyway. I miss the science, the thrill of feeling like I'm on the cusp of something big—bigger than myself. Of knowing that if I kept at it, I could change the world."

"That sounds like something worth fighting for." Her tone was neutral, but she wouldn't break his gaze. There was awareness in her eyes—that she knew he was holding something back—but he'd been right. She wasn't judging him.

He shrugged. "I don't know. Part of it was definitely anger. I was so furious that I was barely functional. I needed to get out of there so badly, I took the first good thing that came along." *On the other side of the world.* "And I know part of it was stubbornness. Greg totally screwed me over and the last thing I wanted to do after all that was to offer up my brain on a platter."

"Now *that* is a disturbing image."

"It's what I would have done if I'd gone to Globalize." Even if it meant continuing the research he loved. Chase shook his head, not sure anymore if that logic held, but not truly wanting to test it either. "I was one stubborn SOB."

"Aren't you still?" she asked, cocking her head at him.

He shrugged. "Not as much as I used to be. Maybe age has mellowed me. And being here has helped a little, too. People end up in Tahoe for so many reasons, but one of the dirty little secrets about this place is that a lot of people here have been burned in some way."

There was silence for a long time. Chase thought maybe she was going to keep pushing. But she didn't.

"I'm so sorry that happened to you," Ann finally said. "No one deserves to be used like that."

"Yeah, well, that's life, I guess." He took another drink. "So what's your story, Ann Smith? Someone swindle you? Make off with your work? Break your heart?" Her face fell, and he knew he'd gotten it right. He hadn't meant to be so flip. "Hey, I'm sorry," he said, sitting up. "Whoever he was, I'm sure he was a jerk."

She shook her head. "It's not like that. I had my heart broken, but not for the reason you probably think. My fiancé died."

"I'm sorry." The words came out automatically, covering up his shock. He put down his beer.

"It was an aneurysm," she went on, clutching her knees closer to her chest now, folding her small body almost in half. "He was twenty-nine, a corporate attorney with a big law firm. He ran marathons. It was the week before our wedding. We were going to be married on Christmas." She paused for a moment. "I had to call everyone and tell them the wedding was off in the same breath that I invited them to John's funeral."

He couldn't even fathom having the strength needed to do that.

"Tell me about him."

Ann looked grateful that he'd asked a positive question. She was probably used to hearing words of sympathy and she didn't seem like the type to want them. "We both went to Michigan, but we didn't meet until after college at an alumni wine-tasting event. John was the first guy I met out here who knew what an actuary was. It was his dad's profession. He was a good man. Conservative, but he knew how to make me laugh."

"What about his parents? Are they . . . ?"

"Still alive? Yes, in Minneapolis. They were devastated," she said. "So was his older sister. I haven't seen them since the funeral. I guess we were all trying to put our lives back together."

"How long ago?"

"Two years."

What would it be like to have his world ripped out from under him? Having someone he loved die was a far cry from having a few years of research snatched away. He'd loved his grandma, of course, but she'd lived a good, long life and her death had been natural. And the closest he'd come to having his heart trampled on was when Heather had left him for Greg. It had hurt, but the fact that he was more hung up on Greg's betrayal than Heather's probably meant he hadn't truly loved her. Somehow all his gripes and annoyances seemed petty in the face of Ann's sorrow.

He slid off the couch and got on his knees, right next to her.

"I hate the almost-widow status," she said. "No one quite knows what to do with me, and honestly I don't quite know what to do with myself. So I work. Try to figure out who I am without him. I mean, what else can I do?"

She looked over to his tree—the one he hadn't bothered to decorate because his family wasn't around. "The worst part of all of this was that all the promise and all the joy of the rest of my life was wrapped up in Christmas. The most wonderful time of the year isn't so wonderful for me anymore. I'm not sure it ever will be again."

When she turned back, her eyes were shiny. She blinked a little too fast. "I love him. I always will. But I'm twenty-nine. I need to live, and living means moving forward. It's been two years since he died, and I'm still figuring out how to get back on track."

She'd been through so much. At twenty-nine he was full of snot and hubris, having just finished the final year of his PhD program. *I'm going to change the world* he'd told his advisor. In retrospect, he'd been such a jerk. And now it had all come full circle. Here he was, hiding out in Tahoe, licking his wounds while a woman with way more humility and guts than he'd ever had was laying her soul bare for him.

"You're brave," he finally said.

"Brave?" she sniffed, her eyes bright with unshed tears. "I'm not brave at all. Just running on auto-pilot."

Those tears shimmering in her eyes threatened to spill, so he held out his arms. "Come here."

Ann blinked and looked at his outstretched arms, then back up at his face. Slowly, she unclasped her hands from around her knees, and without warning, flung her arms around his neck and held on tight. Chase answered by wrapping his arms around her. She was so small, like a little bird fluttering its tiny wings, ready to fly away if he let go.

He didn't want to let go.

He was two years too late to soothe away her hurt—she'd done that all on her own—but he could still show her that she wasn't alone. Her head was buried in that hollow between his shoulder and collarbone. She fit perfectly there, like the spot was tailor-made for her. He wanted to keep holding her. And kiss her. Press his lips to hers and show her how beautiful she was.

Then she pulled back, and reluctantly he let her go.

"I'm fine," she said, doing her best to brighten her expression. She turned away from him, just for a second, and he knew she must be wiping some of those unshed tears away. When she turned back, her face was composed.

Chase sat back on his heels, knowing the moment was over. Which was probably for the best, because how much of an ass would he be if he took advantage of her after she'd told him how awesome her dead fiancé was? *Slick move, Deck.*

"Really," Ann said. "Just look at the two of us. We must be the most pathetic people in Tahoe." She spoke lightly, but he could hear the melancholy in her voice.

"Oh, there are more pathetic people," he said. "Definitely. Like those poor folks wanting to get here for Christmas break who got trapped in the storm yesterday." He paused. "I don't know why you wouldn't go out of bounds with me," he said, grabbing his beer and settling back down on the couch. "You're a damned good skier."

Ann shook her head. "I couldn't."

She wasn't getting off that easily. "You could. You just wouldn't," he said.

"I thought it would be too risky," she finally said.

"No. You're the biggest risk-taker of them all."

"I am not," she insisted.

"Oh, you are, and I can prove it." His lips curled up. "Let's go down the list. You got in a car with a strange guy—"

"Mandy vouched for you."

"—a strange guy and his dog," Chase continued, ignoring her. "A dog you are allergic to, I might add. You could easily have bailed, but you didn't. I gave you medicine that knocked you out cold, yet even when you woke up you stayed with me."

"It was my normal reaction to that medicine. You didn't do anything wrong."

"Then, when the road closed and you could have had the hotel room to yourself, you bribed the desk clerk and snuck me—and Roxy—in to spend the night. You even let me sleep in the same bed with you. Now you're here, telling me your life story. So you're going to tell me you're not a risk-taker?" He sat back on the couch and took a swig of beer. "Like I said, the biggest risk-taker of all."

"You got me to eat," she said softly.

"I did *what?*"

"You coaxed me to eat. And I enjoyed it. I haven't enjoyed food in a really long time," she smiled at him, a bit ruefully. "Also, I'm a pretty stubborn person, and I figured if you cared enough to get nourishment into me, even after I woke up all cranky and suspicious, then you weren't going to hurt me. After that, I knew you were okay."

"Come out of bounds with me tomorrow," Chase said abruptly. "You know you have it in you." He could just see her, flying through the trees as she felt what he felt—that exhilarating rush that overrode everything else. *The same rush he'd get if he touched her. Kissed her. Buried himself in her.*

Surprise flickered across her face, just for a split second, before she tilted her chin up and set her jaw. With the fire behind her she was shadow and light, fierce and wise.

"I will," she said, turning back to the fire. "But just don't keep pressing it, okay. I don't want to think about it too much in case I lose my nerve."

"Okay." He had to get out of there before he did something stupid. Like cover her body with his and kiss her until they both couldn't see straight. He cleared his throat. "I'm going to hit the hay. Why don't you get some rest?" He stood up, waiting for her to do the same. But she didn't budge.

"All right." She looked up at him. "I'm going to enjoy the fire for a while longer."

"Sure." Good. If she didn't go to bed right away, maybe he could get to sleep without dreaming of her beautiful form, naked in the room right next to his. Just make sure it's out before you head to bed."

"Okay."

He wanted to linger. But it wouldn't be smart. "Goodnight, Ann."

"Goodnight, Chase."

CHAPTER 7

Out-of-bounds skiing. The idea conjured up all sorts of images, most of which included her hurtling down the mountainside at warp speed, dodging trees right and left as her thighs burned from navigating the rough terrain. It sounded at once thrilling and dangerous.

Kind of like a certain sexy snowboarder she couldn't get off her mind.

She'd just spent the better part of the last hour talking about John, but she couldn't get Chase out of her brain. What was really weird about the whole thing was that Chase was absolutely nothing like John. But a day ago, she didn't think she and Chase had anything in common either, yet they were finding a lot to talk about. Like their love for the winter season or the best place in Redwood City to get a carne asada burrito.

There was something big inside her trying to burst free, pushing her toward a cliff. She could feel her feet scrabbling at the edge, trying to prevent herself from slipping over. But the strange thing was, she wasn't trying *that* hard to stop herself from falling. Because truth be told, she was feeling pretty trapped in her whole set-up. Work, exercise, home. When she had John, it had been enough to satisfy her, but now it just seemed oppressive.

She'd spent the last two years wrapped up in her own head, trying to keep everything together. Now, this one man with his secrets and his heartache had stirred something inside her. He was just as broken as she was, but he didn't want to admit it. It wasn't much better than what she had done—retreated into herself. Another lonely person at Christmastime.

Coming to Tahoe was a start, but she needed to do more.

Ann stood and marched into her bedroom, unwrapped one of John's precious bottles of Burgundy from where she'd packed it in between her nightgown and her undies, and brought it into the kitchen.

There had to be a bottle opener around here somewhere, right?

She rummaged around in a couple of drawers until she found the one that held all the kitchen knickknacks. And a bottle opener, hooray!

Without even thinking, she opened the bottle, found a glass, and poured a generous helping of wine.

She held it up, toasting the air. "To you, John. To Christmas. And to me and the rest of my life." Then she drank, deeply.

She'd had some last year on their would-be-anniversary, but this year it tasted different. There was more complexity and richness, with notes of cherry and coffee, two of her favorite flavors. The perfect wine to signify her fresh start. She was going to start living again. Right away. Tomorrow she was going skiing out of bounds with Chase Deckert. And whatever happened afterward, well, she wouldn't be opposed.

Tonight, they shared a moment. She thought he'd kiss her, but he pulled away. She still felt the disappointment.

She took another sip of wine. For the past year her focus hadn't been on the physical, but on the cerebral and the emotional—healing herself. She'd stopped eating. Even the simple pleasure of food had been inextricably tied up with memories of John.

And the sex thing was wrapped up with John, too. It wasn't simply that she hadn't had sex for two years. It was that she hadn't even wanted to. Who would she have slept with, anyway? The only single guys she knew worked at her company. None of them were attractive, at least not to her, and she knew enough not to mix business with pleasure.

She could have gone out to a bar and picked up someone just for the night, like Mandy had been encouraging her to do for the last few months. Every time she ended up going out—more than reluctantly—she had at least one or two offers, especially with Mandy greasing the wheels to make it happen. She could never approach a guy with Mandy's ease, but she was all right talking once the guy had been handed to her on a platter. Usually the guy didn't mind talking back.

But even if she connected with someone a little bit, she couldn't bring herself to seal the deal. A couple of times she thought she'd been close, but there was something about the whole thing that just seemed *wrong*, especially after the intimacy she and John had shared.

Somehow Chase Deckert had awakened her lady parts with only his smile, and for the first time since John, she wanted to share all of herself with another person. To explore his body with her fingers, and maybe her mouth.

Ann groaned. How, exactly, was this supposed to work again? Boy, she really was pathetic. Most women would just jump in the sack, get it over with. Kind of like she'd done with her virginity the first time with John. She'd been ready, and the whole V-card thing had seemed like a burden for way longer than it should have. John was the right guy at the right time, but he'd been so surprised afterward.

I was your first? he'd said with something akin to wonderment.

She took another sip of wine. That part of her life was over. Done. She needed to focus on the present. And the present included a hot snowboarder with washboard abs who she very much wanted to be her first. Or second. Whatever.

So she hadn't had sex in a while. So what? Lots of people were celibate for long periods of time. *But lots of people don't have the baggage of a dead fiancé hanging over them, either.*

Still, she had to get back on the horse sometime.

That phrase conjured up some delicious images, mostly of her on top of Chase. Drinking some more wine, she walked to the family room and sat down on the couch, right where Chase had been sitting. If she got close enough to the cushions, she could even smell his masculine scent—pine and mountain air.

Oh, this was a bad idea. Because the wine was warming her stomach, and that warmth crept lower and lower, spreading through her core, inflaming her from the inside. She clenched her internal muscles together, shocked at the jolt of pleasure that coursed through her. When she shifted her body, her hand brushed against her breast, instantly hardening her nipple. Chase's hand would feel so much better.

But she did it again anyway, rubbing her palm in circles over her now-taut bud. A little moan escaped her lips. Roxy, curled up on a big cushion in the corner of the room, gave an answering snuffle. Quickly she put her hand over her mouth, muffling the sound.

If she stayed here like this, she knew what was going to happen—she'd be caught doing what she so desperately wanted to do last night in that hotel room with Chase lying next to her. The thought of him finding her pleasuring herself on his couch filled her with a delicious shame, but what seemed like a better idea was to head to the hot tub, especially with Roxy right there.

Yes, going into the hot tub seemed like an excellent idea. She could warm up, and in the relative privacy of the warm water maybe get some of Chase Deckert out of her system.

Ann took another sip of wine. When she stood, her brain was pleasantly fuzzy. Snaring the wine bottle from the kitchen, she headed upstairs. It took a little longer than she anticipated to find her way back to her room and get undressed and into her swimsuit—so long, actually, that she ended up finishing her first glass of wine and pouring herself another. Ann finally got her suit on and went back downstairs. She couldn't find the light switch for the porch, but at least she remembered where the hot tub was. She went to the back door, a heavy sliding-glass job, unlocked it, and tugged it open.

Oh, it was dark out here! And cold, but the hot tub should be just down the stairs, right? She padded out in her flip-flops and walked to the stairs. As she got closer to the edge of the porch, an automatic flood light went on. Nice—must be motion sensitive. Yes, the hot tub must be right over . . . .

That was her last thought before she tripped and went flying over the edge of the porch.

"Yaagh!" she yelled, her whole body burning with the force of the cold. She floundered around in the snow for a few long moments, trying to stand up. When she finally managed to get upright, the burn had faded to a tingle. It wasn't pleasant, but it was bearable. Thank you, alcohol.

Uh-oh, she'd lost a flip-flop. Scanning the vast whiteness, she saw a tiny dot of black a few yards away. It really went that far? Dutifully, she trudged over to get it and slipped it back on. It was wet and cold, but then again, so was she.

Now where was that hot tub? She walked a few steps and peered through the darkness. No, that was a log pile. Perhaps over here? No, that was a small group of trees. Really? How hard was it to find a great big tub? Just as she was debating whether to go back inside, she rounded the corner of the house, another flood light tripped on, and there it was—a huge round tub surrounded by snow.

Yes!

Her feet were now completely numb, but she'd be warm, soon. She waded over to the tub through the snow, ignoring the tingle in her legs. The tub stood about four feet off the ground, and there looked to be some kind of small staircase on the side, where snow was mounded higher. She examined the cover, well, the two covers. Two covers? She blinked. Back to one cover. Okay, how did this thing open?

Experimentally, she pushed it. It didn't budge. She pushed harder. There was a little give. That was promising. She pushed super hard and two things happened simultaneously: her feet went out from under her and she heard a gargantuan splash.

Oh, crap.

Now she was ass down, feet up in a hole in a giant snowdrift. She was certain the cover had fallen into the hot tub, but she couldn't wiggle her way out of the drift to fix it. Her knees were by her shoulders, both flip-flops had gone flying and two bare feet mocked her from above her head.

After wiggling around for a couple of minutes to no avail, Ann quit moving. She was just digging herself deeper, anyway. What was the probability of this perfect storm of events? The calculation she did in her fuzzy brain made no sense. So she did the only thing that did make sense— she laughed.

And then the light went out.

Roxy was barking. It had started out as a little moan, but now it had turned into a full-on bark. She wouldn't quit. And damn, she was loud.

"Roxy!" Chase hollered from his room. "Quiet!"

But the darn dog kept on barking.

"I mean it, Roxy! Shush!"

She wouldn't shut up.

"Just freaking awesome," he said, sitting up and sliding out of bed. Roxy did this once every couple of weeks. If she saw a raccoon outside or had some weird animal sense that something was wrong, she'd keep at it until Chase went in person to quiet her down. Not even bothering with a shirt, he went downstairs. "Settle down, girl," he said, padding into the sun room where Roxy was barking and pawing at the glass door. "Why are you in here, anyway? See a raccoon out there?"

He rubbed his eyes and looked down only to see footprints. Tiny, human footprints leading from the door, across the porch, and down to the backyard.

"Oh, holy hell," he said, racing back to his room to grab his shoes and a coat.

He ran back to the sun room, pulled the glass door wide open, wincing only a little at the freezing blast of air, and charged into the night.

"Ann!" he yelled. "Ann!"

Roxy barked and ran around him, sniffing the snow on the porch.

"Ann!"

She'd gone down the stairs, that much was certain, but even with the porch light on, he couldn't see her. "Ann!" he yelled again, his voice quickly swallowed up by the darkness.

"Here!" Ann's little voice called. Chase moved fast and Roxy started barking again, racing in front of him.

He followed the black dog around the side of the house to a mound of snow. The light flicked on illuminating Ann, who was buried in a snow drift wearing—Good Lord, was she wearing anything?

He ran to her and grabbed her by the arms, pulling her out of the drift. And realized what she had on. Make that what she *didn't* have on. No shirt, no shoes—nothing except two tiny scraps of soaking wet purple fabric that would have done little to cover her at the beach. Even in the dim light he could see her lips beginning to turn blue. "Ann! What the hell are you doing?"

"I was t-trying to g-get into the h-hot tub, but I s-slipped." And, wait . . . was she actually *laughing?* She was on the verge of hypothermia and she was laughing. He didn't know what to make of that, so he countered with righteous indignation.

"If you wanted a soak, you should have asked me for help."

She stopped laughing and shook her head. "N-no. You were s-sleeping."

"It doesn't matter," he said, realizing that talking wasn't helping matters. What *would* help was to get her warmed up. "We have to get you inside." He scanned around for her shoes, but didn't see them. And in his haste to get outside, he hadn't brought a towel, either. Without asking her permission, he simply scooped her up into his arms. God, her flesh was freezing cold!

"W-what are you d-doing?" she asked, as he walked back to the house. "The h-hot tub's r-right t-there."

"The tub's a blunt instrument. I drop you in there in the state you're in, your skin burns like fire and your heart could go out. We have to do this slow and easy."

"Y-you d-don't need to c-carry me. I'm f-fine."

"Like hell you are. You can barely speak!"

He got to the porch door and let out a loud whistle. In a few moments, a dark streak came bounding out the woods, right towards him. "Good girl," he said. "Inside, Roxy."

Roxy skittered up the steps and raced into the house. He knew she'd head right for her favorite spot by the fireplace in the family room. Chase carried Ann inside, then slid the door shut with his elbow. He walked toward the stairs.

"W-where are w-we g-going?"

"My room. You have to get warm."

She made a motion like she wanted to be released, but he damn sure wasn't going to let her go. Her skin was still ice-cold, and he needed to warm her core.

"Come on," he said, easing her onto the bed and working the wet knots on her swimsuit. "Let's get these things off."

Ann didn't protest, just let him strip off her suit and watched him with a vaguely bemused expression. She wouldn't be laughing when the feeling came back to her extremities. Quickly, he tucked her into the bed, jumped in behind her, and arranged her back-to-chest.

His flesh burned where it touched hers. He focused past the pain by imagining his heat seeping into her, warming her from the inside out.

When he thought she was ready, he wove one leg between hers, wrapping his body around hers for maximum coverage, and held her as close as he could, his arms tucked around her ribcage, right under her breasts.

The breasts he'd only gotten a brief glimpse of when he'd taken off her clothes.

The breasts he'd been daydreaming about.

No. Warm her up. Think about something else.

But his face was right in her hair. Her sweet-smelling hair he just wanted to sink his fingers into, which sent a shot of lust right through him. Oh, but she smelled faintly alcoholic, too.

"Are you drunk?"

"N-not anymore," she said. "I think the c-cold knocked it out of me." Then she shifted in his arms and moaned a little.

"You okay?" he asked, his voice coming out more gruffly than he'd anticipated. Probably had something to do with the deep ache that had formed in his crotch. She might be freezing, but she could probably still feel a hard-as-nails rod poking into her backside.

"H-hurts," she whimpered, barely breathing. Ah, there it was. The awful feeling of nerve endings regaining sensation. Like a thousand hot pokers jabbing you at once.

Immediately, he snapped back into caretaker mode, rubbing a hand up and down her arm to get her to focus on something else. The pins-and-needles thing was the worst. He'd only been outside for a few minutes and his feet had gone through the whole range of sensations already. "Feels like every single one of your nerve endings is burning."

All she could do was nod.

"I'm sorry, Ann. Just stay with me. It'll pass."

"'Kay," she whispered.

After a while, she stopped shivering, and slowly, he felt the warmth return to the parts of his own body that touched hers. He scooted back a little, then tipped her flat on the bed, trying to keep her as decently covered with the sheet as he could.

"Feeling better?" he asked, searching her face. She wasn't smiling, but she didn't look like she was in pain.

She nodded slowly. "Yes. The burning's stopped, but I think my body's in shock. I don't feel pain. Just . . . empty."

"Yeah, I've felt that before. Like the nerve endings don't know what to do with themselves now that they've been firing for so long and so hard."

"Exactly."

"That'll pass, too. It'll take a while, though."

"Okay." She was looking at him so seriously, her eyes intent, her lips set. "You didn't call for help."

"No. I figured I'd find a way out." Pause. "But you came, anyway."

Who was this woman? The woman who'd lost and lived. The woman who gave the impression of being afraid of everything, but was really afraid of nothing. When he'd found her out in the snow, she'd been laughing. *Laughing.* He wanted that kind of courage. That kind of strength.

"Yeah. Thanks to Roxy," he said. They stared at each other for a while longer. "Anyplace else I can warm you up?"

She wouldn't break his gaze. Instead of blushing or stammering or retreating to the safety of her own room, she lifted a hand. "Here."

"Sure." He captured her small hand between his and pressed, imparting his warmth to her while she watched, her mouth a little open. It didn't take long. Finally, he released her.

"Here." Slowly, she raised her other hand. He warmed that one, too. When he slid his thumb over the sensitive area inside her wrist she trembled and her eyes closed, just for a moment. Then she opened them and showed him everything—her need, her vulnerability, and her desire.

"Here." One little finger pointed to her lips.

He ran the pad of his thumb over her lips and she shuddered. "Here?"

She nodded. *Yes.* An invitation he couldn't deny.

So Chase covered her mouth with his.

CHAPTER 8

Yes. Oh, yes.

No hesitation. No confusion. This, here and now, was the only thing Ann wanted. Well-meaning friends kept telling her after John died that she'd know when she was ready. She'd nodded and thanked them and murmured, *mmm, yes, you're so right* without really understanding what they were saying. Tonight, she finally did.

When Chase opened her lips with his, she welcomed it. Welcomed the gentle slide of his tongue over hers. Welcomed the taste of mint and man. Wanted so much more from him than he was giving.

She slid her hand up his chest, every ridge amplified by the lingering sensitivity of her fingertips. He gave a shudder, but didn't deepen the kiss. So she ran her palm along his jaw, reveling in the texture of his beard. Then she wrapped her hand around the back of his head and pulled him closer. *More. Please, more.* But he didn't give her more.

Deliberately, she moved even closer, painfully aware that the only thing between them was part of a crumpled sheet. He'd feel so good covering her, his weight pinning her down as he pressed his whole body against hers. And that image was enough to make her nipples harden. He had to feel them against his chest, but he didn't touch her. Her breathing grew ragged, and her fingers clenched in the sheet by her side. For the first time in two years she wanted more, and the man she wanted it from wasn't giving it to her.

"Please," she whispered, lips against his.

"I'm trying to be gentle," he gritted out.

"That's not what I need right now." Because she wanted this. Badly. Desperately. And she needed to show him how much. So she pressed her lips to his again, opened them and darted her tongue inside his mouth.

He groaned in his throat, low and deep, and eased her into a deeper kiss, his tongue stroking harder. *Yes.* But before they got too far down that road, one big hand slid up her arm to tangle in her hair. He loosened her hair bands and tugged them out, then ran his fingers through her curls. For just a moment he leaned back and drank her in. She loved what she saw in his eyes—desire and need—knowing for certain those sentiments were reflecting back in her own.

Chase kissed her jaw, her neck, the hollow of her throat, and everywhere he touched shivers that had nothing to do with cold washed over her in waves. He was half on top of her now, and his weight felt just as good as she thought it would.

And then his warm, wet mouth was on her breast and she gasped. Had it ever felt like this before? Pleasure amplified so intensely she could hardly bear it. When he stopped sucking and just blew, her nipple became such a tight little peak it almost hurt. He did the same thing with the other breast and it was agony—all of the pent-up sensation without release. But he had no pity, just kept touching her, making her *feel* everything.

When Chase had both nipples hard and taut, he made a noise of approval in his throat. Ann didn't realize she was holding her breath until Chase ran his thumbs over their tips in lazy circles.

She cried out, and he covered her mouth with his again, stroking and plucking her nipples in time with the slide of his tongue. Ann ran her hands up his back, lightly gliding over the ridged muscles of his shoulders and sides, wanting him to shiver the way she was. Her reward was a mighty groan so she got serious, pressing harder before sliding down and cupping his ass.

That got a reaction. He slid a big hand down her body and swept his finger through her folds. She knew how wet she was. Obscenely so. But she wasn't embarrassed. Not with him.

"It's been a long time?" he asked, moving down and wedging himself between her legs.

"Yes," she whispered. Two long, empty years.

He lifted her knee over his shoulder and his facial hair scraped the sensitive skin of her inner thigh. "Let's make it count, then."

When he swept up with his tongue she nearly lost her mind. No, that came when he zeroed in on that one special spot designed to make her fall apart. And fall apart she did, breathlessly fast, in a starburst of feeling and emotion so intense her body shook of its own volition.

She was still recovering when Chase slid up her body and kissed her neck. "Are we done? We can be done."

"No way," she said, reaching for him. She wanted more. If he was willing to give.

"You sure?" he asked, searching her face.

She nodded. "Yes."

He gave her that look again—the one she knew meant he wanted her—and reached over to his bedside table. "Let me do the honors," he said, pulling out a foil packet.

"Wait," she said. "I want to see you first . . . "

"Okay."

His shirt was half-open so she helped it the rest of the way, pushing it first off one broad shoulder, then the other. When he'd shrugged it off she leaned back and simply admired his masculinity—the trail of hair that started mid-chest and went down, down, down below the waistband of his boxer briefs, which sported an impressive-looking bulge. The sculpted six-pack of his abdomen, on display just for her. The hard muscles of his thighs, honed from hours boarding on the mountain. He was absolutely magnificent.

Ann reached out to touch. It was even better now that her senses had been grounded and her brain wasn't as fuzzy. She slid her hand down and cupped him right through his boxer briefs. He was big. Solid. Just like the rest of him.

"Please," he said. He'd asked so nicely, so she pulled his drawers off. When her hand wrapped around him, skin to skin, his gaze burned through hers right before his eyes slid shut in pleasure.

She hadn't wielded such power in a long time. It felt good.

While he was hot and hard in her hand, he kissed her, drew her close and smoothed his hands down her back while she slid her palm up and down his length.

After a few long minutes of her stroking him he finally pulled back and slipped the condom on. "You know we can still stop," he said, covering her mouth with his again.

"I want this," Ann said, in between kisses. "I want you."

"I don't want you to be sorry later."

Ann stopped the kissing, leaned back, and clasped Chase's face in her hands, a tacit demand he look at her. "I won't be. I swear." *Not with you.*

Heat flared in his gaze. "I'll make it good for you."

"Show me."

One more long moment passed between them and then he kissed her neck, making her gasp. He'd hit *just* the right spot. Her nipples, still sensitive from his earlier play, hardened back up fast. His warm mouth fastened on one while he played with the other. He took his time, drawing out her pleasure, making sure it was good for her, just as he'd promised.

She reached down to her folds and began to stroke, then gasped as one of his long fingers pressed up and into her.

"You like touching yourself, don't you?" he murmured around a breast. He tugged his finger out, then pushed it back in slowly, drawing the sensations out.

"Yes," she breathed, wondering if he'd known all along. And that made her even hotter.

"Keep doing it," he said, curling that same finger up until he unerringly found that place inside that made her crazy.

A second finger joined the first. Curled and stroked in the same way. His mouth and hand on her breasts. Her own fingers on her clit. "Too much," she said, taking away her hand.

"Not enough," he said, withdrawing his fingers. Holding her open, he aligned himself for entry, his broad head pushing on sensitive flesh. "Not nearly enough." And then, after a long slow slide, he was inside her.

Ann's flesh tightened in protest, even as she relished the sensation of being stretched wide. Her body wasn't her own anymore. An overwhelming onslaught of pleasure so intense it verged on pain washed over her.

And then he moved.

Another layer of pleasure materialized, one that came only by being filled utterly and completely. And he did, his powerful glide underscoring the strength in his hips and thighs, finely-tuned by hours on the mountain.

"Touch yourself again," he demanded in a tone that sent shivers through her.

She slipped her hand between their bodies. She was as taut as a bowstring, ready to go off at any moment. And so was he.

All it took was mere seconds before she went over the edge, in what she dimly realized through her haze was the best orgasm of her life. Chase followed a second later, thrusting into her one final time before emitting a low groan.

He rolled onto his side, tugging Ann with him and kissing her temple. "You okay?" he asked.

"Yes," she said automatically, still on a post-orgasmic high. And then she realized something. For the first time in what seemed like forever the question didn't bother her.

And when she said yes, she actually meant it.

CHAPTER 9

"The key to boarding—or skiing—out of bounds is never to fly solo," Chase said from the top of the Lake View run at Alpine Meadows.

Ann nodded. She was paying attention to what he was saying, but the fact that everything seemed clearer and crisper today was more than a little distracting. Even the pine trees looked superimposed against the bluest of blue skies. Lake Tahoe was outrageously gorgeous—blue and clear in the distance. The snow glistened bright white on the mountain. But the man standing in front of her pointing down the mountainside was the best view of all.

Even with his bulky snow gear hiding his physique from sight, she remembered how he'd looked. Remembered every inch she'd seen. His goggles were up on his helmet, revealing brown eyes that fairly sparkled with excitement. He'd trimmed his beard in the morning before they left for the mountain and it sat close against his skin. Unbidden, the image of Chase's cheek brushing against the inside of her thigh materialized in her mind.

Last night she'd gone into their encounter with a sense of anticipation, of wanting simply to get it over with so she could move forward. But it had turned into more. So much more.

She'd expected to feel a lot of things after having sex for the first time after John. Guilt. Relief. Sadness. A sense of closure, maybe. She'd felt all those things, but they'd passed by in a flash. Mostly what she'd felt last night, aside from a deep sense of satisfaction, was peace.

It hadn't been what she'd expected, but it had been what she'd needed.

In fact, she'd almost immediately fallen asleep in Chase's arms, another rarity.

And when she'd woken up in the morning she was still calm. So was he.

Just kissed her with a smile in his eyes and said perfectly normal things like *good morning* and *I hope you slept well* and *we'll want to get on the mountain early today, so why don't you take the first shower?*

Actually, for a man who'd been seriously burned in life and love, on the face of things he seemed remarkably calm about everything. He was certainly cynical about his partner selling him out and his girlfriend leaving him—but who wouldn't be? Contrast that with when she'd told him about John. She'd seen real pain in Chase's eyes, and his simple, heartfelt *sorry* and his sensitive questions about John's life had packed more punch than almost anything anyone else had ever said about his death.

Even now, when he was telling her about all the ways she could be killed while skiing out of bounds, he was composed. But she'd seen firsthand the edge he had underneath, and she wanted to see more of it.

"You always have to be with someone at all times in case of an avalanche or an accident," he said. "And you take turns. First you go down a couple hundred yards. Then your partner goes. Got it?"

"Don't go alone," Ann said, remembering the multitude of times she'd done just that. "I wasn't intending to."

He gave her an appraising glance and cleared his throat. "Today you're not, but you know, you might get some ideas to . . ." he paused and gave her a sly smile, ". . . maybe go it alone sometime?"

It took a moment for her to realize he was teasing her. About sex. About *masturbating.* "Why would I go it alone when I have you to go with me?" she said, a smile curling up on her own lips. Oh, this was fun.

"Going it alone can sometimes be . . . liberating," Chase said, his lips twitching. "But I wouldn't recommend it in this case. Now, where was I?"

"Going it alone."

"Right. Don't. Next," he said, back to business. He held up a small electronic device. "This is a transceiver, also known as an avalanche beacon. You go out of bounds, you wear one. Here," he said, handing it to her. "I put fresh batteries in it for you."

Anything that could help with finding her location she instantly loved. "Thanks! Where do I put it?"

"In here," he said, picking up a backpack and zipping it open. "This puppy's loaded with dual nitrogen airbags which you can deploy in the event of an emergency."

"You sound like an airline stewardess," she said with a laugh.

Chase just gave her a look.

"Sorry. Yes. Deployment. Got it." She puzzled over the backpack. "How do I work it?"

He indicated a red cord. "Just pull here."

"All right." The bag looked new and was likely pretty expensive. "Did you buy this just for me?" she wondered.

"I borrowed it from a friend. We can stick your probe and shovel inside."

"Great." She popped them in the backpack.

"Don't you want to ask me what they're for?"

She shook her head. "When we had some down time yesterday afternoon I did some research on my phone. I'm very well aware they are for poking and for digging out avalanche victims."

He actually looked pleased that she knew this macabre information. "You really are Ms. Worst Case Scenario, aren't you?"

"I wouldn't have put it that way, but I guess I am. I just like to be prepared."

"I see," he said, watching her carefully. "So you know the risks involved?"

"*You* clearly do."

"I teach a course at the resort on backcountry safety."

"Ah. Well, I'm aware there are risks, but in the limited time I had I wasn't able to dig up all the information I needed to calculate the probability of being caught in a fatal avalanche." She thought that if she did the calculations she might second-guess her decision. Now she wished she'd done the calculations anyway. More information was always better than less.

"Gotcha. I was worried that all the backcountry gear and warnings would scare you, so I reviewed some avalanche studies and figured out that given the conditions—moderately dangerous—and the two or three runs we're likely to do this morning, the odds of either of us triggering a fatal avalanche is between 1:20,000 and 1:5,000." He said this calmly, watching her to gauge her reaction.

He'd done research for her—research he knew she'd need to feel even more secure than she already did. And then the thought struck her—she *did* feel secure. She'd been willing to ski out of bounds with him even without knowing all the risks. That she might trust him after knowing him such a short time both thrilled and terrified her. She swallowed. "You did the calculations for me?"

"I had help. There's a great white paper written by two Canadians and a Swiss guy affiliated with the WSL Institute for Snow and Avalanche Research."

"That is . . . " *Hot.* She licked her lips. "Super geeky," she finished lamely.

He just shrugged. "I figured that knowing the numbers would make you comfortable."

"Yes," she said. It did. It really did. Everything about the man made her comfortable. The strength in his capable hands. The guarded honesty in his eyes.

"All right, I threw a flare into the bag too, just in case. Not that I think we'll run into any issues today. Avalanche control was out at 6:30 A.M. setting off their charges. You hear the noise?" Ann shook her head no. She must have been sleeping like a log. "We're not heading too deep into side country, anyway. I know this area well, and I've never seen any breaks out of bounds here on the front face. Most of the rough stuff happens on the backside."

"I trust you," she said, believing the words as they came out of her mouth.

Chase gave her a little smile, made sure she knew how to use the beacon, and adjusted the backpack on her shoulders. Before she knew it, he was giving her some last minute advice.

"Steer clear of the tree wells. They can be really deep and dangerous."

She nodded, realizing that when it really came down to what she was about to do, the balance of trust was pretty skewed. Chase was the expert, not she. If anything, it was risky for him to be putting his trust in her, a virtual novice when it came to this kind of thing. But here he was, ready to lay his life on the line that she'd be able to find him and dig him out in case of an avalanche.

She waited for the little pit to form in her stomach. It didn't. She blinked, only a tiny bit surprised. "Okay."

"Okay. Good. I'll have eyes on you the whole time, and I'll be there if anything goes wrong. Which it won't." Then he stopped and cocked his head at her. "Ann? You okay? You looked strange there for a minute."

"I'm good. I'm good. Really." She offered a tentative smile. "And Chase? No matter what happens, thank you. For everything."

Something flared in his eyes. Something she liked very much. So when he stepped forward, gear still in his arms, and kissed her, really kissed her, right on top of the mountain, she tipped her head up and welcomed his lips on hers. Welcomed the scratch of his beard against her cold-sensitive skin.

She slipped her one free arm around him, loving the feel of his solid form under the padding of his snow clothes. Oh, he felt nice. He smelled nice, too. She'd never be able to walk into a winter forest again without thinking of Chase—snow and pine and musk and man.

Finally he pulled away and smiled down at her. "You ready?"

She nodded. "Yes."

His smile widened. "Then let's do it. I'll go first so you can see the distance you should be going ahead, all right?"

"Go," she said. "I know you're dying to."

"Damn right I am," he said. "You're going to be great, Annie. Just great." He pulled a full face mask over his head and adjusted his goggles over it. Then he slipped on his pack, clipped in his bindings, and with a war whoop went plowing down the mountainside. Snow flew up and to the sides as he carved through the fresh powder. His technique was solid—crisp turns, long easy glides—but it was the restraint of his obvious power that really got her. The power he'd kept in check for her last night.

And she surprised herself by wanting him all over again, right then, but this time she wanted to feel everything he had to give. And to return it in kind.

It took a moment for her to realize Chase had stopped a few hundred feet down and was waving for her to take her turn.

Okay. Yes. She could do this. She pulled on her own face mask and goggles. *Treat it like a slalom.* A forced slalom, where if she missed, it would mean a tree in her face.

Deep breath in. Deep breath out, just like she did before any run. And she barely had time to realize the pit in her stomach *still* wasn't there before she was carving her own snowy path down through the trees.

It was incredibly exhilarating. She took the run faster than she thought she'd have the nerve to do, pushing her body to its limit as she skied her way through the deep, uncompressed powder. She blew by Chase, who shouted out encouragement as she passed, and kept skiing until she'd gone down another hundred yards. She slowed, stopped, and looked up the mountain. Chase was there, watching her. He kicked off and boarded past her, making it look effortless.

The two of them strategically wove and darted before popping out onto an in-bounds run. Chase gave her a nod, and together they raced down until they reached the bottom.

Ann was breathless. Thrilled with herself. Triumphantly, she slid to a stop and waited for Chase. He pulled up next to her fast, covered in powder from his mask to his boots, messy and wet, dirty and rough. She knew she must look the same. She didn't care in the slightest.

"Damn, Annie!" Chase said, pulling off his goggles and mask. "That was awesome. You did great!"

"Let's go again," she said, sliding off her own headgear, wanting to see the fire in his eyes with no barrier between them. She loved that fire. No matter how laid-back he seemed to be, she kept seeing flickers of flame behind the mask. Like last night. And right now.

"You really mean it?" he said, sounding ecstatic that she'd want to take another run with him.

"Yes. I really mean it. I had a lot of fun. What other runs are good?"

He popped off his bindings, picked up his snowboard, and grinned even wider.

"Just let me show you."

CHAPTER 10

"Deckert," Chase said, answering his phone with one hand as he shoved a box of crackers back into his kitchen cupboard with the other.

"Chase? Hello." It was Phil Markowitz. "I'd like to offer you the job."

Crap. He should have known the 650-area code he didn't recognize was Phil's number. He took a bracing swig of beer, signaled to Ann that he'd be back in a moment, pulled on his jacket, and stepped out onto the deck to get some privacy. "Thanks, Phil. I appreciate that. But as I remember telling you, I wasn't there for an interview."

"I'm hoping you'll reconsider."

Phil wasn't going to be satisfied until he'd said his piece. "Fine. Why don't you tell me what's on the table."

Phil laughed. "Straight shooter. I like that." Phil immediately laid out some terms including a generous base salary, bonuses for patents filed and ushering the drugs through the regulatory pipeline, and part-ownership in the company itself.

Am I really worth that much?

He snapped out of it, fast. Phil thought he was a straight shooter, but that was precisely the reason he'd been burned the last time. No way, no how would he play games with Phil. With anyone.

"Well? What do you think?" Clearly, Phil expected him to accept the job right then and there.

Chase leaned on the rail, his gaze scraping over the lake and the sky. "Like I told you before, I think I'm not in the market for a job."

"You really don't mince words, do you?" Phil said.

"Nope. And neither do you," Chase countered.

"That's why I like you. I could get you more money, but something tells me you wouldn't really care."

"You're right." It was never about the money for him.

"Look," Phil said. "I get it. You want autonomy. I'd want the same thing if I were in your position. I can give you that."

"How?" Chase challenged.

"You know the costs of research of this magnitude. Before we even get this to market we have major research to conduct, and once we even get something worth pursuing we then have FDA trials and a ton of regulatory crap. But what we don't have are Wall Street analysts to pacify because, as you're well aware, Alliance is a privately-held company. There's a board of directors of course, but I'm the majority shareholder. I will give you everything you need to do the research you think is valuable."

"You mean what Alliance thinks is valuable." Chase knew the way the game was played.

"That's not what I'm saying. I've seen your work. Hell, I've cited your dissertation in team meetings. You'll have what you want, when you want it, with minimal interference from me and the board."

Chase sighed, annoyed at himself for even listening to Phil. Only two days ago he was furious he'd been tricked into the interview, but now he found himself being tempted by the passion he once had—might still have—for his research and for the desire to man up and move on. "Nothing against you or Alliance, Phil, but—"

"Think of all the good you could do with our resources. All the changes you could effect. All the lives you could save. We need you, Chase." Phil knew how to go right for the jugular, and that bastard knew he'd hit his mark. "So before you tell me no, just think about it," Phil said. "But don't take too long. Can you tell me by Monday?"

Chase couldn't even wrap his head around making that decision so fast. Strange, though, he'd done the exact same thing when he'd left Silicon Valley. He was just up and gone overnight, but under very different circumstances. "It's going to take longer than that, but how much longer, I don't know," he found himself saying. Was he seriously considering this? He'd better get off the phone with Phil before he promised him his firstborn.

"Fine. For you, I'll wait. Think about it." Phil hung up.

Phil Markowitz wasn't a man used to hearing the word *no*, that was for sure.

Why was he even giving this opportunity a second thought? It must be because it was right before Christmas, and without his family he was definitely feeling lonelier than normal. But he had to look at the big picture. He was content with where he was in life—for the most part. He had enough money to live on, a job he liked, a house to live in, and fresh air to breathe.

Being content was different from being happy, though. And he sure wasn't happy.

He was a different man now than he had been even a year ago. Doing good came with a steep price. He'd given everything he had to his research—his life, his work, even his health. He wouldn't make that same mistake again.

He took in a big, cleansing breath of night air. Crisp. Clean. Snow and lake and pine all together. Tahoe was in his blood. His family had been here for three generations. And all it had taken was one year of full-time living for him to realize that he wanted it to be there for three more generations. Forever, if he had his way.

But there was a not-inconsiderable part of him that missed the science. The thrill of discovery. He'd been pushing his body for so long he'd almost forgotten what it was like to push his mind. Being away from his research had given him a new perspective, and using his brain in a different way had made him a more flexible thinker. If he ever went back to it, he knew he had the potential to do great things.

Just like he knew he wanted Ann Smith.

Could it be he was even considering taking the job because of her? That was ridiculous. They'd only known each other for two days. Maybe he was more affected by the holidays than he thought, because that wasn't a long enough time for them to form any kind of significant bond. Besides, he'd gone down to interview before he'd even met Ann. No, there must be something internal driving this—something that had nothing to do with a dark-haired woman with a battered heart who weighed and calculated risks even as she routinely disregarded her own calculations to chase after what she thought was important.

Ann clearly knew her own happiness was important, even if she couldn't articulate it to herself.

The real question was, what would make *him* happy?

An image of Ann—her bright blue eyes flashing with excitement as she finished her first out-of-bounds run—popped into his mind.

Ann. She would make him happy.

It didn't make any sense. There was no rationality to it. He just knew.

As if on cue, the sliding glass door opened.

"Hey," Ann said, peeking her head onto the deck. "Everything okay?"

"It is now," he said.

She held the sliding door open as a welcome, he came back inside, and before he knew it her mouth was on his and she was moaning into him, and man, it was sweet. *She* was sweet, wrapped around a core of steel.

He slipped off his jacket and speared his hands through her hair. She was right there with him, her little fingers fumbling with his belt buckle. One of her knuckles dragged over the bulge in his jeans and a jolt of intense pleasure shot right through him.

He kissed her neck, licked his tongue from her collarbone to just behind her ear, and felt her shiver in his arms. Then he kissed her mouth, opened it with his own. She tasted like he did—dark and malty from the beer—and he was lost, drowning in her. He couldn't help himself from sliding a hand up her shirt and cupping a beautiful breast. Her nipple peaked in his palm, and when he brushed his thumb over the tip she moaned his name. It was like an aphrodisiac. The ache in his groin had reached a fever pitch, but she couldn't get his damn buckle off. He let his own anticipation build further, knowing that when he finally sank into her it'd be even better.

She kicked off her shoes, and it was way too tempting to shove her jeans and panties down, lift one of her knees high over his hip and take her right there against the door. But then he wouldn't be able to savor her, to suck on her nipples, to rub that little bundle of nerves between her thighs until she begged him to enter her.

And he wanted that. To draw it out for her, make it good. She was made for pleasure, her body giving itself over again and again. He wondered how many times he could make her come. How many times he could have her lose control, shuddering in his arms, gasping his name.

He wanted to hear her gasp his name.

She was still fumbling with his buckle, so he stilled her hand and lifted her until she was straddling his waist. She wrapped her arms around his neck and kissed him and kissed him, all the way up the stairs.

Roxy followed them up, wagging her tail. She tried to follow them into the bedroom, too.

"No, girl," Chase said firmly, shutting the door.

In his room—finally—he tipped them both onto the bed. He stopped touching her just for a moment, and clearly that had been a distracting force because now she couldn't get his clothes—or her own—off fast enough. Within moments she'd stripped the both of them and he only got a split second to admire her body before she pressed her naked form up against his.

But just because he couldn't see didn't mean he couldn't touch. He cupped a breast in his hand, then nibbled his way down until he'd wrapped his lips around a taut nipple. One of Ann's hands was holding his head to her chest, and the other—clever woman—had found his shaft and was stroking it up and down in time with the flicks of his tongue.

And when his hand snaked down, fingers delving into her damp folds, she gasped. Chase liked that sound almost as much as he liked hearing his own name come out of her lips, so he dipped deeply into her core, drew out her wetness, and rubbed in lazy circles right where she was most sensitive. She gasped again, said filthy things in his ear, and each gasp and shudder, each moan and whispered plea, made him hotter.

Finally he leaned back and caught a glimpse of her. She had her eyes closed, her hair spread out around her head in a dark nimbus. Her cheeks were flushed and the top of her chest, just above her breasts, was the same rosy color. Her nipples were taut and wet from his mouth, and there was dampness on her thighs from her own arousal. She looked like sex. She even smelled like sex. He nearly came, right then and there.

Quickly, he pulled out a condom from a nearby drawer. "You ready?" he asked.

Ann opened her eyes and appraised him. "Not quite yet," she said, and before he knew what she intended she slid down his body to take the length of him in her mouth.

"Oh, Ann," he said, tangling his hands in her hair as she did something utterly wicked with her tongue. "That feels so damn good."

While she played with him, he played with her—his fingers tweaking her nipples to make her moan around him. He felt her hand slide down his leg—to touch herself, maybe? The thought of her doing that while she mouthed him made him even harder.

She was still working her dark magic on him, sucking and licking until he thought he'd go crazy. Just before his eyes crossed he gently pressed his hand on her shoulder.

When she lifted her head, he pulled her up until her face was close to his. "Are you okay?" she asked.

"Yes," he said, sliding a finger inside her. She was wet and ready for him. He watched her face contort with pleasure. "Are you?"

"I think you know I am," she said, a little hitch in her voice.

He slid a second finger in to join the first. "What about now?"

"Uh huh," she said, still watching him, eyes heavy-lidded.

He flicked her clit with his thumb. "Now?"

She shuddered and her gaze dropped to his lips. "Now I want you to put on the condom."

Her eyes were clouded with desire. As fast as he could, he slipped the condom on, wrapped her legs around his waist and slid home.

"Yes, *please* Chase," she said, shuddering around him.

His name had never sounded sweeter.

Ann lifted up her hips, embedding him more deeply inside. Bending his head, he sucked one of her nipples into his mouth and was rewarded when she simultaneously gasped and clenched her internal muscles around him.

She shifted her hips again, a tacit demand that he move. So move he did, starting with long, slow slides that served to build up the tension and pressure until his world narrowed down to just the two of them, and their bodies moving together.

"Please, Chase. Harder. Come on."

Ann was begging him now, her legs wrapped around his back, her words just ratcheting up the stakes higher and hotter until he was slamming into her so hard he could barely catch his breath.

Then she arched her back and cried out, her muscles spasming around him as she took her pleasure. Half a second later, he was coming too, so hard and so strong that for a minute he thought he'd blacked out.

Chase was still inside her when his vision returned. She was lying beneath him, eyes closed, lips slightly curled up, hair everywhere. He shifted his weight to one hip so he wouldn't crush her, and swept a damp curl from her forehead.

"You—you're all right?"

She didn't move. "Oh, yes," she murmured.

"Seriously, Ann. That was . . . " He swallowed and tried again. "I mean, you're . . . "

"I know," she said, finally opening her eyes. The raw emotion he saw there almost blew him away.

"I wasn't expecting this to happen," he found himself saying. *I wasn't expecting you.*

She seemed to understand what he meant, because she stroked his cheek with the back of her hand. "I wasn't, either. But I'm glad it did."

He was honored. Humbled by her trust. What a surprise this woman was. She wasn't nearly as vulnerable as others thought she was, and she was a lot braver than she gave herself credit for. Maybe by the time the weekend was over she'd see that.

Gently, he withdrew from her body. Her lips were swollen and her cheeks were flushed. She'd never looked more desirable.

"You're gorgeous," he said, running his hand down her arm.

"Don't feel like you need to . . . " She gave him a rueful smile. "I won't hold you to anything you say right now."

"You want to hear truth, so I'll tell you truth," he said, entwining his fingers with hers and squeezing her hand. "That was amazing. And so are you."

She blinked and shook her head. "How can it be that a man I barely know makes me feel so beautiful?"

"Because you are." *More truth.*

"You've made this weekend so special, Chase." She pressed her lips together. "And it's not just this. I mean, not that this isn't wonderful because it is, but I wasn't sure if I'd be able to . . . you know. I mean, after John, there wasn't anyone else, and I—"

"Hey," he said gently, "you don't have to explain. I get it."

She nodded, looking a bit relieved. "I know you do."

"I'm just glad you're having a good time. And we haven't even gotten to the main event, yet," he said.

"This isn't the main event?" she said, her tone letting him know she was teasing.

"Nah. You haven't lived until you spend Christmas day on the mountain with dudes skiing in Santa outfits."

She laughed at that, making him feel lighter, too. "Hmm. Maybe I'll try to figure out whether skiers or snowboarders have more Christmas spirit by calculating the percentages of those wearing Santa hats. Or maybe," she said, a smile playing on her lips, "I could figure out the probability that we can do it again." Her eyes were full of warmth and a frank sensuality he knew *he'd* helped put there.

"Right now?"

In response, one small hand wrapped around his growing thickness. "Right now."

He cleared his throat and leaned into her. "I'd say the odds are most definitely in your favor."

CHAPTER 11

Ann woke up warm and satiated in Chase's rumpled bed. She cracked open her eyes. It wasn't even light outside, but the shower was on. Chase must have to be on the mountain early to teach. Stretching, she gave a little yawn. Funny, she wanted to get back on the mountain too. Going out of bounds with Chase had been a thrill ride—an all-in commitment to trying something new. Now she just wanted to do some skiing for herself, in-bounds, going as fast as she possibly could.

It wasn't so much that she'd put things aside for John—well, except the skiing. It was more like her desires had been subsumed into his. She'd appreciated the wine tasting and the art house movies, but it had all been for John. The one thing that was hers—the skiing—had been placed on the back burner because John hadn't taken to it.

That was what you did for someone you loved. You took the parts of yourself they didn't value and you set them aside.

But then they died and you were left with a husk where your true self should be. And you didn't realize that things were missing until you went looking for them, and they were gone.

Slowly, she was filling in the blank spaces. Those gaps John had filled, but that now needed to be filled by her and her alone. Letting too much of herself be wrapped up in John had been a mistake, one she didn't intend to repeat. She wanted to be whole again.

And being in Tahoe during this season was helping her do that.

She thought she'd done pretty well so far. There wasn't any guilt or remorse with Chase. It just . . . was. No analysis. No calculations, just like it had been with John.

But Ann knew from the moment she'd met him that Chase wasn't like John. John would argue with anyone who had an opinion different from his

69

own. She had a feeling that Chase's live-and-let-live attitude would mean he probably wouldn't bother. Not that he wasn't confident, but he seemed to want to do things for the pleasure of doing them, not for the prestige or because he cared what anyone else thought. His technically perfect but utterly exuberant run down the mountain pretty much summed him up. And there were other differences between him and John. Chase was bigger. Quieter, too.

Her brain began to revolt at the idea of a side-by-side comparison of the men. They were different and that was okay. John had been the kind of man she'd needed when she'd met him five years ago. And despite the near-baring-of-souls last night, it was too soon to tell whether Chase was the kind of man she needed now. All she knew was that she liked him. More than liked him.

The water stopped running and a few seconds later Chase emerged, backlit from the bathroom light. His hair was wet from the shower, and he had a towel wrapped around his waist.

"You're up," he said. "I'm sorry I made so much noise. I wanted to let you sleep."

She shook her head. "No. I need to get up anyway."

"You're coming with me? Good," he said giving her a tantalizing glimpse of ass and upper thighs as he dropped his towel to put on his drawers. "If you want a ride to the resort, you'll have to get a move on. I'm due up there at seven-thirty."

She scrambled out of bed and went to get dressed. There weren't many things that could top Chase's bare chest in the morning, but fresh powder at Alpine Meadows might just be one of them.

Ann was on the mountain early enough to get first tracks—the first run of the morning down the mountain with the freshest powder. This time she enjoyed it even more. Chase introduced her to a guy named Dave, one of the equipment rental specialists, who set her up with a wider pair of skis which handled fresh powder better than her racing pair. It took a run or two to get used to the thicker feel. She didn't have to be as precise with her technique because the skis were much more forgiving. If she were still racing that'd be a dangerous thing, but this weekend she was just here to have fun and get her groove back.

And get it back she did. In spades.

By the time lunch rolled around she was exhausted, but exhilarated. After she'd grabbed a sandwich and a drink from one of the stands at the bottom of the mountain she went right back up the lift to get in a few more runs.

At 2 P.M., tired and happy, she went back to the equipment rental station to return the fat skis.

She was at the counter talking to Dave when a prickle of awareness passed over her.

Dave looked over her shoulder. "What's up?" he said, giving a nod to whomever was standing behind her.

She didn't have to look to know it was Chase.

"You liked 'em?" Chase asked.

Finally, she turned. Chase looked just as good as he had when she'd left him in the morning—a little weary, but satisfied. She nodded. "I could really get used to a pair that thick," she said. "But I'm afraid my technique would go down the tubes."

He shook his head. "Imagine what you could do with those skis and your technique in top form? You'd own the mountain." He popped her skis up on the counter. "Get us out of here, Dave. We have plans for the rest of the afternoon."

"We do?" Ann asked as Dave finished up the return.

"You bet we do. Come on," he said, wrapping a big arm around her shoulders and steering her out of the room.

"Where are we going?"

"Someplace cool, but we have to stop at the house first."

"All right," she said, hopping into the cab while he threw his gear in the back of the truck.

They got back to the house relatively quickly and let Roxy out for a walk. The dog was glad to see them, wagging her tail and rubbing her head on Ann's legs after Roxy had done her business. Ann didn't mind. Roxy had made it clear that Ann was her kind of people, and who was Ann to argue with that?

After changing into regular clothes and feeding Roxy, Chase went downstairs to throw some gear in his truck and then all three of them hopped in to go for a ride. They didn't go far. Just down Route 89 to a winter recreation area where Chase parked between two giant trailers, each holding matching snowmobiles.

"Here," Chase said, motioning for Ann to join him near the trunk. When she came around, he wrapped his hands around her waist and lifted her so she was sitting on the bed. Then he pulled out something she hadn't worn in years.

"Snowshoes!" she exclaimed, holding her foot out. Chase strapped on one big, mesh-like shoe to her boot. "The last time I saw a pair of these was in my parents' woodshed."

"Oh, yeah. Vermont. You get a lot of snow there."

"Not so much in Sacramento."

Chase shook his head. "No. But, as we've already established, Tahoe was my playground."

"Lucky," she sighed, holding up her other foot so he could strap on the other snowshoe. "East Coast snow isn't always as powder-heavy. Sometimes the mountain was a sheet of ice."

"You have to be pretty damned skilled to ski it properly," he said, grabbing his own snowshoes and buckling them on.

"C'mon, girl," he said. Roxy jumped out of the cab and bounded toward them. Chase shut the door and locked up the truck, then led her and Roxy down a wooded path.

"Where are we going?" she asked, snapping the top of her jacket shut. It was cold—about thirty-five degrees—but not unbearable, and already she was starting to warm up from the exercise of tromping through the snowy woods.

Chase pointed to where telephone poles marked a path up the mountainside. "There."

"What's up there?"

"Eagle Rock. Definitely worth the trek."

"Let's go, then."

They began to walk. Chase helped her ford an icy stream over mounds of snow-covered branches, and then the real hike began. Up they went, slipping and sliding in the deep snow, buoyed only by the snowshoes. It was slow going. Despite being up to her muzzle in snow, Roxy looked like she was having a ball, barking happily and racing up faster than she or Chase could manage, even with the snowshoes.

Halfway up the side, Ann turned to look down. The mountain wasn't that steep and they hadn't gone that far, but she was still breathless.

"You can make it," Chase said, a hand at the small of her back. "Only a little bit farther."

Ann nodded and kept going upward through the trees. They weren't that far from the road, but it was quiet up here. The snow seemed to act as insulation, sucking away all the sound until the only things left were their breathing and Roxy's occasional bark. Finally, they got to the top. Ann glanced down the other side where the telephone poles continued in a line.

"Not there," Chase said, pointing to a steep outcropping of snow-covered rock up and to the left. "Here." He took her hand, and helped her navigate the near-vertical climb. Ten minutes later, hot and winded, Ann stood triumphantly at the apex of Eagle Rock.

She undid the top few snaps of her jacket and breathed in the clean, fresh mountain air. It was icy in her lungs, clear and true.

When she finally caught her breath and was able to focus on her surroundings, she was treated to a 360-degree view of Lake Tahoe. Snowy pines stood regally, bedecked in white finery. The white-painted mountains rose and fell, creating a jagged horizon. And the lake itself sparkled in the distance like a winter star. She turned to Chase, who stood quietly next to her, eyes gleaming as he took it all in.

"Like it?" he asked, his voice breaking the silence.

"It's just beautiful, Chase. Thank you for taking me here."

"Only locals know this place. Usually you can see footprints all over the side of the mountain, but we must be the first people up here since the storm. Come on. Check this out." He helped her walk over to a giant fallen tree. She followed his lead as he leaned back against the trunk, her winter jacket cushioning her against the wood and snow, and tilted her head back to look up. The sky was still bright, but part of the moon peeked out from behind a far-off mountain.

There was a solemnity in the stillness, a gravity she hadn't quite anticipated. This was life, in all its beauty and realness. Chase had brought her here. Showed her the splendor in the simplicity on this quiet Christmas Eve. She couldn't have asked for a more perfect gift.

"Thank you," she whispered, tears inexplicably pooling in the corners of her eyes, making them sting. She blinked fast to keep them at bay.

She sensed his movement and turned to him. His lips met hers, warm and firm.

Her heart swelled and she couldn't help the little breath that caught in her chest or the tiny tear that escaped and ran down her cheek. Before she realized what was happening, Chase had pulled away. Gently, he brushed the tear off her cheek and smiled at her.

"It's going to be dark soon," he said. "We should get down the mountain before night falls."

"Okay," she said, grateful he wasn't pressing her to talk.

Chase let out a whistle, and Roxy barked in response. Ann followed the sound. Roxy had found a fallen branch, and was rolling around in the snow with her prize, growling and gnawing as if she'd caught a wild animal.

"C'mon girl," Chase said, and Roxy abandoned the branch, loping along in the snow until she reached them.

Going down was easier than going up, mostly because they could follow the tracks they'd made. It was still tough going, though, and by the time they reached the truck Ann was flushed and breathless again.

"You were right," she said as she removed her snowshoes. "It was worth it."

"I'm glad," was all he said.

"So now what?"

"Now we go home. I'll feed you, we'll take a nice long soak in the hot tub, and go to bed."

Warmth spread through her. It had been a long time since she'd even thought of herself as desirable, and that this beautiful man wanted to be alone with her pleased her more than she could say.

"Okay. Food, a soak, and bed sound really nice."

"Good."

As he eased out onto the main road, a ringing sound came from her pocket. She picked up her cell phone.

"It's Ann."

"Annie? It's Mandy. You doing okay?"

Suddenly, she realized that Mandy still wasn't in Tahoe. "Did you get my message yesterday? Where *are* you?"

"Still at the lab."

"Let me guess," Ann said wryly. "Your experiment isn't done yet."

"Ugh, no. Some of my cultures didn't incubate properly and I lost 14 hours of testing, so I had to redo part of the experiment to get it right. Annie, I am sooooo sorry I'm not there with you on Christmas."

"It's okay."

"Really? Because I am just dying about this." Mandy sounded more than contrite, but the odds were high that Mandy wasn't feeling that guilty. Mandy lived and breathed her lab work, and probably didn't even care that she was missing Christmas.

"Seriously. It's fine," Ann said, taking a quick glance over at Chase, who raised an eyebrow at her. *Mandy* she mouthed.

Chase suppressed a smile.

"Really, Annie? Are you having fun?"

"Yes. Yes, I am." *Way more fun than you could ever imagine.*

"Meet any hot snowboarders yet?" Mandy's tone was conspiratorial.

"Uhhh . . . " Ann said, eying Chase, who was grinning like a maniac now, likely because he could hear her through the mouthpiece.

"Oooh, Annie! That's a yes! I can hear it in your voice. You met someone! Tell me!" Men were the only thing that could drag Mandy away from her experiments. "Spill! Is he hot? Does he snowboard?"

"I, uh, can't talk about that now," she said, her voice low.

"Oh, is Chase there? He won't mind. Hi, Chase!" she yelled directly into Ann's ear.

"Ow!" Ann said, jerking the phone away from her face.

"Put him on speakerphone!" Mandy squawked. "I want to talk to him."

That was such a bad idea. "No. Call his phone later if you want to talk. He's driving now."

"Okay, okay," Mandy said, though she sounded awfully disappointed. "He's taking care of you, right?"

"Yes. He's taking care of me." If only Mandy knew how much.

"Good," she said. "You deserve this. He owes me, anyway."

"Owes you?" Ann asked. "What do you mean?"

Before Mandy could answer, Chase snatched the phone and held it out, away from his ear. "Thanks for calling, Mandy," he yelled at the phone. "Merry Christmas. Gotta go!" He switched the phone off and handed it back to Ann.

"Have you gone crazy?"

Chase just shrugged. "We're almost home."

Ann threw herself back on the seat and crossed her arms under her breasts. Chase's little trick would probably make Mandy believe something was up for sure. "What did Mandy mean when she said you owed her?" she asked.

"Not sure," Chase said quickly. "Ah, here we are. I'll get dinner started."

"All right," Ann said, slightly mollified. She was pretty hungry.

CHAPTER 12

They both took showers to wash away the grime and sweat of the day, and then while Chase started dinner, Ann called her mom and dad to wish them a merry Christmas. Her parents so obviously missed her over the holiday—she could hear it in their voices—but even though she missed them too, she knew she'd made the right decision by coming to Tahoe. When she was done talking to them, she went into the kitchen, where Chase was cooking up some homemade *pappardelle*—thick, medium-length perfectly *al dente* noodles paired with a rich, meaty sauce, also homemade. He made some calls of his own while she tossed a simple side salad.

Chase was back a few minutes later.

"How's your family?" she asked.

"My folks are fine. They're sorry not to have me over for Christmas, but I saw them just last week. And I get why Tommy wanted to be away," Chase said, giving the sauce a stir. "He's been working his ass off, and he needs a break. He says he's coming up here next year. We'll see." He tasted the sauce. "Perfect. Dinner's ready."

"Wait," she said, eying the food. "I have the perfect thing to go with this."

She ran up to her room—the room she hadn't spent one night in—and pulled another bottle of wine out of her bag. She'd stopped thinking of it as John's wine and started thinking of it as just wine, which seemed a bit weird to her, but she went with it.

"So *this* is what you had in your bag," Chase said with a smile as he popped the cork. "I thought it was rocks."

"Just think how much easier it'll be for you to carry on the way home," she said, immediately regretting her presumption. "I mean—sorry—I didn't mean to assume you're driving me back."

Chase shook his head and poured her a glass. "We both know that Mandy isn't going to make it up here this weekend, and I know you don't have another way to get back to Silicon Valley. I'll drive you."

"I'd appreciate it. If it's not too much trouble, that is," she said.

He poured himself a glass of wine and met her gaze. "It's not."

"Thank you," she said, at once cognizant of the empty pang inside her. She'd be leaving in a couple of short days and honestly, she didn't want to. Being up here and especially being with Chase had shown her that she could have a life after John. She'd been ready to move on for a while, but this weekend had just cemented it. No matter what happened after, she'd have new Christmas memories to savor.

That thought filled her simultaneously with both relief and sadness. To cover her mixed emotions, she pasted a smile on her face and raised her wineglass. "And thank you for your hospitality this weekend."

"I hope it's been good," he said.

"Yes." So very, very good.

"Good. Merry Christmas, Annie."

"Merry Christmas."

Chase smiled and took a sip. She loved looking at him. His hair was still damp from his shower and he'd combed it back so it lay in dark waves on his head. He'd trimmed his beard too, making him look less like a mountain man and more like a guy on a GQ cover with his oxford shirt rolled up at the sleeves and unbuttoned at the top. "Believe it or not, the resort is open tomorrow and I actually have a lesson—some client called in last-minute and requested me late today—so I'll have to be on the mountain for two hours in the morning. After that, I thought we could do another couple of runs out of bounds. There's nothing like skiing on an empty mountain on Christmas day. Are you up for it?"

"Yes, definitely. Especially if we're going to see some dudes in Santa costumes."

Now he really smiled. "We will. And that means you'll need even more calories tonight. Hand over your plate."

She let him pile the pasta and sauce high, then helped herself to salad while he served himself. The food was simple, nourishing, and warm—just right for a cold winter's night in Tahoe. Pasta wasn't part of her Christmas tradition, but in the future she might have to add it to her repertoire.

After they'd washed and dried the dishes, Chase lit a fire, and together they curled up on the couch and watched the flames crackle.

If she'd been at home in her townhouse, she knew what she would be doing this night. Exercise. Tidying. Laundry. Work. Every boring, mundane thing she could possibly do not to think about the fact that she was alone on Christmas. Or getting completely drunk so she wouldn't have to think at all. But here in Tahoe she was draped over a sofa in front of a warm fire,

Chase on one side, Roxy by the other and doing the unthinkable—relaxing and not needing to think about the rest of her life because it was already in progress. This was it.

"This is pretty perfect," she told him.

"Yeah," he said. "Except for one thing. Hang on." Carefully, he extricated himself and went into the kitchen. He was back in a few minutes with some crushed tin foil.

A star.

He'd made a star for the top of the tree.

"I think this'll work," he said, carefully reaching up to place it atop the spruce. "You like?"

That tiny, makeshift, tin-foil star was a symbol of hope. A beacon of light shining in the darkness. "I . . . love."

Some odd emotion Ann couldn't quite place flickered across his face, but then he crossed the room and kissed her and everything else melted away, leaving the two of them, here and now. When he speared a hand through her hair, she sighed and eased right onto his lap, the better to wrap her arms around his shoulders and press herself up and into him.

She loved the feel of him—not just the physical, but the aura he projected. The easy-going man with the fire in his eyes when he was talking about something he loved. When he was talking about snow or science. When he was looking at her.

A thrill went through her. She shuddered and he responded, sweeping his hands up and down her back before tugging her long-sleeved T-shirt up and over her head. Passion flared in his eyes.

"You really are gorgeous, Annie."

In response, she took his shirt off, too.

"Every time I see this," she whispered, tracing her finger down his muscled chest, "I think about how many hours you must have spent on the mountain." Then she kissed him, right where her finger had traced. He groaned and buried his hands in her hair more deeply, holding her to him as she mouthed one nipple.

"That feels so good."

Excitement swelled deep inside. *She* was making him feel this way. She licked his other nipple, flicking it with her tongue, and was rewarded when he let out a sharp hiss of pleasure.

Ann was feeling powerful now. In control. And focused, very focused.

"Take off your pants," she demanded. Without hesitating he did as she asked, sliding his jeans down long, muscular legs. He truly was a beautiful specimen, and she took just a moment to admire his body. Then she kissed him, long and deep.

When his hands began to roam, she pushed him back onto the pillows.

"Tonight I want it to be my turn."

He raised an eyebrow. "Your turn for what?"

Her gaze flicked down his body and back up to his eyes. *To watch.* She'd been bold enough until this point, but now she couldn't figure out how to tell him.

Understanding dawned in his eyes. He hooked his thumbs in the elastic of his boxer briefs and slowly, very slowly, he peeled them down.

She'd never been able to take control like this before—never been able to command John with a word, or even with a glance. Chase brought this out in her because he was confident enough to let her take the reins.

Chase had the most intense look on his face, and she couldn't seem to tear her gaze away.

"Look at me," he insisted.

She lowered her gaze, loving what she saw. He was huge, straining to keep himself in check. All his power contained just for her.

"Tell me what you want," he said, and her eyes jerked up to meet his. *Take what you need.*

"I—" she swallowed, emboldened by his stare. "I want to watch you. Like you watched me."

"Be specific."

"I want you to touch yourself."

He wrapped a big fist around his length and gave one easy stroke down and then up again. "Like this?"

"Yeah," she said, her mouth dry. "Please. Do it again."

He did it again, not being gentle about it this time. And he kept going, his gaze on hers until he closed his eyes and groaned in pleasure. It was unbearably erotic, watching him stroke himself while she sat there. And while she watched she got hotter and hotter, her nipples hardening into uncomfortable little points, her core throbbing. Her face was flushed and oh, was she panting? He had to know how hot this was making her. She felt an overwhelming desire to touch herself but she was frozen in place, mesmerized by the movement of his hand.

He stroked a little more roughly, and she must have gasped aloud, because in a split-second she was on her back on the couch, under him. His erection pressed into her thigh as he kissed her neck.

"You like that?" Chase said, slipping a hand right down the front of her jeans and into her panties, which were soaked with her arousal.

"Yes," she said, her voice coming out with an embarrassing breathiness. She'd loved watching him take his own pleasure. Within moments, he found her wet and wanting.

"Annie," he groaned, and before she knew it, her jeans and panties were off and she was laid bare for him.

He sat back on his heels on the couch. "Take off your bra."

His demand sent another surge of desire coursing through her. Ann did as he asked, angling herself to unclasp her bra and peel it off.

"Beautiful." His eyes glittered. "Cup your breast now. Easy, there. That's right." She raised her hand and cupped her breast. "Good. Now rub your thumb over your nipple. Keep rubbing." She complied, closing her eyes to the sensation. "No. Keep them open. I watch you. You watch me. Got it?"

Ann opened her eyes and nodded. *Yes.*

"Slide your hand down your belly." She did, slowly, feeling the anticipation build. "Now touch yourself the way you like." This was different than the first time he'd asked. This was her, exposed and vulnerable. But she trusted him, so with only the slightest bit of hesitation she slipped her finger between her thighs. "Yes. That's right. The way you want to show me."

She delved and rubbed, circled her swollen flesh again and again until she was so close to going over she could feel herself heading toward the edge.

He'd begun to stroke himself again with long, hard pulls, and his desperation made her desperate too.

"Chase, please," she said, her voice a broken, breathless plea.

He took a condom out from his pants pocket and slipped it on. He wrapped her legs around his waist and positioned himself at her entrance.

"Ready?" he whispered, his voice gruff.

"Yes," she said, without hesitation.

First he claimed her lips and then he claimed her body, plunging inside and filling her so incredibly full she thought she'd burst. Still, she needed more. And more is what he gave her.

Hips thrust again and again, pinning her to the sofa with each downstroke, giving her no time to catch her breath. Faster and harder Chase drove her close to the edge, and in a few moments she went over, clutching at him as she spun out of her own head into a crazy burst of sensation.

Chase came right behind her, thrusting inside once more before his big body shuddered, then stilled. He slowed his breathing and wrapped his arms around her, enveloping her in warmth. For a few long minutes, they stayed like that. Not moving, only breathing. Her gaze swept over the tin foil star on top of the Christmas tree, but all that truly registered was Chase still inside her, his weight grounding her.

Rough in bed.

From almost the first moment she'd seen him, she knew this was how it was going to go. She'd figured out how raw he really was underneath it all—the man who rejected greed, who traveled halfway across the world to do something good for others. And he'd done something for her, too. He'd given her the space and the means to find her true self, a self she thought was gone. And she'd found it.

Now. Here. Tonight.

CHAPTER 13

Chase and Ann were on the mountain early the next morning. After placing her in Dave's capable hands to choose a fresh pair of skis to try out, he walked over to where he was going to meet his first—and only—client of the day. Even after Ann was gone, he could still smell her scent, clinging to him like snow to a pine.

"Merry Christmas, Jenna," he said to the lesson coordinator. "Who am I with today?"

Jenna, a sporty redhead, smiled at him. "Gaper. Never seen him before. Requested you personally for this morning. Paid triple when I told him you weren't planning on working today, so thanks for coming in. He's over there." She pointed with a gloved hand to a tall man with his back toward them. "And Merry Christmas right back at you."

"Thanks, Jenna," Chase said, walking over. The guy was dressed in brand-spanking-new snow gear—there was even a tag hanging off the side zipper of his jacket—and he had an equally new-looking snowboard by his side. Killer model. Chase himself had test-ridden a friend's board when the model was released just before the season began. Nice edges. Good curl. The man turned slightly and Chase recognized that salt and pepper hair. It wasn't. It couldn't be.

Oh, but it was. Phil Markowitz in the flesh. And by his side was a gangly, younger-looking man—Phil's personal assistant, whom Chase had met when he visited Alliance.

Chase had that jarring sensation of being caught out—of his old life encroaching on his new one. Silicon Valley was fine from a distance, but any time it crept into his day-to-day life in Tahoe, a tingle of discomfort edged up on him. He didn't much like the feeling.

"Hi, Phil," Chase said, trying to sound casual as Phil turned all the way around and sized him up with his intelligent gray eyes. "What brings you to Tahoe?" he asked, knowing full well it wasn't the fresh powder.

"What do you think?" Phil said. "You, of course. Not that the scenery isn't breathtaking." He swept his arm around, as if to encompass the beauty of the mountain. "But talking over the telephone is so impersonal. I'd rather see someone's face when I speak." Phil handed his wallet and cell phone to his assistant, who pocketed them and scurried back toward the lodge.

Chase put down his board and crossed his arms over his chest. "I told you I needed some time."

"You did. And I could hear in your voice that you weren't going to give my offer the attention it needed."

Chase gave him a hard stare. "The offer I didn't ask for?"

"Hey," Phil said, "I'm not trying to trick you into anything, but I could tell that taking you away from Tahoe was going to be a challenge and I don't meet my challenges half-assed. So I figured I'd come to your turf, lay everything on the line, and see if I could convince you."

"You didn't have to come up here on Christmas and pretend to want a lesson to get my attention."

"I think I did," Phil countered. "I've bought your time—at three times your hourly rate, I might add—so the least you can do is to teach me how to stand up in this contraption while I tell you a little more about Alliance Biotechnology, and convince you that you'd be the perfect fit for our team."

"Fine. You can talk to me. But you have to let me call the shots on the mountain. First things first. Show some respect for the sport. Your equipment's not a contraption, it's a snowboard. Got it?"

Phil smiled again. "Got it."

"And second," Chase said, reaching around to yank the tag off Phil's pocket, "let's try not to have you look like a total tourist, shall we?"

"Not a tourist. Okay."

Chase sighed. The man looked way too eager to get started, likely so he could talk Chase's ear off for the full two-hour lesson time. But to Chase's surprise, Phil actually let him start the lesson the way he wanted—with an introduction of the equipment and the mechanics of snowboarding. After fifteen minutes they moved on to balance, then heel turns and toe turns.

Before Chase knew it, their time was up. As he walked Phil back to the checkout area, he realized that Phil actually hadn't talked his ear off about the opportunity, the company, the team, or the product. Was Phil trying to show him that he'd be a good boss? That he'd have all the autonomy he wanted?

"You're a great teacher," Phil said.

"Thanks. I'm sorry we didn't get a chance to talk about the

opportunity," Chase said, half-meaning it. After all, Phil had hauled up to Tahoe to try to convince him to take the job, and he felt a little guilty about getting so caught up in the lesson that he really hadn't given Phil a chance to speak.

"Well, you cleared a lot of things up for me," Phil said.

"Are you rescinding the offer?"

"No." Phil pressed his lips together. "But I would like to modify it."

Chase shrugged. "Like I told you before, more money isn't going to make me take the job."

"I'm aware of that," Phil said, handing off his board to his assistant, who'd scrambled onto the snow to join them. "So what do you want?"

Chase thought for a moment. "If I could really have anything I wanted? I'd want science for science's sake."

"Get the medicine to the people, is that it?"

"Yep."

Phil didn't laugh. Instead, he made some kind of motion with his head and his assistant stepped a respectful ten feet away. "Maybe you should go teach at a university. Get funding through the government to work the way you want."

"Been there, done that. It's never enough money and it's all academic. Plus I can't stand grant writing."

Phil nodded. "I think I see the problem. You want to focus on real, non-academic science, which requires plenty of money, but you don't want the money to actually get in the way."

"That pretty much sums it up."

"Come work with me. I'll make sure you have whatever you need, and I sure as hell won't screw you over like that former partner of yours. You want to leave Alliance? You leave on your own terms." His gaze sharpened. "I won't deny that Alliance needs to make a profit. We're a business, after all. But my endgame is to get the medicine to those who need it most. In fact, I've already pledged any malaria medication we develop to the World Health Organization. They'll get it at cost, no more than that. We'll make our profits some other way."

"How?"

"Malaria isn't the only disease responsive to artemisinin derivatives. We've had some promising developments with our malignant hepatoma studies. I'm curious to see how any derivative you synthesize will stack up against what we already have in the hopper."

There was silence for a moment while Chase weighed what Phil had just said. He'd been so fixated on the malaria problem he hadn't even contemplated what good his research could do in other spheres—namely liver cancer. "You want an answer now, don't you?"

"No. I need my lawyer to draw up some fresh papers. Thanks again,

Chase. I really enjoyed the lesson." And with that, Phil was off, his assistant trailing behind him.

Chase watched him until he disappeared into the crowd. Sneaky bastard. He'd let Chase do his thing and hadn't pressed him, giving him a taste of what it would be like if he were to go to Alliance.

But Alliance was in Silicon Valley, and the thought of going back almost gave him hives.

Except that she would be there.

No. It was too much to process in too short a time. In a day he'd be taking Ann Smith home and returning to Tahoe, alone.

Then he'd go back to his regular life, boarding and hiking and living free in Tahoe without her.

Wouldn't he?

CHAPTER 14

Ikeda's marionberry pie tasted different to Ann this time. Promise and regret, happiness and sadness all rolled into each flaky, tart-sweet bite. It tasted like *him*.

After a few halfhearted bites, Ann pushed the plastic container toward Chase. He nodded briefly. *No thanks.* She placed the container on the ground. Roxy eagerly gobbled up the pie before laying her head on Ann's feet.

Ann sighed. Ever since they'd woken up on this gray Monday morning, Roxy had clung to her like a shadow, as if she knew Ann was leaving. In the house, Roxy had lingered over her breakfast and taken her sweet time doing her business out in the woods. In Chase's truck, she'd done everything to show Ann some love, poking her head between the seats to gaze at her imploringly, rubbing up against her legs when they stopped to stretch. Ann scratched the big dog behind her ears. Roxy whimpered and sighed.

I'm going to miss you too, girl.

A little tickle hit the back of her throat and automatically, she reached for the little blister pack in her purse. One pill left. If that didn't signify *the end* she didn't know what would. With finality, she popped the pill through, swallowed it, and tossed the empty pack into a nearby garbage can.

She glanced up at Chase, but he was staring out at the parking lot. He'd been doing a lot of staring that day—anywhere but at her, the clearest signal he could give that he didn't want to talk. And what would she have said to him, anyway? *Hey, I've known you for less than a week but I'm crazy about you, and could seriously see spending the rest of my life with you.* No. She couldn't. And she knew he couldn't either.

"We'd better get a move on if we want to get you back to the Valley at a decent hour," he said, without looking at her.

She nodded. Right. The holiday was over, and so were they. A lump formed in her throat, but she pushed it back. She couldn't be unhappy. She had no *right* to be unhappy. She'd set out with hopes of getting through Christmas and establishing her mindset firmly in a post-John world.

To live as herself, fully and unashamed.

And she was closer to doing that.

This had been a pivotal weekend for her, and she was wise enough to recognize that she'd turned a corner. Thanks to Chase. And thanks to herself.

If she'd learned one thing from John's death, it was that she couldn't dwell on things she couldn't control or change. Never again would she lose sight of who she was to make someone else happy. She loved skiing and she'd be back to Tahoe soon, on her own terms, to continue exploring the thing she loved. And she was going to take a class to learn how to cook Italian food.

Chase's home was in Tahoe, and her home was in Silicon Valley, and that was that. Not only was the distance too great, but Chase hadn't even said anything about continuing what they'd shared.

So no matter how amazing and intense the weekend had been, it was over. And she'd be wise to take a deep breath and move on. Ann was an old pro at moving on now. She'd had two years' worth of practice doing just that, after all.

Funny thing was, this time she didn't want to.

Before Chase knew it, he was parked in front of Ann's townhouse. He looked up at the building in the late-day sun. The taupe, two-story affair looked like every other place in Mountain View—tidy, boring, and dull. "Nice," he said, trying to be polite.

"Thanks. John and I bought it right before . . . " She stopped. "Well, you know."

Chase nodded. Yes, he knew. He shoved the warring emotions aside. "Let me get your bag." He slid out of the cab. The weather was nice here, the air clear and crisp. Not as nice as Tahoe, but then again, few places were. When he'd lived in Menlo Park he'd had a dull little place like Ann's. Of course, he hadn't seen it much, given that he was working nearly all the time.

He followed Ann to her front door. Inside, there was a staircase leading up to the main level of the place. Roxy was hanging out the open window, whining at Ann's retreating back.

Chase went around to the bed and lifted Ann's suitcase out. Her bag was a lot lighter without all of the wine, but he carried it inside and up the staircase for her anyway, placing it underneath an elegant-looking hall table.

"This is it, I guess," he said, trying not to make the words sound as final as they actually did. "Thanks for coming up this weekend. I hope you had a good time."

Ann was watching him carefully, her expression guarded. "Goodbye, Chase."

He gave a short nod. "Goodbye." He went back down the stairs and reached for the door handle, but something made him turn back.

Ann stood at the top of the stairs, looking small and lovely and sad. A moment went by, and then his legs were moving of their own accord. Just as he walked up, she walked down. Then his arms were around her and his lips were on hers and he simply inhaled her, desperately trying to hold on to whatever he could get. She kissed him back with so much passion it blew him away.

Finally, reluctantly, he pulled back, still holding her.

"Chase," she said, looking up at him with luminous eyes.

"Yeah, Annie?"

"Stay," she said simply.

He stiffened. "For how long?"

"For tonight. Or longer. I—I don't want you to go." She took a deep breath. "I think there's something between us and I want to see where it could go."

Chase dropped his arms and looked at her for a long time. It seemed like it would be the easiest thing in the world—to just stay with her. But he couldn't wrap his mind around what that would mean for him.

What he and Ann shared over Christmas was incredible, but it was only a long weekend. In Tahoe he had finally found his bearings, and if he wasn't the happiest guy in the world, well, at least he wasn't miserable.

He needed time to think. And if he stayed with Ann he knew he wouldn't be able to do that, because he wanted her so badly it muddled his mind. All she had to do was to kiss him and he'd be lost. Whatever decision he made this time had to be on his terms.

Ann was still standing there, barely breathing, waiting for him to speak. She'd laid everything on the line for him, showed him how vulnerable and yet how fearless she really was. The realization that he simply didn't measure up shamed him.

"I can't," he finally said, his voice breaking. "I want to, but I belong in Tahoe. I'm sorry."

Not wanting to see the hurt in her eyes, or for her to see the confusion in his, he turned and left, the door closing behind him with a resounding thwack.

Roxy gave him an accusing stare when he came back to the truck alone. He opened the door and found himself face-to-face with a dog hell-bent on escaping.

"No, girl," he said, holding her collar as he climbed into the cab. "Sit. Stay."

For once, Roxy refused to obey his commands. Instead, she ran to the open window and stuck her head out. When he started the truck and began to move, she howled as loud as all get-out.

"Shh! Quiet, Roxy! Sit!"

But she wouldn't sit. Just howled all the way down Ann's road until they were on the highway. Then she jumped into the back and sank into a depressed silence.

The ache in his chest stayed with him the whole ride home. A soak in the hot tub and two beers tired him out enough to get to sleep. But when he woke in the morning, the ache—and the emptiness that went along with it—returned and it hurt like hell.

CHAPTER 15

Chase took a swig of coffee from his mug and stared out across his snowy lawn, over the trees, to Lake Tahoe glistening below him, vast and blue. The water was gorgeous, sparkling in the early light.

The morning view usually did it for him, but not today. Not since he'd dropped Ann Smith back off in Mountain View at the beginning of the week and simply driven away. Strange, he'd thought he was doing all right up in Tahoe. At least until Ann came along and he'd caught a glimpse of what real happiness actually was. It echoed the way he'd felt when he was in his lab, except with even more contentment and satisfaction. Even living in the most beautiful place on earth, with nature as his playground, he hadn't really understood. Until he'd spent Christmas with her.

And he'd thrown it away.

A chill wind blew, rattling the trees and shaking snow and ice from the branches. His cue to move. He went back inside and shucked off his coat. Just as he was gathering up his gear to head out to Alpine Meadows, his telephone buzzed in his pocket. He checked to see who was calling. Up popped a name he knew well: Greg Frobel.

Silicon Valley was determined to have her way with him, wasn't she?

Like always, Greg didn't get the picture. You couldn't just call someone up after two years and chat like old times. Chase really didn't want to talk, but unless he dealt with this now, Greg would probably keep calling. He clicked on the phone.

"Deckert," he answered.

Greg didn't miss a beat. "Chase, man, it is great to hear your voice. Glad you didn't change your cell phone number. How are you?"

"Do you really want me to answer that?" he said, letting true surliness creep into his voice.

Greg cleared his throat. "Maybe I should get straight to why I called."

"Yeah," he said. "Maybe."

"I'm calling to offer you an amazing job at Globalize," Greg said, in his best used-car salesman's voice. "I have authorization to offer you half a mil, plus stock options and a generous benefits package."

Yeesh, when it rained, it poured. To cover his surprise, Chase gave a mock sigh. "And I thought you knew me so well."

"Oh, right, I forgot. You're above the money," his old friend said, used-car salesman's voice slipping.

"And you'll take all you can get."

Greg was silent for a moment. "Not everyone shares your values, Deck."

Like ethics? "I guess not." All of a sudden, exhaustion hit him. He'd slept badly last night without Ann by his side. "What do you really want?"

"You're a great scientist. And Globalize recognizes that." Used-car salesman was back. "Look, I know we didn't part under the best of circumstances . . . "

"You sold my research out from under me." *Stabbed me in the heart. Let me bleed all over the pavement while you walked away.*

"To a great company that offered you a job."

"Where I'd be doing *my* research that someone else owned under *their* direction."

"It wouldn't be like that now. You'd have your own team. You'd call your own shots."

"Let me be clear. When I said *why* before, what I really wanted to know is *why now?*"

"Isn't it time to come back, Chase? You've been hiding out long enough, traipsing around in Zambia, slumming it in Tahoe."

"Don't hold back," Chase said tightly. "Tell me how you *really* feel about my time management during the past couple of years."

"You always did have a way with words, Deck," Greg said, giving him a fake laugh.

"I don't even know why you're calling me. The head of Globalize must know how I feel about you."

"I *wanted* to call you," Greg said, sounding way too smooth for Chase's liking, "to try to put water under the bridge."

"But that's not how you operate," Chase said. "You wouldn't have done this unless there was something in it for you."

"I'm doing this for *you*, Chase."

"Liar."

Greg didn't respond, and Chase let the silence draw out for a deliciously long time.

Finally, he heard Greg's soft exhale of breath on the other end of the line. "Okay, fine. I'm in line for a promotion. You help me, I help you. And is it really that big a hardship to join a great company with amazing resources?"

"You still with Heather?"

"Yes," Greg admitted.

"Things serious?"

"We're engaged. You're over her, though. Right?"

"Yeah." He had been the moment she said goodbye. But he hadn't been able to let go of his research as easily. Still, there was something missing from this puzzle. "Why the hurry? The timing seems awfully rushed, doesn't it?"

"Are you really going to make me spell it out for you? My CEO got wind of the fact that Alliance offered you a position. C'mon, Chase. You remember how awesome things were before the money got in the way." *Before I stole your research.* "Well, the money won't be an issue now. We'll both have plenty. And if not for me, do it for yourself. Do you want to waste your time in Tahoe when you could change the world?"

Fury rose inside him. "Don't spew that crap when you don't really believe it."

"I don't believe it, but you do."

His anger softened. Yeah, he did believe it. Always had. But not like this. He didn't want to change the world if that meant he'd be used as a pawn to one-up another company. If he did jump back into the research game it'd be at the right time for the right reasons.

Greg didn't get it, and honestly, he never would. So he told his former friend the one thing that would make any sense. "I'll pass on your job offer, Greg," Chase said. "It's nothing personal. It's just business."

And then he hung up the phone.

Chase finished his coffee and went to find Roxy. She was sitting by the sunroom door, her head on her paws in the exact same spot she'd been sitting every day since they returned to Tahoe. When Chase approached, Roxy lifted her head, gazed at him for a long moment, and then went back to staring out the glass.

At the footprints in the snow. His and Ann's.

One long weekend and memories of Ann were wrapped up in the place. She was imprinted on his brain—in his house. On the mountain. In his heart. And for Christmas.

When things had gone south for her, Ann had gone back to her regular life—a huge risk she'd taken with both eyes open. When things had gone south for *him*, he'd run—skipped out of town, first to Africa and then to the mountains, to try to forget what Greg had done to him, pretending like he didn't need anything or anyone to make a life for himself. It had all been a lie, and this time he had nowhere to run.

He'd been a fool. He thought he'd been living on his own terms all along by cutting out of Silicon Valley, but until he met Ann he hadn't realized how unhappy he truly was. He hadn't moved on at all, just let the stubbornness and resentment build up inside of him. No amount of pretty scenery made up for his inability to work through what had happened. To push past the anger at being played by someone he'd really trusted. It had taken one long weekend with Ann Smith to show him what he was missing by running away.

Thanks to her, he finally knew what he wanted. He could do this. He *wanted* to do this. Not because it was the Christmas season and he was lonely. But because he'd glimpsed his future and she had curly brown hair and the brightest blue eyes he'd ever seen.

"Better late than never, Deck." Without waiting another second, he picked up his cell phone and dialed a now-familiar number.

"Hey, it's Chase Deckert," he said. "I want to talk."

CHAPTER 16

"Toss the chopped basil into the pot," the chef demanded, sprinkling the herb into the steaming, bubbling tomato sauce. "Like this."

Ann did as Chef Berelli instructed while the silvered-haired woman stood before the nine-person class, watching with eagle eyes.

"Now, you stir," she said, gesticulating with her hands.

Dutifully, Ann stirred, enjoying the aroma as it wafted up. Memories of Chase came back, thick and rich, like the sauce. It would be all right. She'd survived heartache once and she could do it again. Like she told herself before, she had plenty of practice moving on, and that's exactly what she intended to do. Anyway, what had she expected from her first time out of the gate? That right away she'd find someone to love, except this time she'd get her happily ever after? The probability of that was pretty low.

Ann blinked, painfully aware of the heaviness that had begun to weigh down her heart.

The thing was, she *had* found someone right away, and even though she hadn't known Chase that long she knew she could love him. And that the love would continue to grow. He wasn't her rebound guy at all; he was her keeper.

What were the odds of *that*?

"*Bene.* Good," the chef said, one of the few words of praise she'd given all class. "Now you." The woman took the wooden spoon from Ann and handed it to Mandy, whom Ann had sweet-talked into taking this Saturday afternoon class at a local cooking supply store. "Keep stirring." When Mandy stirred a bit too briskly, Chef Berelli snapped at her. "Gently!"

"What a drill sergeant," Mandy muttered under her breath.

Ann tried not to smile. While the chef's mannerisms were a bit over the top, the lesson on how to make fresh *bolognese* had definitely been worth her time. She was pretty sure that with the recipe the chef had promised they could take home, she'd be able to replicate the sauce in her own kitchen. Without the drill sergeant attitude.

"Having fun?" Mandy whispered while the chef was talking with their other classmates about the perfect pasta to serve with the sauce.

Ann nodded. "Yes. Thanks again for joining me. I know this really isn't your cup of tea."

"My arm is about to fall off!" Mandy stopped stirring and lifted the spoon out of the saucepan.

"Keep stirring," the chef ordered.

Mandy gave her a glare, jammed the spoon back in and stirred double-time, but *gently*. "Spill it, Annie. *Something* happened up in Tahoe. I can tell."

Ann dipped the tip of her finger into the pot to taste the sauce. "How's that?"

"I'm not totally clueless, you know." Mandy paused. "Was it Deck?" Ann must have looked stricken, because Mandy's eyes widened fast. "Oh, no! It *was* Deck." She almost stopped stirring for a second, but one glance from Chef Berelli had her going again. "This is all my fault," she whispered.

"It's not, Mandy," Ann said. "How could it be?"

"Because I bailed on you and sent you up there alone. If only I'd been there . . . ."

"Mandy, it's all right," she said, wondering who she was trying to placate more—Mandy, or herself.

"I'm a terrible friend! I've totally fouled everything up. I thought I'd fixed you up. And I thought I'd fixed Deck up, but that didn't work out well either."

"How did you *fix Deck up*?" Ann asked, a gnawing suspicion growing in her gut.

"No, no, not like that. It wasn't a set-up, truly. I thought you'd feel good in Tahoe, Annie. I remembered how much you loved to ski and I knew you shouldn't be alone on Christmas. But Deck? Him, I got a job." She chewed on a fingernail. "Or at least I thought I did."

Now she was really confused. "But he already has a job teaching snowboarding."

"Not that kind of job," Mandy said. "A *real* job. You know he's one of the world's experts on malaria, right?" Slowly, Ann shook her head. No. She hadn't known that. All she'd known was that he was burned out on the research he'd been doing. "Well, I got him an interview with Alliance Biotechnology in South San Francisco. Great company with a focus on malaria research. Deck would be perfect there. But he won't take it."

Ann stood there, head buzzing, while Mandy prattled on about the opportunity, the company, and what an imbecile Chase was for not immediately snapping up the offer. She wasn't as surprised by the fact that

Chase was a hot prospect as she was by the fact that he'd completely neglected to tell her he'd been offered a prime job. Why would he? They'd only known each other for a few short days. It wasn't as if he owed her anything. But the look on Chase's face when he'd told her he couldn't stay kept flickering in her mind over and over again, like a broken neon sign.

Stupid, stupid woman.

Foolishly, she'd thought that reclaiming herself would be enough, but it wasn't. Because yes, she'd found herself, but along the way, she'd found someone else, too. Someone she thought she could be with. And perhaps love.

She almost laughed aloud. Talk about jumping with two feet back into reality. Still, she had to look on the bright side of things—the pain of heartache wasn't what she needed right now, but at least it meant she was alive.

". . . but all of his idiocy pales in comparison to the fact that he messed with you." Mandy's voice broke into her thoughts.

Ann shook her head. "No. It's not like that. I mean yes, we had something last weekend, but he didn't mess with me. Or if he did, I messed right back with him."

"I told him to take care of you!"

Chase had taken care of her all right. She hadn't asked him to. He'd just done it. She'd been balancing on her own two feet for so long, trying desperately not to fall, but she couldn't deny how nice it was to have someone to lean on. Only problem was, he didn't want her.

"Mandy, it's fine. *I'm* fine."

Mandy watched her for a few long seconds. "So . . . you're not angry with me?"

"Why would I be?" Ann said, trying to keep her voice light. "You got me out of town over Christmas, got me back on the slopes, and got me my rebound guy. I'd say the weekend was a huge success. And who knows what will happen next? Tomorrow is a new year."

She wasn't being 100 percent honest with Mandy, but Ann knew her words would make her friend feel better. Still, part of what she said was true. Whether she saw Chase again or not, the weekend *had* helped her recalibrate herself. She'd go back to Tahoe again, with or without him, because she wanted to ski. And she was taking this cooking class. All she wanted was to be herself—Ann Smith. And that was what she'd gone up to Tahoe for, wasn't it?

All at once, the door opened with a bang.

Chase Deckert stood there looking as shocked as she felt. Everyone stared at him, and no wonder. Although he'd shaved his beard close to his skin, he still looked like the mountain man he was in a T-shirt that skimmed his frame and worn jeans that hugged his thighs in all the right places.

The instructor addressed Chase in rapid Italian. When he didn't budge, she switched to English. "You cannot be here. This is a private class. You must leave."

"I need to talk to Ann," he said, looking directly at her.

Every head swiveled towards her. Instinctively, she tipped her chin up. How did Chase even know she was here? She glanced quickly at Mandy. Guilt was written all over her beautiful face.

"Chase called me yesterday and I told him where we'd be without realizing you two . . ."

"I cannot have you interrupting my class," the chef said. "Go." She made a shooing motion in his direction. Chase didn't move.

"I'm not leaving until I talk to Ann."

The other people taking the class couldn't decide who to stare at now that there was a show-down happening right before them. Eyes flicked back and forth between Ann and Chase, Chase and Chef Berelli. Chef Berelli and Ann. Finally, Ann couldn't take it anymore.

"I'll go."

"If you leave," Chef Berelli warned, "you do not come back."

"I paid a hundred dollars for this class," Ann protested.

Chef Berelli merely crossed her arms over her ample bosom.

"Please," Chase said, his gaze fiery. "Ann, I—" He glanced around. Ten pairs of eyes were staring at him, but when he shook his head she knew he was going to continue. "I hadn't planned on doing this in such a public place, but I just wanted to let you know that what we shared last weekend meant something to me. I'm sorry I hurt you. I know I hurt you, didn't I, Annie?"

She couldn't speak, so she merely nodded.

He nodded too, and ran a hand through his hair. "I'm so sorry. After everything, that was the last thing I wanted to do."

The room was silent except for the soft sound of sauce bubbling on the stovetop.

"Because you forced me to figure out what I really want, and that's you."

She couldn't move. Couldn't even breathe, for that matter. Was this really happening?

"On Monday I couldn't stay. It was just a weekend, and I hadn't sorted it all out in my own head. I needed some space and some time. As soon as I had that, I could think. And all I could think about was you." He took a step toward her. "Your passion for living is in everything you do, even if you don't realize it. And it took me less than a week without you to know I need that in my life. I need *you* in my life."

"Chase," she finally croaked out. "I—"

"You don't have to give me an answer now. I'll wait." Before she could say anything else, he turned and walked out the door. Beside her, she heard

Mandy's soft exhale.

"Good," Chef Berelli said, turning back to them with a smug smile. "The man is gone. Now where were we?"

"No," Ann said aloud. Maybe he could wait another hour, but she couldn't. "I'm going." And without any other hesitation, she ran out the door after Chase.

What were the odds of Ann finishing her class, coming out and telling him to take a hike? Chase tried some rudimentary calculations, but none of them made any sense in his jumbled brain. Probably because he had no clue what she was thinking.

The only things he knew for certain were that she looked more beautiful than he'd ever seen her, with her hair down and her apron hugging her gentle curves, and that coming back to Silicon Valley made sense. This was the first honest thing he'd done in two years, and it would serve him right if laying himself on the line for her came back to bite him in the ass. As it was, he'd cut out of the kitchen classroom before she'd had the chance to tell him no.

Once he'd gotten his head screwed on straight, it had taken him less than twenty-four hours to make the decision to come back to Silicon Valley, accept the job at Alliance, pack up his gear and get down here. Forget clothes or a place to stay. Forget the rest of the snowboarding season. He had one goal in mind: getting back to Ann.

And you couldn't even wait for her answer. Wimp.

Chase sighed. What was he supposed to do now? Roxy was in the car with the windows cracked open. He should let her out so they could take a walk while the class finished up.

He turned down an aisle filled floor to ceiling with colorful crockery which only seemed to mock him with its cheerful hues.

"Chase!"

"Ann?" Chase turned around and there she was. Without warning, she launched herself right into his arms.

He wrapped his arms around her and held on tight, lifting her off the floor. Nothing had ever felt so good or so right. An indescribable swell of emotion surged through his very being—happiness to the core. He buried his face in her hair. "Oh, Annie."

Then he set her down and carefully, so carefully, cupped her face in his hands. Her blue eyes were smiling up at him so he kissed her, deep and long. She kissed him back with equal parts tenderness and passion, so sweet and real he didn't know how he'd lived even a day without her.

When she finally broke away, she looked up at him. "Are you truly here?"

"For real." He swallowed. "I took the job. I guess Mandy told you about it."

She nodded. "Yes. But why didn't you tell me you were even considering it?"

He took her hand. "I didn't tell you because at the time I didn't want to take it. I didn't want to be back here. But all that resentment I'd built up, all the anger—it wasn't really about Greg. It was about me. About losing control over my work and my life. I was a stubborn ass, but it took a while for me to figure it out."

"What made you change your mind?"

"Part of it is the science," Chase admitted. "And Phil, the CEO of the company I'm joining made it really easy. He wrote it into my contract that I can work remotely up to two months every year, so I can spend part of the winter season in Tahoe if I want. But it was really you, Annie. You did this for me. Showed me that the most important things in life you have to work for. Fight for."

He couldn't quite read the look in her eyes.

"Annie? Say something, please."

"I think I'm falling in love with you, Chase," she blurted out.

He wrapped her up in his arms again, wondering what he'd done to get so lucky. "Lord, Annie, me too." He pulled back, gauging her reaction. He saw happiness, and relief. "Look, I'm not sure how this is going to work out. I mean, I'm supposed to start work next Monday and all I have is a duffel bag of clothes, a black Lab and a truck, but we will make this work. We *have* to make this work."

"I asked you before—" she started, then stopped and took a deep breath. "I asked you before if you'd stay with me and you said no."

"Are you asking me again?"

She nodded.

He searched her eyes. They were filled with promise. "Got room for a dog, too?"

"I stocked up on antihistamine medicine," she said. "Just in case."

"Ah, Annie," he said, drawing her close enough to feel her heart beating against his chest. "Kiss me again."

When she did, so deep and so real, he knew everything was going to be all right. Because they were together, and that mattered more than anything.

Tomorrow would be a new year and Ann was his future. He knew he'd never run from it—or her—again.

New Year's in Napa
A West Coast Holiday Series Book

ELISABETH BARRETT

ACKNOWLEDGMENTS

First, thank you to Jennifer and Tasneem who continue to go above and beyond. Visiting Napa was truly a blast with you by my side! Thanks to Alex at Jarvis Estate for the amazing tour. Thanks also to AB, Kelly McClellan, Denise Johnsen, and Kimberly Bowden for your knowledge and expertise, as well as to my amazing beta readers, Suzanne Turner and Lia Riley. Your feedback was, as always, invaluable. Extra thanks to Marina Adair, Jules Barnard, Shawntelle Madison, Jennifer Probst, Jennifer Ryan, and Nalini Akolekar for providing huge amounts of encouragement and support. A huge shout out to Cynthia Mutti and Emily for your expert assistance with the cover. In addition, thanks to Michael, Matt, and Suzanne for all the copyright help, both for this book and for *Christmas in Tahoe*. To all of my readers for continuing to take this journey with me—thank you. And to Jonathan. Your incredible support, love, and partnership makes me happy every single day.

CHAPTER 1

You can do this, Mandy, Amanda Aligheri told herself. *Just go. Walk up there. Say hi. No big deal.* Her feet refused to do her brain's bidding, staying stubbornly planted at the end of the shaded stone path that led to the visitor center and tasting room at Flynn Winery. *Pretend it's all part of the plan.*

She still didn't budge.

Okay, time for the big guns: *you promised Annie and Chase you'd stop in.*

That should work. It had to, because she always, always kept her promises.

Nothing.

She took a deep breath and examined the visitor center a hundred yards ahead at the end of the path. It was beautiful—a stone-and-wood affair cut into the hillside with a jutting second-story deck overlooking the valley. This early in the rainy season, most of the foliage was still emerging, but the structure blended into its surroundings almost organically. Classic Napa.

Mandy closed her eyes, imagining the microscopic neurons firing in her brain, the electrical signals racing to her extremities via numerous synapses, instructing her feet to go.

Move.

Nope.

She opened her eyes and sighed. Chase's dog, a beautiful black Labrador retriever named Roxy, looked up at her and whined.

"I'm trying, Roxy," Mandy told the dog. "I really am."

This trip to Napa was supposed to be relaxing—at least that's what Annie and Chase had promised when they talked her into joining them the week between Christmas and New Year's. Unfortunately, relaxing had never been Mandy's strong suit, and circumstances were making it even more challenging now.

Crushing guilt permeated almost every aspect of her daily life whenever Mandy left work, but this time her laboratory had erupted in chaos once her devoted grad students realized she wasn't returning immediately after Christmas. She'd already fielded over a dozen phone calls asking about everything from operating certain equipment to interpreting interim results from various experiments. Further, the gas pipe in Annie and Chase's town house had sprung a leak, so Mandy had taken Roxy in order to keep the dog out of harm's way. Mandy was glad to help, but she had to scramble to find a new reservation, since the hotel she'd originally booked didn't allow pets.

And now, on top of everything else, she was going to have to see Liam Flynn. In some ways, this was the most stressful thing of all because she and Liam had *history*.

Two years ago when she was visiting Chase in Tahoe on a rare break from work, Liam had joined them and they'd hit it off immediately.

After a perfect day racing down the slopes at Alpine Meadows together, on the last evening of her visit in front of a roaring fire at Chase's cabin, Liam had taken her in his arms and kissed her—a breathtaking, toe-curling, openmouthed kiss that was the closest thing she'd ever come to an out-of-body experience.

The problem? Liam Flynn was an all-or-nothing kind of guy. He'd actually told her he was in for the long haul, and *that* she simply couldn't do. No long haul. No commitment. Just work until she got her research squared away.

So despite *really* being into Liam, she'd turned him down, ignored the hurt and surprise in his gorgeous green eyes, and spent a lonely, celibate night in Chase's guest room.

She hadn't seen or heard from Liam since.

You should never have gone to Tahoe in the first place.

No. She couldn't think like that. This was her life, and she needed to live it, not stay trapped in her laboratory day and night working on her research, no matter how much pain she could mitigate or how many lives she could save. Repressing her emotions and suppressing her needs wasn't healthy. That's why she was here—to make a change, *any change*, because if she didn't, she was going to crack.

Except change required action.

Roxy nudged Mandy's calf with her muzzle and whined again. Mandy didn't budge. "Still working on it," she whispered.

The sweet dog must have understood, because she simply lay down, put her head on her paws, and looked up at Mandy with sorrowful, dark eyes. Mandy stared back for a beat.

Okay, now even the dog was making her feel guilty. But this clearly wasn't happening, so she should just turn around, get back into her Prius, go get her laptop, and find a WiFi connection so she could alleviate her stress by getting some work done.

It might be cheating a little, but since getting her life more balanced was a *New Year's* resolution, she didn't have to start following it for another five days, anyway…right?

Just as she was garnering the strength to leave, the sound of a motorcycle engine caught her off guard. Oh, that unmistakable rumble. Based on the tingle that ran down her spine she knew it was a Harley, something she couldn't resist. She'd wait to see what model it was, take a good, long look, then head back downtown.

When the bike came into view a few moments later, she was glad she'd stayed.

The motorcycle—an early '70s Harley Sportster—was over-the-top gorgeous, with what looked like the original red paint, beautiful chrome pipes, and a ten-inch overspringer front end. Its rider was gorgeous, too—a big guy completely at ease in the seat. But as bike and rider came closer, she realized she'd made a critical mistake, because there was no missing Liam Flynn's broad shoulders or that chiseled jaw underneath his skull cap's strap.

Crap.

Liam drove right up to the edge of the stone walkway, eyes sparking in recognition, gaze smoldering. He cut the engine, and silence hung between them, thick and heavy.

"Hey girl," he finally said, the corners of his lips curling up in a sexy smile. "Miss me?"

And Mandy remembered all over again why she'd been tempted. Heart pounding, she struggled to find a suitable comeback, but before she could even open her mouth, Roxy leaped up and raced over to the bike, straining at her leash. With a grin, Liam reached down and gave Roxy's head a friendly rumple. Roxy wagged her tail like crazy and barked with joy.

He'd been talking to the dog.

Mandy's cheeks burned, but Liam didn't appear to notice, since Roxy was jumping up to lick his face. Liam laughed at Roxy's exuberance, a deep reverberation that carried through the damp air.

Liam's laugh matched his looks—big and bold. Auburn hair made a striking contrast to deep green eyes. A hint of stubble on his jaw, the same color as his hair, added a bit of rough. Huge hands looked capable of anything. Though he was still sitting on his bike, his six-three frame simply commanded the space from the top of his black helmet to the tips of his steel-toed boots.

If she were in the market for a guy—which she absolutely, positively wasn't—she might actually consider Liam Flynn. Aside from his easygoing attitude and his amazing mouth, which she knew from intimate experience, he had a sharp light of intelligence in his eyes and a smile so friendly and welcoming you couldn't help but be drawn in.

Except she wasn't going to be drawn in because nothing had changed, at least not on her part, and likely not on his, especially after she'd rejected him point-blank. Anyway, in a few days she'd head back to Silicon Valley, and Liam would stay here in Napa.

Besides, given her insane work schedule—self-imposed, to be sure, but insane nonetheless—flying solo was better for everyone, and on those rare nights out, she was glad to act as wingwoman for any friend who might need some assistance. All it typically took was a glance and a smile. But pretty soon she'd get distracted, and it was time to hand the guy off to her friends and get back to the lab.

Liam Flynn was not the kind of man you handed off to anyone.

"Back up, girl," he told Roxy. The black Lab obeyed immediately. Liam moved up a few feet to park his bike on a patch of dirt, and swung off, making sure the kickstand was down securely. He took off his helmet and put it into a satchel attached to the back of the bike. Then he turned, pulling off his gloves as he came toward her.

He seemed bigger than she remembered, his black leather jacket stretching over his wide chest, his worn jeans skimming his long legs just right.

"Hello, Amanda," he said, eyes squarely on hers, his face now an impenetrable mask. "Long time no see."

An intense combination of awkwardness and desire flooded her. She pushed back at both. "It's been a while."

"Two years."

"That sounds about right." Then she smiled, an offer of peace she hoped he wouldn't refuse. "I seem to run into you whenever I'm on a break from work."

He didn't bite, but his gaze swept her up and down, and eventually came back to settle on her face. "You still doing the scientist thing?"

Unable to help herself, she tilted her chin up. "Are you still doing the wine thing?"

There was silence for a moment, and then he laughed, breaking the tension. "Forgot what a smart mouth you had. Missed it."

Relief almost made her light-headed. She had enough to worry about this week without adding discomfort around Liam Flynn to the mix.

"Chase sends his regards," she said, glad to be back on neutral ground. "He and Annie are stuck in Mountain View dealing with a gas leak. I came up early with Roxy so she wouldn't get sick."

"Got a heads-up you'd be arriving with my favorite Lab," he said, bending down to scratch Roxy behind the ears. The dog went crazy again, wagging her tail madly and trying to get closer to Liam for more of whatever he was dishing out. "When did you get here?"

Even crouching down he looked enormous, and she was embarrassed to admit her mouth watered a little.

"This morning," she said.

"What have you done so far?"

"Nothing. Just checked into my inn and came up here."

"Flynn Winery's your first stop? I'm honored." He gave her an easy grin, pure Liam.

"Well, the wedding's going to be here," Mandy said, mostly so he wouldn't think she was at the winery solely because of him. "I figured I'd check the place out before the happy couple arrives."

"Hmm," Liam said, as if he could see right through her. "Why don't I walk you up to the visitor center and we can get you and Roxy settled. Would a tour suit you?"

"How long does it last?"

"About an hour. Why?" He raised an eyebrow. "You got someplace important to be?"

"I was planning to go back to the inn. See if I can get some work done before Annie and Chase get here. I figure as long as I'm being forced out of my laboratory and I can't run any experiments, I might as well analyze some data. I'm currently doing two parallel statistical analyses on…"

She trailed off, finally noticing Liam's hard stare. She'd seen that look before in Tahoe when she'd tried to beg off a backcountry run. There was nothing to do in the face of that look but cave, especially since in her heart, she knew work was just an excuse to avoid deeper issues.

Besides, learning about the winery would be interesting, and could help kick-start her get-Mandy's-life-back-on-track plan. And she hadn't been completely fibbing to Liam; visiting might actually give her some clarity about her maid of honor duties when Annie and Chase got married in a few months. If there was one crimp in her plan, it was that she wouldn't be able to keep her mind off Liam if she had to spend an hour with him while he oozed magnetism.

Her eyes narrowed. "You're not the tour guide, are you?"

"Not today," he told her with a half smile. "We're a little short-staffed because of the holidays, so I'm in the tasting room until midafternoon."

"All right, then," she said. "I'll take a tour." What else was she going to do? Her friends weren't here, and the Internet was out at the inn. When she'd called the front desk to let them know, she'd gotten a very polite apology and a little chuckle. *This is Napa,* the woman had said. *We go at our own pace here.* Clearly, this was wine country's way of telling her to quit working and get her Zen on.

If Liam knew that she was struggling with this—with *him*—he did a good job hiding it. "Great," he said. "Bring Roxy inside if you like. We're a dog-friendly establishment."

He placed a hand on the small of her back and guided her up the path, Roxy trotting beside them. Mandy stiffened at first, then allowed herself be escorted.

She'd forgotten how persuasive he could be, and it wasn't all physical, either—his mind and his mouth were just as convincing as his body language. In Tahoe he'd even talked her into an out-of-bounds run, technically allowed at Alpine, but pushing the limits of her comfort zone. Ultimately, the thrill of the run had overridden her annoyance at being handled.

Liam looked out over the property, and she did the same—from the hills blanketed in fog to the manzanita blooms just beginning to unfurl—then he opened the door for her. "You know," he said, "most people would kill to be in wine country over the holidays."

She knew. This time of year, things were quieter in Napa, but festive in a down-to-earth kind of way. Christmas was over, but her little inn on First Street was still bedecked in lights and evergreen, and the holiday decorations were still up at Flynn Winery, too. Two wreaths woven from grapevines hung on the giant double front doors, and garlands of green were draped over the doorframe. She stepped in, and her eyes were immediately drawn to the Christmas tree—a ten-foot Douglas fir glittering with old-fashioned tin ornaments shaped like bunches of grapes and tiny wineglasses hanging upside down from red velvet ribbons. Its piney aroma permeated the room, adding to the post-holiday splendor.

That scent, more than anything, made her feel homesick. Her family always had a huge tree as the centerpiece to the holiday, and so many memories of the season were wrapped up in that Christmassy smell.

To her, Christmas meant getting back to La Jolla, surfing with her sister Nicole, and just hanging out with her mom and dad. She loved her family, but as wonderful as they were, home wasn't a good place to think. So she deliberately cut her visit short to come up here on this soul-searching mission.

Which, so far, wasn't going according to plan.

As if on cue, her phone buzzed and she stole a quick glance at the number. It was from her lab, another question from her grad students, no doubt. She shoved the phone back in her pocket. She'd deal with it later.

"I just have a lot going on at work right now," she said, almost cringing as the words left her mouth. How many times had she used that excuse without even thinking about what it implied she thought of others, not to mention what she thought of herself?

"Hmm," he said again, ushering her into the cavernous room, which was a combination visitor center and gift shop. There was so much to look at— numerous placards and maps, presumably detailing the history of the winery—and so much for sale, including bottles of Flynn Winery's famous cabernet sauvignon, baseball caps sporting the winery's logo, and of course, all the obligatory wine accoutrements including cork art, bottle stoppers, and wine screws.

A slight man behind a desk on the far side of the room stood as they approached.

"Hi, Liam!" the man said.

"Hey, Jeremy," Liam responded. "Got another one for the tour."

"Great! I'll let Jennie know she'll have seven instead of six."

"Here's where I leave you," Liam said. "The tour starts right here in five minutes, but come by the tasting room after and I'll hook you up with some cab. Catch you later."

Not bothering to wait for her response, he turned and sprinted up a nearby staircase, giving Mandy a prime view of his backside.

She was still staring at Liam's ass when Jeremy cleared his throat. "Feel free to look around the shop while you wait, miss," the man said. "I'll let you know when things are about to start."

Suddenly, the huge bin of corks by the register looked *fascinating*. "Thank you," she murmured.

Seeing him again wasn't as bad as she'd thought it might be, but things weren't completely comfortable, either. She liked things ordered and reasoned, and the effect Liam Flynn had on her was neither. When Chase and Annie arrived, they would, of course, want the four of them to hang out, and then she'd be forced to chitchat with Liam when what she really wanted to do was to feel his lips on hers, and to discover if that insane chemistry they shared two years ago was still there.

Bad idea. Really bad.

Because he was still the same man, and she was still the same woman…albeit one trying to make a minor change in her lifestyle—the operative word being *minor*. So she'd play it cool, ride out the week, and then return to Silicon Valley come the new year, just as she planned.

She wouldn't be tempted by Liam Flynn and his easy smile.

Not even a little.

CHAPTER 2

With those beautiful eyes, legs that wouldn't quit, and a smile that would melt ice, Mandy Aligheri was just as gorgeous as she was the last time he'd seen her. She was also just as smart, her intelligence evident with the sharp gleam in her baby blues, obvious with every word that came out of her mouth.

Liam liked intelligence.

Unfortunately, her brains were surpassed by her stubbornness.

He'd never met a woman more determined to close herself off, which kind of went against his credo, not to mention Napa Valley's, which valued going with the flow, enjoying each unique season, and living life to the fullest each day, every day. To wit, the half dozen people gathered around the polished wood tasting bar this afternoon. His guests were two locals—unusual at any time of year, but welcome nonetheless—a couple from Iowa on their first trip to Napa, and an older man and woman—not together—both up for the day from San Francisco. All of them were having a great time, smiling, laughing, and most of all relaxing in one of the most beautiful spots on earth.

Not Mandy.

He'd known it was Dr. Amanda Aligheri standing at the end of his winery's path from the moment he'd seen her—not by the golden braid down her back or the black Lab at her feet but by her slim shoulders thrown defiantly back in permanent challenge.

Funny enough, Liam also liked challenges.

Chase had called him in the morning to let him know they'd be late, and asked him—on both his and Ann's behalf—to take care of Mandy if and when she showed up. He doubted Chase would have asked if he knew what had happened between him and Mandy up in Tahoe.

Liam had been attracted to Mandy from the moment he met her—the way she was always on Chase's case to own his destiny, her take-charge attitude, and her skintight ski pants. He even liked the way she compartmentalized her life into discrete chunks—work, play, sleep...until he kissed her and she turned him down even though she'd just told him how much she liked him. It was then he realized she'd left no room in all those compartments for a personal life.

He wouldn't lie—it had stung.

But he'd gotten over it, and regardless of their charged past, he was always glad to help out a friend. Chase was a good man—solid as a rock and at one point in time, a killer snowboarding instructor. When Liam had started boarding in Tahoe, Chase hooked him up with gear, with lessons— even with backcountry boarding buddies so he wouldn't have to go off-piste alone. Somewhere between the beers, the snowboarding, and watching each other's backs on the slopes, Chase had morphed from teacher to friend. Of course he was going to look out for the guy—it was why Liam had offered the winery as a wedding venue despite the fact that it typically didn't do private events. He'd look out for Chase's friends, too.

And despite her earlier rejection, that included Mandy.

But taking care of her was a difficult prospect.

She seemed to be wound even more tightly than last time, but he'd rise to the occasion. *Think, Flynn, think.*

Winter was called Cabernet Season in Napa for a reason—the pace was slower, and locals and visitors alike had access to the best that the valley had to offer. The week between Christmas and New Year's was a mini-high season, but still mellow. If he were a tourist, this is the week he'd choose to visit. With the harvest, crush, and fermentation complete, and the juice just sitting in oak, there wasn't much to do for winemakers but devote plenty of time to visitors.

Speaking of visitors, Mandy would have to wait.

Liam shot a smile at the middle-aged Iowan who had bellied up to the tasting bar ready for the next wine in his flight, and gave him a generous pour of the cabernet franc. He waited patiently for the man to swirl, smell, and sip.

"This spent twenty-one months in French oak," Liam informed the man. "What do you taste?"

The man wrinkled his nose. "Shoes," he said bluntly.

Liam laughed. "Nice one. Yeah, I taste that too—leathery, earthy. I like the cab franc. It starts out tough, but it grows on you."

"Oh, let me try, Norris," the man's wife said.

"Here," said Liam, pouring them a merlot. "Try this, then go back to the cab franc. I think you'll find the taste develops over time as the wine warms slightly and takes on a little oxygen."

"I like this one better," the wife said, after sipping the merlot. "It tastes smoky. Like a distant campfire."

"Awesome description," Liam told her. "Want to write the label copy for Flynn?" She tittered a little. "I'm serious. The more descriptive and specific, the better." The woman blushed and Liam smiled. "Can't wait to hear your thoughts on the final pour—our award-winning cabernet sauvignon. Let me know when you're ready."

"Hey," came a soft voice with a tap on the shoulder. Liam turned to find his sister Stella looking up at him. The sad resignation that had been in her eyes since she and her ex split for good three months ago wasn't there, even though Liam knew she wasn't completely over him. Guess she was getting better at hiding it.

"Hey, yourself," he said, cupping her upper arm, letting her know he was there for her. He'd erase the pain if he could, but he knew only time would heal that wound. Still, she just kept forging ahead without complaint—without really even talking about the breakup, actually.

With her straight dark hair and quiet demeanor, his little sister was so different from the rest of their red-haired, charismatic Flynn clan. Even so, their relationship was strong—had been since Mom brought Stella home from the hospital and he'd held her for the first time—and had only grown stronger since Liam moved back to Napa seven years ago to help his family run the winery when their dad had needed the extra hands. The best thing he could do for her right now was not to treat her like some breakable object, like their dad did. He let go of her arm.

"You done in the stockroom?"

Stella nodded. "We're in good shape for the rest of the week—we have plenty of the cabernet sauvignon left, and we haven't dipped into the chardonnay that much. The only thing we're low on is the merlot, so I sent George to grab a case of it from storage before he leaves for vacation."

"Great. We'll be able to take a full inventory in January when the winery's closed."

"You know," Stella said thoughtfully, "things will be really quiet then. Maybe you can use that time to work on that software you've been talking about."

Liam shook his head. "Dad made it pretty clear how he feels about that." A year ago, after struggling through the end of a tough harvest, Liam tried to convince his dad to let him build a regression model that could identify correlations between the quality of the wine as judged by its scores, and the massive number of inputs generated at the winery, such as soil moisture, sugar measurements, soil nutrients, and pest activity, which ultimately could direct future vineyard management. It was an elegant, twenty-first century solution to viticulture that not only could help Flynn grow better grapes and make better wine, but with the aggregation of data across other vineyards, could also help their neighbors. Only problem was, Dad was strictly old-school. In his mind, the best way to predict wine quality wasn't by using new technology, but by doing it the old-fashioned way—with his own footprint in the vineyard.

"Ugh, Dad is so stubborn," Stella complained. "He's all *change is bad*, like we're in the dark ages. It's insane. Meanwhile, there's no way we can move from where we are now to achieving cult wine status without utilizing new technology. A couple of great scores from *Wine Spectator* are super, but we're going to have to work even harder and smarter to take Flynn Winery to the next level."

"I agree," Liam said. "But Dad's set in his ways. It took forever to get him to implement modern software to keep track of things on the production side. And you remember how suspicious he was when we set up online ordering—and now most of our orders come via the web!"

"Look, I've said this before: do it anyway. We already have all the historical data, which I'm happy to input once you have the model built. It'll be painful, given that we have everything on scraps of paper or in Excel files, but I'll do it. When Dad sees how much the model can help, he'll change his tune." She set her jaw, and for a moment, Liam got a glimpse of the old Stella. He liked seeing her this way, admired the way she was pushing him forward even while she herself was faltering, but his relationship with their dad was more complicated than Stella understood.

"I don't know. Maybe." Truth was, if he didn't have his dad's full support, he wasn't even sure it was worthwhile. What if he put in all that time and effort, and his dad rejected the model? It would be months of his time down the drain. Still, he couldn't get rid of the nagging thought that what he envisioned building wouldn't just facilitate the way Flynn Winery did business, but had the potential to revolutionize the entire wine industry.

"You're as stubborn as he is," Stella said with a sigh. She pushed her hair behind her ears. "So, are you good here, or can I go deal with party prep?"

It was an annual tradition at the winery to say good-bye to the old year and hello to the new with a friends-and-family-only bash on New Year's Eve. The party was a huge deal to their family, who used it as a way to thank close supporters, and to serve as a gesture of goodwill to the neighbors. Typically, things in Napa were fairly low-key, but the Flynn end-of-year party was more glitzy than anything they did the rest of the year. Everyone dressed up for the fancy sit-down dinner, the entertainment in the form of a local rhythm and blues band, and of course, the wine. Opening the Flynn cellars was a rare treat, and folks came to try those hard-to-get vintages more than anything else.

When their mom was alive, she'd pulled out all the stops to ensure the Flynn party was incredible, but since her death five years ago, Stella had taken the reins. Liam wasn't sure Stella would be up for overseeing the planning this year, given her recent divorce, but she seemed to be all right. Maybe working on something fun—something that looked toward the future—would be good for her.

He embraced her and kissed the top of her head. "Sure. Go."

Stella accepted his hug without question, but almost immediately, he felt one of her small hands pushing him away. She extricated herself quickly, and then he pulled back and turned to follow her gaze.

Mandy was on the other side of the bar watching them with wide eyes, a strange smile touching her lips.

Before Liam could introduce them, Stella ducked her head. "I'd better be going," she said, and disappeared behind the wood-paneled door that led to the staff-only section. Not a surprise. Stella wasn't much for talking to strangers. It's why he typically took the tasting room shift when they were short-staffed, leaving Stella to work behind the scenes where she was more comfortable.

"Hey," he said, walking over to Mandy. He leaned his forearms on the tasting bar to be at her eye level. Almost imperceptibly, she stiffened. He ignored it. "How was the tour?"

"It was…good," she said. "Informative."

"That's what we strive for." The other folks at the tasting bar seemed settled, so he pulled out a glass from beneath the bar. "Want to try some cabernet franc?"

"All right."

He poured generously, then placed the glass in front of her on the wood.

"Thank you." He watched as she took a sip, her face neutral.

"If you don't like that one, I'll get you some of our reserve cab to try," he offered. "It'll make a believer out of you."

Her gaze softened. "I like this one, but the reserve? Are you sure you want to waste it on me?"

"You know about the reserve?"

"Of course. Much of the reserve wine produced at Flynn is purchased by subscription in advance by the winery's loyal customers, leaving only a handful of cases available for the public," Mandy said. She was reciting the Flynn Winery tour guide handbook word-for-word, and he should know. He'd written it. She continued on. "The last reserve cab produced by Flynn Winery was rated a 93 by *Wine Spectator* and sold out in a matter of weeks. I guess you saved some for special occasions."

Liam just stared at her and she flushed. She must be used to this—guys freaking out when she showed them her intelligence—but he wasn't freaking out. In fact, he was more than intrigued. Time had done nothing to diminish his attraction to her. He couldn't act. Not when she'd already turned him down once. But there was nothing in his man code that said he couldn't admire.

"Talk about steel-trap minds," he murmured. "What else did you learn?"

"I'm guessing you already know this stuff," she said, her voice wry.

"Yeah, but it sounds better coming out of your mouth. Tell me."

She moistened her lips. "Ah, okay. Flynn Winery was founded fifty years ago by your grandfather, who wanted to use his experience and expertise in the wine industry for his own label. Initially, the winery focused only on cabernet sauvignon grapes, but has expanded to include numerous other varietals, such as cabernet franc, chardonnay, and a gewürztraminer which is made into very small batch dessert wine. Since its founding, the winery has grown in size and scale, but still remains a family-run operation." She paused. "I could go on, but it'd probably bore you. Anyway, I told you it was an informative tour."

"Wow," he muttered, then blinked. "Well, you sure earned that reserve. I'll pull it out later when Chase and Ann get here."

"It's all right," she told him. "You don't have to."

He did, but telling her might invite more protestations, so he dropped it. "I'm here until two thirty, but afterward, I'd be glad to take you for a walk. Show you parts of the property you didn't see on your tour."

"I could do a walk. But are—are you sure your friend won't mind? I don't want to step on any toes."

It took him a moment to figure out what—or rather *whom*—she meant. "Stella?"

"If Stella's the brunette who just left, then yes."

Liam lowered his voice so the other visitors wouldn't hear. "Stella won't mind," he said. "It's good for her to have some time alone. She's coming off a bad breakup and working is like therapy for her. Dad's thrilled she's actually functioning."

Mandy was quiet for a moment, taking in the information. "She's your…sister?"

"Yep," he said, letting his lips curl up at the edges, unable to resist baiting her a little. She didn't blink, although her shoulders relaxed a fraction.

"You two don't look alike at all," she pronounced. Her tone was neutral, without a hint of jealousy.

"Nope. I got all the Irish, and she got—well, I don't know what she got."

"Genetics at work," Mandy said succinctly. To her, that probably explained everything. A look of sympathy crossed her face. "Anyway, I'm sorry she had a bad breakup."

"Yeah, me too. Unfortunately, her ex-husband is our assistant winemaker, and pretty invaluable to our operation, so kicking his ass is out of the question. So she suffers, and we have to watch her suffer. And let me tell you, watching someone you love get hurt is definitely worse than being hurt yourself."

"Yes," she murmured. "That's so true." She paused and she looked as though she was going to say something else. Then the moment passed, and she was back to her usual, cool self. "Thanks for this," she said, indicating the wine. "Roxy's waiting for me outside, so I'm going to head to the porch and enjoy my glass out there. See you later."

And she turned with a swish, all legs and attitude, and Liam stifled a groan. There were definitely sparks between them, and if there was even the slightest chance she was interested in him, he'd jump, consequences be damned.

But as it was, he just had to smother his ego, make her stay in Napa comfortable, and come New Year's, let her walk out of his life…again.

CHAPTER 3

After the final pour of the afternoon, Liam told the group—with an apologetic smile, of course—that the tasting room was closing. A few final tasting notes and sales later, he closed the bar and went outside. Mandy was exactly where she'd been for the past hour—sitting on the bench, staring out at the countryside, her glass of cab franc still mostly full.

"How are you doing?" he asked.

"All right," she said, wrapping her arms around her body. "A little chilly."

"You could have stayed inside where it's nice and warm." *With me.*

"I like looking at the hills. And Roxy's trying to keep me warm." She pointed down. Sure enough, the big black dog was lying over both of Mandy's feet.

"You train her to do that?"

"The clever thing figured it out all by herself," Mandy said, looking up at him and shooting him a breathtakingly beautiful smile that went straight to his groin. *Keep it together, Flynn.*

He cleared his throat. "You ready for a walk?"

"Sure. Where are we going?"

"There are some great trails in the hills, and I can show you the experimental vineyard."

"Experimental vineyard?"

"It's where we test out varietals, hybrids, and grafts before we plant the vines in our regular growing fields."

"Kind of like your laboratory?" She sounded intrigued.

"You might say that," he said with a smile. "And bring Roxy. She'll love it up there. You don't even need to leash her."

"Okay then."

Liam grabbed a couple of bottled waters from the tasting bar, then led her through the small staff parking lot behind the main building.

"Nice bike," Mandy said, nodding at his Harley. She didn't seem to be joking, but he didn't know her well enough to tell.

"Thanks. It's a '72 Sportster. Found it in a friend's barn. Sweet-talked him into selling and did the restoration myself."

Mandy nodded and walked around the bike. "Original engine?"

"Of course. It's the heart and soul of the bike."

"I know. The Ironhead—998 cc air-cooled OHV forty-five-degree V-twin. Doesn't get more classic than that."

Whoa. He didn't know this Mandy—the one who could rattle off the stats for his motorcycle as easily as she could shut him down with a smile. "Where'd you learn about motorcycles?"

"My dad likes working on them. He's a mechanical engineer. To him, they're like elegant puzzles." She scoped out the bike from a different angle. "The engine's mounted directly to the frame, right? Can you feel everything?"

"Yep. Tons of vibration, so I only use her for short distances. I have a Fat Boy I take out for longer trips. That bike just sings. You ride?"

She shook her head. "No, never. Dad always said they were too dangerous, so I just…appreciate."

Liam took careful note of the way she was eyeing the bike, barely able to drag her gaze away. And then a thought struck him—the obvious thrill she'd gotten on the off-piste run at Alpine Meadows two years ago, the gleam in her eyes while she was ogling his motorcycle. Could it be that careful, analytical, uptight Dr. Aligheri had an untapped wild side? *Interesting.*

"C'mon, girl," he said to Roxy, who was sniffing the wheels of one of the winery's pickup trucks. With a happy bark, Roxy raced over to him, wagging her tail.

Mandy didn't say anything else about the bike. Just hitched up her bag on her shoulder and followed him and Roxy. When they reached the bottom of the hillside, she stopped short and stared at the rocky dirt path that went straight up. "You didn't tell me I was going to need some major hiking gear," she said.

"Once we get to the top it's flatter. And I promise the view is worth it." He paused. "Plus, I have treats."

"It better be chocolate," she said, sounding only half joking.

"I have some trail mix with chocolate-covered raisins in it. For Roxy, I have a strip of rawhide. But we can forget it if you want. It's a challenging hike and if you're not up for it…" Very deliberately, he paused and waited for her reaction.

"No, no, I'm game." She took a deep breath. "Let's do this thing. Come on, Roxy."

And up she went, scrambling a little as she navigated the wetter patches, picking her way around some stray rocks, but never stopping. Suppressing a smile, he followed her up, trying hard not to stare at her ass encased in a pair of jeans that fit her like a second skin. Damn, but the woman was built. He hadn't forgotten that.

But what he *had* forgotten was how she didn't even seem to realize it. In Tahoe, everywhere they went, people ogled her, even stared outright. Honestly, it was hard not to. He'd done a double take himself when he'd first seen her on the top of the mountain at Alpine Meadows—a blonde, winter vision. After Chase made the introductions, Liam had given him *such* a look. True to form, Chase simply shrugged, as if hanging out with genius scientists who looked like models were an everyday event.

"We can rest," Liam offered, when they reached the top.

"No, I'm good," she said, panting a little. "I just haven't had the chance to walk in a while." She eyed him up and down. "Though you didn't even break a sweat, did you?"

He shrugged. "Winemaking's pretty labor-intensive, and we just came off harvest season. I need to be in shape for that."

"Unfortunately, there's no requirement that says I have to be in shape to work in my lab." She gestured down the trail. "What's that way? Will Roxy be okay?"

Liam nodded. "Yeah. It gets a little more woodsy, but the path is clear. She should be fine."

"Okay. It's just that I'm responsible for her and I don't want anything to—oh!" she gasped, finally noticing the scenery. "It is *so* beautiful."

"On a clear day, you can see up to St. Helena. Too bad there's so much fog today."

Mandy peered over the side of the hill. "We're only up another, what, three hundred feet?"

"Yep, but you can see most of the property from here. Look straight down, and you'll see the visitor center and production facility." He pointed to the left. "Over there's our experimental vineyard, and right behind it is my dad's house."

"He lives on the property?" She looked up at him and smiled sheepishly. "That information wasn't part of the tour."

He nodded. "We need a little separation between work and our private lives. Anyway, I live here, too." He pointed to the right. "That's my place. It was the old production facility up to about fifteen years ago. I converted it into habitable space when I moved up here."

"Convenient."

"Sometimes." It was great living on the vineyard—most of the time— but especially during the spring and fall months when things heated up, work-wise. He'd never shirk his duties, but there were times when he needed some space and distance. That's why he had a vacation place in Tahoe. "Come on," he said, gesturing to the path that would take them along the ridge. "I have more to show you."

In silence, they walked along for a few more minutes. Twigs and damp leaves crackled softly underfoot, and in the brush, a few winter birds shared their songs. At last, they reached a straightaway, where Liam stopped to point out a large natural outcropping of rock.

"So," he said, leaning against the side of the boulder. "Seems a little corny to ask, but what have you been up to for the past couple of years?"

"I'm still a postdoc at Stanford," Mandy said, tucking a loose strand of hair back into her braid.

"Tell me again what your research is about. You gave me the high-level download in Tahoe, but I'm afraid I forgot."

"It's only interesting to me, anyway," she said, a gentle smile on her face. "I work on skin grafts using human tissue for genetically non-related donors. They're called allografts," she said.

"Skin grafts are used after someone's been hurt?" he asked.

"Yes," Mandy said, nodding. "They've been used for wounds, trauma, infection, burns—even cancers."

"Grafts help speed up the healing process?"

"And make the wound look better. Except there's a problem. Because the donor and recipient have different DNA, there's always the risk the allograft will be rejected by the patient's immune system, which can make an already sick or physically traumatized person worse. Plus, doing two procedures is painful, not to mention expensive."

"If the DNA is an issue, why don't you just take skin from one site and transplant it to another on the same person?"

"That kind of graft is called an autograft and they're done all the time," Mandy said. "With autografts, the risk of rejection is virtually nonexistent, but there are still problems. For one thing, the patient may not have enough skin to use, especially if they've been in a serious accident, and for another, there are two surgical sites, which increases pain and risk. I've spent my time studying what happens if we completely strip the allograft of any DNA, thereby making it nonreactive with a human immune system, with the goal of creating a one-shot allograft made of naturally occurring materials. After years of study, we actually did it, and we just applied to the FDA to do a clinical trial." She stopped. "I'm sorry. Once I start to talk about my work, I always get caught up in it."

"I asked," he said. "Anyway, I don't mind hearing about what you're doing." With her bright eyes and flushed cheeks, she was truly gorgeous. He wanted her to keep talking just so he could see her bloom. "So will the trial be approved?"

"I think so." She bit her lip. "I hope so. I think it has the potential to help so many people."

"You sound like Chase," he said. Chase's work was in the field of malaria, but he had the same sense of excitement as Mandy did when he spoke about his research.

Mandy shrugged. "I guess Chase feels like I do. If you're passionate about something, it's hard to stop."

Passion. Something he had in spades, but couldn't seem to figure out how to harness, at least not where it counted. Guilt coursed through him, slick and ugly. Just like he always did, he took a cleansing breath, trying to smother the pit that was forming in his stomach. In a few seconds, the pit was gone.

"Chase told me you got him his current job," he said, picking up a medium-sized stick from the ground.

She shook her head. "He got the job by himself. I merely recommended him for the position."

"And you got Ann to go up to Tahoe last year," Liam mused. "Seems like you do a lot for other people."

"They're my friends," she said simply.

"They think a lot of you," he told her. "Chase actually asked me to look out for you. Try to get you to relax."

"I'm not surprised," she said, the corners of her mouth turning down a little. "He's worried about me. So is Annie."

"You know why?"

"It's because I work all the time. Seriously, *all* the time. Nights, weekends, holidays. And if I'm not working, I'm volunteering at the hospital."

"Not on Christmas, though?"

"No. Not on Christmas," she said, and her whole body seemed to lighten. "I went to Southern California to visit my family. I have a sister. She's, well, she's kind of like my other half. We're fraternal twins, actually, but we look a lot alike."

"Huh," Liam said. "You never told me you were a twin." Visions of two beautiful, brainy, stubborn women danced in his head.

"It's not a secret," Mandy said quickly. "It's just—it doesn't come up in conversation a whole lot. She's very different from me."

"How?"

"Well, for one, she doesn't work as much." She laughed a little. "And she has a boyfriend."

"And you don't?" he gently probed.

She shook her head. "Nights, weekends, and holidays, remember?" She took a few steps forward, toward where Roxy had disappeared. "Roxy?" she yelled. "C'mon, Roxy!"

After a few long moments, Roxy finally appeared around a corner, a giant branch in her mouth. She dragged it over and dropped it at Liam's feet. Then she looked up hopefully, wagging her tail in eager anticipation.

"Too big to throw, girl," he said. "But here. I have one!" He brandished the stick in his hand high above his head. Roxy went nuts, circling around and around under the stick until Liam threw it down the path. Fast as a fox, Roxy raced after it. In a moment, she ran back and presented the stick to Liam. He obliged her, throwing it farther this time.

"You know she's going to keep after you if you play with her," Mandy said, amusement coloring her voice.

Liam shrugged. "I don't mind. I like her."

"I like her, too," Mandy said. She waited until another round of fetch and return was completed. "Okay, your turn. Tell me what you've been doing since we last…well, since we last saw each other."

"Same old, same old." He threw the stick again.

Mandy actually laughed at that. "No way. You're definitely the kind of guy to work toward something. Tell me what you've *really* been doing."

He loved that—the way she cut through all his crap every time. "Okay, I'll tell you," he said. "Flynn Winery has been working to expand its operations. This year we're on target to produce roughly nine hundred cases of wine. Next year, I want us up to twelve hundred. It's small potatoes compared to some of the huge commercial wineries, but for us, it's a big increase in scale."

Roxy bounded back with the stick in her mouth. Liam threw it again and when Roxy dashed into the woods and out of sight, the two of them kept walking.

"How are you going to do it?" Mandy asked.

"Through a combination of things. Twenty-five acres of vineyards we planted years ago are finally ready for harvest. We also plan to purchase some additional grapes from independent growers in the valley. The grapes have to be handled differently if they're coming from off-site, but we've done it in the past, and I think we did a decent job of getting them from vine to crush within a few hours."

"What's prompting this change?"

"We won a couple of industry awards," he said, trying not to sound braggy.

"Oh, don't be so modest. You won quite a few awards. I heard all about them on the tour."

"Remind me to give Jennie a raise," he said with a smile. "Seriously, though, I think it's my own restlessness. We've seen some serious success in the industry. Yes, we've gotten some nice awards. We've gotten some good scores, too, but in my mind, we have the capability to go the distance. Make a cult wine. We're so close, I can taste it."

At that moment, there was a sharp yip, then a low whine.

"Roxy?" Mandy shouted. "Come here, girl!"

Roxy came out of the woods, but something wasn't right. She didn't have the stick. And she was limping.

"Oh, no," Mandy cried, rushing to Roxy. "Oh, girl. Did you get something in your paw? Come on. Easy there. Lie down." She got the dog to sit, and lifted her right front paw. "This one, I think? Oh, no, you cut your pad, and it's bleeding really badly. Hold on, Roxy."

"Can I do something?" Liam asked.

"Just keep her calm while I get some antiseptic wipes." She pulled her handbag off her shoulder and rifled around inside. In short order she pulled out the wipes, some ointment, cotton gauze, and surgical tape."

"Man, you're like a one-woman first aid kit," Liam said. "What else do you have in there?"

"Everything," Mandy said. She sounded serious, too. "Okay, hold her steady. I'm going to wipe the wound clean, and it might sting. Ready? One, two, three." Roxy whimpered, but the deed was done.

"I won't be able to apply the ointment with the cut still bleeding up a storm," Mandy said. "But at least the gauze will slow down the bleeding while we get her to a vet." Liam held Roxy, stroking her head, while Mandy used the surgical tape to keep the gauze pressed against the wound. Expertly, she ripped the tape and patted the bandage, confirming it would hold. Seemingly satisfied, she sat back on her heels.

"Okay, girl," Mandy said. "Try to stand up."

Roxy stood, but it was clear that putting weight on her hurt foot was agony.

"Oh, poor thing," Mandy said. "We need to get her to my car, but I don't know how she's going to walk back down that path."

"I'll carry her," Liam said.

Mandy swiveled her head to look up at him. "You will?"

"No problem. She's on the smaller side. She probably weighs fifty-five, maybe sixty pounds. C'mere, girl." Gently, he scooped up the dog, being careful not to hurt the injured paw more. Roxy got what he was doing, since she curled her body to nestle into his arms.

When Roxy was settled, he made sure he was steady on his feet with the extra weight, and then took an experimental step. Fine. "Do me a favor," he said. "I can't see that well in front of me. Make sure I don't trip over a rock, okay?"

"Yes, yes, of course," Mandy said. "Let's go."

They walked back, Roxy in his arms, Mandy by his side. A few times, Mandy grabbed his elbow to steady him. He was man enough to admit he kind of liked it.

"How are you doing?" Mandy asked, looking up at him when they were halfway down the steep hill. "She's not too heavy?"

"She's fine. I'm fine."

"Do you know where the nearest vet or animal hospital is?" Mandy asked.

"There's one on Route 29. I know the way. Let's put her in my truck. More room in back."

"Okay," Mandy agreed.

When they reached his truck, Mandy fished the keys out of his pocket and clicked all the doors open. "Put Roxy in the backseat," Mandy ordered. He did as she asked, then watched as she hopped right in after the dog.

Liam drove as fast as he could to the vet, Mandy in the backseat the whole time with Roxy, soothing, stroking, comforting.

Once they were at the vet, Mandy took charge completely, detailing the circumstances, and dealing with all the paperwork crisply and decisively.

An hour later, they had a bandaged Roxy back in the truck.

Mandy sank into the front seat, face flushed. Several strands of hair had come loose from her braid. Slowly, she pushed them behind her ears and let out a huge sigh. She was clearly exhausted from the ordeal, but through it all, she'd kept her head, and her cool.

"You were amazing," Liam told her.

She shook her head. "I doubt Chase and Annie will think so when they see poor Roxy. Just look at her!"

Liam turned to look at the sweet dog, curled up on the back seat of his truck. "She's going to be fine. The vet said her pad would heal in a couple of days. Just text Ann and tell her what happened. She'll understand."

"I already did. And I found out that she and Chase are still dealing with the gas leak. They probably won't make it up until tomorrow evening." Mandy yawned, then gave him a tired smile. "I don't know why I'm so zonked. You were the one who did all the heavy lifting. I can't believe you carried her down the hill."

Liam shrugged. "It wasn't a big deal. But you can owe me if you want."

"Owe you?" Out of the corner of his eye, he thought he saw her lick her lips. "Owe you what?"

"A day."

"I don't know," she said, sounding reluctant. "What would we do?"

"Oh, I'll think of something."

"I like knowing what I'm doing ahead of time," she said. "I like purpose."

"Okay, the purpose is to keep you from being bored out of your mind doing wine tastings I know you're not into, or freaking out because you're not getting enough of your statistical analyses done. Besides," he continued slyly, "I want to test a theory."

Mandy gave a little snort. "Oh, so you're a scientist now?"

"Are you in or out?"

"You're kidding, right?" Mandy said, clicking her seat belt on. "You haven't even told me the parameters."

"It'll be fun. And *exciting*."

Even through her exhaustion, her gaze sharpened a little at that, and he knew he'd hit his mark.

"Fine. I'm in."

"Good. Meet me at the Oxbow Public Market tomorrow morning at eight."

"Deal," she said solemnly. "Now let's get this puppy home."

CHAPTER 4

The next morning, Mandy awoke bright and early, and at eight a.m. was exactly where she promised Liam she'd be: inside the Oxbow Public Market, close to downtown Napa. She rarely went out, let alone to a place as exciting and vibrant as this, and she spent a few long minutes soaking everything in. Numerous foodie stalls lined the sides and filled the center of the space, a large utilitarian warehouse that was much, much more than the sum of its parts.

Even at this hour, the market was full of life. Shoppers bustled down the passageways, sampling, stopping, talking, as vendors arranged and rearranged their wares. And the food—oh, it was heavenly—from gorgeous cheeses and amazing-looking chocolates to tasty breads and pastries. The artisan goods were incredible, too. One stall had beautiful ceramics on display, and another sold handmade soaps. She wanted them all.

"You made it," said a voice from behind her.

Quickly, she turned and there was Liam, smiling down at her, looking a little scruffier than he had the day before. Reddish-brown stubble covered his jaw, and sharp green eyes regarded her from beneath a mussed-up head of hair. She blinked away the *very* intense vision of him in her bed looking just as he did now.

"Hey," she said, trying to sound normal.

"How's Roxy?" he asked.

"Fine. She slept the whole night without any problems, but she's still having a lot of trouble moving around. I parked in the back lot and left her in the car with the windows wide open."

"Stella's going to keep an eye on her while we're out today. She's great with animals. Did you know she volunteers at our local animal shelter?"

"That's great," Mandy said. "Please thank her for me."

"You can thank her yourself," Liam said, ushering her out a set of doors. "This way."

"We're not staying?" she said, unable to hide her disappointment. "But everything looks so good."

"There's another part to this market," Liam told her as they walked down a long ramp to a parking lot. "We can grab breakfast and then head out. You know, I'm glad you came. I was afraid you'd chicken out."

"No," she said. "I must say, your lack of details intrigued me. And besides," she couldn't resist adding, "the Internet's still down at the inn."

He laughed at that. "Come on, smart-mouth. I'll buy you a coffee and then we're hitting the road." They walked into another market building where Modern Bakery had a storefront. Mandy downed an incredible homemade English muffin slathered with orange marmalade and a bracing cup of black coffee. She'd just finished when Liam checked his phone.

"Stella's outside," he said, texting fast. "We can meet her in the back lot. Come on."

Sure enough, one of the winery's pickup trucks was waiting at the curb. Stella gave a wave from the driver's seat and Mandy pointed to show Stella where she'd parked.

Stella circled around, Liam and Mandy following on foot. When they reached Mandy's car, Liam quickly transferred the dog to the truck.

"Hop in," Liam told her, opening the front passenger-side door.

Mandy climbed in. "Hi," she said, holding out her hand. "I'm Mandy."

The beautiful, dark-eyed woman clasped it. "Stella," she said. "Nice to meet you."

"Same. Thanks again for watching Roxy today." And that was all she got to say before Liam was pressed in beside her, thigh to thigh.

"My pleasure," Stella said. "Now put on your seat belts, please."

Dutifully, Mandy snapped hers on, noting the acute sensation of her side rubbing against Liam's as she did.

When they were settled and back on the road, Mandy cleared her throat. "Please tell me where we're going. I'm dying here." Liam had asked her to dress in layers, and to wear a swimsuit underneath. "Are we going swimming? Sailing? What?"

"I'm not allowed to say," Stella said, pressing her lips together with mirth. "Better ask my brother."

Liam gave her a secret smile and said nothing.

Cryptic. She crossed her arms over her chest. "I'd like some answers," she muttered.

He leaned even closer so his lips were almost touching her ear. "Not having them heightens the anticipation, doesn't it?" he murmured.

She couldn't help the little shiver that coursed through her. He was right, of course, though it still irked her to be left in the dark.

Thirty minutes later, Stella pulled the truck into a small parking lot. "Here we are," she said.

"Thanks, Stella," Liam said, helping Mandy out of the truck.

"Yes, thank you," she echoed.

"Let me know if you have any issues."

"Will do," Liam said. "Catch you later, okay?"

"Sure," Stella said. "If I'm done with decoration duty."

Liam laughed and they both waved good-bye as Stella drove off.

"What's decoration duty?" Mandy asked.

"We have a big New Year's Eve bash every year. It's always a lot of fun—good music, good food, good dancing, and great wine. You should come."

Annie and Chase hadn't mentioned the party, most likely because they knew she'd probably bail. But part of her resolution involved relaxing, and going to a New Year's party might be a great way to ease into it. "I'll think about it," she said.

Liam nodded. "Just know that the invitation stands. This way," he said, motioning for her to follow him down to the river where two long dock-like structures jutted into the water. On one lay a double-person kayak, two paddles, two life vests, and a small cooler.

"What is this?" she asked.

"Cuttings Wharf. Our launching area," Liam said.

"This is the surprise?"

"You like?" He was watching her carefully.

"I like. Very much," she said, and noted that his shoulders immediately became less tense. "But I need to warn you I've never kayaked before."

"Canoed?"

She shook her head. "No, but I have sailed a few times. And I'm a strong swimmer."

"We'll be wearing life vests anyway, but it's good to be confident in the water."

Though she was excited—something new and maybe a little bit dangerous to try!—she was nervous. "I'm confident I can swim, but I'm not so sure about the kayaking."

Liam clapped a hand on her shoulder, his strength comforting. "Don't worry. I have a ton of experience and I can show you—"

"Everything I need to know?" she finished for him.

"Something like that," he said with a smile and let go of her shoulder. "Now grab a paddle and I'll show you the proper way to stroke."

She lifted up one of the long, double-bladed paddles. Liam took the other.

"Keep your hands a little wider than shoulder width apart, and hold the paddle parallel to the water line, like this," he said. She modeled his grip and he gave her a nod. "Now, tip one side in." He dropped his right blade lower. "Dip in, and keep the blade perpendicular to the water. If it's parallel, you won't get as much resistance and you can't move forward." She dropped her blade, too. "Good. Pretend you're pushing through the water. When you've completed your stroke, pull up and out, then dip the other side in and do the same thing." He demonstrated and she imitated. "Find your rhythm. Find the flow. Yes. Excellent."

After a minute of pretend paddling, Liam nodded. "You have the basics. It'll be a little different in the water, but you're a quick study. Let's get your life jacket on." He grabbed the smaller of the two and brought it over to her.

When she had it on, he checked it, tugging on the straps to make sure the buckles were secure, which pulled her a little closer to him. "Good," he said, in that deep voice of his, and before she could even acknowledge the shocking wave of desire coursing through her, he turned away to get the rest of the gear in the vessel.

Liam dragged the kayak into the water and secured it to the wharf. "Hop in," he said. Grateful to have a distraction, Mandy did as he asked, scrambling over the top of the craft and sliding her body into the well. Stretching out her legs, she found she had plenty of room. "All right?" he called from the dock.

"Perfect," she answered.

In a moment, he came over with a tarp-like piece of plastic. "This is a bib," he said, snapping the covering into place around the front of her well. "It'll help keep you dry." She lifted her arms so he could get the bib around her waist. "Okay. Just sit tight for a few minutes."

He put the food into his section of the well and climbed into the kayak. She felt his presence behind her, big and solid.

"All right, let's go!" he said, untying them from the wharf and letting them drift out onto the river. "We'll ride the tide north."

And then they were off. Mandy found a rhythm pretty quickly, and with Liam's powerful strokes from the rear of the craft, they moved along at a fairly good clip. From the smoothness of his paddling—no splashing, no jerkiness—it was evident that he really was experienced, so Mandy just let herself relax and enjoy the glide. It was quiet on the river. Just the sounds of the rushing water, the occasional cries of the birds overhead, the infrequent rush of automobiles closer to shore. There were no other boats, motor or man-powered, and no other people.

"This isn't tourist season," Liam said, as if reading her thoughts. "The commercial outfits generally run from spring through fall. Only locals are out this time of year, and this is a weird week, what with the holidays and all. Too bad, because the kayaking's great. Thanks to the rain, there's more white water."

"White water?" Mandy said, her voice rising up a pitch as a thrilling little shiver feathered down her spine.

"You'll be fine," Liam said. "Besides, we have a ways to go, so there's no use in stressing about it now."

She took a deep breath and did as he said. The water was calm for now, and Liam pointed out things of interest. A lone heron stood by the shore, and farther upriver, a frisky otter twisted and dipped in the water. They took some time exploring the river and some side sloughs, where even more wildlife awaited. Mandy caught a glimpse of three snowy egrets. At one point, the kayak was close enough to the bank that Mandy spied a fat bullfrog in the reeds.

Liam tapped her on the shoulder. "Hungry?"

She took the container of trail mix he offered. "Yes," she said. "Thanks."

They drifted for a while, enjoying the rocking of the water and the soft sounds of the slough. A flock of pelicans flew ahead, their shapely beaks unmistakable against the gray sky.

Once they were back on the main river, a drawbridge loomed up ahead of them, tall and steely in the thin midday sun.

"What's that?" she asked.

"The Brazos Bridge. Get ready."

"For what?"

Liam laughed. "For that white water I told you about."

Before she could say anything else, they were plunged into rapids.

What a rush! Water sprayed in her face and stung her eyes. Her muscles burned from the strain of keeping the kayak bow forward and right side up, until she realized that short, choppy strokes were the name of the game. A jagged piece of wood materialized in the water in front of her. Deftly, she steered around it, then gave it a bonus jab with her paddle for good measure. Her heart hammered triple time, and she strained to hear Liam shouting out orders over the roar of the rapids.

It was wild, exhilarating. As exciting as flying down the slick snow at Alpine Meadows or catching that perfect break while surfing at La Jolla Shores. After the shortest five minutes of her life, they were through.

Safe on the other end of the rapids, breathing fast, heart still pounding, everything seemed sharper, crisper. The intense sparkle of the river, the acute sensation of the wind on her skin. This moment would be etched on her brain forever.

"You okay?" Liam finally asked when the water quieted.

"Yes!" she responded. Even her voice sounded clearer. She turned back to look at him. "That was awesome!"

"I was hoping you'd like it," he said.

She turned forward again, unable to wipe the smile off her face. She paddled hard, away from the bridge, upriver. Although she knew she'd pay for it later with aching arms, she kept pushing herself, making Liam work to keep up.

They continued paddling north, spying a rare night heron, a family of ducks, and way more seagulls than she could count. They crossed under a few low auto bridges, and after an hour, their approach to the city was heralded by a small aircraft landing at the Napa County Airport.

By the time they arrived just south of downtown, Mandy was tired, but happy. Together, they steered the boat to the end of a concrete landing, and Liam hopped out to secure the craft.

"Come on," he said, grabbing her hand in his strong one, and pulling her out of the kayak onto the landing. "Nice job," he said. "I already texted Stella, so she should be here to get the gear any minute. Then we can walk back to Oxbow for some lunch, okay?"

"Sounds good."

She helped him pull the boat out of the water and carry it to the road. In no time, Stella was there, and the three of them loaded everything into the back of her truck.

"Thanks again for helping us, Stell," Liam said.

"Yes, thanks," Mandy said. "Won't you join us for lunch?"

The small woman shook her head. "I have to get back for Roxy. And preparations are really ramping up for the party."

"Maybe I could help you with those later," she said.

"I could definitely use the help," Stella said slowly. "I was so set on showing Dad I could handle things solo this year, I think I bit off more than I can chew."

Mandy nodded. "Great. I'll be there after lunch."

"Sure. Later, then," Stella said. And she was off.

When Stella was gone and they were walking upriver, Liam turned to her. "Thanks," he said.

"For what?"

"For being nice to her."

Mandy shrugged. "She seems like a nice person. And besides, you're both being very good hosts. I'd like to do something for you in return."

They turned onto the First Street Bridge and Liam shook his head. "Again with the doing stuff for others. You ever think about taking some time for yourself?"

At once, the ever-present guilt, the guilt she'd repressed all day, burst free, swamping her brain. Before she could stop it, her mind went *there*, back to the accident. All-too-vivid images of charred flesh, her burning apartment, her sister's agonized face, made her sick to her stomach.

Afraid she'd give something critical away, Mandy stopped smack in the middle of the bridge and grabbed the rail for support. The desire to be back in her lab hit her stronger than ever, and she clenched a fist, willing her mind blank. *Forget about the accident and the lab, just for today. Forget about the calls from the grad students. Forget about everything but yourself.*

When she'd recovered her composure, she braved a glance over at Liam. He must have just thought she was admiring the view, since he was also leaning on the railing, gaze trailing south down the river. Good. The last thing she wanted to do with him was to answer his sure-to-be-pointed questions about her anxiety and guilt.

"Thanks again for the kayaking adventure," she said carefully. "You know, I don't typically do stuff like this."

"Yeah, see," he said, still looking down the river, "I don't really get why that's the case, given that you seem to love it."

"I just don't have time."

Liam turned to her, his eyes narrowed. "Don't tell me that your last vacation was what? Tahoe, two years ago?"

She nodded. Before that, it had been another two years. It felt amazing to give in to her need to break free, but afterward, there was always a price to be paid. Namely, getting back into the swing of her work. She was disciplined. Practical. And that was why she had to tamp down her own desires. Something bigger was at play, and she was wise enough to understand her role.

Yet it was strange that Liam seemed to have homed in on the one thing she truly needed—release. Now if only *she* could get with the program, but the way things were going, it'd take a lot more than a week in Napa to make that happen. She turned to look at Liam, and he was watching her, as if he actually understood who she was.

"C'mon. I'll buy you some lunch," he finally said, motioning for her to join him. When she did, he wrapped his arm around her shoulder. Gratefully, she let him lead. It was easy to focus on Liam, so full of life. She wasn't helpless or weak, not by a long shot. But it was nice to have someone to lean on, at least for a little while.

They sat at the counter of the Hog Island Oyster bar. Liam slurped half a dozen littlenecks and then downed an entire order of fish and chips, but Mandy was content with some seafood chowder and a few of Liam's fries.

"You're not hungry?"

She shook her head. She always felt drained, mentally and physically, after bouts of intense emotion. "Don't worry. I'll get my appetite back before dinner."

"Good, because if Chase and Ann actually get here, I'm cooking tonight."

"Oh?" Mandy said, raising an eyebrow. "And what will you make for us?"

In response, Liam just grinned and winked. More surprises. She had to laugh at that, and he looked pleased with her response.

After they were through and the bill was settled, she went to push herself off the stool, but as she did, every muscle in her upper body groaned in protest.

"I need a massage," Mandy said. Now that she wasn't paddling or hauling or lifting, her arms had begun to ache with an intensity she hadn't felt since the first time she was a strong enough surfer to paddle out to catch her own waves.

"I can arrange that for you," Liam said. "But I also have something else that might work."

"What's that?" Mandy asked.

"You'll have to come over to my place to find out."

"Still testing your theory?" she said teasingly.

He smiled that secret smile again. "Maybe," was all he said.

CHAPTER 5

Liam leaned his head back against the side of the hot tub and gazed up into the clear, starry sky—unusual for this time of year. Warm, heated water burbled around him, the soft sound as soothing as the liquid itself. After looking his fill, he closed his eyes. It didn't get better than this—a good day in the books, a glass of his favorite cab in his hand, and a smoking-hot woman by his side.

Well, not exactly.

He lifted his head and opened one eye. Mandy wasn't next to him—she was sitting opposite him in the tub, hair twisted up, eyes closed. Everything below her lovely shoulders was submerged. Her wineglass sat nearby, untouched.

"Aw, c'mon, you don't like the wine? It's one of our best-sellers," he said, trying to get her to laugh.

"I just need to let my arms soak for a while longer," she replied.

He'd forgotten how stiff and sore first-time kayakers could get. Not only that, but she'd spent three hours after lunch helping Stella string up lights for the party "Let me help," he said. Slowly, he stood, put down his wineglass, and carefully waded across the tub. He sat down right next to her, not touching her, though he desperately wanted to.

"May I?" he asked, reaching for her shoulders.

"You don't have to."

He pressed his lips together. Would she ever let down her guard long enough to allow someone to take care of her? And it wasn't really a surprise to remember how very much he wanted her to drop her defenses, not just for anyone, but for him.

"Well, okay," she said, when he didn't say anything. "If you really think it'll help."

"It'll help," he said firmly. "Face away from me," he said. "Ready?"

"I think so."

When his hands clasped over her shoulders, she tensed. He waited until she relaxed and then began to knead her stiff shoulders, starting shallow, then increasing the pressure. When her shoulders dropped a bit more, he stroked his thumb up the nape of her neck and then worked his palms down her upper arms, her skin slippery silk under his fingers.

She gave a little moan, which he took as encouragement.

"You okay?" he asked, zeroing in on her triceps muscle.

"Yes. Oh, that…that feels *so* good."

He went deep into the triceps, trying to draw out the ache with firm strokes. Then he did the other arm, which resulted in additional sighs of approval.

"Here," he said, turning her shoulders so she was facing him again, then taking one of her arms and using his fingers to massage the muscles from her shoulder to her wrist, paying careful attention to her forearm. Mandy closed her eyes, so he did the other arm. When he was done, Liam surveyed his handiwork. Mandy was lying limply in the tub, her head leaning back against the edge as if she didn't have the strength to hold it up. He slipped an arm under her neck to make her more comfortable, and he was rewarded when she sighed and settled into the crook of his elbow.

My woman.

In the past two years, he hadn't found anyone else who might make him truly happy. He was honest enough to admit he wanted it all, but *all* included a woman who felt the same way about settling down as he did. Sure, he'd had a few girlfriends, but none he felt suited him long-term. And he preferred to break it off sooner rather than later if he knew it wasn't going to work out.

But this felt good. This felt right. Except for the fact that they hadn't worked out.

"Tell me again why we didn't happen?"

Mandy didn't open her eyes. "Because I turned you down."

He loved her smart mouth, but he also wanted a real answer. "Yeah, about that. Why?"

"I don't know."

"Yes, you do."

"Because I work too much." Eyes still closed.

Liam shook his head. "I'm not buying it. You didn't need to tell me that. You could have just slept with me and ditched me afterward."

"I would never do that." She said it simply, stating truth. And that's what he liked the most about her. Her moral code was just as strong as his—so rare these days.

"Why, then?" he pressed.

Mandy finally opened her eyes and looked up at him, and though her gaze was conflicted, she spoke evenly. "Because you're wonderful."

Wait, what? "You turned me down because I'm *wonderful?*"

She shook her head. "You kissed me. And then you said something I wasn't ready to hear. Not from you. Not from a man I could—" She broke off and turned away.

"A man you could what, Amanda?" he asked, his voice soft. She was tough—tougher than he was, which made this admission all the more surprising.

She finally turned back. His lips were mere inches away from hers. All she needed was to say the word and he would close that small space, and they could explore what she'd rejected two years ago.

The doorbell rang.

"That must be Chase and Ann," he said, not even bothering to keep the annoyance out of his voice. *With crap timing.* "I'll be right back." Carefully, he extricated his arm, pulled himself out of the tub, and wrapped a towel around his waist.

Then he turned and went into the house, leaving the woman of his dreams alone.

Love. A man I could love.

Mandy watched Liam disappear through the sliding glass door, still staring at his back. Forget about his intelligence—he was a Michelangelo sculpture, hewn from marble. Winemaking must be *very* labor-intensive, because he was in unbelievable shape. She'd gotten a prime view of his chest when he answered the door in his swim trunks—well-defined pecs and a six-pack to die for, lightly dusted with a fine mist of hair. And those arms, undoubtedly honed from lifting barrels and cases of wine.

This is what you gave up two years ago. Idiot.

Every look, every gesture he made reminded her of Tahoe. The way he'd leaned into her ever so gently. The way his mouth had slanted over hers. *Give me everything,* he'd said. And she'd bolted. Because the timing wasn't right. But the way she lived, the timing would never be right, and that was just wrong.

Why was she tempting herself with something she couldn't have?

Maybe you can have him.

The words hung there in her mind, like a balloon over a cartoon character in a comic strip.

She'd almost melted when he'd given her that intimate, sensitive, and very charged massage. And thinking about those big hands kneading and smoothing *other* parts of her body made her hot.

Envisioning his tongue following his hands made her even hotter.

Liquid heat raced through her veins and went south in a hurry. She rubbed her legs together, trying to get rid of some of the ache that had taken up residence in her most private spot, but the water and the friction just made things worse.

No. You can't have him. But you can *do something to get him out of your system.*

Without even thinking, she clambered out of the hot tub, grabbed her towel and her dry clothes, and scampered inside. She practically ran to the bathroom and shut the door behind her, then locked it. In seconds, she'd dropped the clothes and her towel, cupped her breasts in her hands, and pinched both nipples right through the damp fabric of her bikini top. She bit her lip to stop from gasping as a fiery, desperate pleasure washed through her. This release would be welcome. *Necessary.*

It didn't take long before her nipples were aching and her breasts were heavy with need. She was going to do this, right here, right now. She leaned back against the bathroom door and slipped one hand right down her bikini bottom. She knew how to do this, how to start slowly with the gentle touch of her finger on her clit. How to get herself wet and ready.

But here, in this locked bathroom in Liam Flynn's house, with her friends mere feet away maybe waiting for her, maybe wondering where she was, she didn't need to be slow. It only took a fingertip on her very swollen flesh, and she was already halfway there, spurred on by visions of Liam Flynn and the sheer illicitness of what she was doing.

Closing her eyes, she circled her clit again and again, imagining it was Liam's hand on her breast, pretending it was his fingers delving into her slickness, visualizing his mouth covering hers to muffle the screams of pleasure when she climaxed.

It only took a few moments—seconds, really—until she came hard enough to see stars.

A split second later, a knock sounded. Her eyes flew open, and she jerked away from the door as if it were hot lava.

"Mandy?" Liam's voice was muffled through the wood. "You okay?"

"Just changing," she called out, praying her voice didn't sound like she'd just furtively masturbated right under his nose.

"Sure. When you're done, we're all in the kitchen."

"I'll join you there in a minute."

Better make that two. Because one glance in the mirror and it was obvious that she'd done something other than change.

The stranger staring back at her was a different person. There was a spot of crimson on each cheek, her hair was a mess, and she was still breathing hard. This woman looked passionate. Earthy. *Real.* This woman didn't have to steal her pleasure in doses she felt she didn't deserve. This woman didn't lock herself in her laboratory and deny herself a life. This woman had an eye toward the future instead of being trapped in the past.

It shamed her, this stranger.

This could be you.

But it wasn't. And no matter how much soul-searching she did this week, it might not ever be.

Mindful of the fact that her friends were waiting, she slowly, carefully stripped off her damp bathing suit and washed herself off. By the time she was dry and dressed, she had her game face on again.

When she opened the door, laughter carried through the house. She took her time making her way through Liam's place, as much to see the rooms as to fully compose herself.

The space was interesting. He'd kept the original brick exterior and gutted the interior, rebuilding from the inside out. The house was designed for entertaining, with a huge, lofted living room built around the original chimney. The framed wine labels and valley maps on the wall reflected Napa's history as a seat of agriculture. Even the furniture looked like Liam—huge leather couches and clubby chairs. She would have liked to do some more exploring, but she'd spent far too much time alone already.

Besides, her stomach was rumbling.

Delicious aromas of garlic, tomatoes, onions, and spices emanated from the kitchen, and Mandy simply followed her nose. Warmth hit her as soon as she crossed the threshold of the room, and Annie hurried over right away.

"Mandy, hi!" her friend cried. "Thanks for taking care of Roxy." Ann embraced her and Mandy let herself be engulfed in slim, strong arms.

After Ann's fiancé died three years ago, only a week before their planned Christmas wedding, Ann had shut herself off from life, but over the past year—after meeting Chase in Tahoe—Ann had definitely blossomed. Some changes were obvious. Her blue eyes seemed brighter, and her dark hair, always lovely, was a long, shiny mass of beautiful waves. But other, subtle changes, like the happy glow that seemed to light her from within, were undoubtedly due to Chase.

Chase was smiling—even through his beard she could tell because the corners of his eyes were crinkled up—but he was more contained. Quieter. But he'd changed, too, since meeting Annie. He seemed more willing to take risks—to put himself on the line.

"Hi, Chase," she said, giving him a little wave.

"Ditto what Annie said about Roxy. Thanks for taking her up for us."

"Well, the vet says she's going to be fine," Mandy said, "but I'm so sorry that she got hurt."

"We should have warned you that she loves to run into bushes," Chase said.

"I only wish I'd had her on a leash."

Ann shrugged. "We never do. And how could you know something like that would happen? Just let it go. You did us a huge favor by taking her off our hands while we dealt with the gas issue. I'm just glad the repair guy finally figured out where the leak was and was able to seal it off."

"You're welcome, then," Mandy said.

"Hey," Liam said, stirring a pot on the stove top. "Where's your drink?"

"I think it's by the hot tub." And then she flushed all over again, remembering why she'd left it in such haste. Liam didn't seem to notice.

"I'll find it later," he promised. "Want another?"

"Sure."

"Good," he said, placing a cover on the pot and pouring her another glass of the cab. "Chase and Ann? What are you two drinking?"

"What kind of beer do you have?" Chase asked.

"Aren't we supposed to drink wine when we're in wine country?" Ann questioned.

"Nah," Liam said. "Most locals drink a lot of beer. We even have a saying that goes, 'It takes a lot of great beer to make a great wine.' So I say drink whatever makes you happy. Will an IPA suit you?"

"Definitely," Chase said.

"I'll have what Mandy's having," Ann told him.

Liam was a great host. He poured wine. He made witty jokes and talked politics, at ease in his own skin, every gesture completely unself-conscious, so unlike the men she usually met in Silicon Valley who were either way-too-slick finance guys or awkward engineers.

At some point Liam produced a cheese plate and came to sit beside her on the couch, arm stretched out behind her neck. Across from them, on another couch, Chase had one arm wrapped around Roxy, who was lying with her head in his lap, and the other one around Ann, who was smiling up at him, love written all over her face. He bent his head and kissed Ann, a long, lingering kiss filled with warmth and passion.

There was nothing better than seeing two friends so happy, but honestly, even with Liam there, she felt like a third wheel.

"The Cowgirl Creamery Mt. Tam goes great with the reserve, doesn't it?" Liam said gently, pointing at the cheese.

He's trying to make me comfortable. "Yes," she said, grateful for the distraction, but unable to look him in the eye after her sojourn in the bathroom. "It's very tasty."

"So what are you two up to tomorrow?" Mandy asked Chase and Ann when they finally stopped kissing.

Ann tore her gaze away from Chase. "We had to move a bunch of appointments because we didn't get up here until today," she said. "I'm afraid we're booked solid."

"Have to squeeze it all in before things shut down for New Year's," Chase added.

"But we'll be able to join you for dinner," Ann said. "I hope."

"Maybe I should just head back to Silicon Valley," Mandy said. "I could easily take Roxy with me. It might be good for her, since the vet said to keep her off the hurt paw for the next day or so."

As soon as the words left her mouth, she regretted them. More than ever, it was obvious she needed to get her life in order. If she left now, she might never get back on track. In her pocket, her cell phone weighed down her jeans, a physical reminder of everything she'd left behind.

"No, please don't go," Ann said. "We'll be able to hang out once our appointments are finished. Besides, we have spas and restaurants to check out for the bachelorette weekend."

"Don't cut your trip short on account of us," Chase added.

"Okay," Mandy said, almost glad she didn't have an excuse to leave.

"We just have so much to do," Ann said, her brow creasing. "Even with our jam-packed schedule, we may not be able to fit everything in."

"Then I don't think we should worry about the bachelorette weekend planning this trip," Mandy told Ann. "I can take care of it when I'm back home. It'll just take a few phone calls."

"Why don't I help you?" Liam interjected. "That way everyone will get their work done, and still be able to have dinner together. And *I'll* take Roxy."

"I have Roxy," Chase said possessively, rubbing the dog's head.

Liam nudged her knee with his. "Guess it's just you and me then."

"Great!" Ann said, relief evident on her face. "You two can hang out together, and just relax while we get our wedding stuff done."

Mandy's chest tightened again. Relaxing wasn't exactly likely, because Liam Flynn wasn't out of her system. Not by a long shot. The whole goal of her Napa trip was to figure out how to set limits and boundaries for her work, not blow the walls all to pieces. Liam's charged glances and intimate touches weren't exactly conducive to *moderation*.

She could ditch everyone. Go off on her own and work on her plan. Unfortunately, one glance at the blissful look on Annie's face made her realize she really didn't have a choice. Instead of taking the time to ruminate on her life, which hopefully would lead to a more organized and balanced schedule, she was stuck tooling around Napa with Liam Flynn as her escort.

"It won't be so bad," he said, as if reading her mind. "I promise."

Mandy nodded and drank deeply. She had to swallow hard to get the wine past the lump in her throat. Because no matter how charming and handsome Liam was, or how happy Annie and Chase were, there was one thing she was afraid she couldn't move past.

Herself.

CHAPTER 6

A knock sounded on the door to Mandy's room at the inn promptly the next morning at ten. She peeked through the peephole, then swung open the door. Liam stood just outside, his auburn hair shining in the waxing light. He had on his leather jacket and a pair of worn jeans, and he'd shaved.

Too bad. She kind of liked the scruff.

Last night, alone in her room, she'd resigned herself to what the rest of the week had in store. If she couldn't get her life in order, she might as well have some killer eye candy to soften the blow. She could always take another few days later in the month to get her plan back on track…if her grad students would stop calling. This morning, she'd fielded one ridiculous question about reagents and one less ridiculous one about liquid nitrogen. Still, that was two too many for a vacation she'd planned for months.

"So are we going to head to downtown Sonoma to check out spas for the bachelorette weekend?" she asked, stepping out of the room and shutting the door firmly behind her. She picked her way down the cobblestone path that led around the main building of the inn, Liam right beside her.

"You mentioned you could figure that stuff out by phone, so I thought we'd go for a ride instead," Liam said. Mandy stopped dead in her tracks and he stopped, too. "Don't worry. You're dressed fine."

"You're…" She stopped and moistened her lips, watching him carefully to see if this was a joke. "You're going to take me out on your Fat Boy?"

"Yeah. You in?"

Unable to speak, she simply nodded. A hundred reasons why she should

"

say no flickered through her mind.

She dismissed all of them without a second thought.

"C'mon, I parked over here." He gestured to the street and kept walking.

A thrill of excitement lanced through her entire body as she followed after him. No purpose. Just fun. "You know I don't typically—"

"—do stuff like this," he finished. "So you mentioned." He stopped and turned. All at once, he was dangerously close. "I have one question: what's stopping you now?"

"Nothing." She took a calming breath. "Let's go."

He didn't gloat, didn't even crack a smile, just turned and continued on. Smart man.

And then her breath caught in her throat, because there it was before her, that beautiful machine, full of power and life.

Even in the fog-muted light, the glossy paint shone and the chrome gleamed. Oh, and that engine—an eighty-eight-inch twin cam. It was a beast. Forget about playing it cool—Mandy almost salivated at the mere thought of feeling all that strength firsthand. She reached out and ran her fingers lightly over the leather seats, more satisfying than it had ever been before. She wasn't politely admiring her dad's bike or watching a video online. This was here. This was real. And today, she was going to ride.

"Please tell me you have another helmet."

He unfastened a leather side pouch and pulled one out. "Here," he said. "Got one just your size."

Of course he did. Nodding, she fastened it on. This was it. No going back. *Good.*

He threw his leg over the bike and gestured for her to join him. She climbed onto the raised seat behind him, trying to imitate his movements.

Even up a few inches, she hadn't realized how closely she'd be pressed to him. She edged back a little, but a big hand on her thigh stopped her.

"Don't," he said. "The closer you are, the easier it is for both of us."

"Okay," she said, scooting forward again. Tentatively, she slipped her arms around his waist. That must have been the right thing to do, since he started the engine and the bike roared to life.

"Ready?" he shouted.

"Yes!" She was ready. More than ready. This was the apotheosis of everything she'd dared to dream about, but never had the courage to actually try.

Liam kicked off and nothing could have prepared her for the thick, hot rush that went straight to her head and came back down, flooding her senses, making her feel so very alive. Every nerve ending awakened, every sensation amplified a hundredfold. *Endorphins and adrenaline.*

She shoved her science brain aside. Who cared? It was everything she'd imagined it would be—exciting, dangerous, and above all, *fun.*

Liam turned left and the bike angled sideways. Instinctively, she tightened her arms around him, his hard heat comforting under her fingertips. He'd done this for her—given her this experience.

"You're doing great," he yelled over his shoulder.

She squeezed his waist to let him know she'd heard.

And then everything floated away—all her insecurities, her guilt, her anxieties about her work, life, family—as they zoomed up the Silverado Trail. Cool air whipped her cheeks, the bike throbbed between her legs, and she reveled in the sensation of being completely immersed in this experience. This was all there was—her, the motorcycle, and Liam Flynn.

Liam expertly controlled the powerful machine, keeping it steady and smooth on the turns, letting the throttle open up on the straightaways. And every time he let it rip, the bottom fell out of her stomach. She loved every second of it.

Riding on the bike felt so different from riding in a car. Out in the open, she could feel everything—the changes in air pressure as they got higher, the cool shade from the redwood trees. There was a good deal of fog this high, and a few times they went right through a clammy patch of moist air.

After they'd ridden for about an hour, the sun was out in full force and the fog had mostly burned off. Liam turned right and pulled up a long, steep driveway to a small parking lot nestled at the top. He cut the engine and swung off, then helped her off the bike. She was shocked to find her legs were actually a bit wobbly.

"It's the vibration," Liam said, holding out his arm for her to take. Gratefully, she took it while she got her walking legs back. "Feels a ton better than the Sportster, thanks to the softail's hidden rear suspension, not to mention the shock absorbers along the axis, but for first-timers, it still can be intense." He cleared his throat. "Did you like the ride, Amanda?"

She looked up to find him watching her carefully, waiting for her response. "Are you kidding me?" Trying to describe what she was feeling was nearly impossible, so she settled for the most general truth she could. "I loved it."

"Good," he said, satisfaction punctuating his voice. He paused, and for the briefest of moments, it seemed that he was about to kiss her. A split-second later, he blinked and the haze in his eyes was gone. "I have something else to show you," he said. Gently, he took her by the shoulders and turned her around. "Look."

"Wow," she breathed. With the fog cleared, a gray-blue sky shone through a lightly wooded picnic area—a picture window overlooking Napa Valley. She looked up at Liam. "Is that—"

He nodded. "Yep. The view you've been waiting for. It won't disappoint, I promise. Are you good to walk?"

"I'm good," she said.

"You go ahead. I'll join you in a minute."

She went right up to the edge of the mountain, and her breath caught in her throat.

The whole valley lay spread out before her, miles of shimmering golden brown in the winter sunlight. There was downtown Napa, many miles south of where she was standing. Route 29 cut a straight path right through the valley. And splitting the land in a crazy crisscross pattern were the vineyards, patches of earth carved into the rich soil where farmers had grown grapes for over a century and a half.

It was magnificent—all that barren beauty, the end of one cycle of life showcased in dramatic twists and twirls of wood. Come spring, the vines would once again bud with color and life and leaves and grapes, starting the cycle afresh.

She'd missed this. All of it. For years. Shutting herself away shouldn't be what she was doing with her life…what Nicole *wanted* her to do with her life. While the rest of the world was moving forward, she'd been trapped in her laboratory. Her research was important, yes, but she'd closed herself off to so much.

Sadness swept over her in a wave. Maybe it was the excitement of the ride, or the fact that this was the first time in a long while she'd done something for herself that didn't involve her research, or the heady aroma of the crisp mountain air, but all of a sudden, tears pricked at the corners of her eyes.

She couldn't do this. Wait, yes. Yes, she could. It was exactly what she'd come to Napa for, but not now. Not in front of him. As surreptitiously as she could, she touched the corners of her eyes, ensuring they were dry.

Footsteps crunched on the wood chips and Liam came to stand beside her, looking out to the countryside.

"You like?"

"Yes. Very much," she said, not looking up at him in case she lost it again. "Where are we?"

"A friend of mine named Mike Gordon owns these vineyards. The views are much better here than at our place, so he lets me come up whenever I want."

"That's very nice of him."

"Yeah," he said, with a laugh. "It also might be that for many years while Flynn Winery was ramping up production of its back acres, we bought Mike's entire harvest for a ton of cash."

She smiled a little at that. "It might be."

"It's not as black and white as I'm making it sound. Around here, business and personal relationships kind of bleed together." He surveyed the view. "Look your fill," he said. "When you're ready, I'll be at the picnic tables."

Ten minutes later, she fully collected herself and went over to join him. There was a small cloth on the table on top of which, in classic picnic style, were a couple of fine-looking cheeses, some charcuterie, a loaf of crusty bread peeking out of a paper bag, and what looked like quince paste. In his big hands, Liam was carefully slicing a ripe pear with a pocketknife.

"Hungry? I figured we could have lunch up here before we continue on."

She nodded. "I could eat."

Wordlessly, he handed her a slice of pear. It was sweet, but firm.

"I don't drink while I'm riding, but I brought some Calistoga. Have you had it before?"

"Sure." The fruit-flavored sparkling water was popular in Silicon Valley. "Do you have any lemon-flavored?"

"You bet. That's my favorite, too." With a smile, he poured some of the fizzy beverage into a paper cup and passed it to her.

"Thanks."

She broke off a chunk of bread and spread some cheese on top—soft, gooey stuff that practically melted in her mouth.

"Good?" Liam asked, when she was stuffing her second mouthful in.

"So goorrd," she mumbled.

"Ah," he said, and spread some cheese on his own hunk of bread.

She swallowed and put her bread down. "What does *ah* mean?"

"I think I'm beginning to understand you."

"Oh?" she said, raising an eyebrow. "Why don't you enlighten me?"

"You say you like order. You profess to believe only in purpose and reason. In science. Yet someone gives you a chance to let go and you jump in with two feet, like yesterday on the river. You're starved for excitement, for *life*. Why don't you let yourself be free? Why did Ann and Chase have to hijack your life to get you up here?"

"It's complicated," Mandy said.

"Yeah?" Liam said, laying his forearms on the table and leaning forward. "Try me." Evenly, his gaze met hers.

And then she was struck by the craziest of thoughts: she could tell him. Her guilt had been festering for so long, and whether it was the ride or the morning or maybe even the weather, this felt right.

"Your sister's suffering," she said. "I know what that feels like." *Deep breath, Mandy. You can do this.* "There was an accident."

Liam didn't blink. "What kind of accident?"

Mandy went on quickly before she lost her nerve. "My sister, Nicole, came to visit me over her spring break. Saturday morning, I went to get some coffee while she slept in. While waiting in line at a nearby coffee shop, I actually felt her scream. I didn't know what had happened, but I knew it was terrible."

"What?" Liam asked quietly.

"An electrical fire. While I was out, she woke up and took a shower, then blew her hair dry. The wiring was old. The firefighters told us the blaze started in the walls and spread fast because of the insulation and structural materials. The worst part was that Nikki actually got out, but she went back in to save my fish. *My fish.*" It was just like Nicole to put everyone else—even a fish—before herself. "She ended up with third-degree burns over more than twenty percent of her body, mostly on her left side."

"She needed a skin graft," Liam surmised. "Did you—?"

"No. I couldn't. If we'd been identical twins, we would have shared the exact same DNA and I could have donated skin to her, but as it is, we don't even share the same blood type."

Mandy shook her head, remembering how impotent she'd felt. "So she had an allograft from another donor. Her body rejected it, so she had another surgery. Graft after graft. Infection after infection. I can't imagine her pain, but watching her go through it was absolute agony. The truly amazing part was that she spent the rest of the spring and summer recovering, but come fall she was back at school. I mean, how can you even comprehend that kind of strength?"

Liam was still watching her intently. "Your research?"

"Because of Nicole," Mandy confirmed. "It wasn't that difficult to switch laboratories, especially since my PhD research was in immunology." At Liam's stare, she clarified. "Some aspects of my old research were relevant to what I'm doing now, specifically graft rejection. Anyway, my adviser vouched for me and I was lucky enough to get a fellowship doing what I wanted. Since then, I've made it my mission to improve graft technology so others won't have to suffer as much as Nikki has."

"When did all of this happen?"

"Two and a half years ago."

"The spring before we met in Tahoe," he murmured.

Mandy nodded. Going to Tahoe that year had been her way of trying to return to normal—whatever *normal* was—but she'd felt guilty the whole time she was there. "I don't want to give up my research. I love it. Even before the accident, I loved doing research, but I haven't been living my own life. The sacrifices have been…extensive." The tears she was trying to hold back finally burst free and spilled down her cheeks.

"Hey," Liam said, standing and coming around the picnic table to sit by her side. "Here." He handed her a paper napkin and wrapped his arm around her shoulders while she wiped her nose and blotted her face.

"I'm sorry," she said with a sniffle. Talking about it was one thing, but showing it—all her insecurities and anxieties laid bare for him to see—was another. He should be running, but he wasn't. Instead he moved closer and squeezed her shoulder harder.

"I'm not," he said. "My only question is why you didn't tell me this before."

Mandy gave a little shrug. How did you explain to someone that you'd put your happy emotions on lockdown and thrown away the key? "I'm not sure I could have. I mean, when I met you, it had just happened."

Liam leaned back and searched her face. "You don't think the fire was your fault, do you?"

Mandy looked down, unable to meet his gaze. It was her apartment, wasn't it? If she'd only warned Nicole not to use that outlet, or was there to tell her that she was more important than the goldfish, or something, *anything* that could have gotten her out of there, things might have turned out differently.

"No. No way," he said, shaking his head. "How could you have known the wiring was faulty? Had you used the same outlet before?"

"For my electric toothbrush." She hiccupped a little and wiped her eyes again. "Look, rationally, I can try to convince myself it wasn't my fault. But there's a constant voice in the back of my mind that says otherwise."

The corners of his mouth went down and stayed down. "Is that why you just stopped…having fun?"

"At the time, I didn't think of it like that. I saw it as me focusing on something that could help others like Nicole." But she could see that dividing line in her life so clearly. She went to events now, but only as a means to an end—to set up a friend or wrangle a connection. People who didn't know her well thought she was the life of the party, but the fun wasn't for her anymore. It was for others. She'd closed off part of herself when Nicole got hurt without even realizing what she was doing. And now the loneliness gnawed at her.

Liam squeezed her arm, reminding her of his presence. It was comforting. "Need another napkin?" he asked, holding one out.

She shook her head.

"So, how is she?"

"She has some pretty serious scars, but she hasn't let that slow her down. She teaches high school at our alma mater in La Jolla. Biology. She's got such a way with those kids." When Nicole asked her to come down to do a guest lecture, Mandy witnessed how Nikki's students hung on her every word. "She still surfs when she can get out there. And her boyfriend's a really good guy."

"Sounds like she's in better shape than you are."

Mandy let out a sad laugh. "She is. She's moved beyond it. I haven't, and I don't know why. That's why I'm here, if you really want to know the truth. Even before Annie and Chase asked me to come up, I knew I had to get away. Hijack my *own* life, you know?"

"Yeah. I know."

They sat there for a while, letting the sun wash over them. Liam left her alone, not talking or prodding, but just being. It felt good.

When the chill started to creep in, he helped her up, and together, they rode back down the mountain. For once, her mind was a blank. No lab, no research, no plan. Just the bike and the wind and her arms around Liam Flynn.

She didn't even realize they were back at Liam's place until he helped her off the bike and took off his helmet, then undid hers.

"You okay?" he asked, his voice gentle. "I hope I didn't push you too hard."

"You didn't." And if he did, well, it wasn't any further than she tried to push herself. "The ride was amazing, Liam. Truly."

He was amazing, and why they weren't together was no mystery. It was because of her. Because she'd said *no* two years ago even though she'd desperately wanted to say *yes*.

How had she gotten here? To a place filled with regret, with years of missed chances, of roads not taken, of a life not truly lived? She was still young. There was so much time. And she didn't want to look back two years or four years or forty years from now and realize she'd made yet another mistake.

Liam reached out and pushed a strand of hair behind her ear, his hand lingering on her jaw, his gaze intense. Instinctively, she knew he wouldn't press. Not him. If she wanted this, she had to seize it. Show him she was ready.

Without letting her brain get in the way this time, she flung her arms around his neck and pressed her lips to his. And then he had his hands through her hair, and his mouth was slanting over hers, deepening the kiss. A sweet heat coursed through her, and it was even better than the last time he'd done this because she was walking in with her eyes wide open. With purpose.

She opened her mouth, wanting to take everything he had to give, and he gave, his tongue sweeping in to claim what was his, what had been his before, except she was too wrapped up in her own head to realize it.

This is what you've been missing.

His arms slipped around her back, holding her tight, and she was enveloped in his heat. He smelled like wind and sky and leather and man, and she wanted to grab on and not let go. Everything she'd been holding back came pouring out—her passion, her need, and most of all, her desire for this one man. All this time, there hadn't been anyone else. No one could compare to Liam Flynn, who gave and gave without holding anything back.

Finally, he tore his lips away from her and groaned. "Mandy," he said, his voice breaking. "Are you sure you want this?"

"Yes," she said. More than anything.

CHAPTER 7

Liam Flynn still had the power to blow her away with his kiss. His mouth was everywhere—on her lips, her cheeks, her neck—searing where he touched. He practically dragged her through the door and she went willingly, kicking it shut with her foot. Now that she'd let it all loose, there was no turning back.

Not that she wanted to.

She slipped her fingers up his shirt, pressing the flat of her hand on his stomach. He groaned and she felt him rumble under her palm. She went further, loving the way his muscles tensed under her touch, and snaked her other hand between his legs.

He captured her wrist in his hand. "You keep that up," he said, eyes glittering, "we're not going to make it upstairs."

"So?" she said with a laugh.

"So the floor's cold and my bed's warm."

"You sold me."

Even with them both trying, it took a long time for them to make it through the house. When they finally reached his bedroom, Liam backed her up to the bed, still kissing her, and gently pushed her down. He went back to shut the door and then came toward her, watching her carefully, testing her with each step to make sure she was ready.

"Change your mind?" he asked.

"No way," she said. "I want this." *I want you.*

She loved the way his eyes darkened in pleasure, turning a deeper green. "I know you wouldn't do this otherwise. And," he said, leaning over to kiss her mouth, "I'm honored."

He stood up close to the edge of the bed, waiting, and she understood— she had to make the first move. She got up on her knees.

"Come here," she said.

When he stepped into reach, she gripped his shirt in her fist and pulled him closer. She tipped her head up and kissed him once on the mouth, very deeply, giving him no time to adjust, then pushed him away. Now that they'd established that she was here and more than willing, she got serious, fast. "I want to see you," she demanded. "Take off your shirt."

With a little smile, Liam pulled his shirt off in one smooth motion. Lord, he was beautiful, all lean muscle and sinew. She'd seen him last night, but had been too much on emotional lockdown to gawk. Now she looked her fill—her gaze lingering on those well-defined abs, that magnificent chest. She reached out and traced the line of his pectoral muscle to where it hit his sternum, but only for a second.

"Now your pants," she said.

His nostrils flared, showing her how much he liked her bossiness. Slowly, he unbuttoned his jeans, then slid them down his hips. She drank him in, eyes skimming the dark red line of hair that trailed down until it disappeared into the boxer-briefs that sat low on his narrow hips. His thighs bulged ever so slightly, and he was bowlegged, which only added to his charm.

"You're..." She swallowed. "You're beautiful."

"I think you have this backward," he told her with a smile. He placed a knee on the bed next to her, making it dip deeply, wrapped his hand around her thick braid, and gently tugged. "Will you let me take your hair down?"

She wanted that—for him to see her that way. In response, she slipped the rubber band off the tip and placed it on the coverlet, eyes on him the whole time. Then he reached out and slowly unwound her hair, loosening the strands. When he finally had it all free, he ran his hands through it, admiring his handiwork, and she shivered from the contact of his fingers on her scalp. She knew she looked different with it down. Freer. A little younger-looking, maybe, which is why she wore it back all the time. Liam must have liked what he saw, because his gaze sharpened.

She smiled and wrapped her hand around his neck, bringing his face close to hers. "For you," she said, then touched her lips to his so sweetly. But it went from sweet to carnal fast with the dip of her tongue into his mouth, and the brush of her palm up his thigh. All at once, she pushed him back onto the bed and straddled him. He laughed when she took complete charge, and she laughed along with him, cupping his face in her hands and kissing him everywhere she could comfortably reach. Yet even though she was on top, he simply dominated, paying thorough attention to each and every part of her lips, from the bow to the corners, his hands on her hips holding her down.

He kissed her breathless until she was panting, desperate for more.

She finally raised her head. "You're really, really good at this."

"Oh?" he said, his eyelids at half mast. "We've barely gotten started." That sleepy look had been a deception, because in one smooth move, he flipped her onto her back. He propped himself up on his elbow and surveyed her. "My turn to see you," he said, pulling her shirt over her head, unclasping her bra, and tugging down her jeans and panties. When she was completely naked, he simply stared for a beat. Then two.

He skimmed a hand down her arm, his thumb grazing the side of her breast. "Knew you were gorgeous, but not like this." Instead of embarrassment, her body responded with desire, blood rushing to every sensitive point under his perusal.

And then his lips met hers as his hand closed around her breast. Her nipples were aching points of need, something he discovered all too quickly. Clever fingers rubbed across first one hardened tip, then the other, the intimate contact making her long for more. Wordlessly, she pushed up into him, willing him to pinch, to twist—anything more substantial than that maddeningly light erotic contact he was giving—but he wouldn't budge. Just continued to torment her until she was practically panting.

His mouth left hers and went to her ear. "There's so much more, isn't there? So many layers. I could torture you for hours. Make you beg." A shiver of excitement, of pure desire, snaked its way down her back. She would like that, more than she could ever admit. "But for now, I think I'll take pity on you."

Then he wrapped his lips around a taut nipple and sucked. Hard.

Hot, dark pleasure rushed straight to her sex and she heard herself cry out. He was merciless, priming and sucking one breast, then doing the other, working her over until she was damp and achy between her legs. Unbelievable. And he hadn't even touched her clit yet. She squirmed to try to get some relief, but he merely threw a huge thigh over hers, preventing her from any kind of self-stimulation.

She was shaking now, and just when she thought she was going to actually have to beg, he slid down her body and spread her thighs wide.

"Liam—" she started, suddenly acutely aware of her vulnerability.

He met her gaze and wouldn't look away. "Please let me do this for you," he said.

"Okay," she whispered.

She was wet. Dripping. So easy for him to slide one finger in, and then a second, testing her, stretching her. And then he bent his head to taste.

Insane pleasure coursed through her. She reared up, but he caught her hips, forced her to feel everything he had to give. The hardest thing for her to do was just accept, but once she did, it was easy to let go. He knew exactly how to heighten her sensation, rubbing the pads of his fingers in *just* the right place, swirling his tongue against her flesh until she came apart in his arms incredibly fast.

He gently withdrew from her body, began to gather her up, but she wasn't done.

"I want to touch you," she said. "Please."

"I'm all yours," he said, then leaned back, his trust in her evident with his relaxed smile.

Without hesitating, she tugged his briefs down and wrapped her fingers around his hard heat. He was beautiful—large and proportional—though he didn't seem overly conscious of it. And then she touched, fisting his length in long, easy strokes, lazily running her thumb over the tip. She took her time, too, wanting to draw it out, wanting to please him the same way he'd pleased her, and he didn't seem to mind. Just closed his eyes and gave a low, appreciative hum.

But when she trailed her fingers with her tongue, *that* got a reaction.

"Mandy," he said, his voice sounding strangled. Encouraged, she licked just under his head, and thrilled when he shuddered. She ran her tongue down his length, then dragged it back up again, wanting desperately to know how long it would take for him to lose control. After several minutes of teasing, she finally got down to business, taking his head fully in her mouth, then allowing as much of the rest of him to slide in as she could handle. This was clearly his undoing, because he groaned and palmed her breasts.

Shocked to find she was aroused all over again simply from mere caressing, she reached between her thighs to stroke. It didn't take long before she was ready for a second time.

Liam must have recognized how close she was, because he speared his fingers through her hair and gently pulled her off. In seconds, he had her flat on her back.

"Protection," she gasped.

"On it," he said, already reaching for his night side table. He pulled back, and in a few moments, had a condom on.

She was primed, but still he went slowly, sliding into her willing body inch by delectable inch, filling her so completely there was room for nothing else.

When he was fully seated, he kissed her and smoothed her hair back from her face. "You okay?" he whispered.

"Yes," she said, squeezing her internal muscles around him, desperately trying to get him to move. "Please."

He kissed her once. Twice. A third time, watching her closely. Satisfied she was all right, he flicked his hips just a fraction so that he went even deeper.

"Come on, Liam."

He adjusted himself over her, his shifting pleasurable agony. "I don't want to go too fast," he said.

"If you don't go faster, I'm going to lose my mind."

"Greedy girl." This, said like an endearment. She thought he was going to torture her by staying stock-still, but he gave an experimental slide out and in. Oh, yes, she liked that very much.

"More," she demanded.

Carefully, he angled her hips to meet his thrusts, encouraged her to wrap her legs around his back, then moved into her, slow and deep, drawing out the sensations so artfully, she knew she was in the hands of a master. She followed his lead, shuddering in his arms when he withdrew, urging him back in with words and hands.

Liam was as smooth in bed as he was out of it, stimulating her with whispered words, coaxing her upward with the easy slide of his hips. And upwards she went, so high, so fast, it was a wonder she could even breathe.

At some point she stopped thinking and just started feeling, and that was best of all. There was no awkwardness, no embarrassment, just complete and utter *rightness*.

He was moving faster now, his back a mass of hard muscle as he strained against her. She tilted her hips to move against him, which made him rub against all of that sensitive flesh at the apex of her thighs. It took only a few more moments before she gasped and went over the edge. He was right with her, giving one last explosive thrust before shuddering and going still.

Carefully, he withdrew from her body, gathered her up in his arms, and folded a sheet and blanket over both of them. He smoothed the hair from her temple and gently kissed her lips. It was a revelation—this aftercare, this attention. She shouldn't be surprised. This was Liam Flynn, the man who'd asked her for everything because he wanted to give everything in return.

And the biggest revelation of all was that she was ready to accept it.

"Stay through New Year's?" he murmured.

She nodded, acceptance coming so readily in a way that even a day ago would have been unfathomable.

Yes.

CHAPTER 8

Liam lay in his oversize bed as the rain tapped softly on the roof and ran in rivulets down the sides of the skylight. He'd been in this position a thousand times, but it had never felt like this. Satisfaction. Contentment. Peace.

Because of her.

Amanda Aligheri was tucked against him, her golden curls spilling over his pillow, his arm under her neck. She felt good there. Right. He tightened his grip and pulled her closer, surprised at the intense wave of protectiveness that washed over him for this strong, seriously self-sufficient woman. Mandy sighed and nestled into his body, rubbing her face against the side of his chest.

Mandy didn't need him, but she wanted him, and had given herself freely, unreservedly, to show him how much. A gift he didn't deserve.

She stirred against his side, eyes still closed. "Mmm…what time is it?"

He glanced at his watch. "Five."

One eye cracked open. "Why is it so dark outside?"

"Sunset happened fifteen minutes ago, and it's raining."

"Ah." She closed her eye and buried her face in his chest again. "I'm hungry."

"Same," he said. "Why don't you get cleaned up and I'll check in with Chase to see what the plan is for dinner?"

"Okay," she agreed, sliding out of bed, still partly covered by the sheet.

"Shower's that way," he said, pointing to his bathroom. "There are spare towels in the closet."

"Thanks."

The sheet slipped from her body and she padded off to the bathroom naked. Liam stared, mesmerized by the curve of her hip, the sweet roundness of her rear, before the door shut behind her. He groaned, fighting the desire that came so thick and fast with her. She seriously had no idea how gorgeous she was.

In a moment, he heard the shower go on, and then she was humming some '80s song, completely out of tune. He sat up and plumped the pillows behind his head. This was easy, her, here with him. So easy, he almost forgot how hard it had been getting started.

Liam had no doubt that Mandy gave a hundred percent to whatever endeavor she tried, but he also knew that she was most likely to put herself last. Not that he thought she'd do it intentionally, but the idea had crossed his mind that when she went back to Silicon Valley, she'd once again immerse herself in her work and forget all about what they shared here.

Which meant that he was going to have to do his best to make sure she didn't forget. So that when the time came for them to talk about next steps, there would actually *be* next steps.

Liam leaned over the side of the bed and fished around in his jeans pocket for his cell phone. Clicking it on, he dialed Chase's number. Chase picked up after a few rings.

"Hey, man," Chase said, "how goes it?"

"Great. Just great." No need to tell his friend that he and Mandy had just shared intimate carnal knowledge of each other. "What's the plan for dinner?"

"Oh, yeah, well, about that. Annie's kind of tired, so we're going to call it a night. Hope that's all right with you."

Tired. Right. "Uh, sure," Liam said. "I'll ask Mandy if she wants to join me for dinner, then." He tried to sound as casual as possible.

"Yeah, that's great. I'm sure she'd like that. Thanks again, man, and catch you tomorrow."

The phone clicked off, and Liam sat there for a minute, smiling. More time alone with Mandy he absolutely wouldn't refuse.

When she came out of the shower a few minutes later, warm and smelling of his soap, he told her about Chase and Ann's disappearing act.

She actually laughed. "This is exactly what I did to Annie when I sent her up to Tahoe with Chase," Mandy said. "I guess I'm getting what I deserve."

Liam shook his head. "Nah. What you deserve is a good dinner." He gave her a kiss, then hopped in the shower.

When both of them were clean and dressed, and after Mandy dealt with a work phone call, Liam took her to ZuZu, a tapas bar and restaurant in downtown Napa, right on Main. The restaurant didn't take reservations, and even on a rainy midweek night in the dead of winter, the place was packed. Despite—or maybe because of—the rain, everything seemed more intimate. It was almost as if he was sharing a secret with the crowd. *See this woman on my arms? She's mine.*

They slipped into the last two seats at the bar and immediately ordered a glass of Spanish muscat for Mandy and a lager for him. Before the drinks arrived, Mandy turned and surveyed the place.

"I like it here," she said.

"Good vibe," he agreed. With its patterned tile floor, yellow-painted walls, and narrow staircase leading up to the second level, the restaurant had enough charm to draw locals and tourists alike. The atmosphere was great, but the excellent food certainly didn't hurt, especially given the fact that Napa was a foodie town. And a drinking one. Behind the bar, a hundred bottles of wine were carefully displayed, labels out, showcasing the best domestic and international offerings. "What do you want?" he asked her as she looked over the menu.

"I have no idea," she said, scanning the menu. "Everything looks good."

"What do you say I pick some of my favorites, and if we're still hungry, we can order more."

She put the menu aside. "Sounds great."

Liam got some olives and almonds and salt cod to spread on crusty bread. He could never resist the *gambas al ajillo*—smoky, spicy Gulf shrimp—or the black paella with seafood, so he got those, too. At some point, each of them ordered another drink. He liked watching her eat—slowly, savoring each bite.

Later, stomachs full, brains fuzzy, they stumbled half dazed into the street. The rain had mellowed into a fine mist, so Liam quickly popped open his big umbrella, shielding them both.

"Let's walk," he said, wrapping his arm around her shoulders and tucking her into his side.

They crossed the street at Fifth and went to the water, walking the river path for a block. It was quieter here, away from the street and the cars and the crowd, the river rushing past, a murky chasm in the dark.

"Thanks for dinner," she said.

"My pleasure."

She looked up at him. "I believe it's traditional for us to kiss now," she said.

He obliged her by bending his head to brush his lips against hers. She tasted faintly alcoholic, and a little bit spicy. He deepened the kiss, and she grabbed on tight, pulling him close. The soft weight of her breasts pressed against his chest, and he buried his free hand in her hair. She'd worn it down just for him, and that pleased him more than he cared to admit. It was just hair, but it seemed to symbolize everything about her that had been wound so tightly and now had been let free.

Finally, still hanging on to him, Mandy tilted her head back and sighed. "This evening is just *awesome*," she said.

"You're only saying that because you're drunk."

"No way," she said. "I'm not drunk. I have a wooden leg. Didn't Chase tell you?"

"No," he said, bemused.

"I can drink him under the table. Maybe that's why he didn't tell you. Not that I do it often, mind you."

"I don't mind," he said. "Seeing you drunk would be…illuminating."

"You think?" she said, and even in the dark he could see the twinkle in her eye.

"Yeah, we should do it sometime. I have the greatest wine for getting hammered."

She laughed at that, and he wrapped his arm around her shoulder again and led her down a path back to Main Street, strolling toward his truck, which was parked near Downtown Joe's, a well-known local hangout. Even though the weather was awful, the crowd spilled out onto the covered outdoor patio.

"Out on a date on a school night," she said. "If only my friends could see me now."

"You're not thinking about your research?" he teased.

"A little, especially since my grad students can't seem to keep it together while I'm gone. I think they've called me half a dozen times in the past couple of days," she admitted, shaking her head. "But don't come down so hard on me. I know I work too much, and now you have a better understanding as to why, but I'm going to try to do a better job of taking time for myself." She paused for a minute. "Still, I think it's normal for people to have a hard time separating work from their personal lives. I mean, you lived in San Francisco, right? And it seems even worse in Silicon Valley, where everyone walks around surgically attached to their smartphones."

He knew. The BlackBerry beeped at midnight and you answered the e-mail. Or you texted your friends with last-minute plans that inevitably fell through because someone had to go back to the office. And on the off chance you did go out and have fun, you had to take pictures and post them to every single social media outlet.

Mandy squeezed his waist and looked up at him. "So maybe I'm tipped a little too far over toward the work side of the work-life balance, but a lot of people have the same problem. Don't you think about your grapes all the time?"

"During growing and harvest seasons, sure." They were back at his truck now. He opened the passenger side door for her.

"C'mon, you don't think about them now even a little?" she said, climbing in. "Or when you're bottling? Or distributing? Or at the start of planting season?"

He shut the door and walked around to the driver's side. Of course she was right, but not for the reason she thought. When he shook out the umbrella and got in, it was obvious she was waiting for him to answer. "Okay, okay, I get your point," he said.

"So you *do* think about work!"

"I think about software, actually," he said, knowing this was going to open up a whole new can of worms. But if anyone was going to understand, it would be Mandy.

"Software?" Confusion colored her expression. "Like for your business?"

"Exactly. There's something I've been thinking about doing, kind of a big data analysis of our vineyard, maybe even our neighbor's vineyard, to see if I can improve our viticulture."

"Wouldn't you hire someone for that?"

"No, I'd code the model myself."

Mandy blinked. "I didn't know you were a tech guy."

Liam shrugged, trying to play it off as no big deal. "Yeah. Before I came up to help my family with the winery I did the whole start-up bit." He left off the part about how good he was. How he made tech lead only a year out of college, and was one of the first ten members of a company that ultimately went public with a big bang. He'd made a bundle, not that he advertised that fact. "You're still looking at me funny."

"Well, I never would have pegged you as the engineering type."

"Sorry to disappoint you," he said, his voice wry.

"No, no, it's fascinating." She tucked her hand into his. "Why'd you stop doing it?"

He took a deep breath. She'd revealed her secrets. It was his turn now. "We'd just had our IPO. It was a huge deal. I'm talking New York Stock Exchange-opening, bell-ringing kind of huge deal. That night, we had a party. I was happy, relieved, excited—until I got the call that my dad had a near-fatal heart attack. The next day I gave my two weeks' notice and came up."

"Just like that?"

"Just like that."

"With no fallout?"

He laughed, and it came out sounding a little bitter. "No, there was plenty. My work colleagues were pissed as hell. And my girlfriend was furious, too. So she dumped me."

Expressions of surprise, then compassion flickered over her face. "I'm really sorry to hear that," she finally said.

"Eh, don't be. It was worth it."

"To give it all up?"

"I didn't see that I was giving up all that much. The money was nice, I'll admit. And the camaraderie—that being-in-the-trenches kind of thing—was nice, too. But that wasn't living. It's different up here. Freer. Yes, I still work crazy hours during harvest season, but the rest of the year, my life is pretty great. I'm building a business doing something I like with the people I love. And I still have time for myself. I really couldn't ask for more."

"But you have given something up," she said slowly. "Something you think about. So what's stopping you from writing code again?"

He pulled his hand from hers. "It's complicated," he said tightly, jamming the key into the ignition and turning the engine to get the heat going.

She shook her head. "I know you have time to ski and bike. Why couldn't you spend some of that time coding?"

"It might not work."

"No. If that were the case, no one would ever do science. Next." A dismissal out of hand. And rightly deserved. He moved on.

"My dad's not jazzed about the idea. He thinks if it ain't broke, don't fix it."

"So you're not starting because of your *father*?" Mandy settled back into her seat and crossed her arms over her chest. He knew that look; it was one he'd given her on countless occasions. "Okay, what else? Lay it out."

"If I do this, I'm going to want to go big. That takes time I might not have."

"Uh-huh." She didn't sound convinced. "Anything else?"

"That about covers it."

Mandy shook her head. "All I'm hearing is that you're afraid of your own success."

"Damn that smart mouth," he said, half jokingly.

"I call 'em like I see 'em," she said coolly. "I also find it ironic that a man who has been less than subtle about me taking time to live for myself wants to work more but can't find the time."

"Is this the 'own your own destiny' pep talk you gave Chase?" he asked. "You know he still talks about that lecture," Liam said, trying to defuse the tension.

"I just want everyone to reach their potential," Mandy said. "And to be happy. If you're not happy, make a change." She looked out onto the damp, dark street. "I certainly wish I'd done it sooner."

"I'll think about it," he said reluctantly.

"Good." The word was final, signifying an end to that conversation. "So what now?"

"Since we got ditched—"

Mandy cleared her throat.

"Since Ann and Chase were too tired to make it out tonight," Liam amended, "we're on our own until tomorrow afternoon. Any suggestions on how we use that time?"

Mandy's face softened. "We-ell, my room at the inn is very comfortable."

"I have a better idea. Why don't we stop by the inn to get you some fresh clothes, and then you come back to my place, curl up with me in my very large, very soft bed, and spend the night listening to the rain falling on the roof."

She reached out and took his hand. "That sounds perfect."

CHAPTER 9

The rain was still falling the next day, splattering over the pavement, drenching the dark earth and soaking the hills. In a month or so, mustard flowers would bloom, carpeting the valley in yellow. Napa was always so beautiful in early spring. He could just picture Mandy on the back of his bike, her arms wrapped around his waist, as they drove up Route 29. Maybe they'd spend the day in Calistoga at the hot springs. Or perhaps they'd drive up to Mendocino. Her face would light up when she saw the ocean from the cliffs, he just knew it.

Dr. Amanda Aligheri was amazing. She had shown him who she truly was—loyal, brilliant, a total knockout, and amazing in bed—and Liam knew he needed more of her in his life. She didn't seem at all interested in his former job for its prestige—only that he wasn't achieving his true potential. She simply encouraged him to pursue his dreams, not because they'd make him rich and famous, but because they were his.

Now she was standing with Stella, organizing tickets for the big raffle they always had on New Year's Eve to auction off a case of Flynn Winery's finest. Proceeds went to the local animal shelter, and the raffle was typically one of the highlights of the party. As if on cue, Mandy turned to him and gave him a brilliant smile.

Liam knew she must be stressing about her work. It was one thing to say you were going to change, but doing it was something else entirely. Yet here she was, helping his family instead of working in her laboratory or trying to relax. If she wasn't actually having a good time, she was putting on a pretty good show, though something told him that after what they'd shared, Amanda wouldn't put on a show for him. She'd say what she thought, and mean what she said.

At that moment, Daniel Flynn, patriarch of the Flynn family, strode through the door. His once-auburn hair was turning gray, and he walked a little more stiffly than he had in his younger days, but he was still in decent shape, at least on the outside. There are some things you never forgot as long as you lived, like getting a phone call at three in the morning that your dad had just suffered a near-fatal heart attack and was in the ICU at Queen of the Valley Medical Center.

"Liam!" Dan exclaimed in his large voice. "Just the man I wanted to see. How are the caves looking? We want them spick-and-span for the party. This is the one time of year we open them to the public, and we definitely want to be looking our best."

"They're in good shape, Dad," Liam responded. "I had George help me clear out the junk—it was pretty minimal, by the way—and wash everything down."

"Good, good," Dan said. "Good time of year to do it, too. We'll have a productive January once things settle down."

"Actually, I was hoping to talk with you about that," Liam ventured. Stella's pep talk hadn't done the trick, but strangely, one brainy, beautiful scientist's initiative to change her own life had given him a much-needed kick in the pants to change his. "I think January would be a great time to get started on that regression model I spoke with you about earlier this year."

Dan gave him a look of annoyance. "Not that again, Liam. I told you before, we don't have time to deal with that."

Liam frowned. "But you just said—"

"We're going to have a productive January, and that means I need your head in the game."

"My head will be in the game, but I think the winery could really benefit from—"

"Not this year, son," Dan said and his eyes lit on Mandy. "Oh? Who have we here? A helper?"

Mandy picked her head up from her task and regarded Dan Flynn. If she heard any part of their discussion, she did a good job hiding it. "Hello," she said, crossing the room to shake his hand. "I'm Amanda Aligheri, a friend of Chase Deckert's."

"Yes, Chase. Good man," Dan said, before turning to Liam. "Why didn't you tell me we had a guest?" But before Liam could answer, Dan continued. "You a scientist, too?"

"I am, actually. I'm a postdoctoral researcher at Stanford."

Dan looked impressed. "Well, then, that's just great. Have you had a tour? Have Liam or Stella shown you around? Are you going to join us for the big New Year's Eve bash?"

Mandy laughed at his dad's barrage of questions. "I have had a tour, thank you, but Liam has also been kind enough to show me the grounds. And I'm planning on staying for the party, right?" She looked directly at

Liam.

"You're staying," he said firmly, and was rewarded by a very self-satisfied smile.

"Say, I'm about to make my rounds to check the barrels," Dan said, completely oblivious to the subtext. "Why don't you come along? There's some science-y stuff you might enjoy—acidity, alcohol levels, that kind of thing."

"I'm a biologist, not a chemist, but I'm sure it'll be interesting." She turned to Stella. "Are you okay for now?" Stella nodded. "Great. I'll be back soon."

As soon as Mandy and Dan left, Stella turned on him. "Way to stand up to Dad," she said, her sarcasm winging its way across the room.

"He is so damned stubborn," Liam said. "He thinks my coding is going to screw everything up no matter how many times I tell him it's not."

Stella tucked a stack of tickets inside a cardboard box. "I don't know why you're waiting for his permission," she said.

"I don't want to upset him."

"He's not going to have another heart attack, if that's what you're worried about."

"I know that," Liam said, though deep inside he had a nagging feeling that his dad still wasn't in the best of health.

"You should stop letting him treat you like an employee."

"I *am* just an employee."

Stella shook her head. "What about the $500,000 you put into Flynn Winery three years ago?"

"That was a loan."

"And I guess the $300,000 you put in a year before that was a loan too?"

Liam was silent. The money wasn't doing him any good in his bank account, and had been meant to help take the small winery to the next level. It had paid off. They'd been able to purchase additional acreage and plant more vines. Besides, he had plenty more in the bank.

"You don't just work here, Liam," Stella continued. "You own this place, and you'll inherit it when dad dies."

"Which hopefully will be a very long time from now," Liam said. "I don't want to cut his life short by stressing him out."

"And in the meantime, you're stressing yourself out," Stella said, sounding totally exasperated now. "I bet Mandy Aligheri doesn't sit around on her ass, waiting for things to change!" And with that, she jammed the rest of the tickets in the box and stalked off with a flick of her dark hair.

Liam sighed and went to the tasting bar. He leaned over, snared a bottle of cab and a glass, and poured himself a hefty serving.

Stella, as usual, was right. How much of her prodding was because her own life wasn't going according to plan, and how much of it was because she really loved him, he'd never know. But she sure was right about one thing: Mandy would never sit around on her ass waiting for change. She'd go out and grab it with both hands. She'd come to Napa to do just that, and despite how serious her issues were, she was doing it.

Mandy didn't need him to coax her to break free; she was trying it on her own schedule. And here he was, trapped in a life he'd chosen, but one that wasn't as fulfilling as he'd hoped.

Hypocrite.

A vision of Mandy, laughing with pleasure on the back of his bike, seizing what she could in the minimal time she had, filled his mind. He'd bet anything that as soon as she got back home, she was going to make a list or a chart or *something* to help her get back on track. And he couldn't even find the time to write some lousy code.

He'd deal with this. Somehow, some way, he'd convince his dad that the regression model would be worth the time. And then he'd start coding again like he'd wanted to since he left San Francisco.

Mandy returned with his dad an hour later, flushed and happy, talking about varietals and temperature and fermentation. She wasn't part of this world, and if you'd asked him two days ago if he could ever see her fitting in here, he would have said no. But she'd proved him wrong—she'd been kind to his sister, charmed his father, and won his heart. She would fit. She'd fit anywhere, and her willingness to adapt continually surprised him.

"She's got a good palate, this one," Dan said, patting Mandy on the back. "I say we keep her."

"Maybe she doesn't want to be kept," Stella said, tossing the words over her shoulder as she passed them by with a box of candles in her hand.

Liam followed Stella with his eyes, but Dan turned. "I'll go after her," his dad said.

"Don't," Liam said. "She's fine." But Dan had already followed her out. Liam sighed.

"Hey," Mandy said. "She can handle him, and herself, too."

"My dad is treating her with kid gloves."

"She'll get over it. And so will he."

"For Stella's sake, I hope it's sooner rather than later. He's just holding her back."

Mandy shook her head. "Stella's a smart woman. I'm sure she realizes he loves her and is concerned about her."

Liam just stared, stunned by the truth of that statement. "For a lady who spends almost all of her waking hours in a lab looking at cells, you sure seem to know a lot about people."

Mandy smiled. "You know I wasn't always so single-minded."

Liam pushed her hair back from her face. "I know. It's just that this is the only way I've known you."

"Let's see if we can change that," she said, stepping forward and tilting her face up. "Say, right now."

Liam made a mock pretense of glancing at his watch. "I got a few minutes. You?"

"For you? Absolutely."

They ran back to his house in the rain, and by the time they reached the door, Mandy was breathless and they were both soaked. Liam had gotten his shoes muddy splashing through a puddle. He didn't care, because she was with him, more beautiful than he'd ever seen her, with her damp hair curling on her shoulders and her eyes promising him everything she had to give.

As soon as he got her inside, Liam kicked off his shoes and pressed her back up against the door, trapping her between him and the wood. Her eyes widened, even more so when he wedged a knee between her thighs, angling his body into hers. Burying his face at the place where her ear met her neck, he breathed in, reveling in her scent. When he kissed her throat, and then bit hard enough to lightly sting, she gasped, her reaction making him rock-hard. He cupped her ass in both hands and pulled her against him, letting her feel how much he wanted her, and she responded by lightly raking down his back with her fingers.

He speared a hand through her hair and tipped her face up. The desire he saw in her gaze mirrored his own.

"You like not knowing what's coming next," he said.

"Yes," she admitted on another gasp because he had one hand up her shirt and was now thumbing a taut nipple through her bra. She moaned and pushed into him, wordlessly demanding he continue. He obliged her, stroking until the damp fabric became an impediment and he simply yanked down the cup to feel flesh on flesh.

Ah, that was better, especially when he rolled her nipple and was rewarded with a desperate moan low in her throat. He licked her neck, collarbone to ear, feeling her shiver with each decadent inch.

"Do you know how long I've waited for this?"

"Two years?" she retorted.

He kissed her, nipping her bottom lip for her impudence. She just laughed and nipped him back. And then her cell phone rang.

"You need to get that?" he asked.

She thought for a moment. "No. Let it ring. It'll be hotter if I know someone needs me while we're doing this."

"Adrenaline junkie," he whispered into her ear. "Had you pegged the moment I sweet-talked you into going down that backside run at Alpine Meadows and you couldn't hide how much you loved it." He scraped her neck with his teeth, and she shivered. "You love the excitement." He dragged his mouth back up to her ear and pinched her other nipple, hard enough to make her cry out. "And the danger. Say it. Say you like it."

"Yes," she said, her voice breathless. "Yes, I like it."

Her damn phone finally stopped ringing so he simply devoured her mouth, claiming her for himself, now and always. She was rocking on his thigh in slo-mo, desperate to get closer. He was desperate, too, to feel her, see her. He pulled down the other cup of her bra, pushed up her shirt, and feasted his gaze on her plumped-up breasts before wrapping his lips around the most beautiful nipple. *That* got a reaction—her hands in his hair, pulling him closer. Greedy. He liked that. Known she'd be like this all along, and damned if he didn't get even harder.

He moved his mouth to the other breast and she sighed in satisfaction. "Like that, Liam. Both at the same time."

Demanding, too. He liked that even more.

"Take me upstairs," she ordered.

"Not yet," Liam said, flicking her nipples with his tongue.

"When?" she groaned, sliding the flat of her palm over the bulge in his jeans. He jerked in response, but wouldn't be deterred from his mission.

"I need something from you first."

"What, this?" she said, rubbing firmly now. "I need that, too."

"Later." He snared her wrist in his grasp, removing the distraction. Then he unsnapped the top button of her jeans and slid his hand right into her panties, her slickness smoothing his path. He groaned, she gasped, and he withdrew—only for a moment—to shove her jeans and panties down a little more.

There she was, laid bare for him. He teased her a little, rubbing her clit ever so lightly, then slipped a finger inside.

She grabbed his shoulder and squeezed, her little nails digging into his skin. Her eyes were closed, her cheeks flushed, her hair messy. Just gorgeous.

"What did I ask for two years ago?" he asked, sliding another finger in next to the first, feeling her flesh stretch to accommodate him.

"Everything," she said, her voice a whisper.

"Everything," he agreed. "I gave you a pass the first time, but just so you know, my demands haven't changed. If we're going to keep doing this, that's what I need from you."

He pressed deeper and she made a decidedly unintelligible remark, so he rubbed the pad of his thumb right over her most sensitive flesh. She shuddered in his arms, tried to press closer.

"Please," she begged.

"Uh-uh," he said, withdrawing his fingers. Her body arched into his, but he wasn't giving in. Not until he heard the word. "You know what I want from you." He bent down and sucked the tip of an already-wet nipple into his mouth.

"Liam." Her voice was a breathless plea, and before he realized what she was doing, her hand snaked down to touch herself.

"No you don't," he said, grabbing her hand before clever fingers found their mark. She groaned in frustration, but he only laughed and pinned both hands above her head. Her mouth was swollen, her eyes were closed, and she was breathing heavily, her chest rising and falling with each breath. She was his all right. He just needed to hear her say it.

With one finger, he dredged some of her wetness up and over her clit, stoking the fires even higher, delighting in the way she twisted in his arms. "C'mon, Mandy," he said. "Everything." He thrust one finger deep, enjoying her gasp. "Everything." In went another finger. She gasped again. "Everything." Lightly, ever so lightly, he touched her clit, knowing full well it wasn't enough stimulation to make her come apart in his arms.

"Everything," she finally panted. "Everything, okay? I'll give you everything."

He kissed her then, deep and long, and let her go, pressing just enough with his thumb to tip her over the edge. She drew in a sharp breath before her entire body stiffened in his arms.

He held her when she went boneless. Carried her upstairs where he made love to her again with his mouth and with his body.

And when they were both completely spent, lying in bed as the reverberations waned, the rain finally stopped falling.

CHAPTER 10

It was the last day of the year, and if Mandy were back in Silicon Valley, she knew what she'd be doing—working in her laboratory until she was too tired to work anymore, then calling it a night.

Instead, she was strolling down a lovely little side street in downtown Napa, having just emerged from three heavenly hours of soaking, massage, and primping at a day spa. It was lunchtime, but she was barely hungry. Instead, she just felt sated and more than a little bit sleepy.

"What did you think?" Mandy asked Ann once they were beyond hearing distance of the spa's entrance.

"Good," Ann said, sounding as blissed-out as she felt. "It will definitely fit the bill for the bachelorette weekend." Then she sighed. "The whole purpose of this trip was to do stuff like this. I can't believe we've been here for days and this is the first wedding-related thing we've done together."

"You've been busy," Mandy murmured.

"And so have you," Ann said. "I'm not blind, Mandy. I can tell you really like Liam." Conflict colored her face. "I like him for you, too, but I know how he feels about commitment. Are you sure you're ready to jump back into the game with something so serious?"

"I don't know," Mandy said, honestly. But what she did know was that for him, she was willing to try.

Ann bit her lip. "I just don't want anyone to get hurt." Annie was strong, but she'd always been sensitive.

"You, of all people, should know that it's not possible to predict."

"You're right," Ann said, nodding briskly. "It's just that I'm, well, a little protective of you," she confessed.

Mandy stopped. "You're protective of me? Don't you mean that I'm protective of you?"

"It may have started out that way in college—you, the worldly California girl, me the naive Vermonter. And I could certainly see how you'd feel that way, you know, after John died." Ann paused. "But things have changed. I'm happy. And I want you to be happy, too."

"I'm working on it," Mandy told her. "Seriously."

"That's good, Mandy," Ann said, her tone softening. "And I'm here to help you, just like you helped me. Though I'm beginning to see that you're doing just fine helping yourself."

Right then, Mandy realized why she liked Ann Smith so darn much. Annie was just like Nicole—generous, sweet, but underneath everything, as tough as nails. She'd surrounded herself with women who would bend over backward to help, to care, to support. No surprise, given that she *was* that woman, for so many of her friends, colleagues, and family.

They stood like that for a moment, smiling at each other.

"Am I interrupting anything?" a calm, feminine voice said. It was Stella, who walked right up to them.

"Hi," Ann said, giving Stella a little hug. Stella accepted it, albeit rather stiffly. "I can't believe I haven't seen you this trip yet."

"I've been really busy with the party planning," Stella said.

"Is that what you're doing in town?" Mandy asked.

"Yes. I'm just picking up some last-minute supplies for the event. Turns out the votives we got aren't enough to cover the outside tables, and it's too late to order them online, so I'm forced to go analog. The candle shop's right there." She pointed down the street. "What are you two up to? Out dress shopping?"

Ann looked intrigued. "Should we be?"

"Well, I just figured if you're coming to the New Year's Eve party, you'd want something new. Lots of folks dress up."

"Oh, they do, do they?" Ann said, looking meaningfully at Mandy. "It just so happens I brought a dress, but I have a friend who didn't know she was going until recently."

Stella gave them a sly smile. "Try Cake Plate down the road. There's a killer dress in the window I think would look great on your *friend*."

"Thanks," Ann said.

"See ya." Stella continued down the road.

Mandy blinked. "I think I just stepped into an alternate universe where my friends conspire to dress me."

"Just go with it," Ann said, grabbing her arm. "Come on." She began to walk, tugging Mandy along with her. "If you're serious about Liam Flynn, then I'm serious about helping you not embarrass yourself tonight," Ann said firmly. "The only thing you brought was jeans, right?"

Mandy nodded in affirmation.

"Okay, then," Ann said. "We're going to get some lunch. And then we're going to get you a dress."

Later in the day, with what seemed like hours of time rolling out before her like the fog over the countryside, Mandy stood next to Liam at Flynn Winery's experimental vineyard. The plot of land ran a quarter acre up and down the rolling hills of Napa Valley, and the aroma of wet, loamy earth wafted up, lush and nutrient-rich. Some of the best grapes in the world were grown here, and with every step through the soil, Mandy felt the weight of its importance.

Each row of twisted dark brown vines was meticulously staked and labeled, though some of the annotations written on the signposts seemed like code.

"Chardonnay Graft A Var. 2?" she asked.

"It's a way for us to keep track of what we grow where," Liam explained. "Most of our vines are grafted onto existing root stock, and sometimes we try a couple of different grafts to ensure we get the hardiest plant with the best fruit." They walked down to another row. "See this vine? This one was a gamble, but I took a taste this year. Outstanding. So this vine will be reproduced and planted in our regular vineyard. It's going to make a great wine." He smiled at her. "I wish you'd come before harvest so you could taste the grapes."

"I love listening to you talk about the vineyard. You're so passionate about it."

Liam looked out over the hills. "When I first got here, I wasn't passionate at all, actually."

"Really?"

"Yeah, I mean, I was burned out at work for sure, but I still wanted to code. I never thought I'd go into the family business. That's why I went to school for computer science, not viticulture. I came to Flynn Winery to help out my dad, period. I was just going to stay for a year or two, until he got back to full speed. Then mom died, and, well, I stayed."

"That speaks to your loyalty, but it doesn't speak to your skill. You're really *good* at this."

"I'd be better if I had some data to back me up. " He gave her a small smile. "Anyway, I'm sure by now you've guessed I don't do things half assed. Once I'm in, I'm in. Over the years, it's grown on me more than I ever thought it would. I love my family—it's why I came. But the love of the business is why I stayed. People write code because they want to create, not market. Most programmers aren't very good at the latter, but I don't mind. I like talking to people, love getting them to taste our wines, be part of our family, at least for a little while. Living up here lets me do that. And living in Napa is a pretty big perk of the job."

"Do you miss the city?"

"Eh, not really," Liam said with a shrug. "I mean, I miss the excitement of it. The energy and the rush you get just by walking through the Mission or taking in a Giants game. But I don't miss the entitled attitude a lot of my colleagues had. There was this one guy at my company, fresh out of college, thought he was the ultimate coder. One day, he said—I swear I'm not making this up—'This company's going to have a bigger impact on tech culture and style than Apple.' I just nodded, because people were always saying stuff like that. It was good for me to step away. Living like this," he said, sweeping his hand out as if to encompass the whole valley, "it'd be hard to go back."

"But you miss the work."

He looked out over the landscape and she followed his gaze. Atop a nearby mountain, a lone stag foraged for greenery, its antlered head alternately lifting high to keep aware of its surroundings and dipping into the brush for food.

"Yeah. I miss the work," Liam said. "Told you I did. There really is nothing like writing code, having it sing, controlling the process, knowing what you write will actually *do* something. So I have the itch. I won't deny it. Decent viticulture software already exists for wineries. It's interesting, but I want to take it a step further. Big data fascinates me. See that?" He pointed to a strange-looking instrument at the bottom of one of the vines. "And that?" Another was clipped onto one of the leaves.

"Those are sensors. They collect data and they're everywhere around the vineyard, measuring everything—the moisture, the soil, the plant respiration, the Brix measurement—that's a measurement of sugar, by the way. Each plot, each row, each *vine* in each row, is grown under different conditions. This captures it all. Now imagine the sensors wirelessly uploading to a master program that aggregates all that data. We'd have all the measurements at our fingertips—and not just from this year, but from every single previous year. Given specific weather conditions, along with historical data about earlier outcomes, we could best predict when to harvest and crush. Data is power. Maybe other wineries around here could use the same software. Combine their data with ours. The compilation of that data would be immense, and could help everyone make better wine."

It was the look on Liam's face—that hopefulness. That dream. She saw it so clearly now—his desire to innovate chafing against the constraint of his dad's old-style farming ways. "There's a way you can have everything you want," she said slowly. "But you have to work for it."

"So I've heard," he said wryly.

She shook her head. "I'm not going to lecture you again. All I'm saying is that coming into this week, I made a New Year's resolution. Maybe you'd benefit from having one of your own."

"You have enough of your own crap to worry about, and here you are, worrying about mine. Do you do this for everyone?"

She swallowed hard. "Just for people I think are…special."

He was quiet for a long time. When he spoke, his voice was soft. "You really are giving me everything, aren't you?"

She'd revealed too much, hadn't she? It was too soon to show him this. "It's a character flaw," she said, trying to sound flip.

Liam shook his head, refusing to let her back off. "It's one of your greatest strengths." Abruptly, he clasped her hand in his. "I don't just want you for tonight. Stay the weekend. We can explore, ride, talk."

"Yes. Okay." She squeezed his hand, loving the way his roughness felt against her skin. She was in deep now, and she found, for once, that the guilt didn't come. She wanted to find out where this would go, if there was a future for them together.

There would be time for her research when she got back to Silicon Valley. The cell phone call *had* been from her lab—another crisis that really wasn't a crisis at all. Granted, this was the first time she'd ever been away from work for more than a day, but her grad students really needed to step up and get some autonomy. The lab wasn't going to shut down because she wasn't there to make everything run smoothly, nor could they rely on her to manage their minute-to-minute existence. Distance had made her realize the pressure she'd put on herself to have everything be perfect, to control for every situation. It had begun with guilt, sure, but it had morphed into something bigger, more desperate. There was no room inside for a real human being to live and thrive.

Some changes were definitely in order, just as soon as she returned, but for now, she was content to be present in the moment.

Liam's hand was in hers, solid and warm. It gave her strength. For once, she was in the right place at the right time. Tonight, she'd end the old year, and tomorrow she'd start the new one ready to make an affirmative change with passionate, full-of-life Liam Flynn by her side.

CHAPTER 11

On New Year's Eve, Mandy was ready to go when Liam knocked on her door a little after eight p.m. She opened the door and drank him in. For once, his hair wasn't messy, and he was wearing different clothes—a collared shirt a little open at the throat, a blazer, and a pair of slacks. Not too fancy, but just right for Napa. She liked this cleaned-up Liam, and by the expression on his face, he felt the same way about her.

"Amanda, is that—you?" Liam simply stared at her as if he were seeing her anew.

Mandy nodded and smiled. Her hair floated free in soft waves, and she'd actually put on makeup, something she didn't typically do. She had on a pair of high, strappy sandals, and the dress Stella had suggested. It was black, stretchy, and *just* this side of tight.

"Stella told me about it, and Annie talked me into it," she said by way of explanation.

Slowly, Liam dragged the back of his hand across his mouth. "Remind me to thank them later."

Mandy threw a wrap over her shoulders. "They'll be at the party, right?" Mandy said, stepping outside and shutting the door firmly behind her.

Liam hesitated. "Are you sure you don't need to, ah, get anything else from your room?"

. "Oh, I see what you're doing," she said, for once pleased instead of annoyed that she had this kind of effect on a guy. "No, we are not going back inside. You talked me into this New Year's Eve party. I even bought a new dress. We are going, and that is that. You hear me?"

"Right," Liam said, sounding distant. "Right." In a moment he was back to his usual suave self. He held out his arm for her. She took it, grateful to have something to hang on to while they walked down the cobblestone path to the street.

"Oh, good," she said, when she saw his truck at the curb.

"You thought I'd bring my motorcycle out on a night like this?"

"As much as I like riding it, I'm glad you didn't."

"I'm glad I didn't too," he said, helping her into the truck. "Because then I wouldn't be able to do things like this." He leaned in, pushed her back against the seat, and captured her mouth with his. She went willingly down the rabbit hole, thinking only about how good his hands felt on her, how much better it would be if they could get horizontal. He seemed to have the same idea, slipping his fingers inside the top of her dress. And then she got her head together.

"Liam," she said, her voice a warning.

He nibbled on her neck, just enough to make her shiver with pleasure. "You are so freaking gorgeous, if I don't get you up to the winery soon, we're not going to make it at all."

Laughing, she shoved him squarely in the chest and once he was clear of the door, slammed it shut. Looking seriously disappointed, he went around to the driver's side and got in. But he didn't put his seatbelt on right away. Instead, he turned to her.

She shut him down with a smile. "Drive," she ordered.

Sighing, he clicked his seatbelt into place and dutifully started the engine.

It didn't take long for them to get to the winery. They drove past the valets in front, and went around to the staff parking lot. It was fun to slip in the back door. She felt like an insider and told him so.

"You *are* an insider," he responded. "You're with me."

It was ridiculous for her to thrill at that remark—she wasn't his; she wasn't anybody's—but she did anyway. And for the first time in a long time, the thought of belonging to someone didn't elicit a panoply of negative emotions. In fact, it seemed pretty nice.

They stepped into the main party room where all of the tables were set up for dinner, and found Stella bustling around, making last-minute adjustments to the centerpieces. Stella nodded at her dress approvingly.

"Good choice," she said.

"Thank you for helping me," Mandy said. "You look amazing, too." Stella's dark hair was swept back from her face, revealing her perfect skin. And she practically rocked a fire-engine red cocktail dress, which showed off her slim figure to perfection. Mandy wondered where Stella's ex was, but the quiet woman simply smiled.

"Thank you," she said. "Let's just say my advice to you inspired my own choice of attire."

A large hand curled possessively around her upper arm, Liam's large presence minimizing everyone else's. "Hey Stell," Liam said. "I owe you one."

"You can pay up later."

"Count on it," he said to Stella, who turned and disappeared into the back room.

Liam walked her out of the dining area into the tasting room. The place was jam-packed, with close to eighty people milling around the tasting bar, lounging in the available seating, and doing what they'd come to do—drinking wine. Despite the chilly evening, there were even some folks hanging out on the deck. Liam's dad was holding court behind the tasting bar, laughing and joking and of course, pouring. This was Napa, so none of the men wore suits, but many had on jackets. The women's dresses ran the spectrum from cocktail to casual.

"The place looks beautiful, Liam," Mandy said. And it did. All the work Stella had put into the party showed, from the still-fresh holly draped around the room to the soft lighting of the votive candles to the neon sign flashing over the tasting bar that said *Flynn*.

"You helped," he said.

"Not much," she replied. "Stella deserves all the credit. Where'd you get the Flynn neon?"

"Dad had it custom made a few years ago as a joke. I'm sure Stella was thrilled she could repurpose it for the party."

"This whole thing is amazing. Laid-back, but amazing."

"We try to keep it real," he said with a smile. "Anyway, I think we're about to sit down for dinner. Ready?"

"Yes. And Liam," she said, taking his arm before he could start walking, "thank you for inviting me."

His eyes warmed. "I honestly couldn't imagine it without you."

After wending their way through the crowd, where Liam introduced her to what seemed like everyone at the party, they finally sat down to dinner. She was right next to Ann, who was dressed in a long, flowing gown, which made her look even more fragile and ethereal than usual. Chase, on Ann's other side, kept his arm around her possessively, and Ann just looked incredibly happy to be there.

The food was amazing—several types of winter salads, roasted chicken, grilled steak, and thinly sliced potatoes in a rich gratin, along with a huge platter of vegetables. For dessert, there was a giant buffet of cakes, trifle, cookies, and chocolates.

After dinner, there was dancing. Liam was surprisingly light on his feet for such a big man, and he whirled her expertly around the floor. She thought she'd be nervous, being so near him in public—this was still so new, and it seemed like a declaration of intent the way his hand splayed across her back, drawing her close—but she had to admit she rather liked his possessiveness. *Mine*, his body said. And she responded in kind, leaning into him, laying her head on his shoulder.

He just smiled and pulled her closer.

Five minutes before midnight, she called her parents to wish them a happy new year. She only got in a few breathless *I love yous* before she hung up and the countdown began.

Ten, nine, eight...

Liam squeezed her hand in his.

Seven, six, five...

He pulled her close, eyes glued to the clock.

Four, three, two, one.

The clock struck midnight, and amid all the screaming and cheering and toasting, Liam took her face in his hands.

"Happy New Year, Amanda," he said.

Then he kissed her and the crowd melted away. Like something out of an old-fashioned movie, the band played Auld Lang Syne as they swayed together, wrapped in each other's arms.

This was how her new year was beginning. Not in her lab or running tests or stressing about experiments, but here, being held by Liam Flynn.

"Want to see the caves?" he whispered in her ear when the dance was over. "They're open to the public tonight."

She nodded. "Sure." It'd be fun to see them with him.

Smiling, Liam took her hand and together, they slipped out of the party rooms to the empty hallway.

"We can come and go as we like," Liam said. "At some point, most folks will end up in the caves, sampling our prized reserve wines until my dad shuts everything down at two a.m. But it looks like we're alone, now."

The large wooden doors to the caves were unlocked, and Liam easily pulled one open and flicked on the lights. They stepped inside.

The caves were cavernous and chill, with cool concrete floors and brick walls that soaked up the heat. And at night, they were positively sepulchral. The lamps lighting the passageways cast eerie shadows on the walls, and the musky smells of fermenting grapes, old wine, and oak barrels wafted through the damp air. Keeping her hand in his, he led her through the passages, deeper and deeper into the side of the hill.

Finally he stopped and turned. "We're in the deepest part of the caves. This is where we keep our most valuable reserves. What do you think?"

"I think this is a little creepy," she admitted.

"Oh?" he said, sliding the fingers from his free hand up her arm. "Do you have goose bumps?"

Her skin tingled, and she shivered involuntarily. "Now I do. And I'm a little cold. Perhaps you can warm me up."

He turned to her, his eyes gleaming, his smile dangerous. "Yeah," he said, pulling her close. "I could do that."

And then he kissed her so deeply she felt her knees go out from under her. What was it about this one man that did this to her every time? She couldn't get enough, so she wrapped her arms around his neck and held on tightly.

He pushed her back against the brick wall. "It's kind of crazy, isn't it?" he said, kissing her neck, then her mouth, refusing to let her catch a decent breath. "Knowing how badly I wanted you from the moment I first saw you in that dress tonight. I wanted to drag you back into your room and make love with you all night. We would never have made it to the party and everyone would have known why." At that, her nipples went even harder and he responded by sealing his mouth to hers.

"Liam—" she gasped.

"I've been waiting for hours," he said, slipping his hand up her dress to wrap around her thigh. "Wanting to get you alone so I could do this." He kissed her, a deep, open-mouthed kiss that took away whatever remaining breath she had. "And this." His free hand slid up her waist to cup and squeeze her breast. "And this." The clever hand on her thigh had found its way to the edge of her panties.

Without waiting, he hooked his finger in the waistband and yanked until they slid down her legs. In an instant, one hand was busy between her thighs, pressing and stroking, dipping and sliding through her wetness. His mouth was on her neck, hitting just the right spot under her ear that always made her crazy.

"Oh!" she cried out, as he curled his finger *just so.*

Immediately, he covered her mouth with his other hand.

"Shh," he whispered into her ear. "We don't want anyone to hear and come looking for us, do we? Or maybe..." He slid another finger inside, stretching her deliciously, preparing her for him. "Maybe that's exactly what you want. Ah," he said, cupping her breast once more, plumping the flesh in his hand. Her nipples were so hard they could cut diamonds. "This makes you hot, doesn't it? Knowing that someone could come into the caves any minute, and find us here, just like this."

"Yes," she admitted. She was dizzy with desire, shaking with need. The best adrenaline rush she'd ever had.

He shoved her dress up to her waist, completely exposing her for anyone to see. Slowly, he slid his fingers out, then just as slowly slid them back in again. Her knees buckled and he held her up.

"You're so wet," he whispered, and his words only added fuel to the fire. "You want to do this right here, right now."

She licked her lips, imagining him taking her here, right up against the wall. The illicit thrill of being caught in this most intimate act overrode any kind of common sense.

"Yes," she whispered back. "*Please*, Liam."

"Show me."

She reached for him, fingers fumbling with his fly until finally, *finally*, she got it undone. She couldn't resist stroking him, just a little, until he groaned, his own need echoing hers. "Come on," she urged, pulling him closer.

"Wait," he said, a condom materializing out of nowhere. He slid it on fast, grabbed her thigh to wrap around his waist, and in one long, smooth thrust, was buried inside her. He swallowed her gasp in his mouth and began to move.

With her back jammed against the wall and Liam surging forward, the friction was intense. He was deep, so deep, but apparently that wasn't enough because he grabbed her ass and lifted her high against the wall, forcing her to wrap her other leg around his waist. And the excitement of being handled so roughly was outweighed by overwhelming pleasure so acute it almost verged on pain.

She was full of him—his tongue in her mouth, his cock buried as far as it could go—completely consumed in the moment. She didn't care if someone *did* come in. She needed this—needed him—now. Something welled within her. It started as a tickle, then turned dark in a hurry. He was grinding against her now, the sexiest thing she'd ever experienced, but the pressure was too much. She wasn't going to be able to come.

"Liam—" she said, her voice a plea.

"I have you, honey," he said, slipping a hand between their bodies to stroke her most sensitive flesh. A few seconds was all it took for her to see flashes, bright white behind her closed eyes.

Liam caught her scream in his mouth before pounding his hips hard. And then he came with a groan, thrusting one final time and shuddering against her.

She was still coming down from her high when he brushed his lips against hers.

"You okay?" he asked. Always his first question afterward.

"Yes," she said. Always her answer, the way it should be.

He nodded, probably the only thing he had the strength left to do. "Gonna put you down now."

"All right."

Carefully, he lifted her up a fraction, then slid out from underneath. In silence, they helped each other straighten their clothes. There wasn't anything to say. Now that she'd experienced the most primal act with this devastating man, all else would be tame.

He took her hand and led her from the caves, depositing her outside the women's bathroom.

She went in to survey the extent of the damage, and what she saw shocked her. Her eyes were bright, her cheeks and lips rosy. She looked brilliant and well-loved.

Alive.

Except this time, there was no shame. No guilt. No regrets. All thanks to a few short days in Napa with Liam Flynn.

After the accident, she'd simply shut down parts of herself. Happiness. Joy. Even capacity for risk. Yet life itself was risky. Bad things could and did happen at any time.

Good things, too, if you let them.

Without warning, tears swelled in the corners of her eyes. She was doing exactly what she set out to do, but in a way she could never have anticipated. This wasn't reasoned or ordered, but it was real and true, and she wanted to extend this for as long as she could.

She blinked away the wetness, not because she was ashamed of crying, but because she didn't want to miss another minute of this evening. There would be time to think about this week, and all its ramifications, later. When she emerged, composed and smiling, he was waiting.

"Happy New Year," he said, and kissed her. It felt so good she thought she might cry again.

"You know," she said, mostly to make him laugh so that she would, too, "I don't know how we even did that without you sliding."

He lifted his shoe to show her its bottom. "Rubber soles. The only thing to wear in the caves. Lots of traction."

"Get another pair."

He laughed, then speared his hand through her hair and simply claimed her mouth. She went willingly, melting into him, ignoring the bustle around them. Tonight, Amanda Aligheri wasn't a postdoc grind. She was just a woman out on New Year's Eve, fulfilling her resolution to make this year different.

"Take me home, Liam," she said.

"With pleasure."

He brought her back to his place, wordlessly stripped her, and curled up with her in bed.

She lay there long after he'd gone to sleep, eyes open in the dim light. Everything was different now. Yes, she'd have to head back to Silicon Valley when the weekend was over, but she had a new purpose, a new intent to properly live. *He'd* done this for her—brought color and light to her world. She was looking for it, that was certain, but he'd found her, recognized that, and showed her the best of life. The best of *him*.

"Thank you," she whispered to the back of his head.

Liam gave a grunt, then flipped over and wrapped a long arm around her waist.

It was a new year.

It was a new life.

CHAPTER 12

The long weekend lay before them like a shimmering promise. A final push to cement her New Year's resolutions. She'd started out the post-Christmas week with the twin goals of relaxing and finding balance. Yet days later, that didn't seem enough. She was already working with passion, but now she wanted to live and to love with the same amount. Integrating that into her daily life was key.

Liam was a huge part of that change.

He was sitting next to her on one of the wood benches on the deck at Flynn Winery, looking out over the hillside, his rugged handsomeness played up by his thick sweater, worn jeans, and big boots. Roxy lay at his feet—Chase and Ann had dropped the dog off this morning at Liam's request—and while Mandy watched, he reached down and lazily scratched the Lab's head. Roxy opened her eyes, wagged her tail in pleasure, then settled back down easily.

When he was done with the dog, he shot her a quick smile, then reached out to rub the back of her neck, a generous and charged gesture.

"What do you want to do this weekend?" Liam asked her.

Mandy shrugged and leaned into his side, loving the way his arm felt when he wrapped it around her shoulders. "It doesn't matter." And it didn't. Just being with him was enough to fuel that latent need for a rush.

"We could relax here, that's for sure," Liam said. "But we could head to Tahoe to get some skiing in. I have a cabin there, and I'm sure Chase could hook you up with some gear at Alpine Meadows."

"That sounds great," Mandy replied. "By the way, you wouldn't happen to have a hot tub at your Tahoe place, would you?"

"I sure do," Liam said. "You interested in going for a dip?"

"Very. Preferably late-night." She paused. "Naked."

"Yeah?" Liam said, his lips curling. "That can be arranged." He bent down for what was sure to be a searing kiss, when a buzzing sound came from Mandy's pocket.

"My cell phone," she said. "I forgot I put it on vibrate."

"Just let it go," he murmured against her lips. "You're on vacation."

But she pulled away and checked the number anyway. "It's my lab." She sighed. "I've been ignoring them for days. I should probably take this if I'm staying here longer." She clicked the phone on. "Hello? Yes? Wait, just…just hold on." Something was very, very wrong. Farid's voice, usually deep and resonant, had gone up a full octave. She could barely understand his frantic rambling. "Slow down. The what did *what?*"

"The autoclave blew and shorted the power in our lab," Farid said.

"Okay, but didn't the backup power come on?"

"No. And before you ask, we tried flicking the emergency switch three times."

"The freezers?"

"Down. Everything's down."

"This doesn't make sense. The *building's* backup generator should come on if ours fails."

"It didn't."

"So what you're telling me is that our freezers and fridges are down and that there's no backup power in the entire building? Did you call building maintenance?" Mandy asked.

"We tried, but we couldn't reach them," Farid said, voice still panicked. "And we're in the middle of an experiment right now! We'll miss our twelve-hour time point if we don't have the hood operational."

"How many hours?"

"Two!"

Mandy didn't panic. Instead, she ran through every plausible possibility in her head.

Calling Tim Traynor, the head of their lab, would typically be her first choice, but he was currently on vacation in Bermuda—the very reason her grad students kept calling *her.* Worrying him when she hadn't gotten all the facts sorted would be a mistake, especially since there was nothing he could do beyond what she could do. After weighing a dozen other options in her mind, she slipped into authoritative mode.

"Our first priority is that twelve-hour time point. I'll call Dr. Brecht's lab. See if they can spare a hood and some equipment so we don't spoil our experiment. I'll also ask to see if they have any space in their freezers so our samples don't thaw. Dr. Ainsley and her crew are all out, but I think we have a key to their lab in the big desk in the main room. Grab it, and see if they have any freezer space. Then try again with maintenance."

"Okay, Mandy," Farid said, his voice still desperate. "Please tell me you're coming back. Gemima and I are freaking out."

"I'll be in," she affirmed. Then she hung up the phone. Quickly, she did the calculations in her head. For their experiment, they only had two hours. For the samples in deep freeze, longer—if no one opened the freezer doors. She should call Farid back. Tell him to minimize the number of times they open and shut those doors.

"I'm guessing that was bad news," Liam said. She blinked, realizing she'd been completely lost in thought.

"Yes. Very bad. I have to go."

"But our weekend together…"

"I can't stay. I'm so sorry." Abruptly, she stood, pulled her hair back, and began to twist it into a braid. Roxy picked up her head and gave a low whine. "Sorry, girl. I'm leaving."

"I'll come with you," Liam said.

"No, please, no," she said, pulling a hair tie from her pocket and slipping it onto the end of her braid. "It's a huge mess. It'll take me days to sort everything out."

She'd begun this year with such good intentions. Leave work at work. Balance her work and personal lives. Ridiculous platitudes that meant nothing. When an emergency arose, she chose work every time.

Liam stood, too. "Hey," he said, taking her by the arms. "Relax. You're in no shape to be driving like this."

She shook her head and pulled away. "I'm fine." She was in crisis mode now, and everything else was a distraction.

Roxy leaped up to block her way, getting underfoot when she tried to step around her. Finally, Liam grabbed Roxy by the collar to hold her back. Mandy braved a glance at his handsome face, then wished she hadn't when she saw the hurt in his eyes.

One stupid phone call and she'd shut him out. Locked herself away again. But she couldn't seem to stop.

There was no time to second-guess herself; Mandy turned and stalked back through the winery. Stella was talking to her dad, but Mandy ignored them. Just went to the parking lot and hopped into her car.

Before she knew it, she was sailing down I-80 toward San Francisco. The car felt empty without Roxy in the backseat, but she pushed the sadness aside, focused only on the game plan for when she got back to the university.

The lab was a complete wreck when she arrived. The power *still* wasn't back on, and with no maintenance folks in sight, Farid and Gemima were frantically running around like chickens with their heads cut off, doing their utmost to salvage the tissues and cell cultures by transferring them to the Brecht and Ainsley labs, whose backup power hadn't failed. But they were running out of time…and room.

Mandy called in favors from everyone she knew to get their samples in safe places, but inevitably some were destroyed in transit. It was grueling and stressful, with no time to think, only to act.

She did what she could. Without this research, she was nothing. This was her world.

Later, once most of the samples were squared away and the lab was cleaned up, and the power restored, she curled up on the couch in her laboratory to catch a few hours of sleep before starting the painstaking task of re-cataloging all of her samples. It would take days, and the sooner she started, the sooner she'd be finished.

It was only then that she had time to think about the way she'd torn out of Napa. She hadn't even said good-bye to Liam. Hadn't said anything, really, even after he'd been so open with her. After he'd given her everything.

And there, in the darkness, on her cold, hard couch, with the hum of the backup generator up and running, she finally allowed herself to cry.

CHAPTER 13

"Pull some chardonnay, Liam," Dan Flynn ordered. "We need five cases for that humane society charity auction in a few weeks."

Liam carefully pulled five cases out and stacked them on a waiting dolly. "We promised them ten. Maybe the zin?"

"Okay. Get some of last year's out, then."

Liam shook his head. "That's spoken for already. Remember, we promised fifteen cases to Angele? We're due to deliver next week, and at last count, we only had that many cases left."

His dad scratched his chin, same as he always did when he was thinking hard. "You don't say? We could pull the three-year-old zin, then."

"I've been tracking it. The few bottles available are going for three times list price on the open market."

"Hmm." More chin scratching. "We want to be generous, but we're already doing a lot." He thought for a moment. "What do you recommend?"

"The one from two years ago. It's fruity, but deep, and should be a good sell for them."

"Good," his dad said, nodding. "Pull that."

Liam did as Dan asked. When he was through, he picked up his clipboard. "I think that takes care of everything," Liam said, placing a checkmark next to the last item on his lengthy handwritten list. If it were up to him, it'd all be elegantly digitized.

And thinking of digitizing everything made him think about Mandy Aligheri and how she'd bailed on him two weeks ago to go back to her work in Silicon Valley. Since then they'd exchanged a few voice mail messages—fevered at first, then a little cooler.

It was as if she wasn't herself since she returned to Silicon Valley. Or maybe that *was* her true self, and in Napa she'd only been pretending to be someone else. That promise to keep her New Year's resolution had been a farce. She'd gone right back to doing what she always did.

So had he, and the fact that he wasn't pursuing his passion just rubbed him raw.

"You know, Dad," Liam said off-handedly, "this might be the perfect time to start on that software I've been talking about."

But his dad was off shuffling behind a couple of big crates. "What's that, Liam?"

"The software," Liam said, trying to keep his voice even. "If we had everything digitized, all our data in one place, we could spend less time doing guesswork and more time making great wine."

Dan pretended like he didn't hear. "I'll have to figure out how to spend the rest of this month. Maybe you and I can work out our spring planting schedule a little early?"

"Maybe," Liam said, sliding the pages into a manila envelope. "Or maybe I can work on that model."

He was in the zone now, unwilling to let it go. Coding was in his brain. So what that Mandy couldn't get her act together? She'd inspired him all the same, given him the kick in the pants he needed to get going.

At first he'd been stunned, and then angry at what he'd seen as her betrayal, so much so that he hadn't even gotten started on his own project. But it hadn't been a betrayal at all. She'd been pulled back to her lab through circumstances outside of her control, but working on that regression model was completely within his. It wasn't enough to simply make a resolution to change. He had to actually *do* it.

"Not that again, Liam," Dan said, shaking his head. "I've got enough on my mind without worrying about that kind of thing. Let's just get through the spring and then we'll talk."

"And then it'll be summer and then fall, and another harvest will have passed," Liam argued. "The winery's closed, we're done taking inventory and dealing with back orders. Our work here is minimal. It'd be easy for me to cut out for a couple of weeks and do some coding."

"Coding," Dan snorted. "What you really mean is dreaming up some crazy software program that'll crash all our computers when we install it."

"It's not like that, Dad. It'd be compatible with our current systems. I plan to make an integrated app so we can access everything from our cell phones when we're out in the fields or in the caves. It'd take a while to learn, sure, but once we did, everything would be at our fingertips. The analytics alone would be worth the time. Historical data, including rainfall, soil, Brix measurements, acidity, balance, all in one place. Think of harnessing all that power."

"I need you focused, Liam. This is a big year for us. I need everyone present and accounted for, not off in the clouds, got it?" Dan clasped a hand on Liam's shoulder. He was a tall man, but he still had to reach up to do it. "You'll get back to it someday. Just not now, when we need you the most." He turned away and picked up his clipboard. "I have to go talk with your sister now. Make sure she doesn't have anything else on her mind for me to do."

Liam wouldn't be dismissed. Not this time. He took a deep breath and drew himself up to his full height. "I don't think you're getting what I'm saying, Dad. I'm telling you I'm going to start writing the code this month, not later. Now. And I'm going to finish it no matter how long it takes."

His dad blinked, but held his ground. "We've talked about this," he said.

"No, I've talked, and you've dismissed it out of hand. What I just realized—what I should have realized a long time ago—is that I need to do this, whether you're on board or not."

He'd been so hung up on disappointing his father, in worrying about the strain and the stress it might put on him, but in the meantime, he'd simply disappointed himself.

"Liam!" His father sounded shocked.

"The winery has one foot in the past. I get that. Tradition is important. But it's time for us—for me—to look toward the future." Liam crossed the room so that he was standing right in front of Dan Flynn. Funny, his dad looked a little smaller today, but the emotion he felt was still huge. "I love numbers. I love data. I love analyzing that data to predict future results. And I love you, too, Dad. Can't you see that getting everything into a model like this would help preserve our vineyard's history in a modern, innovative way? We can use these predictive methods in conjunction with your intuition and institutional knowledge to create even better wine. Wine that could achieve cult status. We're almost there, but we won't get there without an edge."

His dad just stood there, looking confused.

"I'm sorry you don't understand what I want to do," Liam said, shaking his head, "but I'm doing it anyway. It's going to work exactly the way I want it to, and it's going to be unbelievably awesome. You'll see."

"I need—"

"No, Dad." He said it firmly, but gently. "*I* need. I love the winery, I really do. But there's a part of me that's missing, that has been missing since I left San Francisco. I'm not asking your permission anymore. If you can't be happy for me, I'm going to leave."

"Where would you go?" All of the wind had gone out of his typically blustery dad's sails. He sounded bewildered. Even a little lost.

"Back to the city," Liam said, realizing the truth to his words even as they left his mouth. "I have a lot of friends who'd let me crash with them while I get this thing off the ground. If you don't want my model, I'll figure out a way to monetize it for the rest of the industry."

"What would your mother say?"

"Honestly? Probably 'go for it.'" Just like Mandy would do for him. "But it doesn't matter what she would say, because I need to live for me, and here's how it's going to happen. I'm going to take the rest of the month off. I'm due up for a vacation anyway. I'm going to spend that time writing the code I need to get this model going. It's going to take a while. No way am I going to get even a fraction of it done in the time I have, but I'll make a dent. Then I'm coming back. And when I come back, I'm going to work with you *and* write code on the side to get this winery into the twenty-first century." He looked his dad straight in the eyes. "I just need to know one thing: when I do come back, will I still have a job at Flynn Winery?"

He'd thrown all his cards on the table. Now his dad knew where he stood and how strong his convictions were. It didn't have to be the software or the winery, and he prayed his dad wouldn't make him choose.

Dan swallowed, his Adam's apple bobbing just like a boy's. "I just want what's best for you. That's all I've ever wanted. The truth is, since your mother died, I needed you here. You're the heart and soul of this place. Not only do you have the palate to make great wine, but you just have a way with people." He shook his head. "I never thought you belonged in software. I thought it was providence when you left your job to come home. But I guess I was wrong. I would never want you to stifle who you are." His dad paused, and Liam realized he was crying. "This winery is yours, Liam. Yours and Stella's. You always have a job here. And Lord willing, when I pass, you'll be the senior Flynn in Flynn Winery."

Liam stepped forward and embraced his dad, hugging him tight. "You won't be sorry, Dad. I promise. I love you." He kissed his stunned father on the forehead, and without another word, turned and left.

He went back to his place, threw a week's worth of clothes in a duffel bag, and grabbed his laptop. He was in the back parking lot, about to hop on his bike, when he ran into Stella.

"Where are you off to?" she asked, eyeing his big bag.

"A vacation that's long overdue."

"I see you're taking your laptop." Those sharp eyes didn't miss a thing.

He wrapped his arm around his sister's neck, bringing her close for a hug. "You're amazing, Stella. Don't let anyone ever tell you otherwise."

"Just come back with something we can use," Stella said. "I want this to be the last year we do everything by intuition alone. I know we need more sensors. You tell me what kinds to order and I'll have everything in place for when you get back into town."

"You rock, little sister." He gave her one final squeeze and stepped away to throw his leg over his bike. "If anyone asks, tell them I'll be back in a couple of weeks."

He started the engine, his Harley's motor the sweetest sound he'd heard in a good long while. It sounded like freedom, like passion. And like a beautiful scientist he realized he couldn't live without.

His heart light, he turned the bike to ride down the winding road away from Flynn Winery.

"Hi, Mandy!" Nicole's happy voice chirped through the telephone. "Thought I'd call before the weekend. Did I catch you at a good time?"

Mandy shifted her cell phone to her other ear, then flicked off the light on her microscope. "Hi, Nikki," she said. "Just finishing up at the lab."

"It's only seven o'clock," Nicole said. "Must be some kind of record for you to get out that early."

"Yes, well, this is the first time in two weeks I'm even coming close."

Nicole paused, then cleared her throat. "I have some news."

"What's that?" Mandy asked, even though she already thought she knew.

"Harry proposed last night."

"Oh, wow, Nikki, that's super!" she said. Nicole deserved this. She was beautiful inside and out, and it was Harry's good fortune that he recognized how amazing her sister was.

"We haven't set a date yet," her sister said, "but we'll need to sit down with a calendar because I want you to be my maid of honor."

"Yes, of course. There's nowhere else I'd rather be than by your side."

"I'm so glad, Mandy. I have more to talk to you about, and I…I don't really know how to say this, so I'm just going to come out and say it. Over Christmas, you didn't seem like yourself."

"Really?" Mandy blinked. "How did I seem?"

"I don't know," Nicole said, sounding thoughtful. "Like your brain was someplace else, maybe? Like a part of you was…missing."

Nikki was right. Something *was* missing, and it had taken seeing Liam Flynn again to show her what she needed all along—someone to balance out her stress and guilt and discipline and purpose. Someone to love.

"I get it," Mandy said. "And I'm trying to make some changes." Or *was*. "Unfortunately, I haven't been that successful."

"What kind of changes?" Nicole sounded intrigued.

"I'm still totally into the research, but I think I need some more time for myself. Nothing drastic. Just, maybe not working nights and weekends for a while." Except since she'd been back, that hadn't happened. But moving forward, something had to give. She only hoped that something wasn't her.

"That's great, Mandy. I think that a change is long overdue. You need to take care of yourself, not just because I want a healthy, happy maid of honor at my wedding, but because I love you." A beat went by. Then two. "Mandy? You still there?"

"Still here," she sighed, suddenly feeling more exhausted than ever.

"It wasn't anyone's fault," Nicole whispered, and Mandy stiffened. "You know that, right, Mandy? It was an accident. A freak accident. I don't blame you. I never did."

How many times had she dismissed Nikki's words out of hand? Had simply ignored the reality because what she felt inside was so much more powerful? Her sister didn't blame her—had *never* blamed her—so why was she blaming herself?

Let it go, Mandy. Just let. It. Go.

"I know," she finally said. And she would keep telling it to herself until she fully believed it. She had to.

"You okay?" Nicole said, her voice gentle.

"Just a little tired."

"Go home and get some sleep. We can talk more next week."

"I'm so happy for you, Nikki. I love you."

"Love you, too."

Mandy clicked off her phone and placed it face-up on the lab bench, brain numb.

Nicole was worried about her. She could hear it in her sister's voice.

I'm trying to change, I swear. But she'd been going about the change all wrong. She'd begun her Napa week with the best of intentions. Get relaxed. Carve out a bit more time for herself. Lose the guilt. She was on a path to do that, but before her plan came to fruition, she'd been dragged back to Silicon Valley. She knew that life had to be integrated into work, and work into life, until she could experience both fully, but she hadn't reckoned on how to make that happen.

She missed Liam. She even missed Roxy. And without anyone to head home to at night, it just didn't seem worth it to leave the lab early. So instead of balancing her life, she found herself right back where she started: locked away in her laboratory.

Until today—Friday—when she realized she'd lost a whole week working without even coming up for air. So much for her New Year's resolution.

And so much for changing who she was. Or who she *thought* she was.

That's why Liam Flynn was so wonderful. With him, she was her truest version of herself—the fun-loving-yet-serious woman who could just as easily hop on the back of his Harley as she could enter into a detailed discussion about graft technology. The woman who looked forward, not back. It wasn't enough to just spend weekends getting herself together; she needed to do it daily, and she knew that with Liam, she could make that happen.

Without thinking, she snatched the phone back up and dialed a now-familiar number. She waited for the phone to ring, fully expecting voice mail to pick up.

Except it didn't.

"Mandy?" Liam's voice rang out loud and clear. "Where are you?"

"My lab. Where are you?"

"Your lab."

It took a moment for her to process that. "I'm sorry, what?"

"I'm downstairs. The door to the building is locked."

"You're here? Right now?"

"That's what I'm saying."

"I'll come down."

Not bothering to pull on her jacket, she tore down the two flights of stairs to the bottom floor and burst through the front door. Liam was standing there, hands tucked into his leather jacket. He stopped, stared at her.

"Mandy—your hair."

Automatically, she reached up, and realized what was different. She couldn't break free from her lab, but in a desperate bid to do something—anything—to act on her resolution, she'd taken to controlling the one thing she could.

Today, it was up in a twist, elegant and unfussy.

"Liam," she said. "I'm so sorry."

"Don't apologize, please," he said, cutting her off. "I'm the one who should be sorry, not you."

"What? Why?"

He shook his head. "I was so hung up on the fact that you just cut out of Napa before we even got a chance to talk. I thought we'd have more time to settle things."

"Settle things?"

"I want to be with you, Amanda," he said. "I want to see where this could go. Where *we* could go. I wanted that two years ago, I…" He stopped and shook his head. "I'm such an idiot. I thought that by letting you go, I was doing you a favor. You chose work over me. It took me until today to realize that this time, it was different." He searched her eyes, looking for something. "It *was* different this time, wasn't it?"

She nodded and he nodded, too.

"It's not a contest," he continued. "There's room for both, except I actually have to be in the picture. Sometimes there are emergencies and you can't break away from work."

"Yes," she whispered. "I couldn't break away. But I should have figured out a way to talk to you about it. I *am* sorry. You deserve to hear that. And you deserve more than this."

"*This* is exactly what I deserve." He stepped forward and ran a hand through his hair. "You don't even know what you did, do you?"

She shook her head. What had she done except leave without saying good-bye?

"You've been working yourself so hard, haven't you?" he said, his voice soft. "It's written all over your face. Anyone with even a fraction of your passion could move mountains. And then I realized, *why not me?*"

He reached out and took her hand. Squeezed it tightly in his.

"You brought out the best in me, pushed me to face what I truly wanted, encouraged me to move past my present and look toward the future. My future, and the future of Flynn Winery, is in that software, I just know it. I don't want to spend the rest of my life wondering *what if?* I want to spend it wondering *what next?* And I want to be with you. Only with you." He swallowed. "Please say you want me as much as I want you."

"Liam," she said, her voice breaking. He still wanted her, even after her disappearing act, and his faith and trust humbled her. "Yes. *Yes.*" So badly. "Up in Napa, I told you I'd give you everything." A tear escaped the corner of her eye and slowly rolled down her cheek. "I meant it. I just need to figure out how to do that. And maybe you could help me try."

"Oh, Mandy." And then he swept her up in his arms, held her close, kissed her hair, her face, her mouth. Finally, he put her down, cupped her face in his hands. "I'm going to stay for as long as I can. When it's time to go back, I'll go."

"But how are we going to do this? I mean, after you go."

"During the weeks, I'll split my time between here and the winery. And we can spend weekends up in Napa. That is, if you're willing."

She nodded. *More than willing.* She understood now. Getting the best out of yourself—out of your life—was possible, if you had someone who believed in you.

"We can do this. We have to do this." He chanted the words like a mantra.

"We *will* do this," Mandy said. "Together."

With that pronouncement, she wrapped her arms around his neck and pressed her lips to his, showing him she was all-in.

This was real, and deep in her heart, she knew this year was going to be different for one very important reason—Liam would be with her. Wrapped in his arms, she resolved to face the future head-on, for him, and most of all, for herself.

For the rest of her life.

Rendezvous in Point Reyes

A West Coast Holiday Series Book

ELISABETH BARRETT

ACKNOWLEDGMENTS

As always, I have so many people to thank for helping me with this book. First, Jennifer, my road trip partner-in-crime—you are awesome, and your perspective on pretty much everything makes my life richer! Huge thanks to all the great folks at Cowgirl Creamery in Point Reyes Station for the incredible tour and the wealth of information imparted about the cheesemaking industry, and to Vandana for the expert medical advice. Thanks so much to my wonderful beta readers, particularly Marina Adair, Alison Ashlyn, and Suzanne Turner for helping to make this book the best it could be. Bonus thanks to Marina Adair and Jennifer Ryan for their publishing advice, and to Tasneem for the technical help. AB, great title! Joan Swan and Toni Aleo, you both rock! Nalini Akolekar, thanks for your support. Huge thanks to Jonathan for, well, everything. Finally, thank you to every single one of my amazing readers and your unbelievable support!

CHAPTER 1

"You want it bad, don't you?" The man's voice was deeply seductive, pervading her senses, oozing into her every pore.

Unable to speak, Stella Flynn simply nodded. She did want it bad. *So bad.*

Typically, Stella didn't give in so easily. She was measured. Controlled. But in the face of this delectable onslaught, she could barely think, barely breathe. For once, she didn't want to check herself.

Not with this.

The dozens of cheeses, packed into the overfull display case in a semi-chaotic jumble, two, three, four deep, called out, enticing her with their deliciousness.

Try me.

Taste me.

To the right she spied a Point Reyes blue and a fantastic-looking Humboldt Fog, a tangy goat cheese with a stripe of ash right down the center. To the left, nestled side by side, sat an aged American cheddar and a creamy Napa Brie, its ivory rind beckoning. On the top shelf was a small stack of heart-shaped chèvre dotted with dried cranberries, a nod to the upcoming Valentine's Day holiday, no doubt. And front and center lay a Rough Ranch original—a circular, sumptuous masterpiece with a rind of pale orange and a center of pure milky sin.

Gorgeous. Her skin tingled and her mouth watered.

When was the last time she'd truly indulged? Honestly, she couldn't remember. But she had needs, just like everyone else. Needs she usually ignored.

"It's okay to want it," the man said, as if reading her mind. "Our Green Leaf is a triple-cream cheese, made of cow's milk from nearby Straus Family Creamery. It has a washed rind and is aged for six to seven weeks in our climate-controlled aging room to allow the rind to ripen and the flavors of the cheese to develop."

Reluctantly, she dragged her gaze from the display to the handsome young man behind the counter. He wore the white apron of a cheese monger and was pleasantly angular from the tip of his sharp nose to his pointed brown beard.

Rough Ranch was known for hiring the best staff, and judging by the expertise of the man helping her, she believed it. While browsing, she'd heard him educating some other customers, and it was clear the guy really knew his stuff.

Several other people were gathered around the cheese counter, tasting, listening, and learning about the cheeses from other knowledgeable cheese mongers while the Wednesday afternoon crowd bustled past the storefront's display in the old grange, now a chic warehouse space that housed some of the best artisanal wares in Point Reyes.

The cheese monger was waiting patiently for her to respond, but she couldn't help her gaze from drifting back to her chosen cheese—that sinfully rich Green Leaf she knew would utterly melt in her mouth.

As general manager of her family's Napa winery, Stella sampled sumptuous wines on a daily basis, but it had been a long time since she'd *eaten* something so decadent.

Since she'd eaten much at all.

Although she and Matt had finalized their divorce three months ago, things still hadn't returned to normal. She was still too thin, too quiet, too sad.

Or at least that's what her brother Liam would say, right before he hugged her and told her everything was going to be okay if she only gave it time.

She wanted so badly to believe him.

"I promise you it's as delicious as it looks," the man said, breaking into her thoughts again. "Want a taste?"

"Yes, please," she said a little too quickly, her voice coming out all breathy.

The guy raised an eyebrow as if he knew she couldn't wait another moment, lifted the cheese to take it behind the counter, and handed her a small, perfect wedge.

She closed her eyes, held the cheese under her nose, and inhaled deeply, trying to imprint the scent on her brain. Then she slipped it between her lips, letting the cheese slide across her tongue.

The people milling around her ceased to exist, and the low thrum of the warehouse faded away as the flavors exploded in her mind.

Musk. Tang. Milk. Grass.

This would be the perfect cheese to go with Flynn Winery's dessert wine. Or the cabernet. Yes, the cab, with its bold, acidic tones, would cut through the earthy base notes of the cheese. *So, so good.*

She must have let out a little moan, because when she opened her eyes, the guy behind the counter was watching her with unabashed interest.

"Mmm, I think you really liked that," he said. "I'm Miles." He smiled behind his beard and waited, an expectant look on his face.

Strange, he hadn't told the other customers his name. So why would he want hers…? *Oh.*

She was so out of practice, it took her a moment to figure it out. He was flirting. With *her*—thin, quiet, sad Stella Flynn.

"Your turn," he prompted.

She should say something witty or fun. Sexy.

"I'm Stella," she managed.

Hoo boy. She was terrible at this. Absolutely terrible. No surprise, given that her body—and her brain—had seemingly shut down every sexual impulse since she and Matt had separated a year ago. Probably even before that, if she was truly being honest.

She'd never been the passionate type, and it wasn't as if she and Matt had ever been hot and heavy. Theirs had been a more cerebral love. Or so she'd thought until she'd caught him cheating on her. With a friend. In her own bed.

Matt had moved on—*clearly*—but since they'd split, she couldn't muster even the slightest bit of interest in anyone.

Miles didn't appear to notice.

"Nice to meet you, Stella," he said, his eyes twinkling. "Want another taste?"

Men, not so much. But cheese? *Please.*

Stella was about to say yes when another male voice spoke.

"Stella?"

Her gaze shifted right. Another man was standing beside Miles, watching her with a strange look on his face.

Jason Roberts, Rough Ranch's owner. Her brother's best friend. Rebel with a heart of gold.

It had been more than a few months since she'd last seen him, but like a good wine, the man only got better with age.

He wasn't wearing an apron, giving her a prime view of the low-slung jeans hanging on his narrow hips and the Rough Ranch T-shirt clinging to his broad chest and shoulders. He was a little leaner than he'd been before the winter holidays, but his hair was the same chestnut brown, slightly tousled, same as it always was. His eyes were the same, too—the color of aged whiskey and fairly glowing with intelligence and intensity.

His gaze was molten hot, just like his expression—an expression she'd seen from him before, but not for her. Never for her. He swallowed hard, as though he was trying to keep himself in check, and good grief, if that wasn't the sexiest thing she'd ever seen.

Something stirred inside her, dark and low and needy, a pang of desire so acute her knees almost buckled.

Whoa.

Her reaction didn't make any sense. This was Jason Roberts, longtime family friend, not some sexy stranger.

Obviously, her body was just confused because she hadn't had sex in forever. Or maybe her brain was misfiring. Yes. That must be it. The divorce hadn't shut down her libido, it had just crossed all her internal wires.

Well, she'd just have to get them uncrossed.

She took a deep breath and pushed away the strange sensations. "Hello, Jason."

Jason was still staring at her as if he were seeing her for the first time.

"I'll go help the next customer," Miles murmured, moving down the counter and leaving them alone.

Jason was her brother Liam's age—four years older than she was—but they'd all grown up together, and Jason had spent more time at their house than he had at his own. He'd been like another brother to her, teasing her, protecting her, and generally being an overbearing pain in her ass. And she knew him intimately enough to know that the look on his face was not normal.

"Are you okay?" she asked.

Jason finally blinked, and his eyebrows went together. "I'm fine." His gaze swept her up and down, and then he shook his head. When he looked at her again, his eyes were clear, the heat gone. "What are you doing here?"

"Vacation."

Jason gave her a look of incredulity. "You? On vacation? Did too much Flynn reserve cab scramble your brain?"

"Nope," she told him. "I'm staying the weekend."

"What?" Now a little crease formed between his brows. "Seriously, Stella. It isn't like you to just break routine. Or to spend a whole weekend away from the winery. What's going on?" He cocked his head in a gesture she remembered intimately from their childhood. The one that meant he was slipping into big brother mode.

She needed to shut him down, fast.

"Don't worry about me," she tossed off. "I have things to do. My schedule's busy. Packed, actually."

As soon as the words left her mouth, she felt bad. She should just tell Jason everything—that the *real* reason she'd taken off during Valentine's Day weekend was that she needed to escape from Napa.

Liam had been pushing her to take time off for months. And no surprise that their father had agreed to her brother's plan. Both of them had been treating her as though she was some sort of breakable object since she and Matt had split.

Though being railroaded by the Flynn men into taking a mini vacation rankled, Stella had to admit that getting out of town was a good idea, especially this weekend.

It wasn't just having to pretend that seeing her ex-husband at the winery every day didn't bother her. Or that being around Liam and his new girlfriend, Mandy, made her feel like a third wheel.

No. It was this stupid, made-up holiday. The one day of the year when you were supposed to declare your undying love. Send a card. Flowers. Chocolates. Gifts.

What a crock.

Love wasn't any of those things. It was trust, plain and simple. Something she'd found out the hard way when hers had been completely abused by her ex.

Truth was, she hated Valentine's Day. And the thought of being trapped at the winery while lovey-dovey couples came to do wine tastings made her want to disappear.

To hide.

This weekend, she wasn't Stella Flynn of the Napa Valley Flynns, with everyone watching her. Judging her. Pitying her. She was anonymous.

No one in Point Reyes knew her, except for Jason, of course, so she wouldn't have to keep her game face on and pretend that everything was okay.

She could be alone and maybe, just for a moment, forget that her life was messed up. That *she* was messed up.

But telling Jason all of this would only underscore how pathetic she was. He'd probably try to intervene and tell her that she couldn't spend the weekend the way she wanted—communing with nature, drinking a little too much, and crying a lot.

He might even call her brother. And while she loved her brother and loved that he cared for her so much, Liam's worrying about her was the very last thing she wanted. Better that he simply think she was vacationing in Point Reyes than know what she was really intending to do.

Jason was looking at her skeptically now, his fantastically ripped forearms crossed over his broad chest.

"I'm serious," she told him. "You won't need to entertain me. In fact, I scheduled some meetings with a few of our distributors." She tried to sound matter-of-fact so Jason wouldn't know she was telling a half-truth.

Jason narrowed his eyes at her. "You're working on your vacation?"

"Not the whole weekend," she said evasively.

"Uh-huh." His tone was dubious. "What else do you have going on?"

"Lots of things," she countered. "I have a plan. I always do."

His lips twisted, and she thought he was going to keep pushing, but to her relief, he merely nodded. "A plan. Right."

"You make it sound like a bad thing," she said primly.

He shrugged. "I don't mind plans. Plans are good. But sometimes it's better to just go with the flow."

"Oh? And I suppose you're the expert on that?"

"You know it," he said, flashing her a grin.

She breathed a sigh of relief and grinned back. She wasn't sure he'd bought her story, but at least he'd stopped grilling her.

"Hang on a second," Jason said. He edged past the cheese mongers, lifted a wooden ledge, and in a moment, had slipped out from behind the counter and was standing in front of her.

He seemed bigger out from behind the wall of cheese, all long limbs and corded muscle. "Come here," he said, opening his arms, and before she realized what he was doing, he'd enveloped her in a big bear hug. "I missed you," he said softly.

Cocooned in his arms, she breathed in his clean, male scent. No matter how long he stayed away, it never changed, bringing back all sorts of memories. Jason helping her plant rose bushes at the end of each set of vines in a new vineyard, Jason talking her into taking a joyride on Liam's forbidden motorcycle, Jason giving her a wink as he swiped one of her dad's prized vintages at the Flynns' big annual New Year's party. He'd been an integral part of her childhood…and now it was gone.

"I missed you, too," she said, her voice coming out a little throatier than she'd anticipated.

"I'm sorry about Matt," he murmured into her ear. Oh, no. Stella stiffened and tried to pull away, but he held her tight, stroking her back with a big palm, soothing her. "Shh—it's okay."

She didn't want to talk about her divorce. Didn't even want to *think* about it until she was alone, but Jason just held on, his body a buffer between her and the rest of the world.

Finally, he pulled back, and with his arms still around her, searched her face.

"He didn't deserve you, Stell."

It was the use of her old nickname that got her. That, and the pity in his gaze—the way everyone seemed to look at her once word of Matt's cheating had spread like wildfire in Napa.

She typically just held her head up, stayed polite and stoic, and didn't give the gossips what they craved. But she found she couldn't bear the scrutiny, not from him. And every emotion that she'd been holding inside for so long came burbling to the surface.

To her surprise and horror, wetness pricked at the corners of her eyes.

She wouldn't cry. She couldn't. Not here, in front of all these people.

Jason must have realized she was about to lose it, because he slipped his arm over her shoulder and without another word steered her down the hallway and through a plain unmarked door.

Don't cry. Please don't cry.

Away from the crowds, Stella jammed her palms into her eye sockets, as if she could physically force the tears to stay inside her ducts.

That and some deep breaths worked, because in a few moments she felt better. When she had fully collected herself, she refocused her gaze. Jason was there, hands on her shoulders, watching her closely.

"I'm okay," she said, shrugging away his hands. "I swear I'm fine." She pushed her hair behind her ears and smoothed down her shirt. "I don't know what came over me."

A lie.

But what was one more on top of all the others?

Eager to change the subject, Stella glanced around. The small room was bare except for a long counter, but through a glass door, she spied another room that was filled floor to ceiling with cheese on metal trays. "Where are we?"

Seemingly reluctantly, Jason dragged his gaze away from her and to the cheese. "In our shipping room," he explained. "Where packages get labeled and logged. The cheese is done by the time it gets to this point, which is why we don't have to wear gear to prevent contamination. He pointed to the door. "But through there is our resting room. The cheese ages there for anywhere from a few days to a few weeks."

"Cool."

"Stell—" he started, but she stopped him with a look. *Don't.*

He pressed his lips together and thankfully kept whatever he was going to say to himself.

"Look, what's your schedule this weekend?" he finally said. "You'll stay with me, of course. There's plenty to do around town. My band is playing a show tomorrow at the Old Western Saloon. And we can—"

"Just hang on a minute," Stella interrupted. "I told you that you didn't have to entertain me. Anyway, I rented a cottage for the weekend."

Jason didn't even blink. "Cancel it."

"No way. Your place sucks." She'd been there a couple of times. A tiny one-bedroom apartment close to downtown Point Reyes Station.

"I bought a house," he said, a smile playing on his lips.

"What?"

"Last October. I must have forgotten to tell you when I saw you in the city."

She remembered that night. It had been right before her divorce, and Jason and Liam had taken her to San Francisco for a night out on the town.

She'd still been walking around in a stupor then, hardly believing that her marriage was truly over. It hadn't been until two weeks after the divorce papers were signed that she'd snapped out of it.

"You're practically family," he pressed. "Besides, how many times did I crash at Liam's place when he was living in San Francisco?"

More times than she could count, but that meant he owed Liam, not her.

"I'm sure you have things to do this weekend," she said.

Jason's combination of looks and charisma had always made him popular with the ladies, and she had no doubt some beautiful woman would be waiting for him to take her to a romantic Valentine's Day dinner on Saturday night.

"Sure, but it'll be no problem to get you into everything," he said. "Look, it's not a question that you're going to stay with me. I'm just sorry that you went to all the trouble to make a reservation to begin with. I want to show you around. Point Reyes is amazing this time of year—few tourists, and the weather is great. A little rainy sometimes, but I know you don't mind that."

Stella hesitated. Staying with Jason would probably be fun, but it would completely blow the rest of her plans to hell. She needed some space—away from Napa, away from her family, and definitely away from people who thought they had her all figured out. "I don't know…"

"If you're worried that it'll be an inconvenience, don't. I have plenty of room in my new place. I'll even cook you a nice dinner one of these nights."

She raised an eyebrow. "Are you saying I need to eat?"

"I'm saying you need to indulge."

"And you're the man to help me do that?"

His lips curled in a wolfish smile. "Definitely."

It was the way he growled the word. Or maybe it was the hungry look on his face. Regardless of what it was, a fluttery sensation began low in her belly and radiated outward.

Jason had always been more than a little wild—the one who pushed boundaries, ran roughshod over convention, and coaxed her into stepping outside her comfort zone, and she could tell by the look in his eye that was exactly what he intended to do.

She was torn.

She'd come here to escape her well-meaning but overbearing family and be away from painful memories on this ridiculous holiday. But to what end? When the weekend was over, she was going back to Napa, where she'd fall right back into the same old patterns.

So maybe spending Valentine's Day weekend in Point Reyes with Jason Roberts was just what she needed. Jason didn't care about convention—never had—and this weekend, she'd be the beneficiary of all of his untamed freedom. She could be his project, let him cheese and wine her on one of the worst holiday weekends for those suffering from a distinct lack of love. And come Sunday night, she might actually be ready to face her regular life again.

Jason must have sensed her caving, because he pressed his case. "Come on, Stella," he said, giving her an incredibly sexy smile. "It'll be fun."

It was impossible to say no to him when he turned on the charm. Plus, it might help her get a grip on her life. She let out a deep sigh. "Fine. I'll stay with you."

"And you'll let me indulge you?"

"Sure," she said, raising her eyes to the ceiling. "Indulge me."

Once again, he ignored her sarcasm. "You won't regret it," he vowed. "We're going to have a great weekend."

"What do you need me to do?"

He pushed opened the door, and once again, they were enveloped in the warmth and noise of the warehouse. "Nothing. I'll take care of everything. You're in good hands."

Big, capable hands.

"Right," she murmured.

He pulled her close, then kissed the top of her head, exactly as Liam might. Except it didn't feel like one of her brother's kisses, because a weird zing swept through her. She ignored it as best she could.

"Come back here after you're done with your meetings, okay?"

"Okay," she said. "I'm guessing it'll be around five."

"That's fine. I'll make sure to be done with work by then." He gave her a crooked smile. "Catch you later, Stell."

When he walked away, she couldn't keep her gaze from drifting to his ass.

No.

As fast as she could, she jerked her head to the side.

You're here to disappear, not lust after Jason.

She let out a deep breath. Seriously, what was going on? She'd never had this reaction to a man before—not even to Matt. And the fact that it was Jason Roberts, well, that was *really* weird.

It was because she trusted him. That must be it. He'd said it himself; he was practically family—her big brother's best friend who was going to indulge her for the weekend. He was familiar and generous and safe.

Except he wasn't safe.

As she walked out of the grange to head to her first meeting, her brain tingled and her body sizzled. Because for some strange reason, Jason's *not* being safe was the most thrilling thought of all.

CHAPTER 2

Something was going on with Stella.

But what that something was, Jason had no idea, and Stella certainly wasn't talking. Which left it up to him to figure out.

He jogged up the stairs to the second floor of the grange—a lofted workspace accessible by a catwalk—and went into his office. He shut the door so he wouldn't be disturbed and ran through the facts as he knew them.

Stella had come to Point Reyes without any warning, looking sadder and more beautiful than ever. She claimed to be in town for work and a brief vacation, but she'd been vague when he'd questioned her about her plans outside of her meetings.

So what was she really here for, and why wasn't she telling him?

He dropped into his desk chair—an old three-legged milking stool that kept him awake on those long evenings when he had to be up way too late creating work schedules or logging cheese turnings—and tipped it onto two legs so his back was against the wall. His thinking pose.

Aside from the sadness, she didn't seem that different. Sure, she had lost a little weight, but she still had that dark hair, cut past her shoulders, long and straight. She had on jeans and a slim-cut shirt over which she'd thrown a cardigan. That was typical, too. And she hadn't been wearing makeup—but of course, she didn't need any. Her dark eyes and naturally long eyelashes, not to mention her luscious pink lips, were all the coloring she needed.

Thinking about her lips made him think about her mouth, which made him think about how he'd almost blown it, completely and utterly.

It had taken only an instant when he'd seen her in front of the counter—beautiful, buttoned-down Stella, his cheese in her mouth, her cheeks flushed, and her expression one of orgasmic bliss. Stunning enough in that unguarded moment to almost make him spill his deepest, darkest secret:

He was in love with Stella Flynn and had been for years.

But he couldn't touch her. Couldn't lay one freaking finger on her because of who she was. Because as much as he loved her, he loved her family, too. Her brother and father were the best of men. He respected them, especially Liam. The Flynns had been good to him, and he knew they'd see him putting the moves on Stella as a betrayal.

Never mind the fact that Stella wouldn't in a million years see herself the way he saw her—as a gorgeous, desirable woman who didn't understand her own worth. Stella didn't think of him as a man. She thought of him only as another big brother.

Jason tipped the stool forward, and the front leg came down with a low *thud*, grounding him once again.

He sighed.

He couldn't have her, so he should just stop thinking about her in that way and focus on the fact that she needed help. Big-time.

Jason stood and opened his office door. Miles, his general manager, was outside on the catwalk, undoubtedly heading to one of their storage rooms.

"Hey," Jason said, stopping him. "Do you need me to be here over the next few days?"

An expression of confusion crossed Miles's face. "What happened?"

Except for emergencies, Jason rarely took time off, so this probably seemed as if it were coming out of left field. "I have a visitor."

"The gorgeous brunette who melted when she tasted the Green Leaf?"

"The one you were practically drooling over? Yes."

"Is she available?" Miles said brazenly.

She's mine, he wanted to roar. But he merely leveled his gaze at Miles. "She's an old family friend." *Steer clear.*

Miles swallowed. "Got it." He cleared his throat, pulled his tablet from his apron pocket, and flicked through their calendar. "Christine's doing both sets of tours tomorrow. We have a class on Saturday, but Suzie is leading it. Oh, we have that Valentine's Day tasting. You're running that, right?"

"Right."

"Okay, and I have Glen and Molly turning cheese this weekend. I'm supervising through next Tuesday, so I think you're in the clear. Take off when you need, but I'll still expect you for the tasting."

"Sounds good."

Miles continued on, but Jason stayed where he was. He leaned onto the railing and looked down to the first floor below, his eyes trained on his bustling cheese counter.

Like a good friend, he'd invited Stella over. She was going to stay in his house, eat his food, sleep in his guest bed.

All of this was great, except for the fact that he didn't want her in his guest bed. He wanted her in his *own* bed, her eyes filled with desire as he buried himself inside her, the way he did in his dreams.

Jason turned away, put his hand on the cool wall, and dropped his head. Thinking about this wasn't wise. It was also exhausting.

He'd hoped that after all this time his feelings for her would have faded. Hoped that all the travel and all the women would have helped him to get over her. But they hadn't.

And it was maddening knowing that the one person he truly cared for was the one person he could never have.

Or maybe it was just penance for who he was.

They'd met when she was in the fifth grade and he in the ninth, Liam Flynn's quiet little sister with the braids down her back and the shyest smile he'd ever seen. His parents cared more about their winemaking empire than they did him, and he'd grown wild—cutting school, raising hell—until he and Liam had become friends.

The Flynns practically adopted him, welcoming him into their home and their lives. For the first time, surrounded by all of that warmth and love and happiness, he stopped acting out, quit looking for trouble, and focused on more important things, like school, family, and friendship.

An only child, Jason loved Liam like a brother, and so it made sense he loved Stella like a sister. In summer, he caught crickets for her in the big fields of her family's vineyards, and together they'd run barefoot through the cold-water creeks. He'd gone to every single one of her piano recitals, as proud of her as Liam was. They'd grown up more than friends; they'd grown up like siblings.

But he wasn't a Flynn. He was a Roberts, and his own family could offer nothing to him but the things he cared about the least—money and power.

Jason left home at eighteen to go to college and hadn't looked back. He traveled everywhere—to New York, Europe, and Asia—learning, cooking, writing, and making music. Yes, he missed the Flynns, but he wasn't ever going to move back to Napa. Not when his parents were there, waiting to pounce on him the moment he returned. He'd stayed away for a decade, doing everything—anything—except making wine.

When he finally got back to the Bay Area, some things had stayed the same, and some things were completely different.

Like Stella.

Gone was the gawky fourteen-year-old, all coltish limbs and frizzy hair. In her place was a beautiful woman, with curves and sass and that same shy smile. Except this time, that smile shot straight to his heart.

He'd come home.

Stella knew him better than anyone, cut through all his crap, and brought out the best in him. Always had. It had surprised him then, how much he wanted her. Shocked him, actually. He wasn't supposed to have those feelings for her. So he buried them, pretended that he still saw her as a little sister, and moved to Point Reyes to start his own business. The next thing he knew, Stella's mom died and she was married—to Matt Barnes, who wasn't fit to lick her boots, let alone share her life.

But it was for the best. At least that's what he kept telling himself, because the feelings he had weren't natural. Not with their history.

So he'd moved on.

Sort of.

There'd been other women—too many women—but none who really mattered.

Then he'd found out Stella was done with her marriage, and those feelings he thought were buried came back with a vengeance.

Jason jerked his hand off the wall.

If he'd known she was coming to Point Reyes, he could have prepared himself. Steeled himself against the emotion that came so fast and thick with her lately. Especially lately.

He took a deep, cleansing breath and tried to think pure thoughts. It was difficult, given that Stella's euphoric expression was on slo-mo replay in his brain.

Seriously, what was *really* going on with her?

Jason whipped out his cell phone and dialed the one person who could tell him—her brother. It was a gamble to call him midday, given that Liam had recently decided to drag Flynn Winery into the digital age with software that would aggregate all of their production data, and he spent most of his time and energy on his new project.

But Liam picked up on the third ring. "Flynn," he answered in a deep voice.

"Catch you at a good time?" Jason asked.

"Hey, Jace. Yep. Good time. Just taking a breather from coding to get ready for V-Day weekend. Predicting some big crowds."

"Uh, yeah. About the weekend," Jason said, slipping way too easily into the role of big brother. "Stella's here."

"What?" Liam sounded surprised.

"I'm guessing you didn't know she was coming," Jason said.

"No," Liam said. "Otherwise I would have given you a heads-up. She just took off this morning. I mean, I've been strongly suggesting that she take a vacation, but she gave me zero warning as to her plans."

"Work. That's what her plans are." *And driving me insane.*

Liam groaned. "Help her."

"I'll try, but she's a stubborn one. Did you know she scheduled meetings with every Flynn Winery distributor she could get a hold of?"

"I'm not surprised. She's been like this at home, too. Spending every free minute at the winery, working herself to the bone, just like she did after our mom died. I think it's some kind of protective mechanism."

"That ass," Jason said. He wanted to both rip Matt's head off for hurting her and pat him on the back for setting her free.

"He's not my favorite person right now," Liam said, obviously on the same page as he was regarding Stella's ex. "And between you, me, and the oak barrel, he's looking for another gig."

"Good. Well, not good. But you know what I mean." Liam would have to find another assistant winemaker before the start of growing season, which sucked, but Stella would probably be happier with her ex gone. At least, he thought she would. She'd seemed pretty teary when he'd brought up the subject.

"Yeah. I know what you mean."

"Back to Stella," Jason said. "I think there's more going on here than just work or her divorce. Any suggestions?"

"I don't know," Liam said. "Just take her out. Show her a good time."

Liam's words conjured up yet another vision of Stella, naked and spread out on his bed, smiling just for him as she welcomed him into her body.

Jason shoved the image away and cleared his throat. "My specialty."

"Not *too* good a time," Liam growled.

He needed a cold shower. Or a lobotomy. "I love her just as much as you do." It was the truth, though Liam didn't know how much, and Lord willing, he never would.

Liam's voice softened. "I know you love her, man. I'm just worried about her, is all. Take care of her. Don't let her do anything stupid."

"I won't. I swear." Jason needed to change the subject. Even the act of talking about this felt like a betrayal, and playing both sides was not good for his mental health. "So let me do the worrying this weekend," he said. "You deal with your business and have fun with Mandy."

When Liam had called him after New Year's to tell him he was seeing someone new, he'd been happy for his friend. Liam was a straight-up guy who deserved someone as loving and loyal as he was, and from what he understood, Mandy was both.

"Yeah, I'll do that." Liam was quiet for a moment. "By the way, I wanted to tell you that Stella and I saw your mom at Oxbow."

Jason stilled. Oxbow was a public market near downtown Napa—a hub for locals and tourists alike, where you could get strong coffee, good produce, fresh flowers, and hot gossip. "What'd you guys talk about?" he asked cautiously.

"The business. Growth. I'll just be happy if we can crank out 1,200 cases next year with our new system, but Optimum's already producing almost a quarter of a million. Impressive. And of course, she asked me if I'd spoken to you."

"What'd you tell her?"

"What do you think? I lied and said no, same as I always do." Liam paused. "But you should really call her."

"There's no point," Jason said. "She'll pretend to care about what I'm doing and then give me the same arguments about why I should come home to work at Optimum. I'm getting too old for that crap."

"You're only thirty-four, Jace. Same as me."

Jason sighed. "I know. I just feel old."

"All the more reason to call your mother and stop this weird estrangement from going on any longer. You've made it pretty clear that you're not interested in joining the family business, and you've established yourself just fine on your own. Isn't it time to let bygones be bygones?"

Liam was only telling him this out of love. He knew that. But reconciling with his parents just wasn't in the cards. He wasn't going back to Napa— not after the hell they'd put him through. These were the same people who'd missed every single one of his band's shows, who'd never once looked at his report cards, who'd left him alone every single Christmas since he was fourteen so that they could travel unencumbered.

So he'd taken the out-of-sight, out-of-mind tack by deleting every voice mail message, text, and e-mail they sent to him. It wasn't the most mature way to handle things, but it was better than being dragged back down again. He'd been in a seriously bad place for years after leaving Napa. A place he never wanted to revisit.

"I'll think about it," he finally said.

"Good," Liam said with satisfaction. "Thanks in advance for dealing with Stella. I know she'll be in good hands with you. I'll catch you later."

Then Liam hung up.

Jason held the phone in his hand for a second, then took a deep breath and jammed it in his pocket, firmly shoving any lingering thoughts of his parents aside. Unfortunately, his brain immediately shifted back to Stella.

"Take care of her," Liam had said. "Help her. Show her a good time."

In other words, torture himself for an entire weekend trying to make Stella happy while hiding the fact that he was head over heels in love with her.

No big deal.

Take care of her.

He could guarantee that Liam did *not* mean physically.

But he wanted to wipe away all that vulnerability, soothe all the pain he saw in her eyes. Except she'd never let him, not Stella.

Well, he could be as stubborn as she was. And his willpower was legendary.

So he'd do exactly what he promised Liam he'd do—take her out. Help her relax. Show her a good time. *Take care of her.* And when the weekend was over, send her back to Napa, hopefully a little happier, a little less stressed. And forget about her all over again.

Until the next time.

CHAPTER 3

Stella stepped out of her final meeting feeling accomplished. She always felt better after a solid day's work, and today was no exception. She'd received good feedback from one of her distributors and increased orders from the other two.

Her truck was parked a little ways down the street, so she started down the sidewalk, pulling behind her a dolly laden with two almost-full cases of wine. Sunset came early this time of year, and only a few people were strolling in the darkening light of downtown Point Reyes Station.

She desperately wanted to call Liam to tell him the good news and to check to make sure everything at the winery was running smoothly. Unfortunately, calling her brother would only mean he'd ask questions she didn't want to answer, like why she'd skipped out without saying anything, and why she'd chosen Point Reyes, of all places, for her vacation, especially when it seemed as if she really wasn't vacationing at all.

She maneuvered the dolly around a big crack in the sidewalk and frowned.

Why *was* she here, anyway? Surely she could have found some better place to hide out for Valentine's weekend. Someplace that didn't include work and Jason Roberts.

Probably. But at least there was no one else here to shoot her pitying glances or ask uncomfortable questions.

She lifted both cases and the dolly into the covered flatbed, slammed the trunk shut, and was about to get into her truck when she heard a woman's voice calling out. Strange. It sounded as if the woman was saying her name.

Couldn't be. She knew no one here except Jason.

"Stella!"

Definitely her name. She turned, and to her surprise saw Jason's mom hurrying toward her.

"Mrs. Roberts!" Stella said when she approached. "Hi. What are you doing here?"

"I need to see Jason," she said, her voice plaintive. "Have you seen him?"

"Oh, I'm sorry, Mrs. Roberts, but I haven't. I'm just here for work." Lying to Jason's parents was practically second nature to her. Both she and Liam covered for Jason and always had; their loyalty was to him, not to his folks.

But for some reason, this felt wrong. Jason's mom was obviously not doing so well. Typically, she looked sharp—hair done, clothes crisp and pressed, makeup tasteful. In fact, that's exactly how she'd appeared a few short weeks ago when Stella and Liam had run into her at the market.

Since then, she looked like she'd aged a decade. Her clothes were a little rumpled, the lines on her face seemed deeper, and there were big bags under her eyes, as if she hadn't been sleeping. Her strain was visible. Even her hands were shaking.

"Are you okay?" Stella asked. "Do you need to sit down? Where's Eli?" The Robertses' driver.

Mrs. Roberts shook her head. "I just want to talk to him. Why won't he pick up the phone? Why won't he answer my e-mails? He can't be *that* busy, and I need him. His father needs him." She was getting more agitated now, wringing those shaking hands.

"I'm sorry," Stella said lamely.

"No, no. I'm sorry for burdening you. It's just that I have no idea how to get a hold of him. I thought he'd be working, but he's not at Rough Ranch. Are you absolutely sure you don't know where he is?"

Stella's cell phone—the one with Jason's text detailing his address and rough directions on how to get to his house—burned a hole in her pocket. She swallowed hard.

"I don't," she lied. Jason was *definitely* going to owe her after these whoppers.

"If you see him, you'll tell him to call me?" Mrs. Roberts asked, her voice pleading. "Please?"

"Of course I will," Stella said. "But I'm not sure we'll cross paths. I'm here for work, after all."

"Ah. Ah yes. Work." Mrs. Roberts nodded, though Stella wasn't certain she even knew what she was saying.

"Are you *sure* you're all right? There's no one I can call…?"

"No. If you talk to him, just tell Jason to call me. Good-bye, Stella. Please give my best to your family."

And she abruptly turned and walked away.

Weird. Something had happened, that was for sure. She'd never seen

Mrs. Roberts anything less than perfectly composed, so her behavior was definitely out of the ordinary. Still, without additional information, she had no idea what was going on.

She could call Liam and ask him if had any information.

But then there'd be those pesky questions to answer.

Not knowing what else to do, she got into her truck and left.

Stella made it to Jason's house in twenty minutes. She would have been there in fifteen, but his road, right off Sir Francis Drake Boulevard, was confusingly windy. It wasn't until she pulled into his driveway, which curved around the back of the house, and saw his truck that she knew for certain she was in the right place.

The house was situated on the side of a hill surrounded by mature oak trees, two stories of wood and glass. It was rustic, blending seamlessly into its surroundings despite its cheery yellow coat of paint and sloping eaves.

A beautifully laid stone path wound from the driveway to the front door, over which hung wisteria vines—in full bloom thanks to the rainy season. Through the trees, she caught a glimpse of Tomales Bay. From the large porch that soared over the hillside, the view of the water would be stunning.

Grabbing her overnight bag from the passenger seat, she walked up the stone path and rang the front doorbell.

Jason answered with a beer in his hand and an easy smile on his face. "Hey, Stella. Any problems finding the place?"

"Not at all," she told him, knowing she'd never hear the end of it if she confessed to getting lost.

He glanced down at her bag. "Is that all you have?"

"Nope. I have some wine in the truck."

"I'll get it." He put his beer down on the hall table.

"You don't have any shoes on."

He simply shrugged and headed down the path. Typical Jason.

She slid her bag off her shoulder. "The full case," she called to his retreating form.

He went around the corner and in a minute reappeared with the case. She'd seen him carry heavy loads before, but she'd never noticed the muscles bulging in his arms, the way his jaw tightened, just a little, as he got a better grip on the box.

It's just Jason.

Stella waited for those awkward feelings she'd felt back at the store to resurface, but thankfully, they didn't. That was good. Sexual tension would make things *uncomfortable*, to say the least.

"What'd you bring me?" he asked when he was closer.

"Some of last year's cab, a couple of bottles of pinot, and some of our dessert wine."

"Mmm." He stepped through the open front door. "Maybe we'll split a bottle later."

"Save it for yourself," she said, following him in. "Ooh—" Eyes big, she took in the sweeping lines of the house. The interior was lovely—a little more modern than the outside, with slate on the floor and cool white walls offset with dark brown wooden accents.

"Sitting room's on the right, dining room's on the left," he said, bypassing the staircase and heading down a big hallway that went right through the center of the house. There wasn't much furniture in either room, probably because he had moved in pretty recently, but she didn't mind the minimalism.

They ended up in a spacious kitchen, and Jason slid the case of wine onto a marble counter. He pointed to a door. "Through there's the great room, and it has a screened-in porch, too. It has a good view of the bay. Come on. Let me show you the upstairs."

"Sure."

He took the stairs two at a time, and she followed him up.

"Here's my room," he said, quickly walking past it and continuing down the hall. "And you can sleep in here."

He pushed open the next door, and she peered in. There was a queen-size bed, a dresser, a night table, and a soaring view of Tomales Bay. "Oh my gosh."

"That's Black Mountain in the distance," Jason supplied.

Stella walked to the window and stood there for a few moments, soaking it all in. It was utterly stunning—rugged and wild—so different from her tidy-but-dull home on a flat residential street in Napa.

From where he stood in the doorframe, Jason cleared his throat.

"Is it okay? There's another room you can use if you don't like this one, but it's in the back and the view isn't as good."

She turned to find him watching her intently. He actually seemed anxious that his place might not meet with her approval, and his nervousness was oddly touching. Quickly, she put him out of his misery.

"It's great, Jason. Your house is gorgeous."

He visibly relaxed. "Good," he said. "I want you to be comfortable."

"Buying a house is kind of huge for you," she said. The Jason she knew was a wanderer, as happy sleeping in a tent as he was in a comfy bed. "Why'd you do it?"

"It just seemed like it was time," he said with a shrug. "Come on back downstairs and let me pour you a glass of wine."

Jason kept all his wine in a big walk-in pantry. Briskly, she scanned the labels, then snared a Stags' Leap cab and brought it back. "This one."

"I knew that was one of your favorites." He handed her an old-fashioned corkscrew. "Why don't you do the honors?"

She did, making fast work of the foil and cork. Then she popped on an aerator, poured two glasses—being more generous with his—and perched on one of the stools at the big counter that split the space.

"Cheers."

They clinked and sipped.

"It's good, but it needs some air," she pronounced.

"So let it sit."

She waited until Jason had taken a big sip of wine before she dropped her news. "I ran into your mother downtown."

Jason froze, his mouth full of wine. Then he swallowed hard. "What?"

"Don't worry," Stella said, waving her hand. "I didn't tell her where you were. Didn't even tell her I'd seen you, actually, and I felt really crappy about lying because she didn't look well. So do me a favor and call her."

At that moment, Jason's pocket buzzed. He pulled out his phone and checked the screen.

"If that's your mother, take it," Stella said.

Jason gave her a dirty look as he clicked the phone on and stepped into the family room. Stella stayed where she was, but she could still hear his voice.

"Hello?" he said. "Oh, hey, Eva. Nothing, you? Ooh, can't this weekend. Another time, then? Great. Talk to you soon. Bye."

In a moment, he was back in the kitchen. "Sorry about that," he said.

"No worries," she said. "So are you going to call your mother?"

Jason ignored her. "Does homemade pizza with Rough Ranch mozzarella and fresh basil sound good for dinner?

"Is that what that is?" An enticing aroma wafted around her. "I don't remember you ever cooking."

"Things change." His phone rang again. It was probably another woman.

"Not everything," she said. "Unless that's your mother."

He gave her another look—dirtier this time—and took the call. It *was* another woman, asking if he was free that night. Once again, he let her down gently. When he came back to the kitchen, Stella fixed him with a glare.

"You're not going to call her, are you?"

"Nope," he said, snaring his glass of wine and taking a sip. "Mm. It's better now."

She let out a sharp breath. "I lied for you."

Jason put his glass down on the counter and crossed his arms over his chest. "You're a real pain in the ass, you know that?"

"If by pain in the ass, you mean teller of truth, then yes."

"Come *on*, Stella," he said, sounding completely exasperated.

"Fine. I'm a pain in the ass. But you love me anyway."

"Yeah," he said, his voice surprisingly gentle. "I do." He uncrossed his arms and sighed. "I'm sorry if I seem ungrateful, but she does this every once in a while. I'm sure it's nothing."

"Why don't you talk to your folks?" Stella asked, genuinely curious. "Hasn't enough time gone by?"

Jason shook his head. "You sound like Liam."

"We *are* related," she said, her lips quirking.

"Yeah," Jason said, but he didn't smile at her joke. Just ran a hand through his hair. "My parents aren't like yours, Stell. They're outrageously selfish, and they're not rational or reasonable. Even though they know I can't stand them and we've never had a real relationship, they're still pushing me to come home. They can't understand that I have a business of my own—a *life* of my own—that doesn't revolve around them or the wine industry." He shrugged. "It's easier not to call instead of giving them false hope."

"They're your parents," she said softly. "And you're an adult. Call your mom. Tell her what you just told me." Her last stab at getting him to do the right thing, but Jason just shook his head no and took a sip of wine.

In the stillness, the doorbell rang.

Jason frowned, but he didn't look surprised. "I'll be right back."

In a moment, she heard the door open.

"Jason," a decidedly feminine voice said. "Marnie's in the car. You ready to go to the pub?"

"I am so sorry, Kelsey, but I have last-minute company tonight."

"Aw." Kelsey sounded disappointed. "Tomorrow then?"

"Can't. I have a show," he said, his voice laced with what sounded like genuine regret.

"Oh, yeah. I forgot about that. We'll catch you there, okay?"

"Sure. Drive safe."

"Good night!"

There was the sound of a door shutting and a car driving off.

"I feel like I'm keeping you from a fun night," Stella said when he returned.

"Nah."

She gave him a dubious look. "I must be so boring compared to your friends."

"You're not boring, Stella."

"Sure I am," she said, her tone flat. "Always have been. Always will be." It was painful to say, but if she couldn't admit it to Jason, who could she tell?

Jason snorted. "Who said that?"

"Matt."

Evenly, he met her gaze. "What else did Matt say?"

"That I suck in bed." The words came out before she could stop them. Heat rose in her cheeks, but Jason didn't blink.

Eyes not leaving hers, he took a long swallow of wine. When he was done, he wiped a stray drop from his lips with his thumb. "Matt's an ass."

He said this matter-of-factly, and her heart gave a little pang. Jason was on her side, just like always.

"He wasn't so great for my ego," she said with false brightness, "but that's okay. I'm kind of done with men, anyway. You know, that whole trust thing and all."

There was no pity in his gaze this time, but something infinitely more complicated. Sorrow and tenderness and something else she couldn't quite put her finger on.

"There's someone out there, Stella. Someone who sees you for who you are. Who loves you the way you're meant to be loved. I promise you that. So don't give up."

She should say something. Thank him for being so nice after she'd gotten on his case about his mom, but there was a lump in her throat.

Luckily, Jason took that moment to open up the oven to check on the pizza. "A little bit longer," he said.

After another couple of minutes—and a phone call from yet another one of Jason's female friends—the pizza was ready.

They ate at the kitchen counter, her sitting, him standing. They talked about their businesses, about Liam and Mandy, about everything, really, and the conversation flowed easily. No surprise, given that she'd known him for two-thirds of her life. She was comfortable with him, relaxed. Even *not* talking with Jason was a million times better than conversation with anyone else.

And the pizza was wonderful—the perfect melding of crust and sauce and that Rough Ranch mozzarella, salty and smooth.

"Is it okay?" he asked her.

She swallowed her bite. "It's delicious. This cheese is incredible, Jason."

He smiled. "Good. You know, I really pushed hard for it. Most of my team was anti-mozzarella."

"What? No. It's amazing."

"That's what I told them," he said. "Well, at least I hoped it would be, so I made a batch and had everyone try it." He shrugged. "They all came around pretty fast once they tasted it."

"I like that you treat your employees like they're your partners."

"Most of them have been with me from the beginning. And they're all as passionate about the business as I am. Honestly, they're like my family at this point."

"Your *family*, hmm?" she said, trying to bait him a little. "Like your mother?"

He didn't bite. "Not everyone is as lucky as you are to have a family they love," Jason said mildly. "So I had to make my own."

"Still, there are always drawbacks to working with your family—or something that feels like it."

Liam and their dad didn't always see eye to eye, and she frequently played the role of peacemaker. She loved them unreservedly, and there was something comforting about knowing her dad and brother always had her back, no matter what, but increasingly she felt as if she was playing the role she was born into without any chance of breaking free.

"True," he said. "But we do all right. Or we have so far."

"You're doing great, Jason," she said, unwilling to push him more.

When they were done with dinner, she took both of their plates to the sink. He was right behind her with the wineglasses.

"Should I just leave them, or do you want me to throw them in the dishwasher?" she asked.

"Leave them," he said, taking them from her and putting them aside. "And relax."

He put both his hands on her shoulders, a familiar gesture he'd done many times before, but it had never felt like this—electrically charged, sending liquid heat right through her cardigan, straight down to her toes and back up again.

And just like that, that strange desire came roaring back.

Her breath quickened and her heart sped up to record time, thumping in her chest so loudly it rang in her ears. And when he started to rub her shoulders, stretching and kneading her tense muscles with his strong hands, her body came alive, nerve endings zinging, screaming along with her roiling emotions.

Quickly, Stella shifted her gaze down and forced herself to remain still, afraid that any movement would give her away. This wasn't familiar. This was new and vaguely terrifying and *definitely* dangerous.

Her whole body was throbbing in time with her heartbeat now, her blood chanting in her veins—*want*—like she'd never felt before, not with him, not with anyone.

It was his touch that had done it, triggered something deep inside she couldn't control.

Stella hated feeling out of control.

She tried to be logical. This wasn't her. This was just her reaction to being in a new environment—in Jason's environment, where his relationships ran hot and were done by morning. *It'll flame out as quickly as it came in.*

But her body wasn't getting on board with her brain.

Her nipples were rock hard and her breath came in short pants. Surely Jason had to see her reaction, or feel it, or *something* given that he was right behind her, so close that his hips nearly touched her rear.

But he seemed to be blissfully unaware. Just kept up the same deep strokes, disintegrating every last ounce of common sense or restraint from her protective arsenal.

Just when she was about to beg for mercy, he stopped. Patted her shoulders and withdrew.

"Good night, Stell," he said, as if he hadn't just shattered her world. "See you in the morning."

And then he was gone.

She stood in the kitchen for a long time, trying and failing to get herself under control. At long last, she dragged herself upstairs. The hall light was on, but Jason's door was shut.

She got dressed for bed. Splashed some water on her face and brushed her teeth. Curled up in the very center of the big bed, her body still aflame, her mind racing, and tried to sleep.

It was a very long night.

CHAPTER 4

Jason woke up the next morning with a fuzzy head, blurry eyes, and the remnants of a deliciously erotic dream that had left him unbearably aroused.

A dream that prominently featured Stella Flynn, who, judging by the sounds of silence, was still asleep in the room next to his.

Ugh, he was hard as a rock. Last night he'd taken matters into his own hands—literally—but that hadn't helped, either. Just made him want the real thing.

The thing he could never have.

He should never have touched her. Never have laid hands on her. Because that made him want her even more.

It didn't matter, though, because *she* didn't want anyone, least of all him.

Not for the first time, his reputation rankled.

Player.

Even though he wasn't anymore, the calls from his female friends certainly hadn't helped her think otherwise.

When he'd first moved to Point Reyes, he hadn't minded the casual hookup culture. Lots of people were artists, craftsmen, or farmers and seemed to be relaxed about almost everything, especially sex. They were welcoming and friendly, and one-night stands were as common as kale at the farmers' market. It hadn't taken him long to realize that having flings made him feel empty and unsatisfied afterward.

So he'd stopped. Instead of sleeping around, he worked. Cultivated friendships. Grew up.

He'd even had a girlfriend for a while. She was a great woman and an amazing artist, but they'd broken up over a year ago for one reason: she wasn't Stella.

Damn, he wished he could tell her everything. She never backed away from telling *him* the truth—the good, the bad, and the ugly. Most people who knew her just saw her as shy. But underneath that quiet exterior was pure steel. She pushed him like no one else—just like she pushed her brother—and no one knew quite how to tease him the way she did, giving him the sweetest smile while flaying him with her wicked tongue. He loved every minute of it.

Groaning, he rose and went to the window and pried it open. The sun was up, its thin light filtering through the gray fog.

He wished for so many things. Some extra space for tastings. A new wire harp to cut the curds. But mostly for courage. To have stayed in Napa and supported Stella more after her mother died. Told her how much he loved her then.

Now it was too late, and the only way he could truly have her was in his dreams.

And what dreams they were. Vivid and bright and painfully real.

Despite the cold air, his cock throbbed, and not for the first time, he wished that his imagination weren't *quite* so good.

Crap, he was getting nowhere, and he was going to be a total wreck today if he didn't take care of himself. Again. He went into the bathroom and turned on the shower. When the water was warm, he stepped inside.

He didn't even bother with the soap. Just wrapped his hand around his thickness and gave a short stroke, then a longer one, the way he'd always dreamed she would. In his mind, Stella touched him as she touched herself, pleasured him with her hands, her mouth, urging him on with her desire. He could envision her now, her mouth open, her eyes closed, her head thrown back in passion as she went flying.

Dream Stella came apart and that image was all it took to send him over the edge. He came hard, spending against the damp shower wall and biting his lip to hold back his groan.

Satisfaction quickly turned to shame.

If Stella knew, if she even suspected what he'd done, she'd be disgusted. And rightly so.

He grabbed the soap and lathered up his body. He hadn't done that decent of a job keeping his desire hidden, and if she was staying with him, he'd need to do better. As it was, he'd almost blown it—again—with that shoulder massage.

Quickly, he finished showering and dried off. There was still no sound from Stella's room, so he threw on a pair of boxer briefs and a pair of jeans and grabbed his phone to check his e-mail.

He felt a tiny twinge of guilt about deleting his mother's two e-mails sight unseen, but not bad enough to un-delete them. He didn't need to worry about his nonexistent relationship with his parents on top of everything else he had going on.

Not bothering with a shirt, he went downstairs to make some coffee. But the moment he stepped into the kitchen, he got a sucker punch to the gut.

Stella was awake and standing there, a glass of water tilted to her lips.

Her hair was still messy from sleep, her eyes a little dazed. She had on pajamas printed with little rosebuds, and her feet were bare. She looked adorable. *Desirable.*

When she saw him, she froze, glass in the air, and stared as if she'd never seen a man's chest before. A deep blush stained her cheeks.

"Morning," she said quickly, and looked away, evidently embarrassed. He should have put a shirt on, but it was too late now.

"Morning," he responded, stepping into the space. "Sleep okay?"

"Yes, thanks." She still wouldn't meet his gaze.

"Want some coffee?"

"Sure."

He rummaged around in the cabinet until he found the ground coffee, measured out enough for two cups, then dumped it in the machine. When he turned back, Stella was at the window, looking out at the woods behind the house.

"It's not raining today," he said, "so maybe after your meetings, I could give you a tour. We could grab some lunch. And don't forget I have my show tonight."

"I don't know what time I'll be done," she said, not turning around. "Can I text you?"

"Sure. Okay."

Man this was awkward. But what did he expect? He'd manhandled her last night, and now she was punishing him.

It was no less than he deserved.

The coffee was percolating in the machine now, dark liquid pinging and dripping into the pot as the rich aroma of the roast permeated the air. He busied himself around the kitchen, getting mugs, some sugar, a piece of toast—anything except trying to make small talk to Stella's back.

When the coffee was ready, he poured her cup first. "Coffee's done."

She finally turned back around. "Jason?"

"Yeah?"

She opened her mouth, as though she was going to say something, then looked down at the mug he held out. "Nothing," she said, carefully taking the cup from him without touching his fingers. "Thanks."

"You're welcome."

He poured the rest of the pot into his own travel mug, then took a bracing sip.

They stood there in awkward silence, drinking their coffee. At some point, Stella went upstairs to get some clothes on.

And he just stood there in his kitchen, trying to figure out how to make this work.

There was no "try" with Stella. He'd just have to do it. He was the one who'd invited her here, who insisted she join him. He needed to make her vacation fun, not awkward.

Which meant no more touching her, period.

He took a deep breath. He could do this. He had to do this. There was no other choice.

Stella bailed on him for lunch and didn't show up at the shop until three, which was probably a good thing. It gave him time to focus on work and to get his head together on how to handle his reaction to her.

He'd be sticking with his original plan: bury his attraction and no touching.

Definitely no touching.

He and Miles were deep in a technical conversation about rind colonization with *Brevi. linens*, a type of bacterium that occurred naturally on the Pacific coast that was integral to Rough Ranch's production of several best-selling cheeses, when he got word from one of his staff members that Stella was waiting for him at the front.

"Walk with me," he said to Miles.

"If it means seeing Ms. Green Leaf, yeah."

Jason shot him a look, but Miles merely grinned at him. "A man can dream."

Now *that* he knew all too well. In vivid Technicolor.

"Forget about her," Jason said, steering the conversation to someplace safer, "and help me figure out how we're going to ensure that we have enough product over the next couple of months. We're already wrestling with the wintertime decreased herd production, and we have our seasonal cheese to think about."

"For the extra milk we'll need, I think we should try reaching out to Everhart Dairy. Their Holsteins are looking good, and they feed the cows organically. They'd fit in with our philosophy, for sure."

"Maybe," Jason mused. "But we don't know if they'll sell to us. Jack Everhart isn't a huge Rough Ranch fan. And even if he decides to sell, we'll still struggle to get the cheese produced. Because *B. linens* is unique to this area, we can't move production inland to our new facility. Plus, we won't know how the milk takes to our techniques until we do some test batches. We could end up wasting a lot of money and even more time."

"We have the money."

"But we don't have the time," Jason said with a sigh. "It's not just the seasonal cheese I'm worried about. It's also filling all the orders for our new subscription service."

"Only two hundred orders have come in so far."

"We just added the subscriptions a month ago. And we haven't done any advertising yet, but we have that *Bon Appétit* ad running in April. I have a feeling that'll generate a lot more subscribers."

Miles shrugged. "Maybe. But who knows? I just worry that if we don't talk to Everhart now, another year will slip by and we won't be any further on our expansion. I mean, what are our other options? Lucky? Wright? Those dairies aren't producing the quality or the quantity of milk that we need."

"Okay, I'll admit that talking to Everhart has merit," Jason said. "And I think we should look into trying to annex some swing space for cheese production right here in Point Reyes. At the rate we're expanding, if we don't deal with this now, we'll just be screwed down the road."

"Let's talk to Greer," Miles said. His head cheese maker. "See what he has to say."

"Definitely. We'll revisit this later, all right?"

Miles gave a nod, and then his gaze drifted away.

Stella stood there, her eyes bright, looking more like the old Stella than he'd seen in a long while. She smiled at him, and he smiled back.

"Hi, Stella," Miles said to her.

Her gaze shifted to his head of staff. "Oh, hi, Miles."

"How was your day? Did you get a chance to explore the area at all?" Miles asked.

Stella shook her head. "Not yet. I had some business to deal with. Maybe I'll get the chance later?" She glanced over to Jason for confirmation, and he nodded.

"We'll get to that this weekend, but we have plans for tonight," Jason told her. "My show, remember?"

"Right," she said, and he noticed that her smile faltered a little.

"Want another sample?" Miles said, a sly look on his face.

"No," Jason cut in, before Stella could say anything. "I mean, I'll take care of the samples later," he amended. No need to have Miles ogling her while she ate. That was a privilege he wanted for himself.

Miles merely grinned, as if he knew all the trouble he was causing. "All right then," he said. "But if you change your mind, you know where I'll be. Bye, Stella. Catch you later."

Miles turned, winked at Jason, and then disappeared into the back.

Cheeky bastard.

Jason turned back to Stella. "Hey," he said, trying to sound relaxed.

"Hey."

"How'd your meetings go?"

"Very well," she said, her composure back. "All the distributors I talked to increased their orders for this season. I'm pleased."

"Everything okay at the winery?"

"I left a list for Liam. I'm sure he has it all under control," she informed him.

"So you're done?"

"I'm done." She held up her hand in the sign of a pledge. "As of now, I am officially on vacation. What do you want to do this afternoon?"

"I was thinking coffee. We're going to be up late tonight."

Her cheerful expression flickered again, as though she wasn't super psyched about going out with him. "Oh, right."

Nope. Definitely not psyched, but he'd talk her into it eventually.

"So, coffee?"

"Coffee sounds good."

"There's a great place around the corner."

"Let's go."

They walked through the grange, cut through a small garden, and ended up on Shoreline Highway, the big road that ran right down the center of Point Reyes Station. The Bovine Bakery was just down the road, a postage-stamp-sized store with amazing coffee and friendly employees.

As soon as they were inside, Stella went straight for the pastry case. "Ohhh, yum," she said as soon as she saw the treats.

"I remembered your sweet tooth," he said with a smile. "Go nuts."

"Have you tried one of those giant cookies?" she asked, pointing to one that looked like chocolate chip.

Jason shook his head. "I only ever get coffee here." Their drip coffee was good and strong, just the way he liked it. In fact, he was here often enough to leave his mug in one of the cubbies reserved for locals.

"Hmm," she said, sizing up her quarry. "I'm getting one anyway."

After they made their purchases, they went outside and sat on the tall curb just off the main road where they could watch the cars and the people go by.

Stella pulled her cookie partway out of her paper bag and took a generous bite, her teeth leaving a perfect half moon in the chewy treat. She ate with her eyes closed, making happy noises in her throat.

"That good, huh?" he asked, trying not to stare at her mouth.

"So good," she moaned.

"Glad you like it."

"Everything tastes better here," she informed him. "The cookies. The coffee. Your cheese."

"You liked my cheese?"

"It's delicious, Jace. But I'm sure you knew that already."

"Yeah," he admitted. He wouldn't lie. There was something deeply primal about feeding her. Nourishing her. "But I like hearing *you* say it."

Her eyes went wide for a moment, then warmed. She took another bite of cookie, smiling to herself. "How was your work today?" she asked, when she'd swallowed.

He gave a shrug. "Eh."

"Something bad?"

"Not really," he said, shaking his head. "Just dealing with a few business issues."

She laughed a little.

"What's so funny?"

"You. Dealing with business issues."

"Why is that funny?" he asked, tamping down a twinge of irritation.

"I thought you moved away from Napa to get away from it all, and here you are, head of your own company. It's all so…I don't know…so *corporate* of you." She shrugged and took another bite of cookie.

"I didn't leave Napa to get away from it all," he told her. "I love working, especially when it's something I'm passionate about. And as much as you may think otherwise, I'm actually pretty good at it."

She turned to him. "Jace—" she started, realizing too late she'd put her foot in her mouth.

He didn't let her continue. "Rough Ranch is doing really well. We've doubled our profits over the last year, and this year, we're on track to double them again. So yeah, that's corporate, but it's the good kind. We don't just talk the talk, we walk the walk by keeping everything local and organic. We may not have the reach of Flynn Winery, but we'll get there sooner than you think."

She blinked. "I've never heard you speak like that before."

"I'm not playing around with this. I want this business to succeed, and the problems I'm facing are real. I guess I could have gone the way of Optimum. Run roughshod over the locals and focused only on the bottom line, but truth is, Rough Ranch is what it is because of our business model and our commitment to the community. I don't want to compromise that. At the same time, I still want to grow the business."

"I get it." She paused. "And I'm sorry if I insulted you. That truly wasn't my intention. It's just that the Jason I knew cared more about adventure and travel than profits and marketing."

He shrugged. "I grew up."

"I'm starting to see that." She took another bite of cookie. "So what are you dealing with? Give me something I can help with…like what's your biggest marketing challenge?"

"Price," he said, honestly. "It's hard to get consumers on board with our higher price points."

"I don't understand," she said. "What are your raw materials? Milk? Cream? How expensive can it be to make cheese?"

"See, that's the mentality most people have. Yes, we use milk and cream, along with rennet—that's the coagulant that makes the cheese separate into curds and whey—and bacteria, but it's the quality of those ingredients that makes it so costly. I can't compromise on the local and organic, and that just makes the prices skyrocket. Not only that, but artisanal makers don't have the economies of scale that larger producers enjoy." He took a sip of coffee. "Price is also impacted by government policies. In other countries, cheese-making costs are subsidized by the government. In the US, they aren't. So when a customer comes and sees that a Stilton from Britain costs $12.95 a pound, but a fresh cheese from Point Reyes costs $39.95 a pound, it doesn't really compute."

"I didn't realize how closely the issues in your industry seem to track the issues we face in the winemaking industry."

Jason nodded. "Artisanal cheese making is a burgeoning industry in this country, so our growing pains are similar to what US winemakers faced a few decades ago. It's not easy, but we'll get there someday."

He looked out to the scene in front of him where a man walking two Irish wolfhounds on leashes was crossing the street. The dogs were huge, almost four feet high at the shoulder, like something out of an old-fashioned novel. Still, it wasn't the strangest sight he'd seen in small, rural Point Reyes. Not by a long shot.

"Jason?" she said softly. "Are you okay?"

He turned back to Stella, who was watching him carefully. "Yeah. Thanks for letting me rant."

"Cookie?" She held it out.

He broke off a chunk, then popped it into his mouth. "Not bad," he said, but Stella had already moved on.

"You know I've been doing all the marketing for Flynn Winery, right?"

"Uh-huh." He snared another piece of cookie and ate that, too.

"I think one of the ways you might be able to combat the price point is to showcase your cheese in informative settings."

"We already do that with our tours."

"Sure, but that's only done locally. People have to come to you, right?"

"Right."

"So go to them. Get the word out. Use social media. Do cheese tastings and demonstrations."

"Where? There are those huge food and wine industry conferences, but we're not ready for those. We need to grow more organically than that."

"My suggestion? Smaller scale, but something with reach." She paused for a moment, and he could almost see her brain whirring. "I have it!" she exclaimed. "Why not pair up with someone else in the food and beverage industry who has a slightly broader reach?"

"There's no other cheese maker quite in our space right now. In fact, we're one of the leaders, not just in this area, but in the country."

"Actually, I was thinking wine. Flynn wine, to be more specific."

"I'm listening."

"Okay, well." Her eyes sparkled with excitement. "I've been thinking of planning a prerelease party for our latest batch of reserve. Maybe with a couple of other wineries doing their prereleases. Join us. Show off your best stuff. We can do wine and cheese pairings and introduce your cheese alongside our wine. You can sample, educate—everything. I'll even help you pick the pairings. What do you think?"

She was leaning forward a little, waiting for his answer. It was a decent plan. Flynn Winery's star was on the rise, and if Rough Ranch could harness some of that power and influence, it could no doubt help them.

"I think it sounds like a good idea," he told her.

"Only good?" she teased.

"Fine. Great," he said grudgingly. "I'll think about it. And in the meantime, you can take a tour. Tell me if you have any other ideas for me."

"All right."

He smiled and went to snare another piece of cookie, but she pulled the bag just out of reach.

"I thought you only ever got coffee," she said with a smile.

"I like sharing with you."

She was quiet for a moment, and her eyes went soft. Slowly she held out the bag. "I like sharing with you, too."

When he broke off another chunk, their fingertips brushed. Such a simple gesture, but one that seemed to have more weight, especially when her cheeks turned a little pink. Was he affecting her as much as she was affecting him? He desperately wanted to know, but was afraid that asking would ruin the moment.

He cleared his throat. "How about I buy you dinner before my show?"

"About your show—" she started, and he knew what was coming next. "I'm not sure it's such a good idea for me to come."

"Nope," he said, shaking his head. "Don't try to weasel out of it."

"I'm not trying to weasel out of it," she said, even though she was doing exactly that. "It's just that it'll be crowded and there'll be so many people, and you'll probably be so busy." She glanced down. "I don't want you to worry about me."

"I'll worry about you more if you're holed up at my house. You need to get out. Have some fun."

"I want to hear you play—really, I do. But bars aren't quite my idea of *fun*. Maybe I could sit this one out?" She looked up, sweetly hopeful. "We could hang out tomorrow night instead."

"Come on, Stella," he coaxed, giving her knee a nudge. "I really want you there."

She sighed heavily. "Okay. But don't expect me to be too social."
"The only person you'll have to talk to is me. Deal?"
She gave him a reluctant smile. "Deal."

CHAPTER 5

Later that night, Stella found herself sitting at the bar at the Old Western Saloon, nursing a glass of wine.

It was a quintessential dive bar, and though the place didn't look like much from the outside, the space inside was warm and inviting, rich in kitsch and history. With its stained glass sign and giant mirror hanging above the bar, a horseshoe mounted on the wall, and its fancy old-fashioned cash register, it felt like an old-time gold rush saloon, and Jason had informed her that's exactly what it once was.

The bar itself was a rich oak, its patina a muted gold, worn down from generations of elbows. Open since the 1890s, memorabilia from the bar's early history in the Old Western Hotel and posters of local bands lined the walls.

Clearly, it was a local favorite, because even on a Thursday night in wintertime, the place was packed with people laughing, drinking, and listening to Jason's blues band play on the tiny stage.

True to his word, Jason had taken her out for dinner at a cute little restaurant in downtown Point Reyes Station. She'd eaten some incredible fish tacos, and that margarita was still buzzing pleasantly around her brain. She should be happy.

But she wasn't, for the plain fact that she didn't want to be here. She wanted to be back at his house, alone. *Hiding.*

The truth was, despite whatever strange emotions were brewing between them, she was comfortable around Jason. But definitely not around strangers. Although her family was well-known and well-liked in local winemaking circles, she didn't have that many close friends. Not the way Jason did, with people calling and texting and stopping by to see him all the time. By contrast, she never went out in Napa. Never went anywhere, really.

Just work and home.

And once Matt left, there wasn't even a reason to go home anymore. So she worked nonstop, trying to forget her failure of a marriage. Her failure of a life.

When had things gotten so complicated? Work and death and divorce and loneliness and longing. Since her divorce—really, since her mother's death—she'd just been going through the motions.

Even the happiness she'd had watching her brother fall in love over New Year's had been a temporary blip, and then it was back to the grind. It didn't help that she seemed to put everyone and everything first—her dad, Liam, work. She'd even put Matt first when they were together, bending her schedule to match his, and because they both worked long hours, that meant she typically only saw him at work.

She should start putting herself first.

Consciously, she dragged herself out of her funk, took a sip of wine, and focused her attention on Jason's band. They were playing a soulful rendition of a famous B.B. King tune, and Jason was taking a solo.

Jason had always loved playing the electric bass and had his own band in high school—performances of which she was never allowed to attend because she was too young.

She'd seen him practicing, though. Even back then, he was good. No surprise, given that he threw himself into every endeavor with passion and drive. Now he was even better. His lean body moved in time with the music; his strong fingers walked all over the frets as if the bass were an extension of his own hand, bending the notes and the rhythm to his will.

A woman in the audience screamed out his name, but Jason didn't acknowledge her. Just kept on playing, nodding his head now as he played some complicated off-rhythm passage, then caught up to the beat, finishing his solo in a whirl of notes.

Mmm. What would it be like to feel those hands on her body?

Wait, what?

Crap. She'd done it again.

She put down her wine and pressed her hand to her forehead, praying that somehow, some way, her brain would figure out that Jason was *not* supposed to be the object of her fantasies.

Ugh, she was a mess. A hot mess who couldn't be trusted with anything having to do with sex.

She wished she could blame this all on Matt, but the real truth was that she was responsible too. Sure, her ex had cheated on her, but she hadn't been that surprised to find out. Sad, but true.

Marrying Matt was the path of least resistance. Her mother had just died, she was lonely, and it didn't get easier or more convenient than marrying the assistant winemaker at your own vineyard. She'd thought she loved him, but honestly, the marriage had always felt more like a business transaction than a love match.

Then again, she'd never been the type to have a passionate fling or to give it all up for love. She'd always been practical. Sensible.

Boring. Frigid.

Matt's words still haunted her.

Jason was still on stage, those big hands strumming away at his bass. She stopped staring at Jason's hands, took another sip of wine, and took stock of her situation. She was here and she was stuck, so she may as well make the most of it.

So what did people do in bars, anyway?

Drink. Flirt. Dance. Maybe find someone to take home for the night for some meaningless sex. Slink home in the morning wearing rumpled clothes, feeling a little dirty and a lot alive.

She'd never done that. Never been brave enough to.

Maybe she should have. If she'd had more experience before marrying Matt, it might have saved her a lot of heartache.

Critically, she surveyed her immediate vicinity. *If* she were going to get some experience, this would be a great place to start. There were a lot of good-looking guys here, fit and handsome in an outdoorsy kind of way, many sporting beards, and most wearing flannel shirts and worn jeans.

She zeroed in on a rugged man at the bar who was leaning forward trying to catch the bartender's attention. He had laugh lines around his eyes and longish sandy blond hair that matched the stubble on his face. He must have sensed her watching him, because he leaned back and caught her gaze. Slowly, he took her measure, once up, once down. She looked right back, taking in his broad chest and his long legs. He resembled a lumberjack. A big, sexy lumberjack.

Except as she surveyed her potential quarry, she felt…nothing. Just an empty space where desire should be. Even *she* knew enough to know that it wasn't normal.

She looked away, but it was too late. The big man was slicing through the crowd, moving toward her with intent. He was at her side in a matter of moments.

"Hey," Lumberjack said, his voice deep. "Buy you a drink? That is, if I can get Ruby's attention. She's awfully busy tonight." He indicated the older woman in the center of the bar, slinging beer on tap.

Stella held up her wine. "I'm okay for now, thanks."

Lumberjack put one huge hand on the bar and leaned in a little, getting in her space. "I haven't seen you around before. You just passing through?"

"For the weekend," she replied, regarding him over her glass as she took a sip. He looked good. He smelled good. And she didn't mind him looking at her like he wanted to eat her up. But she just couldn't get excited about him.

Lumberjack seemed to be oblivious to her inner struggles.

"A tourist," he said with obvious delight. "Well, you're in luck, because I'm an excellent tour guide. I know *all* the best spots." He gave her a wicked grin, leaving no doubt as to his exact meaning. "What's your name, honey?"

"Stella."

"Pretty name," he said, his voice husky. "So what are you doing in town, Stella?"

She blinked, surprised at the power she seemed to wield. It had been forever since she'd felt sexy. Wanted. And it went to her head in a hot rush.

"I came to relax," she told him honestly. "But I seem to have gotten caught up in work and…other things."

Lumberjack raised an eyebrow. "We're going to have to see if we can change that."

Then he smiled, a slow, easy smile, and the promise of meaningless sex—of *experience*—danced before her.

Except it was all wrong. She hadn't thought this through properly, had she? It was a question of desire, and she had none—not for this guy, anyway.

Stella's throat closed up, leaving her mute.

The sad reality was that all her work and lists and plans were as ridiculous as she was. She always did exactly what people thought she'd do. Played it safe. Stayed on task. She was all business, all the time. Always doing the right thing.

She was sick of doing the right thing, but here, faced with temptation, she couldn't do the *wrong* thing. Like go home with this dude. She didn't know him. More importantly, she didn't trust him. And the one person she *did* trust—whom she might actually want to look at her the way Lumberjack was doing—just looked at her like a little sister.

Not for the first time that night, she wanted to be anywhere but here.

Lumberjack leaned in a little closer. "Want to take this somewhere quieter?"

No.

Just as she was working through how to gracefully get out of this situation, a big arm slipped around her shoulders.

"There you are, Stell." It was Jason, and she caught only the gleam in his amber eyes right before he bent his head and touched his lips to hers.

Holy hell.

His lips were warm and firm and demanding. Urgent. A thousand volts of electricity passed through her, shocking her with its intensity. Without meaning to, she gasped, and he slipped his tongue in her mouth—just one small flick. Enough to leave her wanting so much more.

Her brain spun, and she had the crazy sensation of being on a carnival ride—the kind that spins round and round, pinning you to the wall before the floor drops away. She'd always loved that ride, loved the freedom of feeling outside her own body for a few dreamlike moments. But this was different—it wasn't a ride, it was real. And that made it dangerous.

All at once his lips were gone, leaving her dizzy, breathless.

And confused.

She went to search Jason's face for clues, but he'd already turned back to Lumberjack, chest out, swagger on. It took her a moment to figure out what was going on, and when she did, her heart almost stopped.

He was protecting her.

But she'd never quite seen him like this, aggressive and hard. Jason wasn't as physically big as the other guy, but his attitude sure was. It emanated from him in waves, filling up the space and very clearly marking her as his.

His.

A thrill swept through her, followed quickly by annoyance. It wasn't enough that her body went haywire every time he touched her, but now he was treating her like she was fourteen again. Like she couldn't solve her own problems.

Before she could figure out how to get rid of Lumberjack so she could tell Jason off for treating her like a kid, Jason lifted his chin to the other man, acknowledging him. "What's up, Charley?"

Oh, no. Jason knew him. Of course he did. Jason knew everyone.

Lumberjack took a small step back. "Nice set, man." He gave Stella a short nod. "Sorry to bother you."

Charley retreated to his former spot at the bar, but Jason kept his arm around her. In fact, his arm was even tighter now, and she realized that Charley was still watching them.

Jason pulled her close and kissed her temple, a purely proprietary gesture, akin to telling the whole bar that she was off-limits.

Furious, Stella refused to look at him. "What are you doing?" she hissed.

"Getting the situation under control and saving you from making a big mistake." He spoke directly into her ear, his warm breath tickling her skin. "Trust me, you do *not* want to go home with Charley tonight. He sleeps with anything that moves."

"I'm a big girl, Jason. I can make my own mistakes." Her abysmal personal life was evidence of *that.*

She looked up then. Jason's gaze was inscrutable—half angry, half something else she couldn't quite place.

"You're right, Stella. You're a big girl." His voice was dark. "Just answer me this: Do you want him?"

"Who, Charley?"

"Take your pick," he said, jerking his head as if to indicate the entire place. "Any single guy here would be happy to take you home tonight. All you have to do is give them some encouragement and they'd be yours."

The crease was back between his brows, his teeth were clenched so tightly that a muscle ticked on his jaw, and good grief! Stern, commanding Jason was *hot*. His cheeks were flushed—With anger? With passion?—and his eyes sparked fire. Stella's blood raced through her veins and her body throbbed in time with her heartbeat, a sensation she'd never felt before and wasn't much sure she liked.

"No," she breathed, the truth finally hitting her like a ton of bricks. "I don't want them."

I want you.

That admission both thrilled and shocked her.

Jason's expression morphed into something very much like relief, and for the briefest of moments, he looked as though he was going to say something else. But he didn't. Just removed his arm and reached for a glass of ice water the bartender must have slipped there when she wasn't paying attention.

His eyes never leaving hers, he took a long drink, his Adam's apple bobbing with each swallow. She couldn't drag her gaze away. Who *was* this new Jason? This territorial, possessive man who seemed to have come out of nowhere?

Jason finished drinking and put the glass back on the bar.

"I have to play another set. Stay," he growled, pointing at her seat.

She was about to lay into him for ordering her around, but he'd already disappeared into the crowd. That was probably a good thing, because she wasn't sure she was up for a fight. His words had triggered something deep inside—a need she didn't know she could possess. Her lips still throbbed from his kiss, and the rest of her body had gotten on board, too. Her nipples were hard, her sex was clenched, and she was actually panting.

I want him.

The band started up again, but Stella barely heard a note. Just sat there in a state of shock, her body aching. There was no denying her reaction now. She wasn't confused from her divorce. She didn't have any crossed wires.

She had the hots for Jason Roberts.

Okay. Stay calm. Go through your options.

The control freak in her started making lists. She could pretend that nothing was wrong and go about her business this weekend, let him indulge her the way he wanted.

No. That wouldn't work. First, she was a terrible faker, and second, she'd already just proven that she couldn't hide her reaction to him. Every time he touched her she was a wreck.

Next.

She could make an excuse, get in her truck, and head home.

That would be even worse. Not only would that wreck all of *her* plans, but Jason might think he'd done something wrong. And what was she going to do in Napa this weekend, anyway? Hide out from the lovefest going on around her?

Option three?

She could tell Jason how she felt.

Stella wasn't a blunt person by nature. But with her brother and Jason, she'd always been able to tell the truth. She could just tell him what she needed—him. Jason did whatever he wanted, whenever he wanted. Why couldn't she do that, too?

With him.

Okay, no.

For so many reasons. It would ruin their friendship. It would mess things up between him and Liam. And even if he agreed, it would only be temporary. Jason didn't do relationships. One-night stands were his thing, right?

Damn him for kissing her and for messing everything up! Without that kiss, it was all theoretical. He'd just gone and made it real.

She glanced up at him. Jason was playing, focused on the music, but his gaze was squarely on her, eyes hungry.

And then she realized something else.

He wants me, too.

He hadn't needed to invite her to his place. He could have left her alone for the weekend. Taken her out to a token lunch or dinner and left her to her own devices the rest of the time. He hadn't needed to touch her, to kiss her. He knew Charley and could have gotten rid of him some other way.

He wanted her. Except he'd never do anything about it because of their shared history. Despite his devil-may-care reputation, he had a huge noble streak underneath it all.

There was a fourth option. One that simmered on the edges of her consciousness.

I could seduce him.

She wanted him, that much was certain. Those feelings were unlikely to go away, and if they didn't go away, she couldn't get back to her regularly scheduled life.

There were merits to her plan. It would be short and sweet—definitely his kind of fling. Hers, too. She'd just gotten out of a doomed marriage, so she wasn't interested in another relationship. Sleeping around wasn't her thing, but she needed to do *something* to make herself feel like a woman again.

Plus, she trusted him to take care of her. He wouldn't hurt her. He wouldn't expect anything from her except what she was willing to give.

And when the weekend was over, he wouldn't break her heart. Then maybe, just maybe, she could move on with her life.

CHAPTER 6

It was one thing to have a plan, and it was another thing to act on that plan. So Stella ended up simply riding out the rest of the concert and then getting into Jason's truck at the end of the evening for the drive home.

No fewer than five different women had approached Jason after his show. *Five*. All beautiful and friendly and clearly wanting more than simply to hang out that evening. Of course Jason had been friendly right back, but he hadn't gone home with any of them. That gave her a little hope.

Except he'd said zippo about that kiss he'd given her. In fact, he was doing an excellent job of pretending it hadn't happened at all.

Damn.

She'd hoped he'd make it easy. That he would say something suave and witty like he always did, giving her a clue as to whether he would be open to taking their friendship to the next level, but no. In fact, he was acting downright strange. Maybe she'd misread the signs?

She glanced over at him. He had both hands on the steering wheel, his jaw was clenched, and he was staring at the road through the front window. Not angry. Stressed.

She pushed her hair back behind her ears, her movements stiff and jerky, the way she always got when she was nervous. Ugh, this sucked.

"Are you okay?" she asked.

"Fine," he said, his voice short.

Then silence, so thick she could cut it with a knife.

Things didn't get better until they were back at his place, out on the deck. She hadn't really wanted another glass of wine, but she'd accepted the one he'd given her anyway. The glass he was drinking—the first bit of alcohol he'd had all night—seemed to relax him, which was good. The last thing she wanted was more awkwardness.

It was cold, but they threw on their coats and sat on two adjacent Adirondack chairs, looking out into the surprisingly clear night. Myriad stars twinkled overhead in the black sky, and down below, the water was an inky pool in the darkness. In the shadow of Black Mountain, the few scattered lights across the bay seemed even brighter by comparison. From behind the house, an owl hooted softly, then fell silent.

It was beautiful, this dark quiet. Beautiful and melancholy, and yet for some strange reason, she felt completely exposed.

After a while, Jason's shoulders relaxed, and after even longer, he turned to her. "How are you doing?" Jason asked.

"Fine."

"I don't think so."

He was right, as usual. She gave him a sideways look. "Do you want the truth?"

"Always."

She looked out at the darkness again. "I'm not fine."

"Yeah. I got that." He was silent for a moment. "Is it me?"

Yes. "It's everything." She sighed.

"Want to tell me what's going on?"

She shook her head. "I'm a mess."

"No, you're not," he said quietly.

Stella gave a short laugh at that. "I am. And what's more, I've been a mess for some time now."

"What I *have* noticed is that you seem really…I don't know…sad, I guess. Your marriage didn't work out. I get that. But what I don't get is why you don't seem relieved. If it wasn't right, it wasn't right. Shouldn't you be happy you're free to move on?"

He was right—she *should* feel happy. For the first time in her life, there was nothing holding her back. She could focus on herself for once, be the uninhibited woman she always hoped she'd be. But honestly, she didn't know how to do that. It was easier to make her plans and lists than to focus on the tough stuff, the uncomfortable-but-important stuff that took time and energy and work.

"Have you ever thought about getting married, Jace?"

He shot her a strange look. "Yeah," he finally said. "A long time ago."

"I didn't. I know that sounds strange, but I honestly didn't. Not until Matt asked me. I always thought it was kind of crazy in an optimistic way. Sharing the rest of your life with one person."

Jason was silent.

"It was good, at first. I was so happy that he'd noticed me, so happy that he'd chosen me. I thought he saw something in me that I couldn't see in myself. I tried so hard to see things differently. Even taste things differently. To show everyone I'd changed."

"Had you?"

"I thought so. At least for a while. There was this one Flynn wine my dad and Liam were always raving about. I tried it and thought it was crap. Everyone kept telling me it had potential, but I sure couldn't see it. Then Matt talked me into tasting it again. He broke it down flavor by flavor, and I *finally* got what they were talking about."

"So all of a sudden you loved it?"

"No. It was a challenging pour, but at least I understood what they saw in it." She tucked her knees up and wrapped her arms around them. "The early days of marriage are like that. You want so badly to understand the other person, to combine your life with theirs, that you try to see *everything* from their perspective. It's dumb stuff, like squeezing the toothpaste from the end instead of the middle or eating cereal as a midnight snack, but it's also big stuff, like how often to have dinner with your families or when to schedule a vacation. So you try to see things their way. And then you start to do things their way, just to make them happy."

Jason shifted in his seat. "Let me guess. You did everything Matt's way, and he didn't reciprocate."

"It was more than that. I mean, I thought that being married would bring out the best in me. Would—I don't know—truly change me. And for a while, I thought it had. I was feeling more comfortable around our clients. Even getting out more. Going to more parties and things like that." She shook her head. "But it was all window dressing. I hadn't changed. I was still the same person underneath."

"The same great person."

She loved that he saw the best in her. "I'm ridiculous. And everyone knows it."

He frowned now. "What are you talking about? No one thinks you're ridiculous."

"Sure they do," she said, unable to hide the bitterness in her voice. "Shy little Stella Flynn who left home for college and came right back again. Who's attached at the hip to her family. Who married the first person who asked her." *Who can't even keep her husband in her bed.* She closed her eyes. "I wanted to change," she whispered. "I thought I could be someone I wasn't. Someone exciting and passionate."

Jason let out a low whistle. "Matt really did a number on you, didn't he?"

"What do you mean?" she asked, her voice sharp.

"What happened to the Stella Flynn who kept it together after her mom died? Who single-handedly managed Flynn Winery? Who helped keep her dad from going off the deep end until he was ready to take charge again? Who constantly gives me and Liam the butt-kickings we need? You're loving and loyal and strong. None of that's changed, and the Stella Flynn I know would see that."

"There's more to life than taking care of family."

"Your devotion to your family is one of your greatest strengths," he said. "But if you're looking for validation, you don't need it. You do a lot more than take care of your family. You're still playing the piano. You're working. And you're one of the best winery managers in the valley. People know you. They *trust* you. Just because you're not on everyone else's timetable or you got a little off track with a bad marriage doesn't mean you're defective."

She shook her head, not quite believing his words.

"And as for Matt," Jason continued, "he cheated on you, not the other way around. You loved him. Respected him. And he repaid you by dicking around. That's not on you, Stell. That's on him."

Now this she took issue with. "If I'd been the woman he wanted it wouldn't have happened."

"You really believe that?"

She gave a small shrug.

"You're wrong," he said vehemently. "So wrong. That's not what love is. He should have loved you for who you were, not what he wanted you to be. You should never have to change for someone you love." His gaze met hers, and he wouldn't look away. "If you were mine, I'd never ask you to change. And I'd damn sure never let you spend a single night alone."

His words made her brave.

"Why'd you kiss me?" she said, her voice soft.

"About that," he started. "I'm sorry that I—"

She cut him off. "I'm not asking for your apology. I'm asking why."

Silence. "Because I wanted to," he finally rasped.

There was so much pain in his eyes. Pain and confusion and loneliness and neediness, mirroring exactly what he must see in her own, and she wanted him so much she could barely breathe.

Stella leaned toward him. Then carefully, deliberately, she reached out and wrapped her hand around the back of his neck. She left it there for a moment, testing him. Waiting.

"Stella—" His voice was low, dark, but he didn't pull away. "What are you doing?"

"What we both want."

And then she drew his head down and pressed her lips to his.

CHAPTER 7

Stella was kissing him. His Stella, her soft mouth on his, her small shoulder resting against him, and the kiss was even better this time because *she'd* been the one to initiate it. He'd never tasted anything so rich, so sweet.

He pulled her right over the arm of the chair and onto his lap. She came willingly, deepening the kiss, opening her mouth just enough for him to slide his tongue against hers if he wanted.

And he wanted, so very badly.

So he did and was rewarded when she fisted the front of his shirt, pulling him even closer. He buried a hand in her hair like a lover would, the way he'd always wanted, and she responded with a little moan.

His cock came to life, spurred on by her kiss and the weight of her sweet rear end. She could feel it, too, because she made some kind of purring sound in her throat and rubbed against him.

How many times had he dreamed of this? Of having Stella in his arms, taking her mouth, taking *her*. But this was dangerous. Wrong. The ultimate betrayal of a man he thought of like a brother.

He jerked his head back, in near physical pain from the absence of her lips.

"Wait," he managed to get out. "What are we doing?"

Eyes trained on his, she slipped her hand under his shirt and slowly slid it up his rib cage, her soft palm dragging across his flesh.

"I'm seducing you," she said, right before she pressed her lips to his once again.

So, so good.

Her hand inched higher, burning his skin where she touched.

A low sound emanated from between them. It took way too long to realize it was him. Growling.

He jerked away again. "Hold up a minute," he said, pinning her hand to his chest. "We can't do this."

"Why not? I want you." She wiggled her rear against the bulge of his erection. "And you obviously want me."

When she tilted her head toward him again, it took every ounce of his willpower not to bend. "No."

She snatched her hand away and leaned back, hurt written all over her face.

"You don't want me?"

"I—" He ran a hand through his hair and took a deep breath, not wanting to screw this up even more than it already was. "I do want you, Stella. So damned much it hurts. But we can't. Your brother would kill me."

"My brother?" she said, her voice edging up a pitch. "What does he have to do with this?"

"When he finds out—"

She practically leaped off his lap. "I'm a grown woman. Are you seriously telling me that you can't do this because of my *brother*?"

It killed him to say no. Really killed him, but the thought of wrecking everything made him stop cold. "I can't."

"Because of Liam." She sounded more than a little incredulous.

"Right."

He knew she thought he was lying, but there wasn't much more he could say. Or do. His resolve had already been pushed to the limit.

"I'm such an idiot. I thought—" She turned away, her eyes glittery with unshed tears, and walked over to the railing.

He tried to stand, but his cock rubbed painfully against his fly. Crap. A quick adjustment and he was finally able to rise. He walked over to her, just in time to see a tear run down her cheek.

She wiped it away fast. "You must think I'm pathetic, coming on to you like this."

"No." It was brave. Braver than he could ever be. She'd put herself out there for him, laid herself bare.

She shivered a little, stirring up not only his protective instinct but a fresh jolt of desire.

Deep breath. Don't touch her. You've screwed things up enough.

Stella shook her head. "What was I thinking? I can't even seduce anyone properly." Another tear escaped and made its way down her cheek. She wiped it away, turned to him, and steeled her gaze. She was shutting down again, closing herself off, the way she always did, and there was nothing he could do to stop it. "I'm going to bed now."

He wanted so badly to hold her, comfort her, but he forced himself to keep his hands to himself. Just wordlessly followed her inside.

She didn't say good night and went directly upstairs. Footsteps. A door shutting. Then silence. This wasn't known-each-other-for-years silence. This was raw and awkward, the uncomfortable kind where anything you said would just make things worse.

Jason stayed downstairs, doing everything he could to just *stop thinking* for a while. He put the wineglasses away. He drank some water.

But his body was still on overdrive, and the thoughts just kept coming.

Namely that Stella had offered herself to him on a silver platter and he'd declined.

What had he been thinking? That he was noble? That he was saving her? From what? The little devil on his shoulder kept whispering in his ear.

If she doesn't do this with you, she's just going to find someone else.

The thought of that made him sick.

You might never have this chance again.

She wants you. You want her. Take what you want.

It was so tempting.

But the little angel on his other shoulder whispered *wait.*

It was hard as hell, but he waited. And waited, until he thought she was asleep, though it took all of his strength not to go to her.

Finally, he went upstairs. The hallway was dark.

Doggedly, he headed for his room. And then Stella came out of the bathroom at the end of the hall, backlit by the light. Every impulse he'd suppressed—the need, the want—came roaring back like a freight train.

Resolutely, she walked toward him, toward her room. Her face was pale and her eyes were a little red. She'd been crying more. And that just *killed* him.

All of his good intentions flew straight out the window. To hell with waiting.

But Stella wouldn't look at him. Just set her jaw and made as if to walk past him. He stopped her with two words.

"Don't go," he said, his voice sounding desperate to his own ears.

She looked up at him, her gaze tremulous. "Why not?"

Her bravery made him brave. "Because I do want you, Stella. So damn much. And if you walk away from me right now, if you walk away from this, I know I'll regret it for the rest of my life."

She let out a breath—a tiny puff of air—and twisted her lips, searching his face. He let her stare, showing her everything. His confusion, his abject need, and his truth.

She was going to leave. Reject him, just like he'd rejected her on the deck. He wouldn't blame her.

But she stepped forward, tipped her face up to his.

Thank you.

Then her lips met his and he was lost, drowning in her.

He buried his hand in her hair, tilted her head, and took what he wanted from her willing mouth. She responded the same way—urgently sliding her tongue over his in deep, long strokes. One of her hands found his waist, then slid down the back of his jeans to cup his ass.

Stella's mouth. Stella's hand.

The skip of his heartbeat was matched by an answering jolt in his cock.

Years of pent-up longing and need erupted, swamping him in a tidal wave of emotion so thick that he could hardly think straight. But Stella, ah, Stella knew exactly what she wanted.

"Your room or mine?" she asked.

His answer was to press her up against the wall in the hallway, right next to a framed photograph of Flynn Winery she'd given to him when he'd returned from Paris the first time. And as she stood there, looking up at him, his past and present blurred together.

Then he leaned into her, giving her some of his weight as he claimed her lips with his.

She writhed underneath him, pressing her soft breasts against his chest, rocking her hips against his erection, showing him how much she wanted him. One little hand snaked from his hip to his cock, exploring his hard heat. He pinned her wrist against the wall above her head, and when she reached down with the other hand, that wrist got the same treatment, too.

Quickly, he glanced up at her face, making sure she was still on board with this. Her chest was rising and falling in sharp bursts, and there was a look of utter desire on her beautiful face, leaving no doubt that she wanted this as badly as he did.

"If we do this—" she started, then swallowed. "If we do this, afterward nothing changes between us."

What she was asking was impossible. Of course things were going to change. She was everything he wanted, and he wanted to claim her, not just tonight, but for always. But she didn't want that. Could he take her, knowing what he was going to gain and what he was going to lose?

She shifted under him, and that was his undoing. He would sell his soul for another taste of her.

"Swear?" she said, and he felt the last of his resolve slipping. If this was the price he had to pay, he would pay…for the rest of his life.

"I swear." He sealed his promise with a kiss, then went to claim his prize.

He let go of a wrist and unbuttoned her pajama top, revealing inch after inch of smooth skin. When the top was completely undone, he shifted the fabric off her shoulder, revealing one small, perfect breast.

He palmed it and couldn't help from groaning. She was so soft, so beautiful, just as he knew she would be. Her nipple hardened in his palm, and he used his thumb and forefinger to stroke, then pluck the hardened tip. She was the one to moan now, long and low, so he slid the shirt aside further and did the same thing with her other breast, twisting and rubbing until her nipple was taut.

Her eyes were closed, and the most erotic little noises emanated from her throat. He couldn't resist. He bent his head and carefully flicked the tip of one breast with his tongue. She moaned like crazy then, buried her hand in his hair and twisted in his arms, but he showed her no mercy, drawing her nipple in deep and sucking. She cried out, and her cries got even louder when he did the same thing to the other.

He wanted to keep playing, but there was so much more to explore, so he stopped and slid a hand down her stomach, right into her pajama bottoms. She gasped, and he felt the proof of her desire—hot, wet heat emanating from her core.

"Yess—" she hissed, and it was all he could do not to yank down her pants and take her right there.

But this was Stella, and he'd been waiting for this for years. She needed more from him than this.

He scooped her up and carried her the rest of the way to his room, where he laid her down carefully on the bed.

Oh, she was gorgeous, her pajama top falling off her shoulders, her nipples still hard and wet from his mouth.

He pulled his tee over his head, loving the way her eyes drank him in and her breath quickened.

He went for his pants next, kicking them off onto the floor, then edged his drawers over his throbbing cock.

Her mouth had formed a perfect O as she stared at him.

He stood there, trying to gauge her comfort level.

"Tell me what you're thinking."

She looked up at him, then down, suddenly shy. "Last night, I—" she started, then stopped and swallowed. "I touched myself, thinking about you. But my imagination wasn't this good."

He groaned aloud as he envisioned Stella in her bed, pleasuring herself to dreams of him while he did the same to dreams of her. Any doubts he had about this were buried under an avalanche of need.

He shook his head, a smile on his lips. "Do you have any idea how much I want you?"

She glanced at his cock. "I think I have some idea."

She really didn't, but that was okay. She was here, and at least for tonight, she was his. He'd dreamed of this for so long and now she was here, in his bed.

He cupped her face in his hands, took her mouth in a searing kiss. She leaned back, pulling him with her, her hands roaming in his hair, over his back, fingers digging deep when he did something she liked.

He slid her bottoms off, along with her panties.

"Tell me what you want," he said. Above all, he wanted to make this good for her. Unforgettable. "Tell me what you like."

She blinked at him, as if she were surprised by the question. "I like your hands on me," she finally whispered, then bit her lip.

Stella clearly wasn't used to talking in bed, and she *definitely* wasn't used to demanding what she wanted. In fact, she seemed to do better when some of that control was taken away. Maybe if he got another chance this weekend he'd help her break free. For now, all he wanted to do was to love her.

Gently, almost reverently, he smoothed his hand down her arm and back up again.

She shivered at his touch, so he kept on going, first with his hands, skimming over her still-hard nipples, dipping down into the valley of her waist and over the flare of her hips, sliding from the arch of her foot up her calf, her inner thigh.

Tentatively, she parted her legs—a tacit invitation to continue. This was happening, really happening. He raised his eyes in quick thanks to the heavens that he'd been afforded this opportunity.

She was lying there, eyes closed, hair spread over his comforter, her chest rising and falling with each shallow breath.

"May I?"

"Please, Jace."

So he spread her wide and tasted.

She moaned and made to come off the bed, but he held her hips, forcing her to stay still, to watch him worship her body with his mouth.

And she watched, her eyes trained on him, her hands in his hair. Watched as he slowly licked, then sucked, then soothed the heat with gentle kisses.

He waited until her thighs were shaking with need, until she began to chant his name, and then carefully slid a finger inside her.

She came apart almost instantly, her back arching off the bed as she cried out his name. She was beautiful as she came, eyes closed, body flushed, as shudders racked her body.

He'd done that to her. Given her this pleasure.

He kissed her thigh, then her stomach. "You okay?"

She opened her eyes and smiled down at him.

"More," she said. "Please."

"Are you sure about this?" he said, giving her one last chance to call it off, preserve the invisible wall they'd built between them. She had to tell him to stop, because he sure as hell couldn't on his own. But she didn't tell him to stop.

She simply cupped his face in her hands and looked deep into his eyes.

"I've never been more sure of anything."

That was all it took for him to push away the doubt. He got a condom from his bedside table and slipped it on.

He'd been dreaming of this forever. Hoping that somehow, some way, he would get the privilege to touch her, to taste her. Now faced with Stella spread out before him like an erotic offering, he found he couldn't wait a single moment longer.

He edged between her thighs, drew her knees up, and carefully, exquisitely, slid home.

Intoxicating. Heady and rich. But this wasn't a dream. This was real. He was here, buried inside Stella as far as he could go. And she was smiling up at him.

"It feels so good."

He almost cried with relief, but he laughed instead. It wasn't just good. It was incredible. He held on to the moment as long as he could until she began to shift under him. Carefully, he withdrew, then plunged back inside. She gasped, and when he positioned her hips to slide in even deeper, she moaned.

He tried to memorize every minute of this. The tiny beauty mark under her chin. The way she breathed out, just a little, each time he bottomed out inside her body, the depth of passion in her dark eyes. He pulled out, then thrust in deep, loving her sharp intake of breath.

He needed to remember exactly how she looked in this moment, exactly how she felt under him. Because this wasn't permanent, and his memories would have to last a lifetime.

She was moving her hips to meet his now, matching him stroke for stroke, crowding out everything except thoughts of her. Nothing was as good as being buried inside her. He'd known it would be like this from the moment he fell for her. Known how perfectly she'd fit him.

He needed only one more thing to make this complete.

"Say my name," he breathed. "Please."

"Jason," she said.

He withdrew, then plunged back in. "Again."

"Oh, Jace—"

"Yes." That. His name on her lips as he buried himself inside her.

He went faster and faster, and she kept up with him, snapping her hips, chasing down what she was seeking.

Stella dug her fingers into his back—a clear sign she was close—and a few seconds later, came apart even more violently than she had the first time.

Jason clasped her trembling body and pumped, coming so hard it was as if his whole body turned inside out.

He wanted to linger, but she was small, so reluctantly, he withdrew from her body and flipped over to his back where he lay, catching his breath. She slid up beside him and placed her hand on his chest, right over his still rapidly beating heart.

"Nothing changes," she said, looking down at him.

"Nothing changes," he answered, his heart cracking wide open.

Because everything *had* changed. They'd crossed a line, and he was the one who'd have to deal with the consequences for one simple reason— Stella saw him as a weekend fling.

And he saw her as his forever.

CHAPTER 8

Stella woke to the sound of a raven cawing outside. She pried open her eyes. A gray light filtered through the chilly room, and despite the fact that she was wearing only her panties, she was warm and comfortable underneath the heavy blanket, nestled in Jason's arms.

Slowly, she took stock of her body. She was a little sore, but it was the good kind of sore. The sore you smiled about later when you remembered everything you'd done and how good it had been.

Now she knew why there were women knocking down his door: Jason Roberts was a master in bed. She'd never felt so satisfied...or so sated.

It wasn't simply that he seemed to know her body better than she did. It was that he'd made her feel treasured. Wanted. Like there was no one else but her.

Best of all, he hadn't ruined everything afterward with false words and promises he wouldn't keep. He'd sworn that nothing would change, and he would keep that promise. She was sure of it.

It was definitely a little strange being with him so intimately after years of friendship, but that's also what made it easier. There were no expectations of love, for one thing. And for another thing, she had nothing to prove to him—he already knew her inside and out. Moving from the emotional to the physical wasn't the huge deal she'd thought it would be.

Jason was still sleeping, but he was too beautiful not to touch. Gently, she traced the line of one finely hewn pectoral muscle down and around, watching it rise and fall with his breathing.

Something had shifted last night. Something big between them, and it wasn't just the sex. She'd always been connected to him, but here, in the stillness of the room, laid out for her and her alone, he seemed to be *more* somehow.

They'd shared themselves, their bodies.

But things wouldn't be different. She wouldn't let them be different.

Last night had been…well, if not exactly what she expected, then exactly what she needed. Jason had made her feel beautiful, invincible. She'd been right to trust him. He was the perfect man to rebound with. He would be good to her for the weekend, help her regain her confidence, and when she left, well, that would be that.

A strange twinge of sadness panged in her chest.

Stop that.

She knew what Jason was well before this weekend, and she loved him anyway. He was who he always was, and he didn't need to change; *she* did. Thanks to him, she felt as though she was one step closer to doing that.

Gently, she kissed him on the cheek. His eyelids flickered and then opened.

"Hey," he said, his voice still thick with sleep.

"Hey," she responded.

He stretched his free arm up and out. Blinked his eyes a couple of times. "How long have you been up?"

"Not long."

Jason shifted and pushed her hair back, then thumbed her brow, her cheek, her lips, his expression one of wonder.

"You good?"

"Yeah." She kissed his cheek again. "Really good."

His eyes warmed, and he tilted her face up.

His lips meeting hers was delicious. She closed her eyes, soaking in the sensations. It was hard to beat waking up to this. She might even be tempted to make it a habit.

All at once his lips were gone.

"Last night—" he started.

"Doesn't change anything," she interjected before he could say something he'd regret. "You swore."

She didn't want him to feel obligated to her. Obligation was as bad as pity. And she was sure the very last thing he wanted was to have her hanging around after the weekend was over, expecting *more*. It would cramp his style.

"Nothing changes," he said flatly, which made him sound not so much *relieved* as *annoyed*.

"Are you good?" she asked, her voice tentative.

"Yep. I'm good."

He relaxed, so she relaxed, too. "Good."

"We should probably stop saying *good*."

"We should," she agreed.

"Good."

She blew him a raspberry, and he started tickling her, and somehow she ended up squirming underneath him, laughing breathlessly. Until he stopped and she felt his hard heat against her hips. She looked up at him, questioning.

He kissed her, a long, lingering kiss that promised so much more. Finally, he broke it off and groaned.

"Later," he said. "You're probably sore."

"A little," she admitted.

He kissed her forehead. "We'll take it easy, then."

"What if I don't want to take it easy?" she said, a sly smile on her lips, realizing she was already ready for him, primed by his kiss alone.

"Well, then I'd say you'd probably want me to do something like this." He cupped her bare breast in his warm hand and gently squeezed. There was an answering jolt in the vicinity of her lower belly, and then a liquid heat spread through her veins.

"Mmm," she said, sinking so easily into the pleasurable sensations. One night of sex and she already wanted more. Was that her, or was that Jason? It was probably Jason.

His fingers were busy kneading and plucking, stroking and pinching, hardening her nipple and making her body ache so deliciously.

"Or maybe this." He gave the same treatment to the other breast, and she couldn't help the low moan that escaped her lips.

"Or perhaps you mean something like this," he said, his hand slipping between her legs and rubbing her most sensitive spot. Her panties were already damp, but that just made the friction more intense.

Jason flicked her nipples, first with his fingers, and then with his tongue, all the while stroking, first gently, then with more pressure. It was too much, all this attention on her already-sensitized body.

Thirty seconds later, she came hard and fast, closing her eyes against an onslaught of sensation so acute it almost verged on pain.

When she opened her eyes, she found him watching her, an incredulous look on his face.

"That's all it takes for you?" He sounded awed.

"Is that—bad?"

Jason cupped her jaw and kissed her mouth. "No, Stella, that's definitely not bad. In fact, it's pretty hot." He pulled away and swung his legs off the bed, tossing a look her way. "So, you coming?"

"Where?"

"The shower."

The chance to see his magnificent form wet and lathered up was not something she was going to miss.

"Absolutely."

An hour later, still pleasantly mellow from the second orgasm Jason had coaxed out of her using only his wet fingers—*I want to see if I can make you come that fast again*, he'd said—Stella found herself with a travel mug of hot coffee in her hand outside the cheese-making room at Rough Ranch.

The tour wasn't a walking tour, given that they couldn't enter the cheese-making area because of contamination issues, but more like a demonstration and tasting. Instead, they sat in the grange at a long wooden table.

Christine, their Rough Ranch guide, was a gentle, generous woman with curly blond hair who led the group through a detailed history of the area and of Rough Ranch.

A curd-making demonstration was next, and Stella found it fascinating. She hadn't realized just how few ingredients went into making cheese, or the way the milk could be transformed into something so incredible in such a short time. Bacterial culture was added to milk and briefly stirred before rennet was introduced to form the curds. The curds were cut, lifted into molds, allowed to drain and rest overnight, then brushed with more bacteria to colonize the outside of the mold, which made the rind. Aging took anywhere from a few days for the fresh cheeses to a few weeks for the aged cheeses as the bacteria native to the area did its work.

So simple, yet so complex.

But it was the cheese tasting that was a true revelation. Just like wine, each cheese had its own unique flavors and tones. In one, she actually tasted mushrooms and butter. In another, she swore she caught a hint of clover. And in that delectable Green Leaf, she discovered an extra depth to the flavors she hadn't experienced the first time around.

Jason found Stella almost as soon as the tour was over. "You hungry for lunch?" he asked.

"Shockingly, yes," she replied. "You'd think after all that cheese I wouldn't be, but for some reason, it made me hungrier."

Together, they walked through the grange and out to the grassy courtyard behind. The sun had peeked out from behind the clouds, brightening the greenery and warming the air. Stella took off her cardigan and shoved it into her handbag.

"So, what'd you think of the tour?" Jason asked as they emerged from the courtyard onto the street.

"It was amazing." She looked at him slyly. "In fact, I was surprised how much like winemaking cheesemaking actually is." In her mind, Jason hadn't truly left Napa Valley behind; he'd simply taken what he loved and applied it to another medium.

But Jason wasn't buying it. "No way," he said.

"You don't think? Let me try to convince you. In wine you take the grapes and in cheese, you take—let's see if I remember—the milk and cream, sometimes both for your fresh cheeses, the culture and the rennet, right?"

He smiled at her. "Right."

"So the ingredients are different, but the process is the same. Start with fresh ingredients that rely on the land. Grapes are flavored by the earth, the sun, and the rain. Milk is flavored by the same thing, because of what the cow might be eating. Then, mix the ingredients, age them, and the ingredients transform. See? The same!"

Jason laughed. "Not quite."

"Okay, not quite, but you have to admit there are some similarities in the creating process, and *definitely* in the tasting process. In wine, you always taste more than just the fruit. There's the tannins and the oak, just to name two things—those help color the wine, give it depth and complexity. Peach and cherry and oak and butter. Same thing with cheese. I mean, I'm a novice taster, but even still, I could tell there was more to it than just the milk."

"I'll admit that cheese is similar to wine in some respects," Jason said, and she raised an eyebrow at him. "But I make cheese because I like cheese, not because I'm looking for a substitute for something else."

"Okay, okay," Stella said, holding up her hands. "I'll let it go."

"Did you try the Green Leaf again?"

"Of course," she said. "It was amazing, as usual."

"You can take some home, you know."

"Maybe."

"What?" He sounded surprised. "You don't want any?"

"No, I do. I definitely do," she said. "But you only have it in heart shapes for the holiday."

Now he was the one to give her a look askance. "So what? The hearts are cute and people love them."

She shrugged.

"Wait a minute," he said as they turned onto Route 1. "This is coming from the same woman who insisted that Flynn Winery decorate the tasting room for V-Day and have a special, romantic couples tasting. This makes no sense."

"I've outgrown the holiday."

He coughed into his hand and said something that sounded suspiciously like a dirty word.

Damn the man for knowing that she wasn't telling the whole truth.

"Fine." She stopped right in the middle of the sidewalk and looked up at him. "You really want to know? It was almost exactly a year ago that I caught Matt cheating on me."

Jason's dubious expression turned into one of sympathy. "Stella, no."

"In retrospect, I should have seen the signs earlier. I worked all the time, and I thought he did, too. We rarely saw each other. He'd grown…distant. And I pretended that everything was still okay." She shook her head, remembering how naive she'd been.

"That night, he was supposed to take me out for a romantic dinner. We had a reservation at Bouchon, and you know what a hot ticket that is on Valentine's Day." Jason was watching her intently, so she kept going.

"On some level, I knew how much work was affecting our relationship. I wanted us to…I don't know…be different. Better, maybe. And I wanted to look beautiful, so I came home from work early to change. That's when I found him with—" She shook her head. "You know what? It really doesn't matter anymore. I'm over it and I'm *definitely* over him. But let's just say the holiday doesn't have the same luster it once did."

Jason was quiet for a while afterward. "I appreciate you telling me that," he finally said.

"Well, now you know."

"I also know that you're in a different place now."

"Yeah. Point Reyes," she said, her feeble joke falling flat. She wasn't that naive woman she'd been a year ago, but nor was she whole. Not completely.

He didn't blink. "No. A place where you look forward, not backward. Starting now."

And this was the flip side of his knowing her so well. He called her out on everything, turned over every log to find the bugs crawling underneath. But he also knew just how to soothe, how to handle her crazy, and how to make her feel so much better. And he did. She was here to take a breather, to start over, move on.

Honestly, even over the past couple of days, she felt as if she had moved on a little. Being here, away from Napa, had given her strength she didn't know she had. So had Jason.

She cocked her head at him. "You always tell me the truth, don't you?"

"Just one of my many talents," he said with a wink.

"I like your talents," she said, feeling bold.

"Oh?" he said. "Such as?"

It was an invitation if she ever heard one. She stepped forward and wound her arms around his neck, and when she pressed her lips to his, and he responded in devastatingly thorough kind, she began to think that Valentine's Day might not be so bad after all.

CHAPTER 9

Stella expected them to stay in Point Reyes Station for lunch, but Jason insisted on taking her to a mystery location. No matter how much she guessed or tried to trick him into telling, he wouldn't budge.

"Nope," he said. "You'll just have to wait and see." Then he'd smiled, which only served to annoy her. Which he'd known it would do, of course.

Luckily, the drive from Rough Ranch didn't take long. Jason pulled into a crowded gravel lot and handed off his keys to the waiting valet.

"Is this it?" she asked.

"Yep."

Stella got out of the truck and followed Jason around the corner of a big old barn, down a gravel path. In a big clearing, work equipment—a tiny bulldozer and some shovels—were strewn around behind a rope. Nearby, rows of big open-water tanks sat in open warehouses.

"This way."

Jason led her past the clearing to a medium-sized boardwalk on which were arranged about fifteen tables dotted with umbrellas. To the right, half a boat on its end behind a shack looked to be some kind of ordering area with chalkboards detailing the daily specials.

The entire operation was situated on Tomales Bay itself, and down below, the water rippled and glistened in the late-morning light.

"What is this place?" Stella wondered.

"Hog Island Oyster Co. It's a working oyster farm and distributor. You can picnic here, sit at the café, or buy oysters to eat or take away. Do you eat oysters?"

"Cooked," she informed him.

"Ever had one raw?"

She shook her head no.

"If you don't like them, I brought some cheese, bread, and fruit."

Stella glanced at her watch. "It's only eleven fifteen. I can't believe this many people are here already!"

"The place opens at eleven, and it's usually packed from that point on. Believe it or not, crowds are thinner this time of year," Jason said. "Come summer, you wouldn't be able to get a seat at all."

"The oysters must be really good."

"They are. Come on. Let's get a table." They walked to the entrance of the café area, where Jason had a quick conversation with one of the staff members. "We're all set. The tables usually book up months in advance, but they had a cancellation."

Once they were situated at their picnic table, Jason started pulling things out of his cooler. A bottle of prosecco. A couple of fresh lemons. Rough Ranch cheese and grapes and good, crusty bread. "I'm going to the takeaway counter to get some oysters. Stay here. Drink some bubbly. Relax."

"That sounds like an order," she said, a smile on her lips.

"I don't hear you complaining," he said, his gaze heated.

She hadn't minded his orders last night. Nor had she minded the way he'd taken control. He waited for her to blush, which she did as if on cue. Damn the man. Satisfied, he turned and headed to the counter.

Stella looked out at the water, caught up in the beauty, in the friendly chatter of the picnickers surrounding them. A couple nearby—a young-looking woman and her hipster boyfriend—kissed passionately before taking selfies. A family with a newborn baby being dandled on his grandmother's lap. Everyone full of such passion and happiness.

For the first time in a long while, she didn't feel sadness or envy.

Funny what a night of good sex will do.

She felt a little guilty not waiting for Jason before starting drink, but he *had* given her an order. Without too much trouble, she opened the prosecco and poured herself a big plastic cupful. Then she drank. The fizzy liquid tickled her nose and warmed her throat.

Soon, Jason was back, toting two wet bags full of barnacled gray oysters.

He didn't waste any time prepping everything. He quickly slipped on a shucking glove. Carefully, he wedged the shucking knife between the two shells and firmly slid it through. Then he expertly slit the muscle holding the bivalve to its shell, cleaned it up around the edges, and handed it to her.

Stella held the oyster delicately. "Do I just eat it like this? With all the water in it?"

"That's called the liquor. It adds to the flavor."

"Oh. Okay. So I just—"

"Sip and slide." Was it her imagination, or had his voice gotten huskier?

Ignoring that, Stella focused on the shell in front of her. She took a deep breath, held it to her lips, and without thinking too much, let it slide into her mouth and down her throat. It was wet and briny, yes, but it was also shockingly delicious.

Jason was watching her. "What do you think?"

"It was slipperier than I expected," she admitted. "But sweeter, too."

"Did you like it?"

"I think so. Should I try another?"

"Absolutely," he said, shucking a second oyster. "Here. You can try it with lemon, if you like."

She took the oyster from him, squeezed a little lemon juice over it, and then let that one slide down her throat, too. The briny taste was masked a little by the tart lemon juice. "I think I liked it better plain."

"Good girl. Here. I got some small ones, too."

He shucked a tiny one and handed it to her.

"Thanks."

"The small one's not as sweet," she pronounced after she ate it.

"I know," he said, his eyes twinkling.

She licked her lips, tasting salt. "I think I *do* like them."

"That's a good thing." He grabbed another from the pile and slid his knife between the shells.

"Aren't you going to eat any?"

Jason shook his head. "Nope. I'm indulging you, remember?"

"I can't eat that many oysters."

"You can try," he said simply, handing her another.

She took it from him, acutely aware of his eyes on her. She kept her eyes on him, too, watching him as he watched her slide that slippery goodness into her mouth, followed the line of her throat as she swallowed, and when she'd finished, licked his own lips.

"Another."

Wordlessly, he took an oyster from the bag, shucked it, then handed it to her. She did it again, loving the way she felt—sexy, powerful. Desired.

By him.

She'd been blind not to see it before. Utterly blind. Or maybe she just hadn't been looking. But there it was, as plain as day, his need written all over his face.

"I want to see you eat one," she pronounced.

He shook his head. "No."

"Please?"

He hesitated for a long while. "All right," he finally said. He shucked one for himself, and then, keeping his eyes trained on her, slowly slipped it into his mouth.

Hungrily, she watched him devour the oyster, not bothering to hide her expression as his throat convulsed when he swallowed, then slowly, so slowly, wiped his mouth with the back of his hand.

The air between them was charged, electric. She was turned on beyond belief, her nipples hard little pebbles, her sex damp and needy.

"One more," she whispered.

He did it again, slicing open the shell with his sharp knife, then sliding the bivalve down his throat.

She couldn't drag her gaze away if she tried.

"Jason—" she started, her voice pleading.

He raised an eyebrow. "Yeah, Stella?" He was teasing her, pushing her to admit her need. She didn't even care.

"Can we take the rest home?"

"And give up our spot? Hmm. I don't know."

She rubbed her legs together, trying to get some relief. None was forthcoming.

"Fine. If you won't help me, I guess I'm going to have to help myself." She stood.

"Where are you going?"

"To the bathroom," she said, trying to sound careless.

His brows went together. "To do what, exactly?"

"To take care of myself," she said, infusing her words with just enough emphasis to make her meaning clear.

"Like hell you are," he growled, then stood up abruptly and started jamming everything back into his bag.

It took twenty-five minutes for them to get back to Jason's house. Twenty-five agonizing minutes while she was so wound up she could barely breathe.

The instant his truck was parked in his driveway, he pulled off his seat belt, clicked hers off, too, and pulled her right across the front seat of the truck into his arms.

His lips crashed down on hers and he simply dominated her mouth, sliding his tongue in and stroking. His movements were jerky, desperate, one hand in her hair, the other up her shirt.

He dragged down her bra strap and cupped her breast, immediately finding her already-taut nipple, squeezing and twisting it between his clever fingers. She gasped, he groaned, and she felt an answering gush between her legs.

It had never been like this—an unbelievable craving, a want so deep she could feel it in her bones. She slid her hand up his shirt, raked her fingers down his back. He shuddered and pushed her back onto the bench, getting right between her legs.

His eyes were molten amber, his breathing coming in hard pants as he took her in. "What you do to me," he muttered before he kissed her again.

She pulled his shirt off over his head, then traced the muscles of his back and shoulders, loving the way he shuddered a little when she slipped a hand down his jeans to cup his ass.

"We're not going to make it into the house, are we?" she murmured against his lips.

"You got a problem with that?" He kissed her neck, then licked from collarbone to jaw, making her shiver.

"No," she gasped as he hit a particularly sensitive spot.

He was working on her zipper now, edging her jeans off her hips along with her panties, then sliding them down her legs.

This was urgent. Raw. He couldn't wait, and neither could she. As soon as he was done with her jeans, she attacked his, getting his fly open and getting them down his legs as fast as she could.

He was back on top of her in an instant, his cock nudging her cleft, his mouth on her neck.

"Protection," she gasped.

He reached out, popped open the glove box, and pulled out a string of condoms. Ripping one off, he tore it open with his teeth and rolled it on.

Then he tilted her hips up to meet his and entered her in one smooth thrust.

Her cry was muffled by his kiss.

He took charge, one hand on her rear, the other in her hair, pinning her to the bench, and that lack of freedom somehow made her feel *more* free. Her pleasure was in his hands now.

She took everything he had to give, welcomed the heat of him, the hardness, his hips snapping against hers.

She arched her body up to meet his every thrust, showing him how much she wanted this.

There was so much heat, so much friction, and then he hit *just* the right spot to send her flying. She came hard, in a glorious rush of sensation that had her crying out his name.

He followed almost immediately after with a hoarse shout before collapsing on top of her.

In a half second, he'd rolled them over so that he was on the bottom and she was on the top.

"Don't want to crush you," he said, kissing her temple.

She held on tight as she caught her breath, head on his chest, listening to the beating of his heart.

This was crazy. She'd never been like this before in her life—never felt the urgency and need she felt when she was with him.

Jason ran a hand through her hair, pushing it away from her face.

"You knew exactly what you were doing back there," he said, but he didn't sound angry.

She tilted her head up and nipped his bottom lip. "You were the one who took me to eat oysters," she told him, her tone cheeky. "Aren't they supposed to be an aphrodisiac?"

"All I can say is that watching you eat them really turned my crank."

"Nice. A cliché on top of a cliché."

"There's some truth to it, that's for sure."

"Don't deny that you liked it."

"Liked it?" He kissed her tenderly. "I *loved* it."

So had she.

And as she lay there with Jason's strong arms around her, she realized that heading back to Napa after the weekend was over was going to be much harder—and much lonelier—than she originally thought.

CHAPTER 10

Saturday morning found Stella a quarter of a mile deep in the Olema woods, following Jason as he led the way down a dirt trail.

The air was chilly and clammy, thanks to wispy patches of fog that dotted the landscape, but she was snug in her oversized fleece, and getting warmer thanks to their brisk pace. Jason seemed to know exactly where he was going, moving purposefully down the trail, his hiking boots softly crunching on the pine needles strewn on the forest floor.

They hadn't spoken much since leaving the house, which in her mind was actually a huge positive. Jason never felt the need to fill the empty space when silence would suffice. Some of her best memories involved simply walking in the vineyards with Jason and Liam, following in her father's footsteps, watching as he inspected every vine, every bunch of grapes, in anticipation of the harvest.

Jason paused at a fallen tree branch and waited for her to catch up, then took her by the hand and helped her over.

"Thank you," she said.

"You're welcome," he said, a gentle smile on his face.

He didn't let go of her hand, and together, they continued on through the woods.

After another half mile, the dirt turned to clay, which slowly faded into sand. Finally, the trail emptied onto a small, deserted patch of shoreline, about thirty yards long. The beach wasn't huge, but what it lacked in size it made up for with beauty.

A large piece of driftwood—almost a whole tree, it seemed—had washed up on shore, giving the desolate space a sort of sepulchral feel. A few small patches of seaweed and some small boulders rounded out the decor, and the only other occupant was a fat seagull with its face to the wind.

It was quiet and intimate, the perfect space to appreciate a foggy morning on the Northern California coast.

"It's beautiful," she breathed into the cold air.

"Shell Beach. It's a local favorite," he said, with some satisfaction. "I know how much you love the water. I'm only sorry it's so cold."

"I don't mind. It's actually warmer here than it is in Napa."

She glanced over at him, but he was watching the water. The tide was coming in, and with each roll of the waves, the water came up higher and higher onto the shore, leaving bits of shell, stone, and seaweed in its wake.

He walked over to the driftwood and leaned back against the old, worn trunk, crossing his arms over his chest, eyes still on the water. Stella went the other way, close to the shoreline, combing the beach for treasure. She found half of a mussel shell and a purple stone, but not much else worth bending down for. She tucked the two objects into the pocket of her fleece and looked out to the water.

Breathing deeply, she looked out as far as she could see before the fog and the mist shrouded the view.

Funny what a change in location—a change in *perspective*—could do. She'd been living inside her own head for far too long. Forget the gossip and the whispers, the expectations and obligations. She was her own woman, forging her own path. So what that things hadn't turned out like she'd planned? Dwelling on the past wasn't healthy. She needed to look toward the future, no matter what anyone else thought or said, starting now. She loved her family and she loved her work, but they were all-consuming. She'd take time for herself, keep doing the things she loved, make herself happy. Maybe she'd start taking piano lessons again to supplement what she was doing on her own. Or cultivate a few new friendships outside her small existing circle of acquaintances. Friends who'd like her for *her*.

Yes, being in Point Reyes—being with Jason—was turning out to be a very good thing, indeed.

She only wished she'd come sooner.

She glanced over at Jason. He was still leaning against the dead tree trunk, except he'd closed his eyes and tipped his head back against the wood. The man was beautiful, rugged and wild, like the Northern California coast. He belonged here. And being with him made her feel as if she did, too.

It wasn't just the sex, though admittedly, that was amazing. It was everything else, like the way they could just be together and not talk at all. And that he knew her favorite songs and played them for her when they drove around town. He even took her teasing like a champ. He knew her better than anyone, and she fit seamlessly into his life.

Subconsciously, she must have known that coming here would help. She was drawn to him, just as she always had been, a moth to his flame.

She went to stand next to him, leaning back against the driftwood so that their shoulders were touching.

"Thank you," she said.

He didn't open his eyes. "You're welcome."

"You didn't ask me why I was thanking you."

"Okay, why are you thanking me?"

"For this. For everything."

Jason opened his eyes and wrapped an arm around her and kissed her forehead. "You're welcome. Again."

"I feel good," she said, nestling into his side. "Happy." She laughed a little. "I was going to work this whole weekend. Work and throw a huge pity party for myself in an empty cabin."

"I know," he said, his voice sad for her.

"I knew you knew," she admitted. "The weird thing is, I'm not even embarrassed. With anyone else I would be, but not with you."

"Thanks, I think."

"Seriously, Jace. Being with you has made things so much better. I mean, I even went out to a bar. Do you know how huge that is?"

"Huge."

"Totally huge."

Jason shook his head. "Stell, I've said this before and I'll say it again. You need to get out more."

"I know," she said. "Say, maybe you could come to Napa? We could hang out. You, me, Liam, and Mandy, if they're around. What do you say? It'd be fun, right?"

He shook his head and slid his arm off her shoulders. "My schedule's tight," he said evasively, and looked away.

It took a second, but she got it. He never came to Napa anyway, and he wasn't going to make the trip just for her. And she'd probably committed some kind of weekend fling foul by asking him to extend the weekend.

This was a one-off thing. She'd even set the rules, and he was doing what she asked—making sure nothing changed between them.

Which was totally for the best. It's just that she hadn't thought it would feel so…distant.

After a long period of silence, he turned back to her. "You ready to walk back? The cheese tasting starts soon and I need to be there early to set up."

She swallowed hard, pushing back against the lump in her throat, and forced a smile to her lips. "Lead the way."

Stella followed him back down the path. Jason had allowed her a few days of peace, made it a little easier to face going back to Napa. She should feel grateful. So why did she feel like something was missing?

Jason looked out to the group of people sitting in Rough Ranch's test kitchen, all waiting patiently to taste his cheese. Before him was a platter of eight different cheeses, a bowl containing cheese curds, and a glass of whey. Each participant in the cheese tasting had the same arrangement in front of them, minus the curds and whey.

He smiled and held up a wedge of dense white cheese streaked with blue and sporting a snowy white rind. "This is our Bear Valley blue cheese. Pick it up, squeeze it between your fingers, feel the give. Now take a whiff. What do you smell?"

Everyone did as he asked, and then a man in a polo shirt raised his hand. "Butter."

"Good. You?" He pointed at a scruffy-looking man with a grizzled gray beard.

"Lemon."

"Interesting. We'll come back to that in a minute. How about you?" He smiled at the woman in front of him.

"Mold."

He laughed at that. "Nice. Okay. Are you ready to taste?"

The group nodded enthusiastically. "Good. Take a bite. Savor it. Write down what you taste and what you smell. Is it the same? Is it different? We'll talk in a minute."

He stepped to the side of the table where a glass of water was waiting for him.

The cheese tasting was going well. He had a record number of participants—twenty-one, up a dozen from the last time they'd done this event—and Miles informed him that five more were on the waiting list.

He glanced over at Stella, who was sitting in the back row. She'd been subdued on the walk back from the beach, undoubtedly because he'd rejected her Napa proposal.

He couldn't tell her the real reason why he didn't want to hang out with her and Liam and Mandy in Napa. He wanted to—desperately—but going back to Napa would be torture, and not simply because his parents were there. It was because there was no way for him to pretend that they were still just friends, especially around her brother. In fact, it'd be impossible.

Better to keep away from her once the weekend was over, because honestly, he'd never be able to look at her as just a friend again.

He'd ruined himself, but at least he'd helped Stella. She looked a little happier now. Good. He'd wanted to make her happy, to give her exactly what she needed.

And she'd been crystal clear about what she expected—his body, not his heart—which is why he'd had to shut her down when she started talking about visits to Napa.

The group was ready for more discussion, so he walked them through it. He loved this part of the job—connecting with people, sharing his passion. He *would* have been great at Optimum. Probably why his parents wanted him back so badly.

The prodigal son.

That's how he saw himself. As their only son and heir, it was expected that he'd step into their shoes when they were gone, but he wasn't like them. They were cold, corporate drones who'd bought Optimum after a successful stint on Wall Street, and they ran the winery like a company, not a farm. Contrast that to the Flynns' way of doing things, which was land and people first, business second. True, they had a much smaller operation, but they understood the most important thing about a winery—family comes first.

With Greg and Trudy Roberts, it was always about the bottom line.

Family and relationships weren't important to them. They'd ignored him for years in New York, and even more after they moved to Napa, paying attention to him only when he messed up...and then later when they realized how useful he could be. They hadn't raised him, the Flynns had, so as soon as he graduated, he'd given a big *screw you* to his parents' demands that he carry on the family business. Not that he hated wine, but he knew if he stayed, he'd be trapped. So he'd cut out, followed his own dreams.

And now those dreams were real. Rough Ranch was doing well. *He* was doing well.

He didn't have everything he wanted, but no one did. That was life.

But he had this. And for the weekend, he had Stella. A weekend he was going to do his utmost to drain dry.

So he tasted. He talked. He signed almost everyone in the class up for the new cheese-of-the-month subscription that Miles had spearheaded. He wished everyone a happy Valentine's Day.

And when the last person in the class had left, he found Stella waiting for him with a sweet smile on her face.

"How'd you like it?" he asked.

"It was good, Jace. You're good." She tipped her head a little sideways. "You're such a natural at this."

"Thanks. It's fun. Definitely one of the perks of the job. Kind of like the tasting room at Flynn Winery is for you."

"Not quite," Stella said with a laugh. "I'm always grateful when Liam can take my shifts. He's so much better at talking to people than I am."

"You talk to me," he pointed out.

"It's different with you," she said. "It always has been."

He knew it. Just like it had always been different with her. Thank goodness things were back to normal between them. He had only one night left with her, and he wanted to make the most of it.

Stella helped him throw away the trash and pack up the cheese and tasting implements. It didn't take long, but he appreciated the help.

"So are you ready to head home?"

"Sure," she said, grabbing her bag from where it lay on the floor. "That cheese really was delicious, Jace."

"Delicious," he agreed, bending his head and touching his lips to hers. "I'm hoping you'll have the strength for a short hike, and room for dinner later."

"Yes, to both. Are you also planning on serving dessert?" she asked, a knowing smile on her face.

It was that smile. That and the way her gaze slid down his body, slow and sure, then back up again to rest on his lips. Stella Flynn was learning how to flirt. And from the way his body roared to life, she was getting damned good at it.

He smiled back. "I can promise you this. Dessert is something you definitely won't want to miss."

CHAPTER 11

Stella opened the sliding glass door and a blast of warm air hit her as she poked her head in the family room. "Ready?" she called out.

"Almost," Jason called back to her from the kitchen. "Another five minutes."

"Okay." She shut the glass door to keep the heat in the house and walked to the balcony railing. Below her were trees, and in the distance lay Tomales Bay, sparkling dark blue. The sky was still gray and cloudy, but she didn't mind. It was beautiful all the same.

Jason had promised her dinner for Valentine's Day, and he'd banished her from the kitchen while he did the cooking. In a rare burst of indulgence, she'd pampered herself. After a long, hot shower, she'd blown her hair dry. She hadn't brought a dress, but she did have a cute red cardigan that she paired with some jeans and a cotton button-down blouse. She'd even put on some lip gloss. She looked like herself—only happier.

And given that she was outside right now, colder. She shivered a little in her fleece and took a sip of wine, letting it warm her from the inside out.

Ahh. Lovely.

It'd be so easy to get used to this, being here, with Jason.

Undoubtedly the reason she felt this way was because there was an expiration date on this whole thing. Tomorrow she would go home and whatever they'd shared would be over, keeping this weekend squarely in fantasyland.

That was good, because reality was tough. They wouldn't have to deal with things like mortgages and work and obligations because they weren't actually involved.

Nor would they have to deal with that squirrely little issue of faithfulness. After the weekend was over, she would go back to her regular life, and Jason would go back to whatever it was that he did with all of those women.

A tiny pit formed in her stomach at the thought of that, but she quickly pushed it away. *Uh-uh. Don't think like that.*

She wanted no-obligation fun, not something serious, and that went both ways. Good thing no-obligation fun was Jason's strong suit.

She drank some more wine, and a few minutes later, Jason slid open the door. "Dinner's ready."

"Great," she said, coming into the house and shedding her coat. "What'd you make? It's not more pizza, is it?" she teased. "Not that I'm complaining if it's pizza, because yours was delicious, but you've been working an awfully long time. Wait, I know. It's two pizzas!"

Jason just smiled and led her into the dining room. He'd set the table with two seats side by side, lovebird-style. A pair of candles flickered in their candlesticks. And the table was scattered with roses.

"What did you do?" she gasped, taking in the simple but elegant decor.

"I figured it was time for you to start making some good memories."

"This is…it's too much."

"Not for you." Gently, he cupped her face in his hands and kissed her tenderly. "Happy Valentine's Day, Stella."

She kissed him back, even as her heart swelled and a tear trickled from the corner of her eye. Quickly, she wiped it away. "Happy tears."

"I know," he said, taking her by the hand and placing her in a seat.

They had wine and salad, steak and chocolate mousse. And to finish, a perfectly composed cheese plate, complete with tiny portions of Rough Ranch cheese, fresh fruit, and halved walnuts—the ultimate finale to an incredible meal.

"Okay," she said, wiping her mouth with a napkin after the last morsel of cheese. "You definitely indulged me."

"Good," he said with a smile. "But there's more."

"I can't possibly eat anything else."

"It's not food," he said, holding out his hand. "Come on. I have something cool to show you."

Jason snared an oar from his garage, and they walked down to the water in the dark. They ended up on a long dock that extended into the bay, the old weathered boards creaking underfoot.

"Seriously, what are we doing?" Stella asked. "Going canoeing?"

"Nope. Watch." When they reached the end of the dock, he took the long oar and dipped it into the water, then swirled it around. A streak of bright blue lit up the water, then slowly faded away. He moved the oar again. Same blue streak.

"What *is* that?" Stella asked, eyes trained on the water.

"Bioluminescence from dinoflagellates. They're a kind of phytoplankton that live in Tomales Bay and emit flashes of light. On nights like tonight—moonless, cloudy—the phenomenon is really strong."

"Whoa," Stella breathed. "Can I try?"

"Sure."

He handed her the oar, and she dipped it into the water, then moved it out and around. A white-blue streak appeared, then disappeared. And just like that, he'd taken the mood from awesome to sublime.

"It's so beautiful," she sighed.

"I thought you'd like this," he said. "Honestly, it's better if you're out kayaking, but you came so last-minute, I couldn't get a reservation for tonight. They're usually booked on weekends and this being Valentine's Day and all, it was pretty much impossible."

"No, this is great." She didn't want to be kayaking tonight, anyway. She traced the letter *S* in the water, followed by the letter *J*. Then she looked up at him and grinned.

Jason laughed and sat back on the dock. "Have fun."

So she did, swirling and twirling and feeling like a little kid again. She made a few stars and a heart. Then another.

This weekend hadn't turned out like she'd planned at all.

If she'd been left to her own devices, she knew she'd be sitting in her little rented cabin alone, crying her eyes out, just like she had been last Valentine's Day.

She'd planned for some serious wallowing and a lot of soul-searching, but thanks to Jason, she'd regained her sense of self without even trying. He saw the best in her, brought it out, and gave her confidence and strength she didn't know she possessed.

She could face the world again with her head held high. And she could start doing things for herself more often. Not that she wouldn't continue to do things for her family—of course she would—but the one thing she learned was that being a bit selfish worked wonders on her self-esteem.

She owed him thanks.

No. She owed him more than thanks. She owed him everything. He listened without judging, brought out the best parts of her while overlooking the worst. She needed more friends like Jason.

Honestly, she just needed more Jason. But he'd never leave Point Reyes—he'd made that abundantly clear—so this weekend was going to be a one-shot deal.

But that was the deal going in.

Stella twirled the oar faster, wishing the light would streak just a little brighter, a little longer.

When she'd had enough, she handed Jason the oar, and hand in hand, they walked back to his house in silence.

By unspoken agreement, they ended up in his room. She wasn't sure if she reached for him or the other way around, but all at once his hands were in her hair and they were kissing, his tongue in her mouth, hers answering him right back.

She poured herself into him, tasting, testing, showing him how much she wanted to give him with her hands, her lips, her tongue. Everything.

There was no tomorrow. There was only tonight. And both of them knew it.

Wordlessly, he stripped her, then laid her down on the bed and looked his fill. The heat in his eyes was the ultimate aphrodisiac. She twisted on the bed, already damp and needy, but he was in no hurry.

Instead of taking off his own clothes, he simply lay down next to her, wrapped her in his arms, and kissed her, deep and long. She threw a bare leg over his thigh and pulled him close, wanting so badly to feel flesh against flesh. He made her wait, feathering kisses down her neck, across her shoulders, over the tops of her breasts, until she was practically shaking.

Desperate to touch him, she scrabbled at the buttons on his shirt with her fingers. She only managed to undo one button before he captured her wrists in a big hand and held them over her head. She twisted, not really trying to break free as much as she was testing her bonds, loving the delicious feeling of being held down.

And he knew she loved it, because his eyes went molten.

"This gives you freedom, yeah?" he asked.

She nodded. "Yeah," she breathed.

Jason was holding her down, but she was far from helpless. He'd placed all the control in her hands. Or, more accurately, at her lips. She could ask for anything and he'd do it. Command him to be gentle or hard, smooth or rough.

She'd never felt so powerful in her life.

"I want to remember you like this," he said. "Naked and spread out for me. Ready to take whatever I want to give. Telling me what you want me to do to you."

She was turned on beyond belief by his words alone, but then he went and sweetened the pot with a searing kiss that curled her toes.

"How much do you want me?" he demanded, working on his buttons one by one. Each opened button revealed another inch of his chest.

She swallowed to get some moisture on her tongue. "So much."

Jason squeezed her wrists in his hands. The reminder that she was his captive emboldened her.

"I want you more than anything," she told him. Was that her voice? Breathy and seductive. Sexy.

He released her for the moment it took to get off his shirt, pants, and boxer briefs, and when he was naked, he once again clasped her wrists.

Things got serious, fast. "What do you want me to do?" he ordered.

"Say it."

"I—I want you to touch me."

"Where?"

"My breasts."

He ran the back of his hand down her neck, over her collarbone, and just barely skimmed the side of her breast. "Like that?"

"No, please. I need more."

He cupped one, and her nipple instantly hardened in his palm. His quick intake of breath indicated he was affected as much as she was. She arched her back, pressing herself up and into his hand.

"What else do you want me to do?"

"Run your fingers over the tip the way…the way I like. Make it harder."

He followed her instructions, thumbing her sensitive flesh until she was squirming.

"Now put your mouth on it," she breathed.

He licked a path with his tongue over a taut nipple, then blew gently, the cool air over her sensitive tip making her shiver with pleasure.

He did the same thing to the other nipple, and she couldn't help the moan that escaped her lips.

"What else?" he said, his voice dark. "Tell me."

The words spilled out of her, filling the room and heightening her arousal as she told him every last dirty thing she wanted him to do with his fingers, his mouth, his cock. It was complete trust—but it ran both ways. He did everything she asked and more, focused only on her pleasure, the ultimate gift.

He played with her…everywhere, making her shatter in his arms not once but twice, then ramping her back up again with devastating precision, spurred on by her demands, her pleas, her cries.

When she couldn't take it anymore, when every ounce of energy was consumed with holding off yet another rapidly impending orgasm, she finally snapped.

"I need you inside me. Now."

"Stella," he said, his shaking hands belying his control as he slipped on the latex.

And then he was filling her, so smoothly, so deeply, she almost came then and there. She forced herself to hold off until his movements went erratic, and when he came, her name on his lips, all it took was the slightest squeeze and she was there too, breaking around him in the sweetest orgasm she'd ever had.

Afterward, they didn't speak for a long time, but simply lay there in the quiet of the room, the warmth generated by their lovemaking rapidly dissipating in the chilly air.

There was a strange sense of finality to it all. As if both of them knew this would be the last time they'd have each other like this.

Jason shifted so that she was lying next to him, tucked into his strong arms. After a while, he fell asleep, but Stella lay awake, listening to the sound of his breathing, his warm skin under her fingertips.

CHAPTER 12

Stella was leaving today.

From the moment he woke, wrapped up in her small, soft body, that was his only thought. When he kissed her good morning, her sweet-smelling hair brushing against his chest. As he took a shower, readying himself for the day ahead. While he handed her a cup of freshly made coffee with cream without even having to ask how she liked it.

She was leaving. And instinctively he knew she wasn't coming back. Not like this.

They'd shared something real, something raw, but now it was time for her to go. She was going to sail off into the rest of her life, and he'd be left here, alone. Without her.

She stood at the back door, feet bare, coffee cup in hand, watching two cardinals play by the bird feeder. Her shoulders—typically tense—were relaxed, and she had a peaceful expression on her beautiful face. She looked happy. Content. And completely oblivious to his inner turmoil.

"This is awesome," she sighed, taking a sip of her coffee. "I can't believe you get to wake up to this every morning."

"Napa's beautiful, too."

"Not like this," she said, coming to join him at the counter. She leaned back against it, eyes still trained on the birds.

He took a sip of his own coffee, then glanced over at Stella. She fit here, with him.

"Stay," he said.

"Hmm?" she asked, turning to him.

"Stay," he repeated. "Here. With me."

She blinked and put down her coffee cup. "I don't understand," she said slowly.

He put down his cup, too. "It's pretty simple," he said, pushing her hair behind her ear with chilly fingers. "You're not happy in Napa, but I think you're happy here. So stay."

"I can't do that," she said. "My job's there. My life's there. Not that I don't appreciate the offer." She gave him a gentle look and picked up her mug again. "You've always been so nice, and I can't tell you how much that means to me."

Either she had no clue at all how he truly felt, even after what they'd shared, or she was willfully misunderstanding him. But something inside him simply snapped. There was only one way to make her see.

"I love you, Stella," he said.

She gave him a sweet smile. "I know."

"No, not like that." Carefully, he took her mug from her hand and placed it on the counter. "I love you. *Really* love you."

He'd laid it all out on the line. Revealed everything, but she simply stared at him in shocked silence, her eyes wide, her mouth half open.

"Stella?" He stepped forward. "Did you hear me? I said I love you."

She blinked. "For how long?"

"Years. Since I came back from Europe," he confessed. "I didn't say anything because I didn't want to ruin what we had, and I definitely didn't want to screw anything up with your marriage or your family, but I can't hide it any longer. I love you. I want to be with you. Say something." He reached for her arm, but she stepped back out of reach.

"You don't love me. Not like that. You—" Stella stopped and bit her lip. "You broke your promise," she said, her tone hard. Accusatory.

"I can't help it. I thought I could be who you wanted me to be, but I can't hide how I feel anymore."

"Don't do this," she pleaded. "You swore nothing would change."

"Stella, please. I can't help it that I love you."

She visibly flinched. "I'm not looking for a new relationship. I thought you were okay with us just having sex."

No. Her words were like a knife in his heart. She didn't want him. She didn't love him. "Stella, I—"

And in the middle of all of this, the doorbell rang. Neither of them moved. After a few moments, it rang again.

She shifted uncomfortably. "Are you going to get that?" she asked.

"Hang on," he muttered.

He stalked to the door. Whoever was out there was going to get an earful, and explicit instructions to take a hike. Without looking through the peephole, he flung the door open wide.

And got the shock of his life.

Because standing there was his mother, looking uncertain at first, and then as the seconds passed, downright furious.

"So you *are* here," she breathed, her face coloring.

"Mom," he said. Stella was right—she didn't look well. At all. "What are you doing here? Are you okay?"

"No, I'm not okay," she snapped. "I'm here as a last resort because you won't call me."

"How'd you find out where I lived?" His house wasn't exactly on the beaten path.

"All the recent sales are published online," she said.

Damn. He hadn't thought of that. But dealing with his mother was not something he wanted to contemplate right now.

"Okay. You found me," he said, crossing his arms over his chest. "So what do you need to tell me? That you want me to come home? That you want me to join Optimum? Well, I've told you before, it's not going to happen."

"Your father is sick."

He blinked. "What?"

"Stage three colon cancer."

Jason shook his head. "When did you find out?"

"Two weeks ago. He'll go in for surgery next week and start chemotherapy a month after that. They tell me—" She swallowed, and he could tell she was close to tears. "They tell me it's going to be bad. I called. I e-mailed. I texted. Why didn't you respond to me?"

"I—"

"Because you were busy," she said, her voice flat. "And I can see exactly with who." She glared at Stella, who'd come to join Jason in the entranceway. "You lied to me."

"Don't blame this on her," Jason said. "There's a reason why I didn't pick up the phone. Because every time I did, I got a lecture on duty and responsibility. On being a man. On being a Roberts. But you weren't there for me at all. You *or* Dad. So I don't know why you're surprised I'm not more broken up about this."

His mother stepped back, as if slapped. "You never used to be so bitter."

"Yeah, well, if I am, you made me that way while you were too busy making money and ignoring me."

His mom's face crumpled. "We love you."

"You love what I can do for you. Or would, if I came back to Optimum."

"I know you're not coming back," she said, her voice soft. "We screwed up. *I* screwed up. There are too many years between us. Too many lost years, and I can't take any of them back. But your dad has cancer, Jason. Cancer. Can't we put the past in the past? You're my *son.*"

He didn't say anything. He couldn't. He wouldn't.

"You're as stubborn as an ox," she told him. "Always were. But at least I said my piece. You have the information. It's up to you what to do with it. Your father is waiting for you at home. Good-bye, Jason." She gave a nod to Stella. "Talk some sense into him."

Then she walked away.

He turned back to Stella, but she was already on her way upstairs.

"Where are you going?" he called after her.

"To get my bag," she said, heading for her room.

He followed her up. She'd thrown her overnight bag onto the bed and was tossing items into it as fast as she could.

"Seriously?" he said.

"A lot's happened this weekend," she said, throwing in her pajamas. "Business craziness, your mom dropping in, Valentine's Day. You need some time to process it."

"No, I don't." *I need you.*

"Sure you do." She tossed in her cosmetic bag and a sweater and wouldn't look at him. "All of this stuff is emotional. Anyone would be stressed about it. You need some time to think, and so do I." She glanced at his face, and there must have been something in his expression that made her pause, because she stopped what she was doing, reached out, and put a hand on his shoulder. "We're good, right?"

No. They weren't good. Not by a long shot. Because somewhere along this crazy roller-coaster ride of a weekend, he'd moved from simply thinking of her as a dream lover and started thinking of her as a real one. He should have known that just a taste of her wouldn't be enough. Could *never* be enough.

And she was running away from it, from *him*, and he knew why. She was scared, closing back in on herself because she was afraid to break free. Frustration roiled in his belly.

"Why is it that I can see you exactly for who you are, but you can't see me for who I am?"

She withdrew her hand. "I know who you are, Jason," she said, her tone impatient. "The same guy you always were."

"You used to know me, Stella. You used to know me almost better than I did myself, but you don't anymore."

Stella shook her head. "Look, I've got to get back to Napa where my real life is waiting."

"Right," he said angrily. "Some life."

She frowned and zipped up the bag. "What's that supposed to mean?"

"Nothing." He hated that he sounded like a petulant child, but he couldn't seem to make himself stop.

She crossed her arms over her chest. "We've never pulled punches with each other before, so why start now? If you have something to say to me, say it!"

"Fine," he said, his voice heated. "I'll say it. You're going right back to Napa where you do everything for everyone else, and nothing for yourself."

"Says the man who ignores his mother and won't go to see his seriously sick father."

"So you're saying I should sacrifice everything for them?" The *just like you did* went unspoken.

Stella shook her head. "What you're doing isn't healthy."

"Yeah?" he flung back at her. "And what you're doing is?"

"I love my family," Stella retorted. "I'd do anything for them."

"Including repressing who you are and what you need?" Jason shook his head. "You call that living?"

Stella's cheeks were red now. "It's better than the way *you* do it."

"You have no idea how I live my life," he said.

"I've seen enough to guess." Her voice practically dripped with sarcasm. "Eva, Kelsey, Marnie, Chloe…." Methodically, she began to tick off on her fingers the names of all his female friends.

"Right," he said, cutting her off, his tone deadpan. "I'm still the same guy. I never change."

"You know what?" she snapped. "You *have* changed. And I don't think I like this new Jason."

She grabbed her bag, pushed her way past him, and headed down the stairs.

"Why'd you even come here this weekend anyway?" he flung out, sounding desperate to his own ears.

"I shouldn't have," she tossed back. "It was a mistake. A big mistake." She reached the front door and yanked it open wide. "I'm going home," she said. "And if you were smart, you'd take my advice and do the same thing."

He didn't respond.

She turned to him then, her expression one of infinite sadness. "Goodbye, Jason," she said.

The sound of the door shutting in his face was the most desolate thing he'd ever heard.

CHAPTER 13

"Any more questions?" Jason asked Jack Everhart, a burly, soft-spoken dairy farmer with a lined face and an easy gait.

Despite Miles's pushing him to let him join in, Jason had come alone to talk with Everhart, knowing that what he had to say might be better received one-on-one. Plus, he wanted to see Everhart's operations for himself, without being influenced by anyone else.

He was impressed with what he saw. Everhart ran a tight ship business-wise, and the cows—Holsteins—were happy and healthy. Huge milk producers, they grazed placidly on the rolling hills, eating up that clover and nettle that would influence the taste of their milk. He'd had a sample. It was fresh and clean, and the small-batch farmstead cheese he'd tried, which was made right on the premises, was buttery and rich.

Everhart's dairy was huge, covering close to a hundred acres of grasslands here at the Point Reyes National Seashore, and over the past two hours, he felt as if Everhart had walked him through all of them. Not only that, but the man had grilled him nonstop about Rough Ranch's philosophy and business practices. He'd answered everything honestly, but he was exhausted. Still, if everything worked out, his pain would be worth it.

"No more questions," Everhart said. "I think we're good." The big man looked out over a pasture where some of his Holsteins were grazing, then turned back to Jason. "I wasn't looking for a partnership, but you've managed to convince me I need one. I'm not happy with the farmstead cheese we're making."

"It tastes great."

"But I don't have the resources to devote to its production. I need someone like you. Someone who knows how to make the best cheese with the best milk."

"And you have the best milk."

Everhart gave him a wry smile. "I like to think so."

"If you decide to sell to me, Rough Ranch will make the best artisanal cheese we can with your milk. Having tasted it, I think I'll feature a nettle-encrusted rind to bring out the flavors more prominently, at least this season."

"You really know your milk." Everhart's gaze swept him up and down. "When you first called me, I didn't think I'd like you much."

Jason knew. So many of the old-time farmers in the area saw him and Rough Ranch as interlopers, upstarts who didn't understand the value of the agricultural history of the area. Many thought Rough Ranch was a tourist trap—just the latest fad artisanal food in rustic Point Reyes.

That couldn't be further from the truth. Jason had a deep respect for the old ways of doing things, and he made sure everyone he hired did, too. Tourists would come and go, but his commitment to his business would remain. But it didn't matter much at this point. Everhart either knew the kind of man he was or he didn't.

Jason squared his shoulders. "And now that you've heard what I have to say?"

"Changed my mind."

"Good," he said. "I don't think it's any secret that I want the same things you want—namely sustainable farming and preservation of the area's character."

"Thought you'd be slick," Everhart said. "Was ready to tell you to get lost. Glad I didn't."

Jason knew an opening when he saw one. "So do we have a deal?" he asked.

After only a moment's hesitation, Everhart reached his hand out to clasp Jason's. One strong pump and it was done. "Deal. I'll have my folks draw up the paperwork."

"Fine with me," Jason said. It was Everhart's operation, so it'd be Everhart's terms. "You won't regret it."

"I know," Everhart said simply. "Because I've tasted what you can do, and it's damn good cheese. Walk you out?"

"Sure."

Together, the two men walked back across the field to the main barn, behind which Jason's truck was parked. After another handshake and a promise to follow up early next week, Everhart disappeared into the barn to get back to his workday.

Jason pulled out his cell phone and quickly texted Miles two words: *We're in.*

Then he slid the phone back into his pocket.

He should head back to Rough Ranch. Not only were Miles and Greer waiting for him to report on his meeting with Everhart, but he also had a staff meeting to run and mountains of paperwork to tackle.

He got into his truck, fully prepared to head back to town. But his head was spinning and aching, and he wasn't ready to deal with all the noise and craziness of the grange. So instead of turning right, he turned left, hardly knowing where he was going, but finding himself driving toward the water.

He parked in an empty beach parking lot—no tourists this time of year—and crossed the damp sand almost to the water line.

The day was cloudy, gray, and cold. Late February on the Northern California coast. If he were lucky, he'd catch a glimpse of some sea life. Some whales, maybe, on their annual migration. But he saw nothing. It was beautiful and desolate. Vacant.

Just like the emptiness that had taken up residence in his heart.

There was little pleasure for him anymore. Not in his new house, not in the quiet of the winter season, and *definitely* not in his own shallow self. His friends hadn't stopped calling yet, but they would when they realized he wasn't going to go out with them anytime soon. Work was okay, especially on days like today when he had a success, but most days he felt as if he was just going through the motions.

He hated it. Hated the way the isolation permeated his soul. He could feel himself shutting down—slowly turning to stone. Turning into his parents.

When had he gotten so closed off?

He knew exactly when. Two weeks ago when Stella had walked out on him, taking his heart with her.

Wrong. He couldn't blame this on Stella, because really, it was all him. It had always been him.

People saw what they wanted to see—the charm, the friends, the women, the good life. But it was all a facade. Because he'd closed himself off the moment he left Napa sixteen years ago, when he ran instead of staying to fight for his relationship with his family.

Worse? He was still running.

All this time he'd thought Stella was the one who'd given up by staying in Napa, devoting her life to her work and her family, focusing on everyone but herself.

He'd been wrong. Stella was the strong one, worthy of all the love and respect from those who knew her.

And he'd given up—gone anywhere, done anything but face his demons.

His parents weren't perfect. Neither was he, as evidenced by the immature way he'd handled his mother. She'd been right. He *was* as stubborn as an ox, always thinking that he knew what was right for him…and for everyone else. Truth was, he was weak. Selfish. And despite the life he'd built for himself, lonely.

There's a way to fix that.

Go back to Napa, face his past, and try to make some sense of the life he'd left behind.

Old fears rose to the surface. He wasn't good enough, strong enough, powerful enough. They would run roughshod over him like they always used to, second-guess every choice, every decision he made. They wouldn't ignore him anymore—he was too valuable for that, but they would try to use him as an extension of themselves, the way they once had.

No. He wasn't a boy any longer. He was a man, with a life of his own. He'd built a business from the ground up, a life from the ground up, relying on no one but himself. And he was proud of it.

Pride.

The very reason he had stayed away for so long was the reason he was strong enough to return. Whether his parents respected his decisions or not didn't really matter. *He* did. And that was what counted.

Except pride wouldn't work with Stella.

She knew him way too well for him to stand on ceremony. Like no one else ever could, she cut through all of his crap, called him out on every one of his mistakes. She'd tried time and again to help him mend his unhealthy relationship with his parents, but he wouldn't listen.

He'd been so stupid. Yes, she was scared, but that was only part of it. Of course she didn't believe his professions of love. Not when he'd dismissed his parents, along with everyone else in his life. Granted, it was so that they wouldn't dismiss him first, but Stella valued loyalty and trust over everything else.

Which is why he loved her with every ounce of his being.

Stella was everything he wasn't, and it was never so clear what he'd have to do to win her for his own.

He'd have to accept his past and learn to forgive to show her that he was a different man. A man worthy of her love. It was up to him to prove to her that he'd changed, not simply tell her and expect her to believe him.

More than that, he wanted to prove to her that she'd changed, too. That she deserved to have someone love her unconditionally, without reservation.

Either way, he was going back.

For Stella.

And after all these years, for himself.

CHAPTER 14

Stella scanned the supply closet with a critical eye. It was going to be a busy Saturday. Off-seasons for growers typically were, and thankfully, Liam had agreed to man the tasting room.

"One chardonnay and one pinot?" she called through the open door to her brother, who was currently setting everything up for the afternoon.

"Yep," her brother called back.

She stacked the cases carefully onto her dolly, shut and locked the door, then wheeled the dolly into the main room.

Liam was behind the bar, a wineglass in his huge hand. She would have thought a man of Liam's size would have been clumsy, but he was surprisingly gentle. In fact, as of last week, she'd broken her eleventh glass, nine more than he had this year.

Of course, there were reasons for that.

It had been two weeks since her trip to Point Reyes, and she still wasn't back to normal.

And sadly, the thought had crossed her mind that she might never be *normal* again.

Work was all right. She'd gone back to it immediately, trying to pretend that what she and Jason had shared over the weekend hadn't affected her. Orders and tastings and planning their big spring event had taken almost all of her time.

But at night, in her lonely little house, lying in her cold bed, she cried herself to sleep. She missed Jason. Missed his smile and his teasing, his laughter and his warmth. She even missed fighting with him.

She'd gone into the weekend worried only about her issues. Her crossed wires. Her lack of trust. She'd been so blindly selfish, she hadn't thought about how sleeping with Jason would affect *him*.

She'd hurt him. Badly. His look of utter devastation had just wrecked her. And in hurting him, she'd hurt herself.

Jason had been right—having sex had changed everything, and she'd been a fool to think that it wouldn't. You couldn't just sleep with a lifelong friend and expect things to be the same afterward.

Of course it wasn't the same. In fact, it was a million times worse because they couldn't be friends anymore. Not after what he'd told her.

It had taken a mere half a day to get over the shock of his confession. A mere half a day before she realized two things: She loved him the same way he loved her. And she was an idiot for walking out on him.

She'd been so fixated on the idea that Jason had been running from himself that she hadn't realized that she'd been doing the exact same thing. She sold herself short time and again, denied herself love, didn't even think she was worthy of it, not after Matt's betrayal. Maybe even before then.

Now it was too late. She'd ruined everything with Jason. He was never coming to Napa, and she certainly couldn't go back to Point Reyes. Not after what she'd said to him.

As usual, she'd made a complete mess of things.

But she'd keep her chin up and move forward, just as she always did.

"Thanks for dealing with this today," she said to her brother, dragging the dolly behind the tasting room bar. "I know you'd rather be coding, but I have to get the marketing materials ready for our reception. I can't believe it's coming up in a few weeks."

Liam placed the wineglass gently on a rubber mat and looked down at her. He smiled, but there was worry in his green eyes.

"Are you sure you still want to take that on?" he questioned. "I could easily get someone else to do it."

Stella shook her head. "I have it under control."

Liam didn't answer but bent his head, his auburn hair gleaming under the muted lights, and easily picked up both cases, sliding them under the bar where they'd be out of the way until he was ready for them.

He stood back up.

"I'm worried about you," he said bluntly.

"You're always worried about me," she pointed out.

"You've been acting weird since you came back from Point Reyes."

"I was acting weird before I left."

"Yeah," Liam said, scratching his cheek. "But this is different. You seem a little more subdued than usual, and you're usually pretty subdued."

She shrugged. "I went through a divorce. It takes time to heal."

"I'd have thought that with Matt taking that job in Sonoma, you'd be, I don't know, happier, maybe?" He'd left last week, which was a source of both relief and strain.

"I'm not sorry he's gone, but I don't wish him any ill will. I'm glad he found a good position at another winery. But now I'm worried about how you're going to handle the planting this year."

"Dad and I will manage, just like we did before Matt came on board."

"I guess," Stella said, unconvinced. "But we have an additional twenty-five acres this year to deal with."

"We'll manage," Liam repeated.

He opened a fresh bag of crackers and put them into three small bowls. Then he folded the half-empty package and placed it back under the counter.

"I just keep thinking back to New Year's," he said, unable to drop the topic. "You were doing better then. You seemed happier. And now…you're not. Did something happen in Point Reyes?"

She *so* didn't want to go there. "You and Dad are always treating me like I'm going to break," she accused. "Haven't I proven I'm not?"

Liam looked chagrined. "Aw, c'mere, Stella," he said, pulling her in for a hug. "I didn't mean to make you upset. I just want you to be happy. That's all Dad wants, too. And it's pretty obvious you're not."

He dropped a kiss on the top of her head, just as he always did. The way Jason always did. Tears pricked at the corners of her eyes, and she felt something inside her crack.

She didn't want to hide anymore, not from her family, and definitely not from herself.

She put her forehead on Liam's chest, garnering up her inner strength. Then she raised her head and looked him directly in the eyes.

"I slept with Jason when I was in Point Reyes."

Liam stilled. "You…what?" His voice was low. Shocked.

"I. Had sex. With Jason."

Her words must have finally registered, because Liam stepped away and his expression turned from confused to murderous. His jaw was clenched and so were his fists. "I'm going to kill him."

"No, no," Stella said, shaking her head. "It was me. I mean, it was both of us. I wanted to."

Liam's expression softened, but he still seemed on edge. "What happened?"

"It was romantic. Wonderful…until he told me he loved me."

"Sure. Like a brother."

"Like more than that."

Liam blinked. "Whoa."

"I was confused. Afraid. I pushed him away. I wasn't ready to hear it. Not from anyone, and especially not from him." She wiped her face with her hand. "I'm afraid I didn't handle it very well. I'm afraid I haven't handled anything very well lately."

"Let me guess," Liam said. "You gave him the full Stella Flynn treatment."

Stella gave him a look and he gave her one right back. She sighed. Her brother had her number, as usual. "I *may* have accused him of being a womanizer…of not really knowing what love was…you know, all the usual things you say when you're caught off guard." She sniffled a little.

Liam laughed at her sarcasm, but immediately sobered. "Like you said, he *did* catch you off guard. I mean, this was the first time he's said anything like that to you, right?"

"Right. But I still treated him like crap." That started fresh tears flowing. "I suck."

"No, no you don't. You're just under a lot of pressure. You're doing everything, Stella," Liam said gently.

"I'm falling apart."

"No way. You're the heart and soul of this family. You keep us together."

Stella shook her head. "You'd keep it together without me. You have Mandy now."

"But Mandy isn't family."

"She will be."

"Someday," Liam agreed. "But forget Mandy, just for a minute. Forget me. Think only about yourself and answer me this question: Do you love him?"

"Yes," she whispered. "I'm just…I guess I'm not used to thinking of him that way, but yes, I love him. I've always loved him. Except over Valentine's weekend I think I fell *in love* with him, if that makes any sense, but I was too stubborn to admit it. And I was afraid. So afraid he'd hurt me the way Matt did. But it doesn't matter. It's too late."

"It's never too late." Liam took a deep breath, then let it out slowly. "All we ever wanted—all Mom ever wanted—was for you to be happy. If being with Jason makes you happy, then you need to be with him. It may last, it may not. But at least you'll have given it a shot."

She shook her head. "I've ruined everything."

"You didn't ruin anything. If he truly loves you and you truly love him, whatever you said to him won't matter."

"How do you know?"

"Because that's how love works, Stella. It holds fast, even when it shouldn't. It's stubborn. Most of all, it's lasting. You've known each other forever. He'd never deliberately hurt you."

"I want so badly to believe you."

"You don't need to believe me. You just need to figure it out for yourself. And I know that my resourceful, clever, stubborn little sister will do just that." He gave her a genuine smile. "Because she always does."

She wiped a tear from her eye. "How do you always know the right thing to say?"

"I'm your brother," he said. "It's kind of in the job description."

It wasn't. Liam was just awesome.

"So, do you want me to call him?" Liam asked.

"No. I made the mess. I'll clean it up on my own."

"If you need any help, you know where to find me."

"I know, Liam. Thank you."

Stella went out to the balcony and looked out over the countryside. It was still chilly outside, but they were at the tail end of the rainy season, the foliage was green, and flowers were in full bloom. Only the vineyards lay dormant, the rich earth brown, the gnarled, twisted vines dark and bare until summer, when they'd erupt with bright green leaves.

She loved the winery, the age-old rhythm of the seasons, the cadence of the vines as they cycled through growth and harvest. But that wasn't why she stayed.

It was her family. It had always been her family.

They defined her, made her strong. She should embrace that.

But she was also her own woman. There were times for putting family first, and there were times for following her own heart. Liam and her dad loved her. They might give her a hard time about the choices she made, but ultimately, they'd respect what she did.

It was up to her to choose wisely.

She'd be on this land until she died. She knew that with the utmost certainty. And she'd always hoped that she'd have daughters and sons to pass this place down to when she and Liam were gone.

But she wasn't just a farmer. She was a woman, too, and she'd put herself on the back burner for far too long, so wrapped up in hurt and sadness that she couldn't contemplate ever being complete again.

Valentine's weekend in Point Reyes had opened her eyes, showed her there was more to life than work and obligation, showed her that she could come first. She wouldn't forget that again. Nor would she forget the role Jason played.

He'd woken her up like a sleeping vine, cultivated her, nourished her, *indulged her.* And she'd fallen in love with him.

He'd always been there, and she'd always loved him, but it wasn't until she'd left that she realized there was a hole in her heart where his love should be.

She would go to him. She needed to see him, to make things right. Because she did love him. And he needed to know that. She glanced down at her watch. One p.m. She could be in Point Reyes in an hour, maybe less if the traffic was good. Liam would understand. He'd want her to go.

She turned and came up short.

Because there was Jason, standing a mere ten feet in front of her.

She blinked hard. "Wh-what are you doing here?"

"I just came from my parents' place."

A little glimmer of hope flickered inside. "You went to see them? Why?"

"It was time," he said simply.

"Did the surgery go okay?" She was almost afraid to ask.

"Dad's sick. Really sick, and I'd be a liar if I told you that everything was going to be fine, but his doctors are optimistic. Anyway, we worked a few things out." He shrugged. "When I come back for his first chemotherapy session, we'll work out a few more things."

She couldn't believe it. "You're going to visit your folks regularly?"

He ran a hand through his hair, so familiar, such a Jason move.

"You were right, Stella," he said. "I've been an idiot for way too long. I thought that by burying my head in the sand, all my issues would just disappear, but that's not the way things work. Those issues just get bigger until you don't know how to handle them.

"I've been running for way too long and hiding for even longer," he continued. "The truth is, I *have* changed. I'm not the same man I was when I left Napa, and I'm sorry for expecting you to be a mind reader. I know now I can't just tell you I've changed. I have to show you. And I didn't show you hard enough. I let you go on thinking what you wanted to think rather than confront the hard truth, and then I dumped a confession on you without giving you any time to process it."

"Don't apologize," she said in an agonized whisper. "Please."

"I don't want to hide anymore," he told her. "I don't want secrets or lies. I want to be open with you. With everything."

Her heart ached, for everything she'd lost, for everything she'd gained, and for everything she wanted so badly she felt she'd die if she didn't get it. This was love—this topsy-turvy, upside-down roller-coaster ride of emotion that she'd never felt with Matt, with anyone before except with Jason. Her friend.

"We can't go back to the way things were."

"I know," he said. "So I will do my best not to make you feel uncomfortable around me. We were friends for a long time. That doesn't just change."

"But it does. It changes everything."

"You're right. It does." Steadily, he met her gaze. "I have one question: Do you trust me, Stella?"

She swallowed against the lump in her throat. That was it, really. Trust. She thought back to the not-so-distant past, when even the idea of trusting someone again was foreign. And then she looked at the man standing before her, baring himself to her.

"Yes," she whispered. "I trust you."

He took a step toward her. One single step, bringing him close enough for her to see how brightly his eyes glittered. "I told you before and I'll tell you again. I love you," he said. "Really love you. It's selfish and greedy and I know I'm not worthy, but I will fight for you, Stella. Make no mistake about that. I will fight long and hard for the honor of your love in return. But I don't want to pressure you or lose what we shared."

She could scarcely breathe. Could scarcely believe what she was hearing. "You still love me after everything I said to you?"

He met her gaze and wouldn't let go. "Body and soul. You tell me the truth when no one else will. Call me out on every single one of my issues. Make me want to be a better man. Truth is, I went to see my parents for me, sure, but I also went for you. I need you, Stella. I need you in my life, and not just as a friend. I love you."

Her hands were trembling, so she clasped them in front of her. "When you told me how you felt before," she said carefully, "part of me didn't believe you. And the part that did was too scared to accept it. But I believe you, and I'm not scared. Not anymore."

His brows went together. "What are you saying?" he asked slowly.

"That I love you, too."

"Are you serious?"

"Utterly," she said, with conviction. "I love you. I've loved you forever, only I was too blind to see it. These past couple of weeks have been impossible, and it's because I missed you so much. I trust you, Jason. I want you to tease me. Push me. Coax me out of my shell. Because for you, I'll do it. I'll do anything for you, including facing my fears to see if we can make this work. I don't know how we can do it, but—"

She didn't get a chance to go on because before she could say another word she was in his arms, his mouth on hers, and he was kissing her with such depth, with such passion, she couldn't breathe, let alone think, drowning in the pleasure of him.

"I can't believe you actually love me back," he murmured against her lips, his voice filled with wonder. "I've wanted you for so long, Stella. For so long. And you're here. You're mine. But don't change. I love you exactly the way you are."

His words were humbling. Devastating. And of course that made her cry. "Jason, oh, Jason."

"Stell—"

He cupped her jaw in his hand and kissed her again, then wiped her tears from her cheek. "I've been wrapped up in my own world for too long," he said.

"Me too."

"Maybe we could maybe try to wrap ourselves up in each other's worlds for a while. See how that feels."

"I'd like that," she said. "But how are we going to do that? I mean, your work is in Point Reyes, and mine's here."

"I know," he said. She'd never leave the winery, and Jason, of all people, would understand. He looked thoughtful for a moment. "Maybe we could try splitting our time? And when we're ready, maybe we get a place in Petaluma. It's about halfway between Napa and Point Reyes. That way we could each continue to do what we love."

"Yes." There were other choices, but this was a good starting point. She began to see how this could work. How it *would* work, if they were both on board. Jason was watching her with a kind of wonder on his face. "What?" she asked.

He gave his head a shake. "I just can't believe this is real and not a dream."

She reached up to stroke his cheek with her hand. Jason—the man she'd loved forever but only now truly understood how deeply. "It's real."

He kissed her again, longer than before, his hand in her hair, pressing her to his body as if he would never let her go.

She was still a little dazed when he raised his head and glanced around. "Maybe we should go tell Liam before he decides to kick my ass?"

"Just a little longer," she said, pulling him down again.

"Stella," he said, coming willingly. And when his lips touched hers, she knew that it was the start of something big.

The rest of her life. With the man who made her whole.

ABOUT THE AUTHOR

Elisabeth Barrett lives in the San Francisco Bay Area and spends her days teaching, editing, writing sexy contemporary romance, and enjoying time with her sometimes-bearded husband and three spirited children. She is constantly perfecting her home-work-writing juggling act, but in her free time she loves to hike open space preserves, grow orchids, bake sweet things her husband won't eat, and sing in grand choruses.

www.elisabethbarrett.com

COMPLETE BOOKLIST

Other books by Elisabeth Barrett:

West Coast Holiday Series
Christmas in Tahoe
New Year's in Napa
Rendezvous in Point Reyes

Return to Briarwood Series
Once and Again
The Best of Me
Anywhere You Are

Star Harbor Series
Deep Autumn Heat
Blaze of Winter
Long Simmering Spring
Slow Summer Burn